VIKING SON

by

Jay Palmer

Books by Jay Palmer

The VIKINGS! Trilogy:
DeathQuest
The Mourning Trail
Quest for Valhalla

Jeremy Wrecker, Pirate of Land and Sea

The Magic of Play

Viking Daughter

The Seneschal

Dracula – Deathless Desire

Website

http://JayPalmerBooks.com

Cover Artist

Piero Mng

Viking Son

ISBN-978-0-9911127-8-4
ISBN-0-9911127-8-4

To James Paxton,
my knight in the SCA,
respected teacher,
friend forever ...

Viking Son

Chapter 1

"I'm gonna be the greatest warrior ever!"

I leapt atop the big gray rock and brandished my imaginary sword at my deadly foes.

"I'm gonna captain my own dragonship!" little Kal shouted, and he stabbed at me, his invisible blade piercing my heart. I clutched my chest, cried out, and rolled my eyes: *my most realistic death.*

"I'm gonna be a jarl and command fleets of dragons!" Halgrum shouted from the deepest spot, splashing merrily despite the water's numbing cold.

"You fools!" Derek laughed as he swung back and forth on our hanging-rope, shaking the tall, creaky oak shading our favorite swimming hole.

"What're you gonna be?" Kal asked.

"King!" Derek announced proudly.

"You can't be king unless your father was king!" Halgrum argued.

"I'm going to seize Norway and steal his crown!" Derek smiled.

"How?" we asked.

"I'm gonna wait 'til you fools get everything, then kill you ... and take it all!"

Complaints and defiance chorused, but Derek only sneered.

"A man is master of all he can slay!" Derek recited the quote our fathers had drummed into us.

We cheered; that was our favorite saying, frequently shouted by every boy in the village.

Suddenly Halgrum shushed us.

"Thron ...!" Mother's voice echoed across our fields.

"Thron's in trouble!" Halgrum laughed.

"You're not supposed to be here either!" I retorted.

"Little baby better run home to mo-o-o-mmy!" Derek chided in his infantile, sing-song voice.

"Thron ...!" Mother's distant shout sounded angry; all of the boys laughed.

Cursing with the worst swear-words I knew, in a vain attempt to look manly, I pulled my dry clothes over my chilled, wet skin, and dashed across our fields, between our many long, almost-ripe rows of turnips. I couldn't hide my wet hair; I'd be in trouble, but it'd been days since we'd swum at the swimming hole, and summer was almost over. Harvest would mean endless chores, and then heavy snows would freeze our pond frozen solid.

"There you are!" Mother said as I entered our musty, sod-roofed house. "I told you to finish your chores!"

"I fed the pigs!" I argued.

"Did you sweep?" Mother demanded. "All the way into the corners? And don't forget the pantry; it needs a good cleaning before harvest."

Indignantly I grabbed our broom while Mother settled Urd into her crib, and then sat in her chair and picked up the new red blanket she was knitting for Urd. Her needles clicked softly amid the scrapes of my sweeping bristles, but then a strange sound came from outside; ragged, panting twitters of delight, and the slaps of bare running feet.

"They're back!" Ingrid cried, breathlessly bursting inside our house. *"Branwulf's dragon is sailing into the fjord!"*

"Father's home!" I shouted, throwing down the broom.

"Thron, comb your hair and put on your new tunic," Mother threw aside her knitting, but I ran to my bed, yanked up my stained, gray blanket, and shoved my hand inside its scratchy, matted straw. My fingers closed upon my prize: my new wooden sword extended a handswidth longer than my arm, and gleamed from innumerable polishes. Carved out of dense walnut, I'd heated, sanded, and sharpened it until it was razor-sharp and hard as steel. Father would be impressed, perhaps enough to take me on the viking next summer. After all, I wasn't a kid anymore.

"When did you make that?" Mother demanded. "Put it away!"

"I made it for Father!" I argued.

Mother quickly unbraided her long, curly red tresses and brushed them. She'd have burned my sword for firewood long ago, had she seen it, yet I caught a strange, worried look in her eyes as she hurried.

"Put on your striped tunic ... and you can bring it," Mother said.

I hesitated, uncertain. Mother was usually strict, especially about my toys. She never allowed me to play with real weapons; she even yelled when she caught Garand and I stick-fighting. But I wasn't going to miss the opportunity to save my new sword from the woodpile, not if all that I had to do was change clothes. I flipped back the lid of my cedar chest; inside lay my two other trousers, my nightshirt, winter stockings, and my new striped tunic.

"Ingrid, wash the dishes and sweep the dirt," Mother said. "Everything must be perfect when Thorir gets here."

"It'll be ready," Ingrid promised.

Mother threw off her apron, then struggled into an overdress that I'd not seen since the day she'd finished sewing it, bright green with wide red snakes twisting around the collar, sleeves, and hem. She checked herself in the mirror again, carefully examined her slender, motherly face, pushed on her bushy red hair as if to shape it, smoothed her dress over her hay-beige chemise, and then lifted Urd from her cradle.

"Father's never seen Urd before, has he?" I asked.

"No, he left before I birthed her. I hope that he isn't angry; his last request before he sailed was for another son."

"What ...?"

"Nothing, Thron. Put on your leather belt and winter shoes."

Quickly I drug my stiff wool tunic over my head. It was thick and scratchy but striped black and gray, and had a yellow torse sewn around its collar with fanged sea-dragons facing each other. Mother said that it'd give me the strength of real dragons, but I could only wear it when we went someplace special. I had to dig under my bed for my winter shoes and force my feet into them; I didn't like shoes, but I wanted to look my best for Father. Then I buckled on my wide leather belt and slid my prized walnut sword into its place so that Father would see it at once.

"Do we have any fresh meat?" Mother asked.

"Only what's left of the pheasant we smoked," Ingrid said.

"Start a stew with it. Thicken it with two eggs, the good flour, and use the last of the spices; Thorir's first dinner home can't be boiled turnips."

"Do you think he was successful?"

"We won't make it through the winter if he wasn't. Wait, Thron."

Mother turned to face our idols and bowed her head. I looked also; beside our door hung a small rack of painted ceramic figures, our family's tribute to the gods.

"Blessed Frigg," Mother prayed, *"let all be well. Please."*

She paused, silent, and then Mother wrapped Urd in the plaid blanket that Father'd brought back from Scotland. I ran outside, but Mother ordered me to wait. I pushed aside a dirty pig and opened the gate for her, then closed it behind us.

Lots of people travelled our path. Mother had taught me to count to a hundred, and afterwards I'd counted everything in our village. We had two docks, fourteen farms, three ranches, and eighty-three people, when the men were home. During the summer, after the plantings sprouted, most of the men went viking to get treasures. Father had gotten me a brass chain with a real copper coin on it last year, and I didn't take it off until Mother had to sell it. I couldn't wait to see what he got me this year.

Hal and Smiðr rode past, Hal racing away from the fjord, Smiðr riding toward town. We moved aside for them, but both knew Mother and waved. Hal was my old friend; he used to live in our barn, and he waved cheerfully to me, too.

Smiðr actually stopped and spoke cordially to Mother in his deep, growling voice, but he barely glanced at me. I watched amazed; Smiðr was our smith, and us boys called him Smiðr the Sword-Maker. He also forged cooking pots and plow blades, but who cares about those?

Mother walked too slowly for me. She finally made me come back and hold her hand; I complained, but she threatened to send me home, and I knew better than to defy her; my leather belt had more uses than holding my walnut sword.

As we neared the butcher's, something I'd never heard before stung my ears: Lady Hodkins, Derek's mother, was crying, but like I'd never imagined, a miserable, drawn-out wailing. I'd never seen a grownup cry in public.

"Merta ...!" Mother shouted, dropping my hand to run to her. Mother grabbed her ... as if Lady Hodkins would've fallen without support.

"The Danes!" Lady Hodkins sobbed. "*The Danes ...!"*

"Thorir," Mother said firmly. "Did you see him?"

Dumbly I stood there, confused. *See Father?* Why did Mother need to ask? Father always came home on the ship. He'd have wonderful gifts, tell great stories, and we'd all be happy.

Sobbing uncontrollably, and despite Mother clutching her arm, slowly Derek's mother collasped onto her knees on our dirt path.

"Thorir!" Mother demanded desperately, shaking her arm.

Suddenly a scream burst from the village. Something was wrong; Father's homecoming hadn't gone as planned. My eyes widened; *something was wrong with Father!*

"Father!" I cried, and I bolted toward the docks.

"Thron ...!" Mother shouted, but I dashed ahead. Familiar houses blurred past my vision, but I didn't stop until I'd pushed through the crowd standing before our two narrow docks, watching as men unloaded the great dragon.

"Stand back, boy," warned one of the men, but I couldn't wait.

"Father!" I cried out.

"You're Thorir's boy, Thron, aren't you?" the man asked. "Wait here. Your father'll be off soon."

I gasped, seeing their cargo. A man lay unmoving on a shield between them; he seemed to be sleeping, but he wasn't breathing, looked ghastly pale, and strangely ... familiar.

"Is Garad here?" the man asked me.

My throat constricted. Slowly, as if through a winter fog, I remembered the dead man's face: Holbarki, Garad's father. *My best friend's father was dead.*

"Father!" I shouted.

Garad's father moved on, carried past the crowd of onlookers, which I was barely aware of despite their bitter chorus of sobs and whispers. Another pair of warriors came down our narrow dock carrying a large round shield; upon it lay a dead man I didn't recognize, but I couldn't take my eyes off him. Chalk white, mouth open, and his right arm missing, they carried him past me into the crowd.

I stood terrified, aghast, wondering who'd next be carried off the ship.

"Father!" I shouted as I recognized his features.

"Thron?" Father asked, and then I was holding him, my arms tight about his leg. *Father was alive!*

"Let go, Thron," Father said.

I didn't. Tears poured down my face. *Never had I been so scared!* Yet Father never reached down to me. Instead, he lifted his leg, carrying me with him, and proceeded through the crowd. Behind his back, Father and a tall blonde man carried another corpse.

Attached to his leg, Father carried me into Tavern Hall, the largest building ever. Everyone in our village could crowd into Tavern Hall, if all of the tables were leaned against the walls. The tables were set out today, three laden with corpses. Father and the tall man set their burden down upon the fourth.

"That's the last," the tall blonde man said.

"More than we could afford," Father said.

"Come, Thorir, let's get your gear unloaded. We've two more stops today."

Strong hands seized my ribs, pried me off, and lifted me high. As we hugged, I squeezed myself against Father as hard as I could, so hard that he grunted, as if in pain, although that was nonsense; *nothing could hurt Father.* When next I looked, Father had carried me out of the tavern and onto the dock.

Amazed, I stared as he carried me out onto our narrow dock, stepped over the rail, and onto the gigantic ship. Branwulf's dragon was huge, the biggest vessel in the world, and could hold more people than I could count. Doubtlessly two such ships could hold all of the people in the world.

The dragon was beautiful, a real dragon's head turned to wood and mounted on the front, its curling, petrified tail mounted on the aft. Its mast towered, strung with ropes for climbing. Branwulf's dragon rocked and bobbed on the water as if alive, and I dreamt of the day I'd sail on it to find the greatest toys in the world. Father had promised that someday I'd join him, and together we'd conquer England.

Lots of strange men squeezed aboard, lifting chests and

bags, some standing in line, waiting to get off. These warriors were almost as big as Father, whose ancestors were giants, yet none of them looked happy, and some glared at me.

"Hold tight, Thron," Father said, and he spun me on his neck so that my feet hung down his back. Then, with a lot of groaning, he lifted a huge barrel.

"Thorir, let me help you," said the tall blonde stranger, stepping over and taking the bottom of the barrel.

"Thanks," Father said, and he braced, reached down with his other hand, and picked up a large bag. Slowly they inched their way around the other men, and finally down the long dock. They pushed to the outside of the crowd and set their burdens down.

"Vespa!" Father cried.

Mother smiled brightly, though tears drenched her cheeks, and Father ran to hug her with me bouncing against his back. He held her long and kissed her, and the warmth that I barely remembered suddenly flamed again.

"Thank Odin you're home," she said.

"Who's this?"

"This is your daughter, Urd."

"Urd? Your grandmother?"

"I wanted to honor her."

"A good name. A fine daughter. You've done well. Vespa, this is Sammuel, from Finland. We've been like brothers all summer."

"A pleasure, good sir."

"I've heard much of you, dear lady."

"He saved my life."

My eyes snapped open. The stranger was tall and thin with a beard that looked like a new broom with too few straws. He wore no shirt, his once-pale skin now red with sunburn. He wore no shoes.

"You have my deepest gratitude, sir," Mother said.

"Don't believe all he says," Sammuel smiled. "He saved my hide a dozen times. Well, I have to be off; my sea-chest has no lock and I don't like being out of sight of it. Next year ...?"

"I'll look for you," Thorir promised.

"I won't sail with anyone else," Sammuel said.

Father hugged Sammuel long and hard. Finally they released, and Sammuel nodded to Mother, then walked away without another word.

Father turned to Mother. "We lost forty-seven men this year. Almost didn't get back at all."

Slowly he drew my arms apart and lowered me to the ground. Then Father reached toward my belt and pulled out my walnut sword. Quietly he held it up and examined it.

"Did you make this?"

"Yes," I said.

"Good. Vespa, stay here and watch my things ... our things. I have to attend to the fallen."

Mother nodded. Father started to turn away, and then he looked at my walnut sword in his hands.

"Come, Thron. It's time you learned what this is."

* * * * * * * * *

"Stay silent and behind me," Father whispered. "Watch and listen."

My sword in his hands, Father led the way back into Tavern Hall. Shouted orders bellowed from the ship, probably from Branwulf himself, and men hurried to comply. Lines were cast from the dock. The big dragonship floated slowly away, helped by sailors pushing it with oars. I loved watching ships set sail, but obediently followed Father into the gloom.

Four corpses covered the tables. Men clustered around them, muttering softly, a deep rumble that echoed incoherently. The air reeked of blood and decay, and I hardly dared breathe, fearful of interrupting the solemn atmosphere. Never had I seen faces so grave.

I barely knew most of the men, so seldom was I allowed to visit the village. Beside Smiðr stood Digr, who was very fat and owned the biggest farm, and beside Digr stood Brún and Trandill, both of whom were owned by Digr, farmhands that he took viking each year. Rath was there, of course, with his big axe, talking to a couple of older village men whose names I couldn't remember.

"Thorir, we've decided to hold the burials together below Seal Ridge on Thor's Day," Trandill said.

Father nodded. "Who has the sacks?"

"I do," Digr said. "We thought to present them at the funerals, but ..."

"Their families will have enough to think about then," Father said. "Give out the sacks today. Waiting until the funeral will be hard; give them something else to dwell upon."

"Gaceth lived by you. Will you take his sack to Eardai?" Smiðr asked.

Digr nodded.

"I'll take Holbarki's to Grettir," Father said.

"Clamsby said that we could leave the bodies here as long as it doesn't get too hot, so people can grieve properly," Digr said.

"Meet here shortly after the cock's cry," Father said.

"My sons are old enough to chop wood," said one of the

older men whose name I couldn't remember. "I'll send them over to Seal Ridge tomorrow."

The impromptu meeting suddenly dissolved. Without ceremony or words, the men seemed to know that it was over. Two left right away, hurrying out into the open air, while the rest broke into groups, talking quietly. Father stood still as stone, eyes closed, head bowed.

"They were good men, very brave," Father said.

"Except Turhelm ...," Brún interjected.

"We take that to our graves!" Father said harshly.

"Better a corpse than a coward," Brún said.

"True," Father said. "But my lips won't stain his sons with the disgrace of a shipmate."

Everyone nodded in silence. Father frowned, then lifted up my wooden sword, which looked tiny in his hand. He examined it again, then held it out.

"My son made this."

Brún took it, sighted down the length of it, and ran his thumb across its edge. Others came over to look at it. Brún smiled, but the other faces were grim.

"Thron's first key to Odin," Hal said, smiling at me.

"Good start for a warrior," Digr said, taking the sword from Brún and holding it up.

"Does he know what it's for?" Brún asked.

"He will," Father said.

Father lifted me, and turned me to face the morbid tables. I eyed the fallen, and dared not breathe or close my eyes.

"The measure of a man is who he can kill," Father said to me. "See these corpses? Wealth belongs to the last man standing; sometimes we won, sometimes not. This is what happens when we lose. Remember these faces every time you draw a weapon. In all fights, death claims your enemy ... or you."

Clamped in Father's grip, and with all the village men watching, I stared at the horrible, dead faces. Ghastly, they laid motionless, hollow shells of warriors who were no more; pale, sunken, and reeking. I knew only one of them, and he seemed the most horrid. I shuddered, but I didn't turn away.

"I'll remember, Father."

* * * * * * * * *

Dinner was a feast. Father sat at the head of our table while Ingrid served us spicy pheasant stew rich with turnips and onions, flavored with pepper and thyme, and freshly-baked bread.

"Where's Hal and Morgan?"

"Morgan's dead," Mother said, and Father's smile vanished. "Morgan died trying to protect us. Five men, strangers from Lapland by their accent, broke in one night."

"What!?!" Father demanded.

"It's long past, Thorir," Mother said, glancing at me, and Father followed her gaze. "We'll talk about it later."

I fell silent, remembering that horrible night: strange men with swords burst inside when Morgan opened our door to go out. I'd been carving a large oaken cooking fork while Mother wove by candlelight and Ingrid washed the dishes. They killed Morgan, and threatened to do the same to us, if we screamed. They bound Hal with leather thongs and gagged him. I was locked in Mother's clothes chest, but I could hear the nasty sounds. They took Urd, who was then newborn, and promised that they'd kill her if Mother and Ingrid didn't obey them. They stole many of our things, and Mother and Ingrid had cried for weeks.

"What about Hal?" Father asked, frowning, his voice deep.

"I had to sell Hal. It was him or Ingrid, and he was worth more. Digr's wife bought him."

Father lowered his head. "I should've been here."

"You had tasks of your own," Mother said. "Those tasks are doubly important now. What happened ...?"

Father glared strangely at Mother, as if wishing her to continue, but her face was pale, and Ingrid stood frozen behind her, stiff-lipped, fighting back tremors.

"I'll tell you of our summer," Father said sternly.

* * * * * * * * *

"Things went well at first. We sailed toward the western coast of Scotland, where the rivers are less defended. In the second week, we boarded two merchant vessels and pirated all that they had. With fresh supplies, we sailed out to sea and came at Ireland from the west. We landed in the first glow of dawn at a large farm and killed every man there, feasted on swine and chicken, and opened all of their kegs. They had some wealth, apparently, but Captain Branwulf took that.

"It was about the first of May when things went wrong. We'd taken several more farms and another merchant ship, which we kept as a second ship just to carry our booty, when we heard a bell tolling in the morning fog. On a small island, we spied a Christian monastery near a rickety dock, completely unguarded. It was a great site, facing away from the mainland. Branwulf wanted to use it as a base from which we could raid the Irish for weeks.

"That cursed bell was a lure. Hundreds of arrows shot at us as we reached its barred doors, both from inside the monastery and from the nearby woods. Fires sprang up from flaming bottles of oil that they dropped upon us from the tower. Men fell by the dozens, and still we couldn't see our enemy.

"We fled back to the boats, plying oars while arrows hailed. Over half of our company was wounded, including Rath, Digr, and me."

I bolted upright. *"Father...?"*

"I'm well-healed; I took one arrow in the arm and another grazed my side. I was one of the lucky; men were dying for days.

"We sailed out to open sea, hoping to lose ourselves from pursuit; Irishmen seldom give up the scent of blood. Sharks ate our dead. Then a terrible storm forced us inland.

"Blind, not knowing what rocks we might hit, we drove our ships up onto sand at night near a heavy stand of trees. We anchored, ran ashore, and there we spent the next three days, building fires for warmth and sleeping in wet clothes under under dripping pines. After too many cold nights at sea, land was welcomed, although the rain never stopped. One of the men shot a deer and we cooked it while it bled.

"With dwindling supplies, Branwulf announced that we needed another target; the viking season doesn't last forever. We went after cargo ships, since that had been our easiest prey, but we found only worthless fishing boats. Two weeks passed, and our fresh water ran out.

"We raided another farm, but it was no equal to the first. We slaughtered their animals and took them whole onto the ship ..."

Father kept talking, but in my mind I clearly saw both of us viking together. I'd fight beside Father, and we'd charge across England and France leading hundreds of warriors. We'd always be foremost, holding the front line, or in the lead ship. We'd fight like Odin, Villi, and Ve. In combat, none would stand against us; our swords would slice through any armor. Foemen who dared come within our reach would die in pieces. Enemy blood would paint us, and castles and empires would crumble before us! Men would see our courage, our giant-bred strength, and flock to us! We'd be kings, heaped with every treasure on Earth, and I'd never have to plant or harvest another turnip. We'd build a castle on our farm, and Ingrid would serve us roast venison and sugar-dates every night. All of the other kids would sing my praises ... and even Derek would bow down before me!

"We sailed too close to Denmark," Father continued. "Heavily armed and well-supplied, their sailors get to keep all of the treasure that they capture, so their warships are manned only by the best. Rams are mounted on their bows just below the waterline; steel-capped spikes that can tear a dragon in two. One spied us early in the morning, and the chase began.

"We rowed for hours under the hot August sun, and thought we were escaping westward, until we saw another ship there, sailing right at us. Branwulf should've expected it; Norsemen have been raiding south since great-grandfather's days, and too-well the Christians have learned to fight. Pinched between their ships, we steered north and rowed without rest until dawn. But the moon was bright, the night clear, and we couldn't shake them.

"Branwulf decided to fight ... before rowing exhausted us. We'd stolen more than treasure over the summer, so we made ready. Suddenly we turned east, toward one of our pursuers. Both ships turned to meet us.

"Arrows pierced us as we approached, but Branwulf had us hold our weapons until the last minute. We braced behind our shields with four oars strapped to our prow to fend off the deadly ram. Our rowers had precise instructions; if they failed, then we'd sink.

"At the last minute, we flung thirty flaming flasks of oil at them, as the Irish had done to us. Our oarsmen proved their merit, avoiding the spike and keeping our ships apart. Many of their men tried running across our oars, but we met them with spears, and they fell to the fishes. A few made it onto our ship, and they fought like madmen.

"We drove right past their ship and kept sailing. Those of us left fell to the oars and rowed. Our oarsmen, who'd so bravely kept our ships from ramming, had suffered the brunt of the Dane's arrows: half of them were wounded, dead, or dying.

"We shoved them aside and rowed. The Dane's ship was afire, both vessel and crew. The other ship stopped to help them while we rowed as fast as we could.

"That's the tale of it. Our dead we carried home. Branwulf paid us well, which he could easily afford; we started out with one hundred and forty-four men and ended up with ninety-seven, twelve badly wounded. We collected portions for each of our neighbor's widows; sacks of copper coins and jewelry, and Branwulf added a silver coin to each sack. We lost six from this village, four in our last fight, three of whom were oarsmen, and Holbarki, who fell beneath a Danish axe."

* * * * * * * * *

"Show me your sword again," Father said, leaning back in his chair. I ran to get it, eyeing the large bag and heavy barrel that Mother had helped Father carry home; I couldn't wait to see what they contained. I knew that Mother felt the same, but Father liked to delay his surprises as long as possible. I brought him my sword and he examined it again.

"Have you made anything else?" he asked.

He knew that I had; that's what we did at night while the candles glowed. Mother worked her loom while Ingrid spun, and I carved hardwoods; making plates, bowls, spoons, or whatever. Ladles were my specialty, and I ran to the kitchen to retrieve several. As Father turned them over in his hands, complimenting me on my craftsmanship, Mother told him of the pieces that she'd traded for dyes and needles. Father seemed very proud. Then Urd started to cry, and he insisted on holding her again.

Finally, Father had me bring him the big sack that he'd brought home; it was much heavier than I'd expected. Father placed it on the floor between his feet and opened it up; it was full of clothes. He pulled out a long, white nightshirt that shined in the candlelight.

"Silk!" Mother exclaimed, and she took it greedily. He also had several fancy dresses, fine bed linens, and rolls of exquisite cloths for sewing. Lastly, he pulled out a thick coat of fox-skins, and Mother had to try it on right away, and wore it while she hugged him.

I could barely contain my excitement as Father opened the barrel. First, he reached in and pulled out a pair of tall candleholders, solid brass, and set them on the table. Then he pulled out other things; metal pots, fireplace hooks, iron tools, fancy bed curtains, and several small chests and boxes, mostly empty, however one contained lots of sea shell and bronze jewelry, which Mother and Ingrid fawned over, laughing delightedly. It was obviously more than they'd expected, but I waited impatiently.

"I don't know if you'll want this, Thron," Father said to me at last. "Your walnut sword is so nice, I don't know if you'll want ... this one."

Father held up the most beautiful sword that I'd ever seen. Longer than my walnut sword, it rested encased in a wooden scabbard covered with black leather. Its crossguard and pommel of polished iron shined, divided by a grip wrapped in leather thong. Slowly Father drew it; its steel blade flashed in the candlelight. I took it reverently, trembling, as proud as I could be. I held it up, then viciously stabbed at an imaginary foe.

Father laughed loudly.

"Men's hands are stained by the blood of their enemies," Father lectured me. "Impress Odin with that sword ... if you would be honored."

Father lifted other treasures from the barrel, valuable or useful, including a small pouch of two silver coins and fourteen copper ones, but I paid scant attention. Clutching my prize, my paradise was sheathing and unsheathing it, examining every detail of its surface. I hugged Father and thanked him many times; I'd wanted Father to start thinking of me as a warrior, and found that he already did.

* * * * * * * * *

"What did you want us to do...? Let them kill your daughter...?"

I awoke to Mother's voice, unusually shrill and angry. Father slammed the door behind him and Ingrid burst out crying.

"Father ...?"

"Go back to sleep, Thron," Ingrid said. "He'll be back soon. We had to tell him about the men who robbed us."

Bleary-eyed, I glanced about the room. More things than I recalled lay on the table, fancy daggers, metal forks, and matching spoons that Father must've pulled out of his barrel after I was sent to bed. Mother and Ingrid had seemed so happy then; now they seemed sad.

"Close your eyes, Thron."

Knowing not to argue, I rolled over and faced the wall. My new sword, scabbarded, I found still in my hand; I must've been clutching it in my sleep. I couldn't wait to show it to Garad.

Garad! I'd forgotten - *Garad wouldn't be smiling tonight.* He'd have no prizes, no gifts from his father, no tales to tell of his courage and craftiness. I had no idea what I'd say to him.

Ingrid's shadow crossed the wall momentarily as I heard her go to Mother.

"Go after him," she whispered.

Quietly I glanced back at them. Ingrid helped Mother put on her new fox coat; both were crying ... I never understood why they cried so much. I could barely remember the things that the robbers had stolen from us. Whatever they took, the women missed it very badly.

Long I laid there, pretending to sleep as Ingrid pulled the covers tight around me. The flickering candlelight danced upon the wall, and the last thing that I remembered was that I wasn't the least bit sleepy.

* * * * * * * * *

Father hadn't told me bedtime stories for a long time, but sometimes I remembered them. Mornings were when I usually recalled them, somewhere between dreams and awakening, when the world is silent and gray, and I'm warm and tingly, I can still see Father smiling and leaning over my bed.

"One quick story, Thron, and then you must sleep.

"Once, very long ago, our ancestors were giants, as tall as the mountains, with skins as hard as rocks. All men feared us, and cowered in our shadows, and we were the lords of thick forests, where we built great halls and palaces beside the sea. But our hearts were as big as our fists, and eventually we fell in love with human women, who bore us children that were as much human as giant. Generations passed, and each time the human blood grew stronger in our veins, and so we grew shorter, until only the very wisest could see the strain of giants living in our blood. Yet still we were renowned as the mightiest of all.

"Then, one terrible stormy night, in the heart of winter, disaster fell. Jealous of all that we owned, puny mortals attacked our halls and palaces with fire, igniting even the forests around us. We killed them easily, but the rising flames encircled our burning homes, and we stood trapped between raging fires and the stormy sea.

"Having no choice, we piled ourselves and a few possessions into one mighty dragon and set sail blindly into the night. Behind us, fire consumed everything that we owned – all of our wealth and power, our plowed fields, and herds of cattle.

"The sea washed us into this fjord, where we arrived penniless, without even food to feed our children. We sold our dragon for this farm and supplies to last us through harvest. But your great, great grandfather made a promise that first night before he slept in this house; he promised that someday our family would rise back up, reclaim our wealth and power, and again we'd be kings of men.

"That day is coming, Thron. You and me, someday – we are going to viking south to find treasures beyond imagining. Then all men shall fear us, and we'll be giants again!"

* * * * * * * * *

"How did Garad's father die?"

Father glanced over and saw my best friend leaning against his barn door.

"Let's go tell Garad," he said.

"Wait. I want to get something."

I ran to the house, grabbed both of my swords, and ran back out. Father looked at me questioningly.

"I want to give my wooden sword to Garad."

Father smiled slightly and nodded. We walked over together.

Garad's eyes were red, his young face haggard, his hair unkempt. I'd have known that something was wrong just from that; his mother used oil on his hair and fussed whenever he got dirty.

"Hello, Garad," Father said. "Where's your mother?"

"Sleeping."

"Good," Father said. "I think that you should know how your father died. He was very brave and saved all of our lives. He'd want you to remember him well."

Garad said nothing, just looked at the real sword in my hand. I felt ashamed. My father had lived to bring me presents, while his ...

I held out my walnut sword. Garad knew it well. He'd tried to make his own, but a flaw in the wood had bent his when he'd heated it.

"Father brought me a real sword. I ... want you to have this one."

Garad looked at my walnut blade as if it were dung.

"It's proper that you should take it," Father instructed. "Bring your mother over for dinner tonight and I'll give you a steel dagger to match it."

Obediently Garad accepted the wooden sword, and then Father sat between us, his wide back against their barn's side door.

"Your father was a good man and a good friend. I once saw him tear his only tunic in half to bandage a stranger who'd been pierced with a spear. He was a great fighter, too. Watching him fight reminded me of the tales of your grandsire, that your father and I listened to when we were your age. Holbarki liked to throw his weight against his foes, once he had their weapons entangled, and then break them with the strength of his arms. Strong as an ox he was. Few dared wrestle him, and he was crafty, clever with a sword. He could shoot a heavy bow, too."

Father kept talking, slowly, his deep voice carving a picture of Garad's father as a hero, how he always led the way into farmhouses or ran across oars to board enemy ships. I listened, fascinated, but my attention stayed on my friend. Garad sat still as best he could, although his tears rained the whole time. Sometimes he cried so hard that Father had to stop and wait, but mostly he sat silent, tears dripping off his chin. Finally, Father picked Garad up and set him in his lap. By the time that he told how Holbarki had kept rowing even with four feathered shafts stuck in his flesh, his back to an axeman running across the oars, we were all crying, and I'd learned the truth: Garad's father was a hero.

"Go inside soon," Father told Garad as he set him beside me. "Your mother needs you now, more than you know. Don't forget to tell her of my invitation. We'll expect you for dinner before dark."

Father got up and walked back toward our fields. I carefully placed my hand on Garad's shoulder, not knowing if he was aware of me or not.

"We should make a song about your father," I said.

* * * * * * * * *

"Wealthy men don't eat boiled turnips every night," Father said as we walked back to our house, after surveying our ripe fields. "Have you ever butchered a pig?"

"No."

"Well, pick out an old male and you'll butcher him today."

I knew instantly which one would be best, the fat one with the black spot around one eye. I showed him to Father, and he nodded.

"Draw your sword, Thron, and give me the scabbard."

I did as ordered, silent and confused.

"Kill the pig."

I glanced at the pig. He outweighed me and had big teeth and hooves. I looked at the naked sword in my hand, then up at Father.

"Aren't we going to tie him up?" I asked.

"Do you want to end up like Garad's father? You need to learn to fight ... now ... while I'm here. You must learn to defend yourself and your mother ... for when I'm gone."

I hesitated, uncertain. When he was gone? Did he mean that I wouldn't go with him next summer ... or was he talking about ... *when he died?* A shudder ran up my spine*; if it could happen to Garad's father* ... no, I couldn't even think that.

"Foemen don't like to die. The pig will resist. Kill the pig."

I turned to face the smelly beast. He was no different than any of the others, but I tried to think as if he were. *He was my foe!*

With a shout, I charged the pig, my sword held high. He bolted as I attacked, but I was determined; I chased him down and swung my blade hard at his neck.

The fat pig moved faster than I'd expected. My blade gashed the back of his rump, evoking a human-like screech, before he ran off. I turned back and looked at Father, who stood still and silent, watching.

My foe had run to the far edge of the pig-pen, pushing aside the others, all of whom grunted loudly. My mighty sword had done far less damage than I'd expected, but I wasn't going to fail with Father watching. I held my sword out and walked through the muck toward my foe.

The pig backed up against the fence. The other pigs nervously moved away. My foe squealed and grunted as if both crying for help and trying to frighten me. My feet sank deep into the muck; it squished between my toes. Mother would shout angrily if she saw me walking here; good thing that I wasn't wearing my fancy tunic.

The pig bolted past me. I jumped at him and swung my sword, but I only splashed to my knees. The pig fled squealing out of the pen and across our fields. I glanced at Father again, but he said nothing.

I spent an hour running after the pig, hopelessly chasing him, before I gave up. He'd bolt before I got within a dozen yards of him. Finally, I herded him back. It took a long time, and I was hot, dirty, and smelly before he stupidly ran back inside his familiar pen. I followed him in and pulled the gate closed behind me.

The fat old pig made noises like I'd never heard, as if he knew that he was trapped. I held my sword tightly in both hands and slowly approached. His squeals made all of the other pigs nervous, and he tried to bolt, but I moved carefully, keeping him hemmed in the corner against the boards.

Finally I could approach no closer. We stared at each other, unblinking, and I tensed. I had to be patient, and spring like lightning from the clouds. I waited anxiously, my steel sword tight in my grip, more nervous than ever before.

I jumped and swung, and suddenly he came at me. Everything went black – I choked. Pain shot through me so many ways that I couldn't tell where it came from. I heard the pig grunting, but muffled, as if I was underwater.

Father's hands pulled me from the muck. I rose covered in filth, hair to toes; ears, mouth, and nose – all plugged and fouled. Blood leaked from my arm.

"Boys fight, men kill," Father said. "Watch."

I clawed and spat, digging the crap from my face. Shaking my head, I spied Father lift my sword from the muck. He held it up and wiped the blade off with a rag. Slowly he stepped toward the gate.

Suddenly he turned and stepped toward the pig, so fast that I almost missed it. My sword, in his hand, stabbed through the squealing pig, driven into one ear, which cut into the swine's brain. The squeal died instantly ... and so did the pig.

Father and I stared the the dead pig.

"Never forget that we're Norsemen," Father said. "Kill a

beast, you take from it everything it owns. Kill a man, no difference."

* * * * * * * * *

Chapter 2

*   *   *   *   *   *   *   *   *

Again, the bedtime stories that Father used to tell haunted my dreams.

"Ymir was his cursed name," Father said. "Ymir, first of all things, arose from the bubbling waters of Gunningap, where the hot fires of Munspell met the frozen ice of Niflhiem. Ymir wasn't just a giant, he was the tallest and mightiest of all the terrible giants. Ymir was the most evil thing that ever was ... or ever would be.

"Buri was the first man, and he was more than a man – Buri was a god. Buri was licked out of the ice by the great cow, Amundula, and he was best of men; all that is good. Buri married a giantess and fathered Bor the Aseir, who, many years later, fathered the three mightiest Vanir: Odin, Villi, and Ve.

"Ymir hated Buri because he was loved by all. Eventually

Ymir killed Buri; it was the first and most-foul murder. And even though Odin, Villi, and Ve avenged their grandfather and killed Ymir, they couldn't bring Buri back to life.

"You must learn from them, my son; you live in the same world that they were born in. You will face the same evils they faced. Always be wary of friends, distrustful of strangers, and prepared to fight at any time. Always remember, Thron: evil came first, and thus, evil is stronger than good."

* * * * * * * * *

On Thor's day, I awoke before Father and Mother. Even Ingrid still slept. I sat up, then spied my new sword in the folds of my blanket. It felt cold in my hands, but I gripped it tightly; *this was the weapon of a man, of a warrior, the dream of every boy!* Quietly, I took it and crept to the door, removed the brace, and slipped outside.

Thor's day dawned gray and cloudy. I walked out, ignoring the chickens that crowded around demanding their cup of feed. I drew the steel blade and slid my finger carefully across its edge. The sharp metal cut lightly through the tiny swirling lines on my fingertips, and I stopped before it cut deeply enough to draw blood. My sword was deadly; *no wonder that it'd killed the black-eyed pig so easily!* Yet that had been in Father's hands. The worst that I'd done was scratch its back, a dismal failure considering how sharp it was. I should have cut the beast's head off and handed it to Father as a trophy. *How proud he'd have been of me then!*

The hungry chickens pressed about me. I slashed my blade down and the ends of several tail feathers cleanly sliced off. The chick complained noisily and several scattered squawking. I smiled and kicked the others back despite their clamor. I stabbed at the air, then spun around, slaying every foeman who dared face me. *Never again would I fail in Father's eyes! The next pig that I hunted wouldn't have a prayer!*

Swinging wildly, I charged and ducked, spun and jumped. My sword felt like magic in my hands. Dozens of gigantic imaginary foes fell screaming ... and I laughed triumphantly.

Suddenly something hit me in the head and I dropped my sword, crying out in pain. My hand flew to the back of my head, and when I pulled it back, I found that a clump of my hair had fallen out. My hand was glistening red. A wet trickle ran down the back of my neck. I glanced at my sword where it lay on the grass; *blood colored its edge near the tip.*

I started to scream, but I choked it back; *I couldn't tell Father that I'd hit myself with my own sword!* I carefully probed the wound, feeling a small gash, nothing worse. It was bleeding badly, but no worse than my knees when I skinned them. I pressed my hand hard against it, trying to force the bleeding to stop. *I couldn't let anyone know about this!*

An hour later, Ingrid came out.

"Did you feed the hens?" she asked as they ran to her.

"No," I shouted from behind the fencepost, still pressing my hand over my wound.

"Why not?" Ingrid demanded, and then she huffed. "Feed them, and the pigs, and hurry! Your mother wants you dressed for the funerals."

Ingrid went back inside. I looked at the drying blood on my hands and tried to wipe it onto the fencepost, but with little success. I scooped up a handful of dirt and scrubbed with it until it crumbled in my hands, taking much of the telltale blood with it.

I ran to the barn, scooped a cup of feed from the bin, and

flung it at the starving chickens, and then got the slop bucket from its perch and emptied it into the pig's trough, spreading it out so that no one pig could eat it all. They clustered around me, but I pushed through them. The black-eyed pig wasn't there; Father had taught me how to cut it up so that the blood drained properly, and then we hung its pieces in our pantry. Ingrid cooked a whole leg for our dinner with Garad and his mother, which was very sad. Father gave Garad a beautiful dagger, not as big as my sword but polished like a mirror, and told in more detail about Garad's father's bravery. When he walked them home it was very late; Father carried Garad, who'd fallen asleep.

I gently touched my wound; it hurt badly but it wasn't bleeding anymore, so I hoped that I could hide it. I quietly opened our door, crossed to my chest, and pulled off my tunic. I dressed facing them, keeping the back of my head toward the wall, and no one seemed to notice. Then I gently put on my winter cap, stuck my sword in my belt, and hurried outside. My head was throbbing.

* * * * * * * * *

"Keep a close eye on Grettir's place while we're gone," Father told Ingrid. "She and Garad have to be at the funerals, and everyone knows it. It'd be a black deed to rob a house while the family's at funeral, but some men have no honor. Wind my horn loud if any strangers appear, and bar yourself inside."

Father and Mother came out, Father with our axe in his belt, Mother with a basket of fresh-baked bread, and we walked to the village. It grew foggy as we descended, and soon we tramped through a thick mist.

A crowd had gathered before Tavern Hall, mostly quiet, save for the women weeping. Many dressed in white, the traditional color of mourning, and I spied Garad and his mother. I'd never seen Garad dressed entirely in white before, but I said nothing as Father led us into the crowd. Mother stopped to talk to someone in white, but Father vanished into the hall without saying a word.

I didn't know what to do or say. Garad's eyes were red. I went to him, and we stood saying nothing.

Almost everyone in the village stood about; Kampi, his scarred face hiding behind his long, bushy whiskers, stood beside Widow Veðr, who'd lost her husband long ago. Lady Hodkins stood centermost with Øxna, Derek's grandmother, and Derek, all three in radiant white. I wasn't as close to Derek as I was to Garad; I didn't know what to say to him, either. Rath towered over everyone, standing beside his little blonde daughter, Helsa; Ormstunga, Rath's wife, had died of a sickness only two months before, while Rath was viking.

Hal patted Garad's shoulder and mine. Hal said that we both looked much bigger, and then he went on to talk to Gandr the One-Armed. I rarely saw Gandr, a fisherman who owned a small boat. Gandr used to go viking, but he'd lost his arm to a scythe while helping a friend harvest. He lived alone in a small house overlooking the fjord and seldom came into town. Gandr grinned a toothless smile at me, but he said nothing. Tall, youthful Hjálmun stood nearby; he hardly ever talked. All of the boys looked up to Hjálmun, although we knew little about him. He lived on the Widow Igrár's farm and helped her, when not viking.

Igrár stood beside Hjálmun; Igrár was the widow of Farmaðr, who'd brought Hjálmun to our village. Farmaðr had died a'viking two years ago.

Beigaldi, whose husband had died on his first viking after they were married, wandered about, sniffling into a rag. Beigaldi was a sickly woman, always with several babies and many small children around her. She was talking to Katla, who had a huge butt and had never married. Katla had made all of the pottery in our house, and her mother had made our idols of the gods and goddesses.

Halgrum waved at me; he was my best friend after Garad. Halgrum's father grew some leeks and celery, but mostly wheat for flour. Kal, Kampi's youngest son, stood near Beigaldi's eldest daughters: Sjóna, who was as old as Ingrid but very shy, and never left her house unless she had to, and stood by her older sister Skratui, whose dress was as immaculate as ever. Nobody liked Skratui; she was loud, hated getting dirty, and wore strange necklaces, claiming that they gave her magical powers.

Many kids came and stood by me. It was nice; we seldom gathered together. Like me, none of them knew what to do or say. Several reached out to touch my new sword, amazement in their eyes, and stroked the thin leather over my scabbard. I started to draw the blade, to show the boys, but a pair of fingers snapped sharply, and Hal signaled for me to put it away. I obediently slid the blade back into its resting place in my belt. The other kids looked disappointed; if my head hadn't been hurting so, then I'd have been very proud.

Suddenly a drum beat, loud and strong. Another beat followed. Slowly, men with drums, and others with torches, came out of Tavern Hall. The adults made a path and pulled us out of the way as the drummers and torchbearers walked slowly past us.

Finally Father came out, helping carry Garad's father on a tarp stretched between two poles. He walked slowly, stepping evenly with the other men. Some of the women began wailing, and all bowed their heads. Others followed in groups, carrying the bodies of our fallen townsmen between them. When all had passed, everyone fell into line behind their procession.

We walked down the fjord trail, in many places right past the water. I'd been here many times, but never walking this slowly. It grew annoying, intensified by the throbbing in my head. I kicked aside a big stone. Kal picked up a stick and hit each tree that we passed with it, but Kampi snatched the stick from his hand, hit Kal with it, and then dropped it beside the road. The rest of us tried not to fidget as we walked.

Seal Ridge was a narrow, rocky, treeless outcropping overlooking the mouth of the fjord. The men set the bodies onto the grassy lawn below it and pulled out their axes. Already a large pile of wood lay there, but the men vanished into the nearby woods and chopped more. Halgrum and Kal tried to go and watch, but Beigaldi stopped them, scolding them for not reverencing the dead. I stood and did nothing.

Hours passed. My legs ached, but I knew not to sit down; the few children that had dared to sit or play were promptly yelled at. I stood still, hoping that no one would notice me.

Finally the men carried back the newly-cut logs. They carefully stacked the logs against the rocks beneath the ridge, like they were building wooden forts. They also brought lots of dry, leafy branches and dead bushes, which they stuffed inside the wooden forts. Six stacks of wood they piled and leveled; when all was done, they lifted up the dead men, still on their tarps, and set them on top of the forts, upon the thick piles of wood and brush. Then several people came forward and set treasured items on the two remaining woodpiles to represent the dead who'd not been carried home. Finally, everyone stepped back, and one of the older men came forward to speak.

"Brave they were," the man said loudly. "They fought to feed their families, as every man should. They fought to save their brothers, and died protecting us, their friends, as we would've died to protect them. Let no one doubt their prowess or courage. Odin has called them to Him, and no mortal can resist His summons. The Norns have cut the threads of their lives. The Valkyrie have taken their spirits. Now we must send their bodies skyward."

As he talked, Father took my arm and led me to stand by Mother. I glanced behind to the fog-shrouded sea, then to the forests, wishing that I could escape without being noticed, when Father grabbed my head and turned me to face the speaker. I winced, staggering. Father looked puzzled, then snatched off my hat and held me still while he looked at the crusty wound on the back of my head. I knew I was in trouble, but Father said nothing, just slid my hat back over my head and pulled it down in the back. Slowly I looked up at him and saw his angry frown. Then he reached down, pulled my new sword out of my belt, and stuck it in his own.

Ashamed, I lowered my head; *I'd lost the greatest gift that Father had ever given me, the treasure that all of the other kids had wanted to see, and now never would.* It was the worst moment of my life.

The speaker told the great tales. I could only barely listen; the pain in my head stabbed, but I dared not cry out.

Movement distracted me from my misery. Clamsby and several of the other men carried a large table from Tavern Hall. He waved silently at the crowd, and Father pushed me beside Mother, then went off with him, as did many others, back down the fjord trail to the village.

One woman collapsed and had to be carried to the shore, but the speaker droned on. I tried to listen; the old tales were great, full of wicked craftiness and dangerous giants who fought relentlessly against the gods. When they told my favorite, of Thor and Loki's visit to Utgard, I pushed up to the front, but the speaker tended to mumble, and soon I lost interest; Father told it much better than he did.

Father and the others returned, burdened with another table and large bowls and baskets of food, and two men carried a keg. Clamsby tapped the keg with a small hammer, momentarily disrupting the speaker, but he quickly finished. They set the food on the tables and left it there, rejoining the crowd, listening to the speaker.

Although very old and thin, Eardai looked radiant in her white dress. She slowly backed out of the crowd and went to the table. She took a cup, filled it at the keg, and drank the whole cup, then selected a few tidbits of food and came back to her place in front. Several others followed her example, including Grettir, who took Garad with her, and made him drink and take a small wedge of bread and a slice of cheese. Then they returned to their place beside Eardai. Starving, I watched Garad eat, but Father and Mother ignored me. Others began going for food, and I was relieved when Father and Mother started backing out.

We each drank one cup of beer. The beer was weak, but I drank it greedily. Then I reached for some grapes, but Mother caught my hand and put half of a large carrot in it instead. Father took a small loaf of bread, tore it in half, and put half back on the table. Mother took one grape and a slice of dried fish, and we went back.

The day went on and on. By sunset, they'd finished telling the old tales, and other speakers told of the six men that had died. The older men spoke of their lives as young boys, of the pranks that they pulled, of the troubles that they caused, and of the punishments that they suffered. Next, some of the older women came forward; they spoke of the youth of the dead, of the noble young men that they'd grown into, and of the fine husbands and fathers that they later became. Then younger men, including Father, spoke next, telling of their bravery in battle and their cunning swordsmanship, detailing all of the deeds that led up to their falling under the shadow of the Danes, the Scots, and the Irish. Father knew all of them, and described each as a true viking warrior.

The sun set and new torches were lit. Finally, white cloths were brought forward and laid over the four bodies. Two more cloths were brought forward and laid over the treasured items of the missing dead, along with wreaths of colorful flowers. Then three lambs were led into the field. One man came forward and spoke in a strange language, waving his hands over them. Kampi, Hal, and Rath came forward with drawn swords and, at a signal from the speaker, they swept off the heads of the young lambs. The lambs were slaughtered, their bloody pieces arranged beside the bodies. Then buckets of fish oil were brought forward and poured onto the wooden forts, all around the bodies and the tokens of the dead.

"Odin!" cried the speaker. "Deny not these brave men the feasts of Your hall! In Valhalla, as in our hearts, let them live forever!"

Torches were cast onto the biers, and flames roared up, quickly engulfing the woodpiles. Sparks flew skyward. I watched the bodies in the dancing red flames, wondering if I'd actually see their spirits rise into the heavens – I didn't. The flames burned high, then slowly fell to a roaring mass as the tree trunks seared and hissed, dripping sap as the flames ate through their bark into green wood. I was amazed at how hot the green wood burned, but there was so much of it that, once ignited, nothing could quell it.

It started raining an hour after dark, and everyone headed back. It'd been a cool, overcast day, and the funeral fires did little to warm anyone. The men would come back with shovels later and raise mounds over the burned ashes and bones. Father led us back to the table, where we stood in line until Mother could collect her now-empty basket, and then we headed home.

"You were very well behaved," Mother said to me as we walked home. "All of the other children were fidgeting and getting in trouble. You made me proud."

Father scowled. I bowed my hurting head and said nothing.

* * * * * * * * *

Ingrid lifted off the brace and we entered. A hearty smell rose from the cooking pot hung over the fire. Urd slept in her basket beside the loom.

"Thank goodness," Mother said.

Father said nothing. He pulled out his axe and my sword, set them behind the door, and turned his big chair so that it faced away from the table.

"Vespa, take your son's hat off," Father growled.

I froze. Mother looked confused, but reached over and plucked my hat off. Father didn't move or speak. Mother ran her fingers through my hair, and I jumped. Instantly she pulled me into the candlelight, finding the missing hair and the blood-crusted gash on the back of my head.

"Thron!" she scolded.

"Thought that you could hide it, didn't you?" Father demanded. "That's three lashes. Thought you could fool your father? That's three more lashes. Thought you didn't need to properly treat a wound? That's four lashes: a total of ten ... if you come and get them now. Take off your belt and bring it to me."

"No, Father!"

"Saying no to your father: two more lashes."

I remembered Father's lashes; nothing ever hurt as bad. I glanced back at our barred door, but Mother stepped in front of it and leaned against it.

"Twelve lashes," Father said. "Come take it like a man, or it'll only grow worse."

I didn't move.

"Thirteen."

"Father, no!"

"Fifteen."

Slowly, against my will, I reached down and started to fumble with my buckle.

"Don't make me wait!"

"Mother ...!" I whined.

"How'd you get cut?" she demanded.

"It's a sword-cut," Father said. "He hit himself."

I looked back at Mother, surprised to find her expression hardened.

"Sixteen," she said. "And take off that tunic; I don't want it ruined."

Father threatened to jump the count to eighteen before I handed him my belt. He stood up as I pulled off my tunic. His hand caught my arm. I tried to pull away, but he pinned me to the floor and stepped on my back. He raised my belt.

I only felt the first seven lashes before they blurred into a blood-red universe of pain. I wondered if I was screaming and assumed that I was. The next thing I knew, Father had lifted me off the floor and was yelling at me.

"... was bad? You've no idea what bad is, when you fight with a sword, not until you've lost an arm, or maybe your head! Think about that!"

An eternity later, I lay on my bed. My butt hurt worse than my head. Only coals burned in the fireplace; they must've eaten without me and gone to bed. I laid there and cried. Finally I glanced up at the rack of idols, glowing in the dim red light, and wondered if Odin was watching me cry. I pulled my blanket over my head, hoping that Odin's one eye was elsewhere.

* * * * * * * * *

Chapter 3

* * * * * * * * *

Again I awoke dreaming of one of the bed-stories that Father used to tell me.

"Odin is the wisest chief, king of all the gods. Born knowing the nine secret sorceries of the living didn't satisfy him; Odin invented the noose and hung himself until he was dead, but Odin was so strong that he fought his way back from death, stealing the nine secret sorceries of the dead. Combining the secrets of the living and the dead, Odin can create the greatest, the most-powerful magics. He is the Master of Battles, and none has ever defeated him.

"Odin's wisdom told him that he couldn't face Ymir alone, so he engaged his brothers Villi and Ve to help him avenge their grandfather, Buri. And, once they killed Ymir, wisely they used his blood to drown as many of the giants as they could.

"Wisdom is Odin's one desire. To know all things is his

greatest goal. For even the slightest news of Ragnarrock, Odin tore out his own eye. You must learn from him, my son; nothing is as important as knowledge! Always seek the wisdom of Odin: knowing when to fight is as important as knowing how to fight, and never fail to avenge your kin!"

* * * * * * * * *

On Frigg's Day, I awoke early but I didn't crawl out of bed. My head hurt, my butt stung, and I could barely move. But finally I heard Mother giggle, and Father called out from behind their new bed curtains.

"Ingrid, take Thron to the barn. Take your blankets."

Ingrid slowly crawled from her bed. Her blanket wrapped tight about her, she walked over and pulled on my arm. Fire shot through my wounds, but I went with her, dragging my blanket with me.

"Thorir ...!" Mother laughed. "Wait...!"

Yawning, Ingrid pulled me to the door and lifted the brace down. Outside, it was raining, but not hard. Ingrid hauled me around the pig pen to the barn, then paused to hurl a cup of feed at the chickens.

Our barn wasn't as large as our house, but well-built with earthen walls and a thick sod roof. It was full of hay with five stalls, none of which had a horse in them. They held our plow, other tools, and lots of firewood, but little else. Grandfather had owned a cow and three horses, but they were long dead.

"Why do we have to come out here?" I complained.

"It's Frigg's Day," Ingrid yawned. "Frigg is Odin's wife, and she gifts babies to wives who please their husbands on Her day."

"What do you mean?"

"That'll have to wait until you're older."

"I'm older!"

"Lie quiet. I want to catch another hour of sleep, if I can."

I snuggled up against Ingrid, warm between the blankets. Ingrid wasn't much older than I; it irked me when Mother left her in charge, but sometimes I liked her. Ingrid was pretty, with golden hair and creamy soft skin. She played games better than Father, although he always complained that she was only lucky at dice. I liked playing games and grinned as I snuggled up against Ingrid.

* * * * * * * * *

"Still won't give you your sword?" Halgrum asked.

"May not ever get it back," Garad said. "Eh, Sword-Head?"

"Don't call me that!" I shouted at him. "It's still my sword, even if Father won't let me have it! Neither of you have a sword!"

Garad reached down, under the water, and picked up a shiny stone. He examined it, frowned, then dropped it. It hit the water with a plop.

"Well, when I do get a sword, I won't hit myself with it," Halgrum said.

I turned, fists clenched, and Halgrum backed up, but he raised his fists, ready to fight.

Garad sighed, and reached down to pick up another rock.

The creek flowed slowly, the water gently splashing over the big rock into our pools, which we'd dammed to keep from emptying. Two pools frothed; one above, where the cold water first collected, and the bigger one below, which was almost three feet deep in the middle. During planting season, it would swell and flow faster. The icy cold water flowed from the glaciers up on the mountains, but it was a hot day, so the chill felt good.

None of us were supposed to be there. I was supposed to be weeding our back fields, which I'd done for almost an hour before I spied Halgrum visiting Garad in his fields. If any of our parents showed up, then we'd all be in trouble, but it was too hot to pull grass. The cool shade of the trees over the swimming hole made it the perfect hideaway.

Halgrum splashed water at me and I kicked more at him. Garad moved away. Since his father had died, Garad didn't often feel like playing. He'd begun collecting shiny stones; at night he'd grind a hole through them. He hoped to make a necklace that his mother could sell or trade.

I splashed back, feeling the cool water tingle across my sunburnt shoulders. Soon it'd be the dreaded time: harvest. Halgrum's farm was big and grew lots of things. Garad's family grew mostly onions, although they had a small corner field where they grew oats. Turnips were all that we grew, but we raised a lot of them, and Father traded with the other farmers for other things to eat. Soon I'd be spending weeks pulling turnips; none of us would see each other during harvest except across distant fields.

I'd taken a substantial amount of jesting for hitting myself with my sword. Twice I'd gotten in even more trouble for fighting; once with Derek, who weighed twice what I did. But parents don't like us fighting for real, so we were all punished. Few mentioned my sword-wound anymore; I'd fight no matter how many punishments threatened.

"Did your father at least say when you'd get your sword back?" Halgrum asked.

"He never said he'd give it back," Garad answered for me.

"I'll get it," I argued. "It's too little for Father. Besides, I'll need it when I go viking next summer."

"He won't take you viking!" Halgrum laughed. "Derek's father wouldn't take him, and he's two years older than you."

"Derek has to feed cows and horses all summer," I said. "Turnips grow by themselves."

"Doesn't matter," Halgrum said. "Branwulf won't take kids on his ship."

"I'm going," Garad said. "I have to ... to take my father's place."

I looked up at Garad, shocked by the plaintive tone of his voice. He was even smaller than I was; I couldn't imagine him on Branwulf's ship. But if he got aboard, somehow I would, too.

"We'll go together," I said.

Halgrum laughed and splashed.

* * * * * * * * *

"... then Sammuel's sword slashed; the hand holding the dagger fell away, only an instant before he plunged his blade into my chest. The Irishmen pinning me gasped, and in their confusion, I wrenched my swordarm free ..."

Father loved to tell tales at night, sitting with an ale before the fire. I knew most of his adventures now, having heard each many times. Ingrid spun yarn while Mother wove on her loom. I scraped a fine-grit sandstone over my latest carving, removing the knife-marks from the lid for the fine basswood bowl that I'd finished last week. Mother said that it would fetch a fair price, but Father said that it was so nice that he might keep it for himself.

"I could've used it aboard ship," Father said. "We seldom had time to finish our meals. Often we had to lay our plates aside while we rowed, and the flies ate more than we did. Garad's father, Holbarki, lost half of a roasted chicken right out of his lap when a hungry gull swooped down and stole it. Afterwards he claimed that the fowl was poisoned, and Odin sent the bird to spare his life."

"Did Odin really send the bird?"

"No, Thron," Father said. "Holbarki was always saying things like that, even when we were kids, long before he married Grettir."

"Is Grettir really going to sell her farm?"

"I hope not," Father said. "Trustworthy neighbors are rare. But it'll be hard for just her and Garad to farm their fields; she needs a new husband."

"Marrying men are scarce," Mother said. "So many widows these days ...!"

"I'll send Thron over to help once the turnips are in," Father said. "If I could afford it, I'd buy their farm myself, but either she'd have to sell it for half of its value or we'd have nothing left of our own harvest."

"Where would they go?" I asked desperately. The idea that Garad might move away twisted inside me.

"Holbarki had a brother who was a fisherman near Oslo," Father said. "Perhaps he'd take them in."

"Grettir sent him a message," Mother said. "Gandr memorized it and said that he'd deliver it for two coppers."

"A lot of money just to carry a few words," Father grumbled.

* * * * * * * * *

Harvest became my life. Every day Father and I headed out before dawn and didn't return until after dark. Mother and Ingrid fed us in the field, brought us water and ale, and when they weren't cooking or serving, they pulled turnips near the house and barn. They took turns carrying Urd, who now cried more than she slept. It was hard to sleep in our house; Mother had to stop and nurse her every few hours, and Ingrid spent half of her time washing out diapers. Urd had seemed fun at first, but now she was ruining everything. Exhausted, we hardly ate a bite before we crawled into our beds, but Urd seemed determined to keep all of us awake.

Father seemed especially exhausted; he harvested three rows faster than I finished one. Slowly, day after day, rain or shine, we knelt in our fields and pulled turnips. Soon I hated turnips so much that they were impossible to eat. Weeks went by in a dull, mindless, dreary chore, on our knees in the dirt – the same work, the same pains.

* * * * * * * * *

"Garad!" I shouted as he walked up.

"Hey, Thron. How are the turnips?"

"Big and plentiful. Father's pleased. Why aren't you working?"

"Taking a break. Mother's harvesting oats."

"Using a scythe in the rain?"

"No, she's using Father's sickle, harvesting by hand. I hope this rain stops soon; onions are ripe, but they're hard to pull from mud."

"We're almost done. Father says that we'll help you when our turnips are in."

"I wish my father were here."

I stopped talking, just looked up at Garad. standing before me, as the rain slowly thinned our layers of mud. Grettir had tried to sell their farm, but found no one willing to buy it. Mother sometimes went over there just to sit with her. I reached out my mud-coated hand and closed it around a leafy stalk. Pulling carefully, the turnip slowly squeezed out of the mud, pulling free with a long sucking sound. I stuffed it into my bag and inched forward on my hands and knees.

It wasn't fair! Garad's father had been a great warrior!

* * * * * * * * *

"Don't touch that," Ingrid warned.

"It's my sword!" I complained.

"Fine," Ingrid said. "You can play with it all you want."

I hesitated, hopeful but uncertain, and again reached for my blade.

"Of course, I'll tell Thorir when he gets home. You can explain to him that it's your sword."

Furious, I resignedly walked back to the fire and plopped down in front of it; *I hated Ingrid.*

"I'm bored," I complained.

"Why don't you finish the lid for your bowl? You could surprise Thorir and Vespa with it when they get home."

"I finished it already."

"You can do better than that. It needs at least two more oilings."

Ingrid leaned forward, sliding her shuttle of spun wool through the loom back and forth as she worked the intricate mechanism. I picked up the fire-stick and poked at the coals. Slowly I shoved them together, trying to balance the thin, blackened logs on the fire-stick long enough to stack them.

After I'd piled the black coals, I bent close and blew, brightening them, but little else. I blew harder, repeatedly, until tiny tongues of flame rose between the coals.

"I'll get more wood," I said.

"There's plenty of wood right there," Ingrid said.

"It's all green!"

"Dry wood is for cooking."

"But I'm bored!"

"Thorir and Vespa said to stay inside; I'm not taking that brace off until I hear their voices."

"I can take off the brace ..."

"You'll do no such thing! It's getting cold out, and who knows what strangers are on the road tonight."

"It'd be safe." I said. "Everyone's going to Market."

Ingrid sighed heavily.

"Market," she said. "I wish I could see Market again!"

"You've never seen Market!"

"I was born in the city, remember?" Ingrid said. "Before my father's ship vanished, my mother took me to Market every year."

"What's it like?"

"Market's very exciting. People come from all around with loaded wagons and carts. We used to wander from cart to cart all day, just looking at all the treasures."

"Real treasures ...?"

"Sometimes. Most carts were filled with food, fresh from harvest, with goats or sheep tied to their wheels. But they also had copper and brass jewelry, and iron forks and spoons, and piles of cloth woven more finely than this loom could ever do."

"Were there swords?"

"Everyone at Market wears swords. Merchants don't leave

their carts unattended for even a second, and most carts have a watcher, usually a woman, who doesn't trade anything, but makes sure that no one steals from them."

"Do people steal?"

"Yes, but there are always soldiers about; the stocks at Market are always full."

"How long does it last?"

"Months, sometimes until early December. Market starts as soon as the farmers arrive with their harvest, and many rush ahead to arrive early, to get the best stalls and be first in line to trade. But Market doesn't get really huge until mid-October, and then it's crowded all month."

"I wish that I could go to Market," I said.

"I know," Ingrid sighed. "But Thorir doesn't have a wagon ... or a horse to pull it. Still, we'll see many merchants pass by on the road. No one knows which goods will be most prized that year, so some merchants travel slowly, doing trades with farmers along the way."

Ingrid's description of Market flamed my desire to see it. So many people, all with treasures to trade, in one magical place; how could anyone not go? I wished that Father had more money and a bigger farm.

"It's not fair," I muttered.

"Think how Garad and Grettir must feel," Ingrid said. "They don't have anyone to guard their house, so they can never leave their farm. They can't even go into town without coming over and asking one of us to watch their house while they're away."

"They could buy someone," I said.

"It's not that easy," Ingrid said. "My mother sold my brother and I so that she could feed our younger sisters. But my mother questioned Thorir and Vespa extensively before she agreed to the sale; she wanted to make sure that I was going to a good family. Few good houses want to buy servants anymore. Some orphans starve, become thieves, or are sold as oarsmen."

"At least they get to go places."

"Yes, chained to a bench, never leaving the ship, with a whip across their backs if they don't row fast enough," Ingrid explained. "They can never go home, get no spoils, and have no shields to protect them when arrows fly. Does that sound exciting to you?"

Ingrid was crazy, as always; *no man would live like that.* Ingrid set down the shuttle and leaned back in Mother's chair with a heavy sigh.

"Thorir and Vespa have been very kind to me, but I'd give anything to see my mother again, or know what happened to my brother. I'm very much like a galley slave; if I ever fled, then I'd be outlawed. No one would ever hire me, and if I got caught, I'd be outside of the law. Besides, who'd want me, now that I'm fifteen?"

"Do you want to leave?"

"Our house is warm, and we eat every day; many servants aren't so lucky. Vespa and I are close. No, I'll stay here ... and never know what happened to my mother, brother, or sisters."

"You could send a message," I suggested.

"I have," Ingrid said slowly. "Twice ... but I've never gotten a response. They may have moved, or maybe the note was never delivered; I'll never know."

I poked the fire with my stick; it was burning down low again. I felt bad for Ingrid, but Mother and Father never let me go any further than the swimming hole, and I couldn't even go out of our gate onto the road without getting yelled at.

But Ingrid was right; someday I'd leave and find riches in the south, and then I could go anywhere.

"I'll look for your mother," I offered, trying to soothe her. "When I'm old enough, I could go to Market, and maybe take you with me."

Ingrid's eyes widened with surprise.

"You'd do that ... for me?"

"Sure," I answered, wondering why she was so surprised. I wanted to see Market, and if Ingrid knew the way, that would make things easy.

"That's ... very nice of you," she said. "You're growing up into a nice young man."

I glared at Ingrid: I wasn't going to be *nice!* I was going to be strong and feared, like Father, and maybe someday have a ship of my own!

"Thron?" Ingrid asked softly. "You don't ever ... watch me ... while I undress, do you?"

I hesitated, confused.

"No. Why?"

"Never mind," she said absently. "Forget that I asked."

Ingrid was crazy, as I'd always thought.

* * * * * * * * *

Onions stank. Chilled, I pulled another out of the mud. Garad smiled, glad to have me working his fields. Although exhausted after four weeks of pulling turnips, as soon as we were done, Father had ordered me over to Garad's farm to help harvest onions. It wasn't fair, but it was nice to see Garad smile again. Of course, I'd have smiled, too, if someone had helped me harvest in the rain.

Grettir knelt in the mud not far away. Their fields were

only half harvested, and it'd take us another month at the rate we were going. I wished that Garad's father had lived; Holbarki'd been huge, and always rushed to get his harvesting done early. If he'd been here then I wouldn't be kneeling in their mud.

The cold rain chilled my aching fingers. I worked faster, trying to build up some heat. Slowly my bag filled, and then I stood up and headed for their house.

"Show me that bag," Grettir ordered, and I complied. "That isn't full! Get back to work! We have to get these onions out of the ground before it freezes solid, and we'll never do that by carting half-empty bags back and forth."

Grettir never stopped pulling onions as she talked. Garad glanced up at us, shook his head, and I reluctantly knelt back down. Soon my bag would be too heavy to carry, yet I resumed pulling, and snarled when I spied Garad smiling.

When my bag was full to Grettir's satisfaction, staggering under its weight, I stumbled back over their unharvested fields toward their house. Garad's house was much larger than ours, but it was half barn, with only a straw-woven fence to keep the chickens out of their living quarters. They had no pigs, only goats, which Garad milked each morning. They had four beds, but only needed two. It stank like a barn, of course, and their onions stank, like everything on Garad's farm stank. Still, onions are more flavorful than turnips, and Father and Grettir had already traded several bushels.

As I approached their house, I spied Father standing on the road by our gate with many baskets of turnips and onions, and most of the treasures that he'd vikinged; *I prayed that my sword wasn't being traded.* Down the road, a wagon train approached, two covered carts and four uncovered, each pulled by two strong horses. Two men sat aboard each wagon, and the last wagon looked empty. They returned Father's wave and stopped. One jumped down and talked to Father, but they were too far away for me to hear.

If I hadn't had to help Garad then I'd be there now, helping Father trade with the merchants headed to Market.

I pushed open their door and carried my heavy bag inside. It was dark; like ours, Garad's house had only one window, a thin sliver of wood-frame with an oiled lambskin parchment stretched across it, but the light from the doorway showed their interior as I'd seen it a hundred times. Piles of onions, most taller than I, lay stacked on their beds. I upended my bag on the smallest, letting the hard yellow onions pour out. Many fell to the floor. Grettir would've skinned me if she'd seen it; she insisted that we stack them carefully. I quickly picked up the fallen onions, tossed them on top of the pile, and then looked around for something to drink. An empty wooden mug lay by the keg; I poured myself an ale and drank it slowly.

"Thron!" I heard Grettir's distant cry. "It doesn't take that long to empty one bag!"

Reluctantly I drained the mug, picked up my empty sack, and headed out the door.

* * * * * * * * *

In the fading light, I'd almost filled another bag when Grettir shouted.

"Finish filling those bags and then come inside. I'll have something hot for you."

I increased my speed, pulling hard, sometimes pulling two onions at a time; anything to get finished and out of the freezing rain. It was my turn to smile; Garad's large bag was barely half full; *I'd easily beat him to his house.*

Stuffing four last onions into my sack, I hefted it and walked toward Garad's house. Garad made a face at me, but he was too far away to speak to without shouting, so I left him alone in the rain.

Grettir stooped, hanging a pot of ale over their fire. Her ale was weak, but a warm cup of anything seemed tantalizing. I suspected that she was only doing it for me; Grettir was very grateful to my parents for all of the help that they'd given her, including my labor. She wouldn't send me home half-frozen.

She turned to face me and I startled; *I'd never seen an adult so disheveled.* Grettir was as soaked as I; water dripping from her scraggily hair, seeping down the taut lines of her face, her ragged dress plastered to her skinny frame, and every inch from her elbows down was thickly caked in mud. I was no better, but I was a kid; *adults never got as dirty as kids.*

"Thank you, Thron," she said. "Pile those onions carefully. I'll restack them tonight, and maybe we won't have to store any on the ground. That attracts worms, you know, and I won't have worms in my house."

I carried my sack to the closest bed. It no longer mattered which bed I stacked them on; all were piled too high for me to reach. I set down the sack and began pulling out onions, one at a time, and adding to the stack as best I could. At my house, Father had filled and stacked all of our baskets in our pantry, then piled the rest on blankets in the corner, our turnips stacked to the ceiling. Our pile of turnips stretched past Ingrid's bed almost to the fireplace. Grettir had sold all of her baskets, which earned a good price, right before harvest.

"I don't know what I'd have done without your family," Grettir said. "Thorir's such a great man – not that Holbarki wasn't great, but widows must learn to do without, you know. Vespa's a lucky woman."

Her tone left a strange impression on me, as if she were trying to say more than her words conveyed. I stacked my onions silently, hoping that Garad would enter soon. I'd never been alone with Grettir before and felt strangely uncomfortable. She hung a large copper of water beside the ale; Grettir moved very slowly, as if badly hurt, although she'd done nothing but pull onions out of the mud since dawn.

"Are you ... okay?" I asked.

Grettir paused and lowered her head.

"No, Thron, I'm not okay. My husband's dead, and he didn't have to die. Life would've been more difficult without the vikings, but his loss is worse than all our gain. How am I, alone, supposed to raise a son, and what will happen to me when Garad sails south?"

Grettir raised a hand to brush away a tear, but mud caked her every finger. She snatched up a towel to wipe her eyes.

"Look at me," Grettir said. "Drenched, filthy, and sore, harvest only half finished; how am I supposed to work this farm all by myself? How are we ever going to be safe again? So many have died; there are more widows than wives! What'll we do if raiders come to our shores?"

Grettir spun and glared at me, a crazed fury in her eyes, as if demanding an answer, some solution. I stood aghast, frightened, not knowing what to do or say.

"Talking to a boy, Grettir. What are you coming to? You'll be talking to the goats next."

Grettir swung the iron hook holding the pot of water out of the flames, dipped her towel into it, then pushed it back over the fire. With the wet towel, she began to wipe off her face and hands.

"All this rain; not surprising, this late in the season," Grettir continued to ramble. "Makes pulling onions easier, at least. Once it dries up for a few days, then the cold will set in and the ground will freeze. We have to get all the onions inside before then, or we'll have to dig them out of frozen soil."

I understood that; last year it'd frosted early, and Father gave me an axe to dig to free the turnips without damaging them.

"I hope Thorir made some good trades today; I'm almost out of salt. Thron, would you help Garad herd in the goats before you leave?"

"Yes."

"Good boy. Such a cold rain; my old joints are aching. I can't afford to get sick and it'd do me no good, letting you boys take chill. Your mother and I have enough to take care of."

I bent deep, lifting the last of the onions out of the sack. Grettir didn't seem to need a listener to talk. I wondered if it was ever quiet around her; maybe she should take care of Urd.

"Sit down on that bench," Grettir instructed. "Touch nothing until you've washed. I can't wait until this water gets hot; I don't think I've ever been this dirty!"

All that I wanted to do was go home, but I sat as instructed, waiting for Garad. Once the goats were in I'd go home, warm ale or not.

"Poor boy, you must be freezing. Where's that lazy son of mine?"

Garad came a while later, his sack so full that two onions toppled out of the top as he pushed his door closed behind him.

"Don't drop those!" Grettir scolded. "Do you think that bruised onions are easier to sell? Bring those two over here. I'll set them aside for us."

I jumped to help Garad. Together we wrestled his heavy sack to the ground, and then we unloaded it, stacking the onions high.

"Go bring in the goats, both of you," Grettir said before we were done. "The ale'll be hot by the time that you're finished."

Garad opened the inside door, the bottom half of which was strong enough to fence back their goats while the top half was only a wooden frame filled in with woven straw, only strong enough to keep their chickens penned on their side. We went through the barn and lifted off the heavy brace, opened the big outer door, and stepped out into the cold rain. Older goats pushed past us, eager to get into the dry barn, but some ran away from us, and the kids dashed about aimlessly, splashing in the puddles.

We chased them, herding until they fled into the barn. We didn't talk much while herding the goats, but I was greatly troubled. Grettir's words stung in my ears and I couldn't help feeling things were worse than I'd known. *More widows than wives ...?* Had that many men died ... and I was unaware of it?

* * * * * * * * *

Chapter 4

* * * * * * * * *

"Sleep, my son, and dream about Baulder.

"Baulder the Pure is Odin's eldest son. Baulder is so beautiful that women fall in love with him on sight, and even the fiercest beasts of the forest calm before him, and eat from his hand. Songbirds constantly circle him, yet none of their sweet voices match his, and his speech is always so gentle and cultured that mortal women who hear him swoon.

"Yet the Norns, also women, doomed him, for by sacrificing his eye, Odin learned that Baulder was fated to die, not in battle, but unexpectedly, and thus be doomed to Niflhiem. Hel, another woman, will love him jealously. Frigg will try to free him from Hel, but fail, and Baulder, alone of all the Asier warriors, will never be admitted to golden Valhalla.

"Learn from Baulder, my son: never let women control your life, or you'll never join your fathers in Valhalla, and be doomed to Hel's bitter land of darkness, cold, and death."

* * * * * * * * *

Excitement filled me with the first real snowfall. I rushed out and slid on the ice. I loved early-winter snow when it's crisp and powdery and you can play all day just catching falling flakes on your tongue. Soon it'd be deep-frozen winter, the sun rising late and setting early. Snow would bury our whole farm, and I'd be shoveling a path to our barn everyday just so we could keep enough of a fire going to save our pigs and chickens from freezing.

My new tunic was thin, made of the fine material that Father had brought back from Ireland. It wasn't very warm, but I couldn't fit into my old tunic any longer. Garad and I'd been the same height only a few months ago, but I was already two finger-widths taller than he. Father seemed proud, but Mother frowned exasperatedly; my old clothes and winter shoes wouldn't fit.

Father came out and saw me sliding. He scowled, seeing my bare feet in the snow.

"Time that we did something about your feet," he said. "You can't go all winter with no shoes; you'll catch a chill and get sick, and boys don't grow while they're sick."

I followed Father inside; I didn't mind the cold, at least, not yet, but I wasn't going to argue. Mother was breaking apart the fire that she'd used to warm the remains of last night's stew while Ingrid washed our dishes in the basin.

"Vespa, Thron needs new shoes," Father said.

"Merta Hodkins might have some that Derek can't wear anymore," she replied.

I grimaced; I didn't want Derek's stinky old boots. Derek

was older and definitely bigger, but we seldom got along. Derek thought he was better than everyone else since his family had cattle and horses, and Derek liked bullying.

"What should we offer?" Father asked. "Derek can't wear Thron's old shoes."

"Rath might want them," Mother suggested. "Helsa's almost Thron's age and growing like a weed."

Ingrid dropped a bowl, splashing the water loudly. Everyone stopped to look at her, but she ignored us, pulled the dish back out, and scrubbed it hard.

"I can try," Father said. "Rath may trade something that Derek might want. Got to do something, or we'll be wrapping Thron's feet in rags like a beggar."

"Take all of Thron's old tunics, since he can't wear them anymore," Mother added. "Rath may need warm clothes for Helsa as well."

I hesitated, remembering Grettir saying that Rath's wife had died of stomach pains caused by evil vapors. Perhaps he'd be a good husband for Grettir.

"Get your old tunics and shoes, Thron. We're going trading today."

Rath lived in the village next to Clamsby's Tavern Hall. By the time that we arrived, the cold snow was uncomfortable; I kept switching feet, trying to warm one while standing on the other. Father knocked loudly on their door.

"Who is it?" Rath's voice shouted.

"Thorir," Father responded.

Suddenly their door flung open wide.

"Come in, come in!" Rath shouted. "Helsa, ale for our guests!"

It wasn't very warm inside; I shivered, trying to shake the icy chill off my bare feet. Rath had a thick carpet in front of his fireplace and I eyed it enviously, standing on their cold dirt floor.

Helsa filled two mugs from the keg. Rath had six kegs stacked together in a pyramid on a stout wooden frame. Only in Tavern Hall had I seen more kegs in one building.

"How's the turnips, eh?" Rath asked. "Good harvest this year; everyone's talking about it."

"Yes, a fine crop," Father said as Helsa brought our drinks.

"Glad you came by," Rath said. "Can't wait to go viking again. Pretty profitable summer, eh? Here, take a mug, and one for your boy. He's getting tall, isn't he?"

"Thank you, Helsa," Father said, taking a mug. "Yes, he's shooting right up. Going to be as tall as his grandfather, I'd say."

"Well, let's sit by the fire and swap a few stories," Rath said, motioning us to the fireplace.

"Actually, I was hoping to do some trading," Father said.

"Really? What'd you bring?"

"Three of Thron's old tunics and a pair of stout shoes. He's outgrown them, but they're still good for someone small enough to use them."

"Let's see," Rath said, and Father handed him the shoes first.

Rath took the shoes over to his fireplace and sat in his big wooden chair, and Father sat beside him on a crude bench. Rath bent over, holding my shoes close to the light, examining them carefully. Meanwhile, Helsa held out a mug of ale to me, and I accepted it gladly. I tried to smile at her, but she looked away.

"Not bad, a little worn by the toes, with a lot of scratches," Rath said.

"Vespa made these tunics, even spun the wool herself," Father said, holding out the tunics.

Rath set the shoes on the carpet and took the tunics, one at a time. I tried not to fidget but my feet were still cold, so I took a deep drink of ale. It was very strong, but not flavorful. I'd tasted strong brews before, but they were thick and hearty. This tasted half-brewed with too much yeast; green, too strong and thin. I didn't drink any more of it.

"Drink up, Thorir, and have another! It's been too long since we just sat and talked. Remember that fire we built under the pines? We sat up all night then."

Rath closely examined my old clothes. I couldn't get into my fancy tunic anymore and the other one's sleeves barely reached past my elbows; wearing them had been embarrassing. I'd be glad to get rid of them, but Rath seemed to want conversation more than old clothes.

"I remember being cold and wet all night," Father said slowly. "Without that fire, we'd have frozen to death."

Helsa crossed the room and picked up a needlepoint frame. She turned her back to the fire, letting the light shine upon her work, and began sewing. I quietly walked up behind her, careful not to block her light, but glad to stand on the thick carpet before the fire. Helsa was sewing a delicate piece of trim: twisting seahorses whose tails branched into intricate crosshatchings.

"Those were the days, eh? Free of cares and woes, living by your wits or surrendering to the Norns; that's a warrior's life!"

Helsa and I rarely saw each other despite that we lived close by. We seldom talked; she played with the girls and never seemed interested in fighting with wooden swords. Yet she was very fair, with a small, straight nose, bright blue eyes, and long, thin yellow hair.

"That's fine work," I commented softly, trying not to disturb Rath and Father's conversation.

"Would you trade for it?" she asked suddenly, her tone almost defiant.

"I – I don't have anything ..."

"You have turnips," she said. "I'll also accept onions, barley, or wheat, if you have it."

"I'd have to ask Father," I said.

"It's not finished," Helsa said. "It won't take me long, maybe less than a week."

"What do you think, Helsa?" Rath interrupted us. "Do you need new shoes? What about these tunics?"

"I don't need them," Helsa responded without ever turning around, but anger filled her voice.

"Perhaps we should go," Father said.

"No, no, sit down!" Rath said. "Helsa, bring Thorir another ale! We've got lots to talk about."

"Like what?" Father asked.

"Like that damned church bell ... and the ambush."

"What about them?"

"Terrible day, wasn't it?"

I glanced back at Father, sitting on the bench but looking uncomfortable.

"Rath, I have to trade these and get back home before dark ..."

"No hurry!" Rath laughed. "Stay for dinner! Helsa, put on ..."

"Father," Helsa said firmly, "we can't afford ..."

"Shut up, wretched child!"

"Please!" Father interrupted them. "We have to get going. Thanks for the drinks."

"Damn it, Thorir, you just got here!"

* * * * * * * * *

Rath's curses followed us down the frozen street. My feet had barely gotten warm, and the slushy frost stabbed into them anew. Yet Father seemed in a hurry, silent and angry.

Helsa's scream stopped me in my tracks. I spun, ready to run back, when Father's hand clamped onto my shoulder.

"Not our business, Thron."

"But ...!"

"If he kills her, then he'll hang for it," Father said. "A pity; she's a good daughter. But our laws give him the right to punish her, whether she deserves it or not. Our interference won't save her; he'd only hurt her again after we're gone."

"Father ...!" I objected.

"What would you do?" Father demanded, staring at me.

I looked up into Father's grim face and met his glaring eyes. Rarely had I seen him this angry, this resolute. At first, I thought that he was going to hit me, and then I realized that his fury was directed at Rath ... and he was just as angry as I was.

I'd never defied Father to his face. I knew better; the scars of his beatings traced across my backside and still hurt when I thought of them. Yet it seemed wrong, leaving Helsa to Rath's unjust punishments. But what could I do? Rath was a grown man, as big as Father, and many times stronger than I. He'd survived a dozen vikings, and I'd only recently begun to understand what that meant. Yet, when I thought of him hurting Helsa, my gorge rose.

Helsa's scream split the frozen villiage. Suddenly I jerked free of Father's grasp and ran back toward Helsa. I didn't think; I raced as fast as I could.

Something heavy struck from behind, and then I was sliding over frozen dung and dirt. Father landed on top of me, grunting and cursing. I flailed, trying to free myself, but I was crushed, my chest aching for breath under Father's weight. Father drug me to my feet roughly, cursing and shaking me like a rag doll.

"... not listen to me? I said you'd only make it worse! Now look at you! Get home! We can't go visiting while you're covered in filth!"

Father raised his hand threateningly, but then he hesitated, and slowly lowered it. He shoved me back up the road, but he didn't loosen his grip on my arm. Cowed, I walked, half-pushed, before him. I kept expecting blows, yet they never came.

Numb with cold, before we arrived home, Father released my arm, but he stayed right behind me, within reach every step. I opened our gate and closed it behind us, then turned toward our door. What Mother would say when she saw my new tunic covered in filth I didn't want to hear.

"Thron," Father said quietly, laying his hand on my shoulder. "Thron, you made me proud today. You've yet to learn wisdom, but today you showed your heart."

* * * * * * * * *

I startled as Ingrid sat up suddenly, her face hidden in the shadows, but the sharpness of her posture reminded me of my countless awakenings to bad dreams. She visibly relaxed almost instantly, and I glanced back at the fire. The last log was a blackened char but still shined a dull red glow over most of one side. It was the middle of winter, our whole world buried in thick snow, and the sun shone less each day. I wasn't supposed to be sleeping; if the fire went out, here or in the barn, then I'd be in trouble.

Morgan had slept in our barn last year, and kept its fire burning, before he'd gotten killed. Afterwards, I'd offered to sleep in the barn, but Mother had refused. When I was old enough to go viking, she said, then I could sleep in the barn.

I pulled my blanket tight around me, unhappily knowing that I had to go back out into the cold. I'd wear Father's boots again, since I still didn't have shoes, but Father had traded my tunics and boots for a good hide of leather and a thick steel needle. He was making me new boots with a special waxed thread that Mother had spun, but they were still in pieces.

Ingrid arose from her bed, her pale nightshirt glowing like a phantom as she threw her blanket around her shoulders. She came over and sat in Mother's chair before the fire, staring into the glow. Soon she'd fill the iron pot with ale, hang it over the fire, and stoke up the flame with dry wood; Father liked a warm mug to greet him when he awoke.

I glanced over at Mother and Father, snuggled together under their quilts, snoring like always. Mother had loved the bed curtains, but Father had traded them for four huge baskets of celery. Soon they'd awaken and chores would begin. After chores I'd be allowed to sleep for a while, at least until mealtime.

I noticed Ingrid looking at me. She picked up a handful of dry wood and placed it carefully against the red coals. Then she got up, filled the pot at our keg, hung it on the lowest hook, and swung it over the dry twigs and split shavings.

"Don't watch me," Ingrid whispered.

I glanced up at her questioningly. I'd gotten down on the floor to blow onto the coals, forcing the dry sticks to ignite. But Ingrid walked away.

Curious, I followed her with my eyes. She stopped in front of her bed, reached down, and pulled off her nightshirt. She was naked underneath, and the growing flames of the dry, crackling wood illuminated her pale skin. She slowly folded her nightshirt and set it upon her bed, then lifted her blanket and folded it as well. It seemed to take an eternity.

I'd seen Ingrid dress before, but now ... something was different. Something drew my eyes and forced me to stare. I couldn't look away. I hadn't noticed how adult she was, shaped like a woman, tall and slender. The way that she stood, moved and flexed; I sat mesmerized. Ingrid lifted up her chemise and shook it out, then turned around to face me; she was even more woman than I'd realized. I stared transfixed, breathless, and then noticed her eyes looking at me. I thought that she'd be angry and I started to turn away, but her expression surprised me, almost as if she was glad that I was watching.

Ingrid smiled brightly, then slipped her chemise silently over her head. It fell down over her, concealing her nakedness, but I saw nothing but her sleek backside, her round breasts, and the supple gleam of her creamy skin.

I swallowed hard, then looked away. *She'd asked me not to watch.* Why had I? Why was my heart pounding, my breath gasping?

I stood quickly, pulled my blanket tight about me, and crossed the room in three steps. I slipped my feet into Father's big boots and lifted the brace off the door. Swiftly I exited, stepping out into the dark and cold. It was snowing again, the low clouds barely glowing with the first light of morning, but I knew the route so well that I could walk it in total darkness. I pushed through the new snow and stomped a path to the barn, opened its door, and stepped inside. A few chickens instantly clucked at me for food.

The barn fire had burned to a few embers, but I shoved them together and piled kindling atop. Then I picked up a large, heavy log off the stack and placed it in their fireplace. Soon I had its fire going again, enough to keep our sleeping pigs from freezing.

A cock crowed in the distance. Soon our rooster would crow, unless I fed him quickly. I scooped out a mug of grain and threw it onto the dirt. The chickens all came awake suddenly, fluttering their fat bodies down from their perches to feed. The rooster jumped to join them, making several hens scatter. Some of the pigs started grunting; I had to feed them as well.

Yet I stood frozen before the tiny, rising flames, thinking about Ingrid. I couldn't banish her image from my mind. Ingrid got dressed every morning. If she hadn't told me not to watch her, then I'd barely have noticed. Why could I not stop thinking about her now?

* * * * * * * * *

Two pigs were mating. It was uncommon during the heavy snows, but it happened. We watched because we were bored.

Garad and I sat in my warm barn, having built up the fire more than we were supposed to. Both of us were clutching warm mugs and wrapped in blankets. Our ales no longer steamed, but neither of us drank quickly or we'd have nothing left. Going inside to get more ale would be the death of our playing outside, where we were supposed to be, but we'd gotten chilled and decided to hide out in the barn rather than get stuck under watchful eyes. Winter was a terrible time with nothing to do but sit and make things. Sledding was great, but the snow was now hard and crusty; plowing into a snowdrift felt like throwing yourself onto sharp rocks. It hadn't snowed in a week, but a thick fog had settled over the whole village and never let up. I'd made two ladles and a large bowl in the last month, and if I had to make another, I'd scream. There was simply nothing to do.

"Father used to do that to Mother every night," Garad said, watching the pigs. "I used to lay awake, unable to sleep, until they were finished."

"Mother and Father do that every Frigg's Day," I commented.

"Mother wanted more kids," Garad said. "She had three other babies, when she was young, but none of them lived. I almost killed her, and she didn't have any more after me."

"Mother had a few like that," I said. "The last one was only a few years ago. I remember her screaming; I thought that she was going to die. It was the same when Urd was born."

"I heard," Garad said. "Good thing that only women have kids."

"I'm never going to have kids," I said. "Urd is fun, but all she does is eat and cry. She used to cry all night long; I slept with my head under my pillow."

We sat in silence a long while, glancing between the pigs and the fire. I tried to think of something to say, but everything that I thought of we'd discussed a hundred times. I couldn't tell Garad about Ingrid; *Ingrid was the best thing in my life.* Every morning I watched her change clothes. Thinking about her kept me awake all night while I tended the fire. Sometimes she seemed angry at me for watching, yet sometimes she seemed to like it. She often smiled or winked at me, and sometimes she yawned and stretched, or shook her breasts at me, grinning while I sat silent, intent. This morning she actually walked over and dressed right in front of the fire, so closely that I could touch her. I almost did, I wanted to so badly. Yet she warned me almost every day: if I told anyone, *ANYONE,* then she'd dress under her blankets and I'd never again see her naked. I wanted to tell Garad, but I didn't dare; I couldn't bear the thought of losing my morning show. I'd never tell Mother or Father; *they'd punish both of us.*

"What're you thinking about?" Garad asked.

"Nothing," I replied quickly.

"You looked like you were thinking."

"Did not."

"Did, too."

"I was thinking about ... seeing Helsa," I said, foundering for any topic.

"Wish I could see Helsa," Garad said with a heavy sigh. "I haven't seen anyone in so long I can't remember."

"Maybe we could sneak into town tomorrow," I said. "We haven't done that in a while."

"Remember how much trouble we got into last time?" Garad said. "Widow Hodkins told Mother that she saw us, and my mother told your mother ..."

"We'll just have to be more careful," I said. "Come on, we haven't seen Halgrum or Kal for a month, and I want to see Helsa again."

"I'd like to see Helsa, too," Garad said. "Do you think that

Rath is still hitting her?"

"I don't know; I hope not."

"Let's go tomorrow."

* * * * * * * * *

Chapter 5

* * * * * * * * *

Again I dreamed of the stories that Father used to tell me.

"Thor the Thunderer is the Champion of the Gods. He wields Mjollnir, the mighty dwarven hammer that can kill any giant with a single blow. Thor wears gauntlets of giant-strength and a belt made from the tendons of frost giants. Thor has slain more giants than any other Aseir.

"Once, Mjollnir was stolen by Thrym the giant, who offered to ransom it in exchange for Freyja, the most beautiful of all Goddesses. Desperate, Thor humiliated himself and dressed like a bride, covering his manly face in wedding veils. He pretended to be Freyja, and when Thrym the giant brought out his mighty hammer as her bride-price, Thor seized it, cast aside his womanly disguise, and killed Thrym.

"Of all the sons of Odin, Thor is the most like us, because his mother was the Earth herself. Be like Thor, my son. Avenge your honor! Do deeds of legend, no matter the cost, until the sight of you fills your enemies with dread!"

* * * * * * * * *

Thick fog hid us completely as Garad and I snuck unobserved through the center of town. Everyone was hiding inside, protected from the silent, frigid air. The frozen snow crunched beneath our feet so loudly that we couldn't approach any houses. Every shutter was closed, braced, and iced over, yet it was exciting to be anywhere that we weren't supposed to be. Voices came from inside of Tavern Hall, but we didn't dare approach.

My new boots worked great. Father had made them to fit Ingrid, whose feet were still bigger than mine, but I'd wrapped three layers of knitted wool around my feet to make them fit, and the cold no longer bothered; my feet felt warm and dry, even walking in snow.

Long we lurked outside of Rath's house. We both wanted to see Helsa, but we couldn't knock at her door; Rath would tell Father, and then both our backsides would suffer, so we stood freezing, miserable. Our secret adventure wasn't as exciting as we'd hoped.

We wandered around the whole town, finding little of interest. We walked up the road a ways and spied Halgrum and Kal sledding on a hill, but Kampi, Kal's father, was splitting logs outside of their house, and we couldn't get anywhere near them without him seeing us. We watched them sled for a while, and then they all went inside.

Bored, we decided to risk approaching Tavern Hall. We snuck between Rath's house and the hall, trying not to crunch the snow. No shutters existed on this side, so we put our ears close to the walls, trying to hear. Muted voices reached us but nothing discernable could be heard. We knew not to press an ear against the frozen wood; the story of Derek getting his ear frozen to Widow Eardai's house was a tale that we often laughed about.

We snuck around to the back, but from there we could hear even less. Finally, we snuck around to the exposed side. The shutters were frozen solid, but the big fireplace built into the wall was too warm to touch. We pressed our ears against the warm wooden wall beside the hot stone chimney and heard the conversation inside, although we couldn't guess who was speaking.

"There are no unsecured harbors anymore. We attacked all of the ones there were."

"Small raids are a thing of the past. Branwulf needs to join a larger fleet."

"The bigger the fleet, the fewer rewards. What we need is another ship or two, and more warriors to man them."

"We don't have enough men left to man Branwulf's ship next year. Where are we going to get more men? We'll have to join one of the larger expeditions."

"Branwulf will never do that."

"Then we'll get killed."

"What choice do we have? Stay here with the women and children ... watch crops grow? I'd rather face more Irishmen than endure a summer with my wife."

A general laughing followed, then silence. We kept our ears pressed against the wall, and then a loud 'pop' of the fire startled us.

They began discussing harvests and we quit listening. Talk about the vikings was far more interesting, but we couldn't discuss it there. We scampered across the snow toward the docks, eager and excited. Away from the land, the waves splashed over the ice, which thinly covered our bay near the shore.

"Did you hear that?" Garad laughed.

"They need us!" I said, sliding across the icy dock-planks, wary of the icy water.

"We're going viking!" Garad cried, and we laughed and danced upon the frozen boards, ignoring as they crunched under each of our steps.

"I can't wait!" I said. "Father will have to give me my sword back, and we'll sail with Branwulf. We'll be rich!"

"Whatever we want!" Garad laughed.

"Anything we find!" I shouted. "Ours for the taking!"

"The first sword that we find is mine!" Garad insisted.

"The first Englishman is mine!" I replied, trying to look fierce.

"Englishman ...?" Garad hesitated. "We're going to Denmark!"

"Denmark ...? But they have the toughest sailors ..."

"My father won't rest until Danish blood wets my hands."

I stood suddenly still, taken aback by the unexpected depth that Garad's voice sank to, the angry, serpentine hiss that seeped between his teeth. Garad was almost my height again, and thinner, yet suddenly he looked bigger, more threatening, his eyes as cold as glaciers. I couldn't let fear show, of course, so I laughed.

"To Denmark," I agreed. "We'll plunder every castle, and burn it from Skagen to Germany!"

Garad smiled, and we both jumped about, knocking hard snow piles off the icy posts and kicking frozen chunks up into the air. It really didn't matter where we went; all that I cared about was not getting left behind.

Suddenly Garad cried out and seawater splashed high and

wide. Droplets splattered the dock, showering me. Shattered ice floated in dark water which frothed inside of a wide, new hole – *Garad was gone!*

"Garad!" I cried.

I stared at the hole, expecting Garad to surface. The water here wasn't deep; Garad and I'd swum in it many times.

"Garad ...?" I shouted again. *"Garad ...!"*

I cried out and I jumped down onto the ice, felt it crack beneath my feet, and then it shattered and collapsed. I fell into the freezing, stinging salt water. I shoved my hands under, feeling for Garad's quilted coat, his arms, anything ... but I found nothing but icy rocks and slimy seaweed.

"Garad! Help! Help! Somebody, help!"

The water splashed up to my waist, but I bent over, almost diving under; the icy chill stabbed like frozen needles, but I kept reaching. I pushed aside icy chunks and crashed through the thin crusts, but found nothing. My fingers grew numb; *if I didn't find him soon ...*

"Garad ...! Garad ...!"

Suddenly something large crashed into the ice, dousing me with a solid wave. I tripped into the briny froth, but strong hands threw me into the air and dumped me onto the dock. Other men ran up. Excited voices reached my ears.

The man in the water searched quickly, pushing through the thick ice as if it weren't even there. Another man jumped in to help him, but stumbled as he landed.

"Here!" he shouted, and he reached down and pulled Garad up out of the water. Garad was soaked and unconscious, looking dead.

"Water in his lungs!" said another.

"Squeeze it out!" Clamsby shouted.

The man holding Garad turned him upside down and

held him against his chest, then wrapped his thick arms about him, and squeezed. Water poured from Garad's mouth, and suddenly he coughed.

"Back to the Hall," Clamsby shouted, and he reached down and grabbed my arm. "He needs warming up right away."

"I'll get Grettir and Vespa," a man said.

"Tell them to bring warm blankets to take the boys home in," Clamsby said. "One chill a day's enough."

On the march back, I spied Helsa and Rath standing outside of their door, as others were, watching the men drag us back to Tavern Hall. I lowered my eyes and tried not to look at her while I shivered in my soaking wet, freezing clothes, trying to ignore the water splashing inside of my new boots. I'd wanted to see Helsa; *this wasn't how I'd wanted her to see me.*

* * * * * * * * *

I couldn't sit for a week. Father had pinned Garad on the bed with his left hand, his hard knee on my back, and alternately struck. He yelled the whole time, but we only heard the voice of his leather belt crack across our butts. Finally Grettir and Vespa stopped him ... or he'd have killed us both.

* * * * * * * * *

My raw fingers stung from dragging rough sharkskin over wood. In the last month, I'd made four matching trenchers and spoon sets, and Father had never been so critical of my work. Each piece had to be perfect, or he'd throw it in the fire and make me start again. Garad slaved on his farm, his mother always two steps behind him, and yelling so loudly that I could hear her across our fields. Garad looked as exhausted as I; Father insured that I didn't enjoy a single free moment. After staying up all night to tend the fires, I did all of my chores before midday meal, and then I worked on my projects for several hours before I could sleep. Father woke me up before supper, and I didn't dare fall asleep during the night.

Worse, Ingrid stopped dressing in front of me. Well, she still got dressed every morning, after putting Father's pot of ale over the fire, but quickly, by her bed, facing away from me. I feared that I'd offended her, but I eventually suspected other reasons. Every time that our eyes met, Ingrid cast a worried glance at Mother and Father, even while they snored.

I hated Garad for falling into the water. Mother insisted that he was lucky; Garad had struck his head against the dock while falling in, and been swept under it. If one of the men hadn't landed on his arm while jumping into the water, then Garad would've drowned. I almost wished that he had rather than suffer this much punishment. Worse, Father angrily swore that I was staying home this summer; *I'd missed my only chance to join him on the viking.*

* * * * * * * * *

"Soon it'll be spring planting," Father said to Garad and I, standing in the wet grass where the snow was mostly melted. "There'll be no time for you to learn fighting then, and it's time that you did. You're both grown up enough to defend your mothers, if need be. You need to be capable of doing so before I go viking."

Father held three long, thin branches in his hand. He handed one to each of us, then raised his over his head.

"Watch this," he said.

Father swung hard and struck himself across his forearm. Garad and I both winced, yet Father never even flinched. Then he rolled up his sleeve and held his arm out for us to see. Between his forest of dark hair and hard skin striped a long red welt; it must've hurt like hell.

"Do you see me crying?" Father asked.

"No," we replied nervously.

Suddenly Father swung again, first at Garad, then at me. Neither of us had time to realize it, then suddenly exploding pain wracked my body and blackened my vision. I fell, aware only of Garad's scream intermixed with my own.

"Get up!" Father shouted. "Now, or I'll hit you again!"

Gasping for breath, I crawled to my knees. Father had hit me on my calf; it burned like a hot iron. Then another lash, less hard but promising more, slapped across my back.

"Don't make me wait," Father warned.

I spied Garad's tears through my own. Grimacing, Garad was standing on one leg, clutching one hand just below his knee.

"What if I'd used a real sword?" Father demanded. "Your legs would be gone, and you'd be dying. Do you think that steel hurts less? Now come on, it's your turn. Hit me."

We both stood there, dumbly clutching our sticks in our hands.

Again Father struck. Both of us jumped, but to no avail. Instantly pain erupted, this time on our other legs, and again we were both writhing on the ground.

"When I say hit me, hit me!" Father shouted. "No waiting, no excuses. Now get up, and stop crying like babies! You're both going to learn to fight, even if it kills you. Up! Or do you want more?"

We quickly scrambled to our feet, fighting to stand despite welts on both legs.

"Raise your sticks over your heads, like this," Father said. "Good. Now, hit me."

We both swung, but neither of us struck. With blinding speed, Father blocked both our sticks. We looked up at him questioningly.

"Well?" Father asked angrily. "I told you to hit me! Anyone who doesn't hit me in the next minute will crawl home!"

Garad and I glanced at each other, alarmed, and began swinging. A dozen times we tried, but Father blocked all of our blows with ease. Then Garad dropped his stick; Father's hand had barely twitched, but his stick flew, and Garad fell, crying out, clutching his right arm.

"You wouldn't drop your sword in the middle of a fight, would you?" Father asked me warningly.

"No," I quickly replied.

"Time for games is ended," Father said. "Boys play, men kill. You and Garad practice together. Don't pull your swings; if I can't hear you hitting each other then I'll come out and hurt you both. We'll do this again tomorrow. Anyone who can't hit me by then will regret it."

Father walked back toward the house.

"Oh, and you'd better learn not to cry," he added. "I'm going easy on you because you're just beginning. I'll give you a real reason to cry if I see any tears tomorrow."

* * * * * * * * *

Mother and Father went to a village meeting at Tavern Hall. Grettir went with them; Garad was locked inside of his house, as we were in ours, to guard our homes while they were away. Urd slept quietly in her crib.

Urd was getting older, more fun to play with. She'd survived her first winter, walked on two legs now, and knew enough words to let me know whether she wanted a drink or her blanket. Often one of us had to play with her at night, usually Father, so that the rest of us could do our chores. Mother had to work her loom on the table where Urd couldn't reach it, and I had to keep my chisels and files behind me, and stop working if she ran too close.

I laid on my chest, atop my covers, shirtless and aching. Ingrid rubbed the greasy ointment into my back, which was dotted in bruises. Neither Garad nor I had hit Father yet, despite two weeks of trying. Not an inch of my skin was free of black, purple, or green bruises. It hurt to move or sit still. Morning chores were torturous. Ingrid's fingers stung as she pushed into my wounded flesh, the swollen lumps rolling under her touch.

"Lie still," she ordered. "It's good for you."

"Then you try it," I sneered.

"I could, if I wanted to," she said. "But I don't need it, you do; Branwulf won't let you on his ship if he thinks that you can't fight."

I grimaced under her strong fingers, gritting my teeth but trying not to flinch.

"What does it matter?" I sighed. "Father said I was staying home ..."

"It's your own fault," Ingrid said. "Playing on an icy dock ..."

"Garad fell in, not me!"

"Grown men anticipate trouble and avoid it. That's why you're getting left behind; you knew that playing on the dock was dangerous, not just for you, but for Garad, too. You had nothing to gain by taking that risk, yet you went out anyway – that was childish."

Ingrid was right; I'd heard so a thousand times since Father, Mother, and Grettir had arrived at the Tavern Hall to find us shivering, soaking wet on the hearth, and surrounded by half of the town.

"I'll never get to go viking," I complained.

"Nonsense," Ingrid said. "Thorir can beat you, but unless he kills you, he can't stop you from growing up. Someday you'll be a man. You may not be going viking this summer, but if you show Thorir how much you've grown when he gets back, he may start treating you like a man."

"What should I do?"

"Why should I tell you?"

I flinched as her fingers dug into a painful spot, then half-turned to look at her.

"What do you want?"

"You know what I want," she said. "I want to go to Market. If you behave yourself, and do as I say, then Thorir will be greatly impressed. After harvest, perhaps, he'll let you go to Market, and I could go with you ... to look for my mother."

"I want to go to Market."

"You'll have to ask to take me," Ingrid said. "It'd make sense, since I know where it is and what goes on there."

"You get Father to take me viking and I'll take you to Market," I promised.

"Agreed," Ingrid said. "But you have to stop doing stupid things ... at least when Thorir's around."

The thought of Market should've cheered me, but I felt

crushed over not going viking. Garad was only slightly less crushed; Father had told Grettir that he'd take Garad when he was ready, just not this year. We'd both have to spend another boring summer weeding fields while Father went adventuring, and then wait through another whole winter just for another chance to go.

Alone with Ingrid; I'd hoped for such a situation, but now that it'd come, I was too nervous to ask for what I wanted. Yet Mother and Father seldom left the farm; it might be months before I got another chance. I riveted my courage and finally blurted out the words.

"I miss ... our ... mornings."

Ingrid hesitated, and then her massaging hands left my back. She got up, walked away from me, and wiped her hands on her apron.

"I don't know what you are talking about," Ingrid said finally.

I staggered. *Not know? Wasn't it obvious?* She'd watched me, and smiled at me, naked in the firelight.

"You know what I mean!"

"No, I don't."

Her voice was icy. What could I say? She was lying, but ...

"You know ...!"

"I have no idea what you mean."

Desperately I fumbled for words.

"You ... let me ... watch ..."

"Watch what?"

Confused, I stared at her. Ingrid finally turned, sat on her bed, and picked up her knitting basket. She pulled out the mittens she was making and started to click her needles.

"You know," I said flatly.

"I'm not playing childish games," she said, interlocking the yarn, not even looking at me.

Exasperated, I clenched my fists. Was she playing a game? Was this a test of some kind? What could I do ... or say? Why was she denying what both of us knew?

"You let me ...," I stammered, but I couldn't say the words.

Finally I fell silent. If she wasn't going to be honest then I wouldn't talk to her. I stared into the fire, gritting my teeth behind a firm frown. She was just being a woman: unreasonable. I couldn't wait to get away from her.

Yet, as the minutes drug on, I couldn't help recalling the excitement I felt, the thrill of watching Ingrid undress. She made my blood pound ... my throat dry. I missed that more than I missed anything else. I was miserable without it. I glanced back at the heavy brace sealing our door; not even Father could get in without breaking a hole through the wall. We were alone, more than we'd ever been in the early mornings when Ingrid had let me watch her. Why was she pretending not to know?

"I never told anybody," I said finally. "Not even Garad. And I never will; that's a promise. I just ... miss it."

An eternity passed, broken only by the clicking needles, the crackling of the fire, and Urd making noises in her sleep.

"Winter is ending," Ingrid said softly. "You won't be staying awake all night, tending the fire."

I perked up, turning my head to look at her.

"I ... I could wake up when you do," I offered.

"Vespa would wonder why you awoke so early," Ingrid said, never taking her eyes from her knitting. "Then Vespa would turn me out ... I'm just a servant. Without this job, I have nothing. I'd be starving in the streets with no shelter or protection."

I frantically fumbled for some reply, any excuse to see her again. My mind raced, but found only panic and confusion. I wracked my brain for some solution.

"We could ... somewhere else ... *the barn!"*

"It's not safe," Ingrid said. "Thorir and Vespa would wonder where we were and what we were doing. Your friends are always poking around in the summer. Someone would see us ..."

"No one can see us now," I said.

Ingrid looked up at me, her glare severe. I feared I'd said too much.

"I'm already dressed," she said.

The silence after she spoke was deafening.

"You ... you could pretend," I stammered.

Ingrid set her knitting back in her basket. She locked her eyes on me, but she said nothing. She rose to her feet and my pulse quickened. I held my breath, hoping that she'd reach down and pull off her dress.

Ingrid didn't undress. She walked toward me, agonizingly slow, and stopped right before me. She lifted her hands and cupped her breasts through her dress, then inhaled deeply, reached one hand down and cupped my cheek.

Ingrid bent toward me, never blinking, and pressed her lips against mine. Fire shot through my being as if lightning had struck me. Ingrid kissed me long and hard, and suddenly I realized that her touch felt better than all of the times that I'd watched her undress. After forever, Ingrid pulled back, smiling. I grinned from ear to ear. Delight, wonder, amazement; I didn't know how to describe it, save that I was anxious for more.

Ingrid beamed her smile at me, then walked back to her

bed. She sat down, picked up her knitting, then continued as if nothing had happened.

"We can't do ... mornings ... anymore," Ingrid said. "But there may be times ... I'll decide when it's safe. But you must keep it secret; if anybody ever finds out then it'll be the death of both of us. But if you can behave, well ..." Ingrid paused and blushed a little, "I don't want to be a servant forever. There's more than ... mornings. Much more, when the time is right."

* * * * * * * * *

Chapter 6

* * * * * * * * *

I hurried to lift off the brace at Father's shout.

"A bit warm in here, isn't it?" Father growled as he and Mother entered. "You'd better not be wasting firewood."

"Ingrid, put a pot of ale over the fire," Mother said. "It's been a long night."

"What happened?" Ingrid asked.

"Rath was accused of stealing," Mother said. "Losing Ormstunga proved too much for him. Pity; she was a good woman."

"Stealing from your neighbors is unpardonable," Father snapped. "On ship, a man would be thrown overboard."

"Who'd he steal from?"

"Several accused him," Mother said. "Kampi, Eardai, and Merta Hodkins; each says he snuck into their barns at night and stole food."

"Lucky for Rath that Gaceth is dead," Father said. "Gaceth

would've chopped off his hands, like they do in the East."

"No one could prove anything," Mother reminded him. "Dead chickens and carrots all look the same."

"Then where'd they come from?" Father asked. "Rath had nothing left to trade. Helsa didn't know where they came from."

"What's going to happen?" Ingrid asked.

"Are they going to kill him?" I asked.

"No," Father said. "A village council was convened. Old man Ranglátr and Widow Væna presided; both are twice as old as anyone in our village. Rath was sent home, and then we all talked until everyone had their say, and punishment was decided.

"Rath must marry ... or leave the village. He has until the full moon after next to find a bride, or one will be appointed for him. There's no lack of widows these days; one of them must marry him. If Rath can't pick one, then Væna will choose for him."

"Rath's no prize," Mother said. "No woman wants a husband who does nothing but drink and sleep. Only Ormstunga kept him in line."

"Helsa needs a new mother anyway," Father said. "Rath has nothing to teach her; he can barely care for himself."

"Helsa's a good, hard-working girl," Mother said, and she looked right at me. "A pity that she's so young."

I froze, uncertain, and Ingrid glared. Suddenly my skin prickled.

"Give her a few years with a new mother," Father said. "Everything will work out."

They fell into their chairs exhausted, and Ingrid filled their mugs when the ale started steaming. They discussed Rath in detail, Eardai's shrill accusations, Kampi's slow, deep denouncements that resonated throughout Tavern Hall, and Merta's angry insistences that her carrots be returned and compensation paid for her troubles. I merely listened, yet I couldn't stop wondering what Helsa thought about all this ... and what would happen to her.

"Grettir said that she'd burn down her own house before she let Rath into her bed," Mother said.

"Too bad," Father said. "She needs a man to work her farm, and Grettir's strong enough to handle him."

"She deserves a better man than Rath," Mother insisted. "He's a lazy wastrel with no concern for anyone but himself. He wouldn't even make a good servant, let alone a husband."

"Who should he marry?" Father demanded. "Merta wanted him outlawed tonight."

"Beigaldi ... or Læknir," Mother said.

"Beigaldi would lose her only income," Father said, at which Mother snorted derisively. "Læknir's old, but she's Rath's best choice. She could take him with her when she travels. I've always said that Læknir should be protected; healers are hard to replace. Rath pulls a mean bow, and few wield an axe like he can."

"Helsa could learn from Læknir," Mother agreed. "Our village will need another healer when Læknir's days end, and it takes time to learn such skills."

"Læknir's no beauty," Father reminded her. "Rath may not deserve them, but he has standards. Besides, there're other widows about, even in other villages."

"We have more than enough widows right here," Mother sighed. "What terrible times we live in! Costs going up, taxes more frequent every year, and the toll of the vikings is ruining our whole country."

"It'd be worse without the vikings," Father said. "Too

many men on too little land; we'd ruin what precious farmland we have trampling our fields with armies, every noble fighting each other. Grandfather used to tell me tales, when I was young, of summers with almost no harvest, and winters so long and cold that cattle froze in their barns ... or starved to death because there wasn't enough hay. The milder weather has brought more crops and animals, but more children grow to be adults, enough to eat all of our crops and animals in a single season. The vikings maintain Nature's balance, and profit us with treasures from the wealthy lands."

"No necklace is worth a good husband," Mother said, and then she and Father exchanged glances.

"Thron, go build up the fire in the barn, and stay in Morgan's room tonight," Father said. "Ingrid, take some blankets and go with him; Vespa and I want to be alone."

* * * * * * * * *

Morgan's room was dark, but Ingrid brought a grease-lamp and I built up the fire. The chickens had gotten into Morgan's room through a a rotted hole in the wall, but Ingrid shooed them out and blocked the hole with a log. Cold fogged our breath, but I couldn't have been happier; it'd been a long time since Father and Mother had sent us to sleep in the barn. Before, I hadn't wanted to be alone with Ingrid; *now I did.*

Ingrid said nothing; she didn't even look at me. I couldn't wait to kiss her again. Everything had worked out perfectly.

As soon as the fire was burning strong, I turned to find Ingrid tightly wrapped in her blanket. She sat on a bench, away from the fire, leaning against the wall. I couldn't imagine why; our barn was draftier than our house, and Morgan's bed was right beside the fire where it was warm.

"Ingrid ...?" I asked. "Aren't you ... coming to bed?"

Ingrid pulled a corner of her blanket over her face and ignored me.

"Ingrid ...?" I repeated, but she said nothing, hidden inside her wool cocoon.

Was she playing with me again? Wasn't this the opportunity that we'd spoken of, that I'd prayed for? We had all night, and no one would interrupt us! Just the two of us! Alone!

Slowly I approached Ingrid, trepidatious, uncertain. Why was she hiding? I reached out and lifted the corner of her blanket; the crackling fire glistened off of tears running down pale cheeks.

"Ingrid ...?" I asked. "What's wrong?"

Ingrid looked up at me, pained lines creasing her normally-smooth face.

"I can't," she whispered softly.

I wanted to stamp and yell. *This wasn't fair!* I wanted to scream and punch and rant and stomp, but something in Ingrid's voice stopped me.

"Why not?" I asked.

"Vespa'll kill me," Ingrid said. "She'll beat me and throw me out. I'll starve, and you ... and ... Helsa ..."

Ingrid's voice trailed off into wracking sobs and she clutched her blanket tighter.

"Mother'll never know," I said. "I won't tell her, or anyone, I swear!"

Ingrid shook her head.

"We can't..." she sobbed. "Not yet! If ... I ... a ... baby ...!"

I listened intently, but couldn't grasp what she meant.

"What baby?" I asked.

"Our baby!" Ingrid said.

I stood flabbergasted.

"Our baby?" I gasped. "You mean, you could have a baby ... because we kissed?"

Ingrid's eyes widened, a look of surprise transforming her face. She looked at me as if I were crazy, and then her tone changed entirely.

"You ... don't ... know ...?" she stammered. "But ... how can you ... not know ...?"

"Know what?" I demanded.

Ingrid glanced about the room, silent. I looked at her; wet cheeks, bright blue eyes, and honey-golden hair. Something had happened, something that she knew and I'd missed.

"Thron?" she asked softly. "What ... what do you want to do ... tonight?"

I hesitated, swallowing hard despite the sudden dryness in my throat.

"You know," I said. "Like ... our mornings ... and maybe you could ... kiss me again?"

Suddenly Ingrid laughed, somehow delighted and relieved. I had no idea what she meant, but I didn't care. Quickly Ingrid undressed and kissed me repeatedly. *Paradise!* Ingrid smiled and let me look as long and as closely as I wanted. Then she put her clothes back on and we cuddled under our blankets; I felt more than delighted. We fell asleep together: *I'd never been happier.*

* * * * * * * * *

Father stitched a sheath from the scraps of leather left over from my stiff, new boots. Mother wove. Ingrid twirled a drop-spindle, making more yarn. Urd laughed and played with the new rag doll that Mother had made her. I carved, using a curved chisel to gouge out a deep hole that I hoped would become the first of six matching cherry-wood cups. The fire was mere coals, the candles just bright enough to let us work. I kept looking at Ingrid, although I tried not to; *she'd warned me not to look at her ... and to stop smiling all the time.*

Ingrid and I hadn't had another night together since our visit to the barn, but every day she found a moment to kiss me when Father and Mother weren't looking.

Suddenly a distant scream, muted by our thick walls, disturbed our evening. Father jumped up and ran to our door, threw off the brace, drew his sword, and dashed out into the thick snow. Mother shouted warnings, but Father shouted something about staying there, and we stopped at the door and watched him crunch through the deep snow. I tried to follow, but Mother's hand seized my shoulder.

Unexpectedly, I heard a beloved, almost-forgotten hiss – Ingrid had drawn my sword from its scabbard. Mother and I both turned to stare at her.

"Thron should go with Thorir," Ingrid said, and she held out my blade to me.

Mother hesitated, looked from her to me, then took a deep breath.

"Put your boots on," Mother said. "Hurry, and be careful!"

I shoved my feet into my boots, snatched my precious sword from Ingrid's hand, and dashed out. The cloudy night sky hid the moon and stars, but my feet knew every pebble and rut, and my new boots plowed easily through the melting snow. More screams broke the silence; Grettir's voice, mixed with Garad's yells. Then I heard Father yell, and seconds later I burst inside Garad's house.

Rath! Father held Rath pinned to the floor, his sharp sword-point hovering over Rath's chin. Both were shouting at each other, red-faced. Screaming, Grettir stood by her fireplace, an iron kettle threateningly raised over her head. Garad was jumping up and down, yelling incoherently.

"Enough!" Father boomed. "Be silent! Everyone!"

"Get off me, you lout!" Rath bellowed.

Father withdrew his blade and stood back. Rath jumped up, staggered, and then managed to stand.

"He's drunk!" Grettir shouted.

"Stop him!" Garad shrieked.

Father ignored Rath, and with one hand, picked Garad up and sat him hard on his bed. Then Father spied me in the doorway, clenching my naked sword. At first, I thought that he was going to yell at me, but he only nodded.

"Lower your sword, Thron," Father said. "Garad, stop shouting ... or I'll give you a reason to scream."

Father turned back to Rath.

"Rath, I'll take you home," Father said. "We can discuss this in the morning."

"You!" Rath accused Father. "You let them do this to me, this marriage decree! If you'd stood up for me then I wouldn't be here at all! We were shipmates! How could you stab me in the back?"

"Get him out of here!" Grettir screamed.

"Come on, Rath," Father said, reaching out a hand. "Let's get out of here ... until Grettir calms down."

Rath resisted, but only slightly, as Father took his arm and pulled him toward the door. I stepped back, but not far. As

Father heaved him outside, Rath almost fell, but Father held him up, and then held out his sword to me.

"Take this home," Father said. "Tell your mother that I'm taking Rath home."

I took Father's sword without even thinking about it, although I'd rarely been allowed to hold it before. Father started walking Rath down the snow-crusted trail, then he turned back and looked at me.

"You did right, Thron, bringing your sword, but you don't need it anymore," Father said to me, white mist streaming from his mouth with each word. "Leave both swords at home, fetch our cloaks, and catch up with us on the road."

I nodded, hesitating only a moment; Father was trusting me with his sword ... and inviting me to join him. *He'd never done that before.* I dashed back to the house, carefully holding both swords pointed away from me as I ran; I recalled hitting myself with my own sword and didn't want to repeat it. But I wanted to rejoin Father as quickly as I could.

Mother and Ingrid had lit a lantern and stood outside in the frozen air. I slid to a stop before them.

"Father said to leave these here," I held out both swords. "He told me to get our cloaks and bring his to him."

"What happened?" Mother demanded.

"I don't know," I said. "Rath was drunk and Grettir was screaming. I think that they had a fight. Father's taking Rath home ... told me to hurry."

Mother took Father's sword, opened the door and vanished inside. Ingrid, holding the lantern in one hand, reached out and took my sword with her other. Suddenly I remembered that she'd given me my sword and insisted that I go in the first place. Thanks to her, Father had been very impressed, and had asked me to help him take Rath home.

Ingrid had told me, I recalled, that if I listened to her, she'd help me impress Father. I hadn't believed her then, but it was true.

"Thank you," I smiled at her.

Mother came out suddenly, startling me. Good thing that she did; I was about to kiss Ingrid, and Mother would've seen, and then everything would've been ruined. Mother held both of our cloaks in her hands, but she paused, glancing strangely at us.

"Put yours on," Mother said sternly, handing me my cloak, and no sooner did the wool touch my shoulders than she pushed Father's bundled cloak into my arms. "Hurry."

I glanced at her, enough to perceive that she wasn't smiling, and quickly ran off. Worried thoughts assailed me, but I ignored them; *I was going with Father.*

I caught up with them on the road. Father pulled his cloak around him, but paid little attention to me. Rath was walking beside him, and they were deep in conversation.

"What about Beigaldi?" Father asked.

"And have every man in the village cuckold me?" Rath asked disgustedly. "Beigaldi can barely feed all of her children; how's she supposed to take care of Helsa and me? Grettir's my only choice!"

"Læknir's rich, with valuable skills," Father said. "She may not be young, but she'd be a good mother for Helsa."

"Roaming all over the lands, never at home; what kind of a mother is that?" Rath sneered. "If only Branwulf would let us bring women back! I'd have a good Saxon wife!"

"How would you keep her?" Father asked. "Chained to the fireplace? She'd just be a bed-warmer, another mouth to feed."

"That's why I picked Grettir, because she has food!"

"Showing up drunk won't win Grettir's heart."

"Heart? Bah!" Rath scoffed. "In my father's day, women did as they were told! No one gave them choices!"

"Pig-slop," Father replied. "I've heard it all; tying women down with their own hair, whipping them until they begged to be slaves, but I've never seen any man do it, not once in all my life, especially not in his homeland. Those are just stories, like giants and dragons."

"Still," Rath grumbled, "Grettir had no cause to yell at me. I wasn't gonna hurt her! Hell, I was going to propose!"

"You don't want to marry a woman that hates you," Father said. "You want a woman who needs you. Læknir, Beigaldi, Eardai, Merta; there's more widows than wives around here."

"I can't stand Merta," Rath said. "Grettir has the largest farm. She's the best of the lot."

"Yes, but you aren't," Father said. "You've no money and no trade; all that you own is your strength and your house in the village. You don't like farming. You're a good warrior, but except for the vikings, you don't have an income. You'd make a great soldier, but there's Helsa."

"Yea, Helsa," Rath said. "Inherited her mother's tongue, that one did."

"Helsa's a good girl," Father said. "Her needlework's impressive."

"We can't eat off sewing," Rath said. "But she is good; I've thought about selling her."

Father halted in his tracks.

"Don't you dare!" Father shouted. "She'd be a slave with no hope of a future! Even if you found her a decent house, which is almost impossible, she'd be virtually unmarriageable. She'd own nothing but her flesh, and end up a whore, if she peddled that! Helsa could marry a farmer someday; someone

who could support you in your old age."

"I wouldn't marry a woman who was tied to another!" Rath retorted.

"You'd marry Grettir, and she has Garad ..." Father said.

"Kids are different," Rath said. "Kids grow up and move away."

"Not on a farm," Father said. "Believe me; Vespa and I hope to have more kids. Farmers need sons, as Grettir needs Garad. If you do marry a widow with a farm, trust me, you'll want as many sons as she can have working your fields."

Rath fell silent, slogging through the snow. Father and I followed, our faces blasted by frequent, frozen gusts, but we talked no more.

Bundled up in her cloak and carrying a lantern, Helsa met us as we neared Clamsby's.

"Father!" she cried. "Where have you been?"

"What are you doing outside?" Rath shouted.

"I came looking for you!" Helsa answered. "Wandering about in this ..."

"Don't speak to your father that way!"

Father grasped my shoulder, halting me. Helsa came up and took her father's arm. For a moment her eyes met mine; sad eyes surrounded by an angelic face, but Helsa turned away and bowed her head, ashamed to be seen. I understood; not long ago I was drug back to Clamsby's soaking wet, ashamed for her to see me.

Helsa and Rath headed home. Father and I turned back.

"You don't think that he'd really sell her?" I asked Father.

"I hope not," Father said, and then he looked intently at me. "Someday Helsa will make some man very happy."

* * * * * * * * *

I hit Father!

I hit Father before Garad did!

I hit Father!

The hard, frozen ground broke as I struck. The sharp iron point of my pick carved a gully through the dirt. Father would rent a draft horse to plow the main fields, but beside the house and barn, we had to dig rows by hand to get ready for planting. It was exhausting, but Father had said that swinging the pick would be good sword-practice, and today I didn't care.

I'd hit Father!

Father hadn't even flinched when I hit him just above the ankle; he was busy blocking Garad's attack. Garad was smaller than I, but he moved fast; most of our bruises came from hitting each other. We'd gotten better at blocking, so weren't getting hit as often. Before, welts covered us by the end of each day. Now we could fight for hours and only suffer a few bad ones.

Sticks were no longer our only weapons. Father taught us grappling, which hurt far less but wasn't as much fun. I liked grappling; I was bigger and stronger, and I could pin Garad most of the time. Of course, Father could pin both of us anytime that he wanted to, and he wasn't gentle.

Father made us practice after every midday meal. He always watched at first, showed us something new or corrected our stances, and then he'd vanish inside for an ale while we fought. Whatever he showed us, he expected to see done correctly when he came out, or he'd show us again, and then send us to finish our day's chores nursing painful bruises. This happened often, but we never cried in front of him; the one time that we did was a lesson that neither Garad nor I wished to repeat.

A loud crunch erupted from the ground; a rock had shattered when I struck it – *I was getting stronger!*

*   *   *   *   *   *   *   *   *

Chapter 7

*   *   *   *   *   *   *   *   *

Ingrid pressed hard against me as we kissed, knocking the empty chicken's feed cup from my hand, both of us trying not to laugh. We still had to hide, but Ingrid seemed more relaxed, certain that we wouldn't get caught. Another chance was approaching; Rath still hadn't found a willing bride, and Mother and Father would be going to the meeting tonight to hear his verdict. After dusk, Old man Ranglátr and Widow Væna would announce which widow Rath would have to marry, unless he chose to leave our village. I half-hoped that Father would let me attend, but I was even more eager to be alone with Ingrid again.

Laughing, Ingrid wiped the grin off my face, and then pushed me out of the barn. I looked around, saw no one, glanced back, and laughed at her. She stuck out her tongue and giggled, and then came out into the light.

"Grettir!" boomed a deep voice, and a fist pounded on

wood.

We both startled and looked across the field. Rath was back, pounding his fist on Grettir's door.

"Get Thorir,"Ingrid said, and I dashed off. Father was in our back fields, too far away to have heard.

Minutes later, Father and I were running toward Garad's house. Rath had a bolt of red cloth in one hand and was pounding on her door with the other.

"Grettir!" Rath shouted. "Please! I'm not drunk, and I brought you a gift; at least let me give it to you! You can't manage this farm by yourself!"

"I've nothing to say to you!" Grettir's voice shouted from within. "Go away! I'll see you tonight at Clamsby's. We've nothing to talk about."

Rath glanced at us as we ran up, but Father grabbed and stopped me before we crossed onto their property. He held up an open palm to Rath, who nodded back, and then turned back to the closed door.

"Tonight will be too late, Grettir," Rath said. "Tonight I'll be married ... unless you and I can resolve this. Please! I don't want to marry Læknir, Beigaldi, or any of the others! I want to marry you!"

No sound came from within. Father and I glanced at Mother and Ingrid as they came running up the mostly-melted path, but Rath stood frozen in the slush, listening intently for the slightest sound.

"Rath, you listen and listen good!" Grettir shouted from behind her door. "This is my farm, and you'll never get it, not by marriage or any other way! For the last time; go away!"

Suddenly Rath dropped the red cloth and began beating on the door with both fists. Grettir began screaming and Garad started yelling again. Father sighed and shook his head, then motioned for us to stay there while he walked up to Garad's house. Rath was leaning hard against the closed door, almost sobbing, when Father reached out and took him by the arm.

"It's not fair!" Rath cried. "*I didn't steal those chickens …!*"

Father slowly pulled Rath away, back toward our house. Father never said anything until he got back to us, Rath blubbering, walking unresisting.

"Thron, go get that red cloth and give it to Ingrid; it has to be cleaned and dried so that Rath can present it as a bride-gift."

Rath seemed tormented by Father's words, but I ran to get it. The cloth was rich cloak material; good thick wool, brightly dyed, with an ornate iron broach pinned to one corner. I snatched it up and ran it back to Ingrid. Inside our house, Father made Rath sit in his chair while Mother served him ale.

"Rath, you need a wife," Father said. "Helsa needs a mother, and there's plenty of women who need husbands. You've had almost two moons; you can't wait any longer."

"I'd have made a good farmer," Rath whined.

"You'd be good at anything," Father agreed.

"They're going to stick me with Læknir."

"I suspect so," Father said. "She's our only healer and she's getting old. She needs a strong hand to help her get around, to handle her horses and carriage. And she needs a good fighter to protect her; these lands aren't safe anymore."

"You know what they'll say," Rath said bitterly. "In a land of widows, poor stupid Rath couldn't find a wife."

"Mean people say mean things no matter what happens," Father said.

"Have you even spoken to Læknir?" Mother asked.

"Læknir hates me, just like all the others," Rath said.

"Is she opposed to the marriage?"

"She says it's good for the village," Rath scowled.

"It is," Father said. "It'll prove good for you, too ... in time."

"Great," Rath said with little conviction. "I'll end up her slave for the good of the village."

"No one knows how these things turn out," Father said. "In two months, the viking season begins, and we'll be leaving anyway."

"I don't understand Grettir!" Rath complained. "I could plant her fields in half the time that it'd take her and Garad!"

"Grettir's made her choice, and it may turn out bad for her," Father said. "She does need a man, a strong man, but ... it's her legal right to refuse a match."

"You have a big night tonight," Mother said. "Thorir, why don't you put on your new tunic and take Rath home? He needs to get cleaned up and ready. I'll come along later, at sunset."

Father nodded and changed his tunic, then buckled on his sword and pulled his heavy cloak over his shoulders. Mother turned to Rath and spoke softly.

"Rath, before you leave, I have one piece of advice for you; I know that you don't want to wed Læknir, but if you have to, then at least try and look like you do it gladly. Everything in your life will go better if you start this off well."

Rath bowed his head and said nothing. Father helped him up, and Ingrid gave him his red cloak material, dried, brushed, and refolded. Rath and Father left amid a deafening silence.

* * * * * * * * *

"Thron, put your boots on and carry the basket," Mother said.

"W-what?" I stammered, surprised. "You ... want me to go ...?"

"Yes, of course," Mother said firmly. "Ingrid's a grown woman; she can watch our house and Grettir's. What'd you think? That I'd leave the two of you *... alone?"*

I froze and glanced at Ingrid, but she quickly turned away, suddenly straightening the bowls on the shelf.

"Hurry and dress," Mother said. "We don't want to be late. Oh, and you two won't have to sleep in the barn ... together ... ever again."

I didn't know what to do or say. I just stood while Mother brushed her hair in the mirror, until she turned and looked at me. Instantly I jumped to pull on my boots, silent, but my mind raced – *what did Mother know? How did she know? What was I to do?*

My boots on, I turned to the door, but Mother stopped me and straightened my tunic.

"Bring your sword," she said. "You're escorting your mother, so you should be armed. Besides, you'll want to appear grown up tonight. Helsa's getting a new mother, and it's proper that you should witness it."

Ingrid choked, emitting a loud, barely-stifled half-sob. I glanced at her; she wasn't even pretending to straighten bowls, just standing before the chopping board, her back to us, crying. I looked back at Mother, her stern face glaring accusingly.

"Your sword ...," she reminded me.

I snatched up my sword, stuck it in my belt, and Mother

stepped away from the door, then turned to stare at me. I hesitated, then jumped forward to open it for her, and she handed me her basket and sauntered out like a queen departing her castle.

Ingrid turned to look at me, her red cheeks drenched with tears. I felt like crying myself; more than anything I'd wanted to be alone with Ingrid, but that might never happen again. I wanted to say something, but Mother was waiting. Reluctantly ... I closed the door between us.

As we passed Garad's house, Mother spoke sharply.

"Walk beside your mother, Thron."

I did, but I kept my eyes downcast.

"You're growing up, Thron, and it's time that you learned the truth," Mother said in an imperious tone. "Men rule this world, even here in Norway, where women have rights. But women are the trainers of men. What did you promise Ingrid in exchange for her ... *pleasures?*"

I stared at my feet as I walked.

"It doesn't matter," Mother said. "You won't keep your promise. She's been training you to obey her, to take full control of you. I know, because that's what I did to your father, what all wives do to their husbands. Someday some woman will seduce you, and you'll walk into her trap with both eyes open, like every man does. Yet who that woman is, what property she has, and what family she comes from – that you must choose carefully.

"It's difficult for men to admit; no man would say so, or his friends would scorn him, but choosing a wife is choosing a trainer. You need to insure that she'll be an asset to the family, not some cheap trollop looking for a purse to support her. Ingrid has nothing, while Helsa's father owns his own house in town, and Læknir will teach Helsa healing skills on top of her embroidery; valuable skills for a farmwife.

"Did you really think that I, your mother, could miss the way that you look at Ingrid? I'm surprised that your father hasn't noticed. He'd get rid of Ingrid tonight, if he knew. Turn her out into the cold; is that what you want, for Ingrid to freeze and starve?

"Think of your family, Thron. Think of your future ... and your children. You're a free farmer with no land-debt. Many work their whole lives and never acquire the status of your birth. You can't disgrace your station by marrying a slave, anymore than you'd waste your time pursuing a noblewoman. You're a peasant; that may not mean much, but it's more than most have. This infatuation with Ingrid has to stop."

I wanted to refute Mother, but I held my tongue. I was a man, able to make my own choices, and no one would ever *'train'* me. *Mother was wrong;* I would be with Ingrid, and if Father turned her out, then I'd go with her.

I couldn't lose Ingrid. *She was so beautiful, so delicious ...!* I yearned for her with every breath. I saw her every time that I closed my eyes, and in my dreams her naked body pressed hard against me while we kissed. *I'd do anything to keep her!*

* * * * * * * * *

"Læknir," Widow Væna announced.

Rath smiled suddenly, turned to Ranglátr, and they shook hands. Then Rath faced Læknir and bowed deeply to her; she tilted slightly forward in return. Rath stepped closer and held out to Læknir the thick roll of red wool that Ingrid had cleaned and refolded. Læknir smiled, and accepted the fabric with silent serenity.

I looked at Læknir closely; her face was wrinkled as a walnut shell and twice as crusty. She was tall and thin, frail-looking, with curly strands of gray hair sneaking out from the yellow scarf tied under her chin. Looking at her ... oldness, I understood Rath's reluctance. Apparently, Rath was taking Mother's advice, and pretending to be glad. Whether Læknir was pretending or not was a mystery. To all appearances, she seemed content with the arrangement.

Old man Ranglátr lifted his ale and commanded a toast. "Raise now your mugs and celebrate! Let us drink to this blessed union; may it endure forever!"

We all drank. Clamsby even stopped refilling mugs to empty his own large tankard into his mouth, and then he returned to his trade. Behind him stood a table with many gifts for the betrothed; new yarn, eggs, mead, and spices, but hidden on the floor, under the tablecloth, I spied an even bigger pile, including three live chickens - Clamsby's payments from everyone who came to witness the wedding. I suspected that Clamsby earned more for his ale this night than ever before.

Rath and Læknir's wedding immediately followed the toast. The couple stepped forward, stood together, and Ranglátr spoke words so ancient that I couldn't understand them, and then he gave a long and boring prayer to Odin and Frigg to bless them both. The widow Væna walked around the couple, hitting them lightly but constantly with branches from a fir tree. I puzzled over this; it seemed odd, so I nudged Mother and looked up at her questioningly.

"To ensure that their love will remain evergreen," Mother whispered to me. "Listen to Ranglátr and he'll explain."

"... And now may the blessings of Thor, son of Earth, rain

upon you both," Ranglátr said, and he reached into a small wooden box then lifted his hand over their heads and sprinkled a pinch of sand upon them both. I couldn't believe it; if Mother had caught me pouring dirt onto her best dress then she'd have killed me, but Rath and Læknir only looked at each other and smiled.

Old man Ranglátr continued, but through the crowded hall I spied Helsa, standing in front beside Rath, almost hidden by Kampi's great cloak. She was radiant, dressed in pink and yellow, smiling brightly. I suspected that Helsa was delighted to be getting another parent, someone who might control Rath's drinking and temper. Yet I was equally troubled; both Father and Mother seemed unusually interested in Helsa. Ingrid didn't seem to care for her at all. Whatever their problems were, I was just glad that I wasn't in the middle of it.

I hoped that Helsa noticed my sword.

"For the blessings of Freya, most beautiful of all goddesses, I crown you with these holly wreaths," Ranglátr said, and he placed upon each of their heads a crown of prickly leaves, heavy with bright red berries, and laced with white ribbons. "May they remind you always that from the scratches that life gives us are born the brightest gifts that we ever receive."

I'd never seen this before. I'd been to other weddings, but always in the spring, and those wreaths were made of colorful wildflowers, but few flowers bloomed in snow. As I looked around the room, difficult because it was so crowded, I noticed fresh holly strung over all the rafters, and many bright banners.

Ranglátr went on, blessing them many times over, and finally Rath and Læknir spoke, repeating his words.

"I vow truth and faithfulness to my beloved wife," Rath

said, and he went on for some time reciting promises, but I didn't pay much attention. Clamsby walked up behind me and glanced down. I quickly looked away; the last time that I'd seen him he'd fished me out of the frozen water by the dock.

"I vow virtue and obedience," Læknir began when Rath was finished, again repeating Ranglátr's prompts. I briefly wondered about this; how much could they mean what they were saying if they were just repeating whatever Ranglátr said? Everything was subdued, as if only the barest of rituals were being bothered with. But, if our rituals weren't all-important, then why did we bother with them? Wouldn't our gods be displeased?

All of the other marriages that I'd witnessed were daylong affairs, with lots of food, drink, and drummers. I loved drumming; around a great bonfire, all of the drums in the village available for anyone who wanted to pound on them, and there was always someone to take over once your hands got sore. A dozen drums, all pounding to one beat, echoed across the night sky, exciting and delightful. Dancers jumped and stomped around and around the fire, constantly circling, until they collapsed from exhaustion. I loved to dance at weddings, but I doubted if that would happen tonight.

Finally the new broom was brought forward.

"This broom," Ranglátr said, holding it aloft, "is the symbol of a strong house, of all that civilized people aspire to. It is the symbol of family. It will sweep away the old to make way for the new, and brush the happy couple into their new lives, then clean their home of dirt as a marriage must be constantly cleaned with forgiveness and understanding. This broom is the doorway to the glorious future that lies before you. Enter, and be joined forever!"

Ranglátr stepped between Rath and Læknir and set the broom reverently upon the dirt floor behind them. I squeezed forward to watch; *I loved this part.*

Rath and Læknir turned around, faced us, and smiled. They took each other's hands, and as one, they jumped over the broom.

Disappointment filled me. Rath did a slight jump, but Læknir merely stepped over the broom, but everyone cheered as if she'd jumped high and wide. Tavern Hall exploded with joyful shouts and applause, Clamsby banging his heavy hand on a table as hard as he could. Everyone smiled – *Rath and Læknir were married.*

Adults pushed forward, and I used the opportunity to slip away from Mother and Father, toward the back wall where I'd spied Grettir watching silently from the rear. Garad stood beside her, as expected, but not far away huddled Derek, Halgrum, and Kal, all looking as discomfited as I. I veered toward them, knowing that Garad would soon be able to escape his mother in the confusion.

"Won't take much of a wedding bed for those two," Derek said sarcastically as I approached.

I grinned wickedly, although not sure what he meant; Derek usually said mean things, and I didn't want to appear ignorant.

"Stupid waste, old people marrying," Halgrum said, wiping foam from his lips onto his sleeve. "Still, Clamsby brews good beer; almost makes being here tolerable."

"This isn't a marriage," Derek sneered. "Læknir's a jailor, Rath's punishment for being a thief."

"Too bad his prison's so old," Halgrum said, and they both broke up laughing.

"Yea!" Kal laughed, and I joined in, although I doubted if

Kal understood any more of their sarcasm than I did.

"So, been locked up on your farm?" Derek asked me. "Haven't seen you in months."

"Twice," I groused. "First the funeral, and then Garad fell in the water ..."

"Oh, we laughed about that one!" Halgrum said. "You idiots!"

"Garad fell in, not me!" I defended myself. "If not for him, we wouldn't even have been seen."

"Yea, Sword-head wouldn't do that!" Derek snickered.

"No, Ice-ear," I retorted.

Derek's smile inverted and an angry look crossed his face. He rose up to his full height and clenched his fists, but he could do nothing with so many adults nearby. I smiled, knowing how much he hated the name 'Ice-ear', but the moment quickly passed. Garad came up and shrugged; Grettir still stood by the back wall, close enough to watch, but apart. I suspected that she wouldn't be offering her congratulations to the newlyweds; the story of Rath's drunken invasion of her house had circled our district several times, and the tale of his pounding on her door only hours before his wedding would be the gossip of the countryside for months.

"Hello, Snow-swimmer," Halgrum said to Garad.

It felt good to hang with the other boys. The last time that we'd all been together had been at the swimming hole before harvest. We talked for almost an hour undisturbed. Greatly impressed with my steel sword, I let each of them hold it, but we huddled close so that none of the adults could see that I'd drawn it from my scabbard. Garad and I told them of Rath's visits to Grettir, and Derek laughed so hard that he spewed a mouthful of beer over Kal's head. He said that it was an accident, but he didn't sound sorry.

"Hello," Helsa said.

We all stopped laughing and turned to face her. No one said anything; her appearance had startled us. Helsa stood looking at us, forlorn, her shoulders sunk, as if sad and tired.

"C-c-congratulations," I finally stammered.

"Thanks," she murmured absently, and then the silence continued.

"It won't be so bad," Halgrum spoke up. "Læknir travels all over the county; you'll get to go more places than we do."

"Yea, I guess," Helsa said. "I just wish that it were over. They're married. Why can't everyone just go home?"

The bitterness in her tone was unmistakable. Helsa was tired, sick of all this attention to a problem that she wished no one knew about. This forced marriage might prove best in the long run, but having it shoved in her face, in front of the whole village, must be extremely tedious.

"Læknir healed my mother when she was sick," Kal said suddenly, and Halgrum winced.

"She wants to teach me her secrets," Helsa said, as if fearing an unhappy doom.

"It - it's a good skill," I said, "for a farmwife."

Helsa's eyes snapped open. She glared at me, and Derek suddenly laughed. I didn't know what to say, just stood there with my mouth open. I was just repeating what Mother had said, not thinking how it sounded.

Helsa turned and stormed off into the crowd. Derek laughed hysterically, so loudly that all of the nearby adults paused to stare at us. Halgrum was smirking and Kal started laughing just to join them. Garad looked shocked. I felt bad for Helsa, but mostly embarrassed; I couldn't face the guys, so I walked away, pushing between the adults.

I made my way to Clamsby, and he smiled down at me.

"Well, young Thron, you're looking bigger each time I see you," he grinned, and he reached down and took my mug, filled it, and handed it back. "What's that? A sword? Be going viking soon, won't you?"

"Not this year," I mumbled.

"Not yet, you say?" he asked. "Speak up lad; the hall's too full for quiet talk. Well, I say that you're big enough to come by some night for an ale, you and Grettir's boy. Drinks are on me, for your first night. Then we can talk about some trading, so that you can come more often."

"Thank you," I said.

"Now, you be careful with that sword; keep it sharp and oiled," Clamsby said. "A true warrior can be told by the care that he gives his weapon. When next you come by, I'll tell you about the wound that ended my vikings, when I almost got my leg chopped off."

I already knew that story; Father had been there, and told me many times of how brave Clamsby had been, how they wanted to cut off his leg because of infectious vapors, but Clamsby had refused; he vowed that he'd enter Valhalla whole or not at all. It'd taken him months to heal, and he'd endured many sicknesses that burned him from inside until no one expected him to last another day. Yet he fought back, as Odin had, and though his leg had never fully healed, he still had it, and walked with only a slight limp.

"Thank you," I said again, and I slipped away as an empty mug was pushed into Clamby's hand to be refilled.

Helsa was sitting on a bench beside Old Lady Væna, who looked like she was asleep. I couldn't leave with Helsa thinking that I'd purposely insulted her, so I carefully approached her.

"I'm sorry; I didn't mean it ... that way."

Helsa looked up at me; she looked very pretty in her pink and yellow dress, but she was my age, still a child compared to Ingrid.

"I know," Helsa said. "It's just ... Derek ... and ..."

"I know," I said; neither of us had to finish that sentence. "Læknir will make a good mother ..."

"I don't need a mother," Helsa hissed, a quiet whisper that didn't carry amid the noise in the hall. "I'm not a little girl."

"She'll make Rath a good wife," I rephrased.

Helsa sighed.

"Yes," Helsa said. "Father changed so much after Mother died. He's been ... lonely."

"Læknir will fix that," I said. "He'll be busy, driving her carriage, helping her get around. You'll get to meet all kinds of people."

"At least we'll have food," Helsa said.

Something caught my eye – Widow Væna wasn't asleep; she had one eye open and was looking at me intently. I froze, wondering how much she'd heard, uncertain what to do about it.

"Don't mind me, young ones," Widow Væna said, her high, creaky voice barely audible in the bustle. "I'm just a tired old woman, glad to hear young voices. But if you two want to talk privately, why don't you slip out the door and go for a walk? No one will notice, as long as you don't go far."

I glanced at Helsa; her frightened look warned me not to ask.

"No, thanks," I said. "I think I need to find my mother."

I bit my lip; that was a childish thing to say right in front of Helsa, but one look at Helsa's visibly-relaxed expression told me that I'd done fine. I nodded to her and turned toward the crowd, wondering where to go. I didn't feel like seeing the guys again; they'd just tease me, and I couldn't stand Skratui or her sister. Slowly I pushed between the grownups, ended up standing near the warm fireplace, and slowly realized that the only place that I really wanted to be was home with Ingrid, no matter what Mother said.

* * * * * * * * *

Chapter 8

* * * * * * * * *

"Father, are women the trainers of men?"

Father coughed suddenly, spilling some of his ale onto his tunic.

"You've been talking to your mother," he said disgustedly.

I waited paitently, knowing that he'd begin eventually. It was a cool morning, but we were both hot and sweaty; Father had rented a draft horse for the day, but it had to be frequently rested and watered, and so did we. I pulled the stubborn beast while Father wrestled with the plow; already aches and exhaustion hampered us. Mother and Ingrid brought out our food today; we couldn't stop for a midday meal. While we had the horse, we had to get as much of our fields plowed as possible.

The ground wasn't frozen anymore, but it was still cold and hard. Last year's furrows were almost gone, but the burly horse pulled the sharp iron plow-blade right through them. I had a pouch stuffed with turnip greens; the only reason that the huge horse paid any attention to me at all, despite my pulling on his teather. He was all black with massive hooves, and wouldn't even feel my weight if I stood on his back. When he tossed his head, which he did often, I stumbled, yanked off balance, and several times I fell or had his teather jerked from my hands. But, for an occasional turnip green, he'd follow me, and I led him as straight as I could back and forth across our fields.

However, much of the time I spent thinking about Mother's words. Could it be true? Had Father been *'trained'* by Mother? Were women smarter than men, puppeteers pulling our mindless strings?

"Son, women are not the *'trainers'* of men," Father said. "Wives may choose to believe so, but that doesn't make it true. Women are the workers. They get stuck doing the boring, arduous tasks. That's the way of things, no matter who caused it to be. Can you imagine Ingrid and your Mother out here, pulling this plow? They don't have the strength, as I don't have the patience to sweep, cook, or weave. They'd be as unhappy as we'd be, if our places were reversed. We're each what we were born to be, and no fanciful beliefs can change that.

"However, what good would it do to tell them that? Would you go up to Clamsby and tell him that he's not a fighter anymore because of his game leg? No, he knows the truth, and to remind him of it would only insult him. Men didn't make this world, and we aren't to blame for the weakness of women. Yet it'll do no good to flaunt your superiority; a superior man carries his nobility quietly.

"Be wary of women, though. Most may not be as strong as men, but some are. Women can fight; women make deadly, vicious killers. Many are smart, strong-willed, and wicked. They know we desire them, and flaunt their desirability to gain control over us. That's why you must always be strong; you're a free man, and no one must ever master you. Don't trust anyone too much ... ever, and always know what you want versus what others want. Listen for lies, and always scorn those who speak them, especially when lies are intermixed with truths. Odin said *'Never listen to a woman's bed-talk'.* Good words, Thron. When you're old enough, you'll understand."

I laid back against the plow and breathed deeply. Father wasn't *'trained'.* That meant that I wouldn't be trained. Yet still I was puzzled; why would women want to train men? If they could, what would they train us to do?

* * * * * * * * *

"Kill the pig."

Silently I nodded to Father, and then I lifted my sword and grinned. I'd been waiting for this chance to redeem myself. I glanced at Garad, his face a mask of fear and envy. First, I closed the gate behind me and looped its rope securely over its post; this was going to be quick and decisive, not like the hours that I spent chasing the pig the last time. This time I was going to prove myself.

I looked at my prey: a fat, old pig, very large, but aged, one that didn't move quickly. Yet I suspected that he'd move fast when he realized my intent. He outweighed me, but I wasn't afraid. Months of practicing fighting, with countless victories and bruises, had taught me well. *I was ready.*

I approached the pig carefully. He sensed my approach and moved away, grunting irritably. I got him backed into the corner, but knew that he'd make a break for it, so I inched forward slowly.

The pig dashed along the fence, running faster than I'd ever seen a full-grown pig run. I dived at him and stabbed with all of my might. My blade penetrated his side and drove to the hilt. Then something happened that I hadn't expected; the pig kept running, squealing in pain, and I lost my grip and fell into the slop behind him.

The pig bit at my swordgrip sticking out of his side as he ran, and then he flopped onto one side and writhed, trying to somehow push it out. I jumped up and ran to him; far from dead, he was wild with fear, screaming like a human. I reached for my blade, intending to pull it out and finish the job.

His teeth sank into my arm. The bite didn't hurt, but he shook me violently, as if I were my sword and he was trying to pull me out of his side. I cried out and glanced at Father, who made no move to help. Terrified of losing my arm, I desperately grabbed the grip of my sword with my other hand, yanked it out, and began stabbing the pig, repeatedly, until it stopped struggling. Then I wrenched my arm free of his long, sharp teeth. The pig slumped back; it was still breathing, but bleeding from a dozen deep wounds.

"Keep going," Father said. "A wounded enemy is still dangerous. Kill the pig."

I hesitated, gasped for air, and then steeled myself. I raised my sword, aimed, and stabbed hard and deep, right through its ear into the center of its head.

The pig died.

"You're becoming a fine warrior," Father said.

My arm hurt for days afterward, but I bore the pain proudly. I wasn't a kid anymore: *I'd killed the pig!*

* * * * * * * * *

I opened our pantry door and peered into the darkness inside. The door and wall were thin planks, separating the last five feet of our house, plugged with clay to seal the smoke inside. Pork hung from our pantry ceiling, caked with sea-salt, and baskets of turnips and onions were still stacked over my head, though only half remained of what we'd harvested last fall. It also held a barrel of wheat and two sacks of barley.

I set down the iron smoke-pot, which I'd just filled with fresh coals, on the flat rock, dropped some thin cedar shavings and a few blades of fresh grass into it, and closed its lid. Smoke seeped out through the holes punched through the smoke-pot's lid, and I quickly closed the door. That smoke would keep out the insects while our meat cured.

Father had promised Garad that he could kill the next pig. I was a little jealous, but I understood. Still, I couldn't wait for my next chance.

Father finally came into the house, walking slowly and wearily. He said nothing, simply sat down hard in his chair and stared at the fire. Planting was always tough; even my back was aching from burying the tiny seedlings that Mother had sprouted. Hauling heavy buckets of water back and forth was torture. Both Mother and Ingrid had helped for most of the day; both were now resting, as they'd been for hours.

"Where were you?" Mother asked.

"I saw some more footprints by the backfields," Father said.

"Footprints ...?"

"Strange footprints," Father said. "Boots, big ones. I saw some a few days ago but dismissed it as hunters. Today I found some new ones and thought that I'd best check them out."

"What'd you find?"

"Nothing. From our property, they go up into the hills. I tracked them for a few miles, but the trail vanished."

"Who'd be back there?"

"Could be anybody; most likely some peasant or escaped thrall. Harmless enough, unless they take to thieving. Eventually I'll find them."

"Take your sword," Mother said bluntly.

Father looked down and nodded.

Ingrid and I exchanged glances. We barely spoke these days; Mother wouldn't leave us alone even for a moment. From behind Mother's chair, Ingrid nodded silently to me, wary of Mother's ever-watchful eyes, for we couldn't afford to get caught again. I didn't know what her nod meant, but slyly, while no one else was watching, I kissed the back of my hand, too softly to make a sound. Ingrid smiled slightly and looked relieved; it was our secret signal to each other. She lightly kissed the back of her hand.

* * * * * * * * *

"Don't you see?" Ingrid exclaimed. "If you found whoever was stalking around the back fields, and dealt with it properly, then Thorir would respect you for it."

"How can I deal with them properly?" I asked. "I don't even know who they are."

"You need to find them first," Ingrid said. "You can follow their tracks and discover where they lead. Then you could hide in the forest and spy on them."

"What if it's someone really big?"

"Don't let them see you," Ingrid said. "Come back secretly and tell Thorir who it is. Then he can get Rath and the other village men, and they can chase them away."

It made sense. I'd impress Father and he'd start to see me as a man. Maybe he'd even change his mind and take me viking. Or, he could let me go to Market ... and take Ingrid. Traveling alone with her, without Mother watching, would be paradise itself.

"It'll be hard to get away during planting," I said.

"You may have to wait until planting's done, but before Thorir leaves," Ingrid said.

She glanced around carefully, peered out the barn door, and then kissed me really good.

* * * * * * * * *

Planting took longer than ever. Father hunted for the stranger every day, and I feared that he'd find him before I could even start to look. He went carrying his sword, and traced the hills, looking for tracks of the mysterious intruder, right after midday meal, during the hottest part of the afternoon. Meanwhile, I had to plant and water seedlings out in our fields while Mother and Ingrid planted near the house. It pained me how Mother kept Ingrid and I apart, but there was nothing that I could do about it.

"Thron!" shouted my best friend.

"Garad!" I cried, delighted. "Are you done planting already?"

"No, barely started," Garad said, stepping carefully over the rows. "We've planted the field near the house, but the back field is still unfurrowed."

"How will you get it finished before planting season ends?"

"We'll be lucky to finish before harvest," Garad said.

"What's the problem?"

"There's a thief in the woods," Garad said. "Mother saw his tracks in the back field."

"Father said the same," I said. "He goes off every day to look for him."

"So does Mother," Garad said. "She's out there now, looking, so I took a break."

"Won't she notice?"

"Probably, but I'm exhausted," Garad said. "We get up before dawn, and I cut the ground while she plants and waters. If we could've afforded a plow then we'd have a lot more done by now. I'm worried that we might not have enough harvest this year; onions have to be planted early."

"Glad that we didn't have to plow by hand," I commented, feeling guilty. Garad's father had never failed to plow and plant early. Without him, I couldn't imagine how they'd survive the winter.

"Where's Ingrid?"

I glared up at Garad, but I bit my lip and didn't yell; he didn't know our secret and I had to keep it that way.

"Ingrid and Mother are working by the house," I seethed, looking away. "I don't know why Father cares about that thief so much; nothing's missing, and there won't be any crops for him to steal for months."

"Mother says that thieves are dangerous," Garad said. "If you don't get rid of one, as soon as they appear, soon you have many, and then it's too late. Like the Lapland thieves that killed Morgan, they come at you at night and take everything. Mother said that thieves move into a district in the spring, then wait for the viking, when the men leave. The thief has to be evicted before then."

"I wish I could hunt him," I said. "I'd track his footprints in no time."

"Me, too," Garad said. "But Mother won't let me anywhere near the back fields. She says that it's too dangerous; she can't afford to lose me as well."

"Seen any of the other kids?"

"Kal, Derek, and I were at the swimming hole a few days ago," Garad said. "We tried to signal, but you didn't see us. Thorir was nearby, so we couldn't shout."

"Too bad," I said regretfully. "I could use a swim. Any news of Helsa?"

"Derek says that she's traveling all over," Garad said. "Rath's driving Læknir's wagon across the whole district, and Helsa goes with them. They've moved into Læknir's house; Rath's place is empty. Derek says that Læknir wants to sell it, but Rath doesn't."

"Did Derek talk to Helsa?"

"No, but he says that she's having lots of fun." The displeasure in Garad's voice was obvious.

"Derek talks a lot," I said angrily. "He talks even when he knows nothing."

"Stupid cow-herder," Garad cursed him.

I paused and looked up at the hot sun. My water bucket was almost empty again. Why couldn't it be raining, like it was during harvest? The dread of carrying the heavy bucket back from the well again shriveled my soul.

"Hey, let's go fill up my bucket at the swimming hole!"

"Really?" Garad asked.

"Sure. It's not much farther than walking back to the well, and the water level in the well's getting low."

"Let's go!"

Taking the bucket, we laughed and skipped across the

field toward the swimming hole. The swimming hole wasn't far from the edge of Garad's back field, under the tall trees that grew around the base of the hills. The rocky hills were covered with brambles and brush so thick they would've been easier to climb over than push through, if not for the thorns. I kept an eye out for Father or Grettir, and we swung our path into Garad's fields to retrieve Garad's bucket; if Father or Grettir saw us headed for the swimming hole then we could claim we were both going for water.

We dropped our buckets on the grass, stripped, and splashed into the icy water. The flowing chill iced my sun-reddened skin, and I pinched my nose and sunk to the bottom. The small, round, mossy stones touched my back and seemed to push me back, weightless in the underwater silence.

Suddenly Garad's hands grabbed and pulled me up. Sputtering, I realized that he was frantic again, and struggled to make sense of his babbling. Then I saw what he was pointing at: footprints in the mud; large boot-prints leading away from the water. Recent, because we knew every inch of this pool...

"The thief!" Garad shouted.

"He was here!" I gasped.

"What do we do?" Garad asked.

I swallowed hard. The boot-print was huge and could've been made by a murderer, but Father had told me that real men had to be brave. In my mind Ingrid's voice echoed, telling me how proud Father would be if I found the thief.

"We follow them," I said determinedly.

"But ...!" Garad stammered.

"Stay here, if you're afraid," I said. "I'm going."

"I'm going, too!" Garad insisted.

"Fine," I said, "but we have to be quiet!"

We dressed, then left our buckets behind and followed the tracks. They led down the path that we all used and vanished as the mud gave way to dry dirt. We followed the path; the impenetrable thorns on either side prevented anyone from veering in any other direction. The main path led past Garad's back fields to Eardai's farm, where we seldom went openly, for it could be seen from her house, so we doubted if the thief would've gone there. When the path split, we chose the branch that led away from Eardai's, up into the hills. The thief was probably living there, hidden among the crags, so we quietly slipped up the slopes amid the cover of trees. We were still too close to our houses to find the thief's camp, but the tingle of fear and excitement made me over-cautious. It felt like a game, but better; *this was real!*

Too soon, a distant noise alerted us. We ducked low and slid behind some trees. I motioned for Garad to be quiet, and continued to listen. Someone was close by. Human voices floated in the wind, too faint to be heard clearly, but too loud to be dismissed.

Nervously I crept out, sliding to another tree, low behind the bushes. I didn't dare step into the brush; crunching grass and snapping twigs would alert anyone nearby. Instead, I glanced up and saw a low branch before me.

Waving for Garad to stay hidden, I jumped up, grasped the branch, and pulled myself up. The rough bark scraped and scratched, but I ignored it; all of us boys were master tree-climbers. I prided myself on my reputation for climbing higher than anyone else.

Through all of the fluttering leaves it was hard to see. I had to move slowly to not shake the tree; if the thief saw me, and reached the base of the tree before I climbed down, then

I'd be trapped, and I feared to think what might happen then.

From the heights of the branches, I looked and listened. Our fields were clearly visible from up here, but little else. The hills were confusing; just by looking you couldn't tell solid ground from brambles ten feet thick. Everything looked the same, save for the different colors of leaves. Almost anything could be hidden beneath a single layer of brush. If the thief's camp was in the middle of a dense thicket, then I'd never see it unless I was hanging right over it.

Suddenly I saw something – *someone* – on the next rise. It was hard to see between the fluttering leaves, and the figure seemed hidden, half-buried in tall weeds. I froze, trying to keep my tree from swaying, and finally got a clear look; it was a man, lying on his stomach in the thick grass. He was moving, seemed to be doing something, and at first glance I couldn't tell what. Then I realized it ... *and almost fell out of the tree.*

It was Father. It was Grettir. Father was lying in the tall grass ... on top of Grettir. They were naked. They were ... *Father and Grettir were mating ...!*

I clung frozen, shocked and terrified. What did it mean? What was I going to do? *What would Mother say?* Father ... *mating with Garad's mother?* Why? *Why?*

I couldn't stay there; I was too visible. What would Father say, or Grettir, if they happened to look up and see me? Almost falling from branch to branch, I descended the twisting trunk to the forest floor. Garad waited anxiously at the base of the tree.

"What di..?"

"Shhhhh!" I shushed him, my eyes round as wagon wheels, and then I pulled him back down the trail. Garad didn't object; I was obviously panicked. Full-tilt we ran back

down the slope all the way to the swimming hole.

"What was it?" Garad demanded as we ran. "*What'd you see?"*

I collapsed to my knees beside the swimming hole, gasping for breath. Garad ran up behind me, panting.

"Not fair!" he cried. "What'd you see?"

I didn't know what to say. *I couldn't tell Garad!* But I had to tell him something. My mind raced, but all I could think of was the horrible sight: *Father ... and Grettir ...!*

"What was it?" Garad demanded. "Did you see the thief?"

"Uh ... yes!" I stammered. "More than ... many thieves! A whole army ... I mean, at least five or six! They were big guys, and had swords, and spears, and looked like killers!"

"Mother!" Garad gasped.

Garad turned to run back, and an instant later I realized his intent. As far as he knew, his mother was somewhere in those hills, alone, facing a deadly pack of thieves! But I couldn't let him run back, shouting hysterically; Father and Grettir would know that I hadn't seen any thieves. They'd know that I saw ...

"Garad!" I cried, and I dashed after him. "Wait! Your mother wasn't there! We have to go back!"

"She's out there!" Garad shouted, but he slowed enough for me to catch up with him. When I did, I grabbed him, and we both fell, rolling across the hard dirt.

"You don't know that! These guys' camp was really well hidden; I'd never have seen it if I hadn't climbed that tree, and your mother's too old to climb! We need to go back ... and not tell anyone that we were there, not ever!"

"But the thieves ...!"

I struggled to think of some answer, some lie that I could tell Garad, some lie that would cover up my first lie and make

Garad shut up.

"Those thieves don't want to be found ... so we have time."

"We have to tell somebody! Thorir, or the men in town!"

"No!" I insisted. "We ... we have to deal with them ourselves ...!"

Garad looked horrified, as if I'd suddenly gone mad right before his eyes.

"Us ...?" gasped Garad. "Against six grown men ...? Killers with swords ...?"

"Quiet!" I shushed him. "We can do it. You and me."

"But why?" Garad demanded.

An idea finally came.

"Don't you want to go viking?" I hissed at him. "We'll never get to go as long as Branwulf sees us as kids. Don't you see? This is our chance! Our chance to prove ourselves!"

Garad's expression didn't change.

"Come on!" I shouted urgently, realizing how far we'd run, that we were too close, and that Father and Grettir would come this way eventually. "Back to the swimming hole! We have to think this over carefully!"

Soon I turned my bucket over and sat on it. Garad paced circles around me, whining and complaining.

"But they're dangerous!" Garad repeated.

"Remember what your mother said?" I asked him. "They won't attack until the men leave to go viking. That gives us a few weeks. If we can't think of something by then, we'll tell Father. He and the townsmen can chase them away before they leave."

"We could get hurt ...!"

"We'll be heroes. Think about it! The two of us ... honored and respected ... more than Derek ever dreamed of.

We have to do this!"

"We'll get in trouble," Garad argued. "We'll get killed."

"We'll go viking."

That silenced Garad. He obviously doubted, but going viking was what we wanted more than anything in the world.

"We'll go viking," I repeated. "You and me, together, aboard Branwulf's ship ... with swords and shields of our own ... ahead of Derek, Halgrum, and all the others; think about it!"

"What can we do against six men with swords?"

"I don't know," I answered, "but there has to be a way. Just give me some time! I'll think of something."

"We're going to get in trouble again," Garad said.

"You got us in trouble last time," I accused him. "You fell off the dock ... and I got punished for it. All that I'm asking for is a few days. Just don't say anything ... to Grettir ... or to anyone! If I can't think of something within a few days, then we'll tell everyone. I promise! Just give me a few days; you owe me that much!"

* * * * * * * * *

Chapter 9

*   *   *   *   *   *   *   *   *

I couldn't look at Father. I couldn't look at Mother. I couldn't even look at Ingrid. *What was I going to do?*

Days passed slowly, Garad and I watching each other across our half-planted fields.

While Mother and Ingrid worked by the house, Garad came into our fields, after Father and Grettir had vanished, and we talked again about the dangerous thieves. Again I pressured him into promising that he'd say nothing to anyone; I finally caved his objections, but he wouldn't last long. I racked my brains to try and think of something, but no solution came; I'd lied myself into a corner, and now I had to produce, and defeat, six dangerous thieves, or admit the truth.

I felt helpless. Even the truth was a lie, a lie between Father, Mother, and Grettir, and now I was part of it. I couldn't tell the truth; Mother would be devastated ... and Father might go viking and never return. If that happened, then I'd never get to go south – my world would end, and my life might as well be over.

How could he? I'd admired Father all of my life. He was everything to me – the symbol of what a man should be, of what I wanted to be. He was my icon, my example, my idol. Now I didn't know what to think.

The image of them lying together in the grass, mating like two pigs in the mud, poisoned my thoughts, and blinded my vision. I couldn't close my eyes without seeing them, feeling my stomach turn and head pound. I wanted to be sick.

"Are you sanding that cup or playing with it?" Mother suddenly asked.

I looked down at the cup and sanding stone in my hands, abruptly aware that I wasn't even keeping up the pretense that nothing was wrong. I shrugged without looking up, touched my smooth stone to the wet cloth, then tapped the top of the finely-sifted sand in its box, and began sanding out the chisel-marks more fervently.

"You're being very quiet, Thron," Mother said. "Are you feeling all right?"

"Just ... thinking," I replied.

"About what?"

"Nothing."

"You must be thinking about something."

"I'm ... worried about ... planting. It's not going fast enough, and Garad isn't even halfway finished."

"Oh, you want to help Garad plant?" Mother smiled. "That's very nice of you. I'm sure, when our fields are planted, that you can help Garad."

I gritted my teeth: helping Garad harvest had been bad enough; I didn't want to help him plant, but anything was better than revealing the truth. My lie to Garad was growing bigger. *How long could I keep up this deception?*

Mother went back to her sewing. Father had said little, sitting in his chair, staring at the fire. We wouldn't be up long; planting was hard work, and we'd have to be up with the roosters to start again.

A toe kicked me from behind, and Ingrid leaned over and refilled my ale. I glanced up at her worried expression, but I turned away the instant that I saw her eyes. *How could I face her, knowing the truth about Father? What could I say?*

Another kick, harder, landed before she walked away. I shuddered; lies ruined everything. Soon Garad would blab the truth, and then everyone in the village would know.

I tried to think of some solution – wracked my brains for any idea, but nothing came. I began to despair. Some traps were too complete; once you got into them, you couldn't get out unscathed. Mother would be furious, horrified, shamed and insulted. She thought of herself as a trainer, and was about to be bit by her trainee. Worse, it'd happen in public, and gossip travels; as with Rath's thieving and marriage, soon everyone would know.

Father would be gone soon, and maybe not come back, if word got out. Worse, *he could decide to move in with Grettir, take Garad for his son, and leave me behind!* I couldn't bear that thought, but what could I do? Without the treasures from Father's viking, could we afford to keep our farm?

Ingrid: *what would become of her ... of us?* It'd been days since we were alone, since we'd last kissed. If Father left for good, would Mother sell Ingrid, like she'd sold Hal? *How could I lose Ingrid?*

My brains couldn't answer any of these questions. I needed someone that I could confide in, someone smarter than ...

Ingrid!

I glanced at her suddenly, and Ingrid looked surprised, then quickly turned away. Worried, I glanced at Mother to find her carefully watching me. I looked back at the half-finished wooden cup in my hands and refreshed the sand on my stone.

Ingrid would think of a way. She had to ... or everything would fail.

* * * * * * * * *

Ingrid's mouth fell open and hung in disbelief.

"Grettir? Thorir with ...? *Vespa will kill him!"*

I bowed my head and quickly blurted out the rest of the story, not once looking into her eyes. When I'd finished, Ingrid sat in silence.

"What do I do?" I implored.

"Garad's not the problem," Ingrid said. "He's an idiot; fooling him'll be easy. Vespa's the problem. If she finds out ..."

"She can't find out!" I insisted.

"Vespa's not stupid," Ingrid said. "She knows about us, and no one had to tell her. Thorir's been so quiet lately ... even I knew that something was wrong. You've been different as well; I thought that you were mad at me."

"Me?" I asked incredulously.

Ingrid smiled and kissed me.

"I'm glad that you're not," Ingrid said. "Now, I need to think. First, we have to find a way to silence Garad, to convince him that the thieves have left."

"How can you prove that?" I asked.

"The only way to fight one lie is with another lie."

* * * * * * * * *

No sooner was our last turnip-seedlings planted than I was sent to Garad's. Planting onions was miserable work; the weather had been unusually dry for a Norwegian spring, the ground too hard. We couldn't just dig holes; since they hadn't plowed, we had to break up the dirt as much as possible, scoop it out, fill the hole with water, and then hold the seedling in place while we dumped the loose dirt back into the water-filled hole. Slow, muddy, and laborious, and when combined with endless trips to refill the water-buckets, it became horribly tiresome. Even in the very back fields, I had to fetch water from the well by the house; Grettir wouldn't let us near the swimming hole. The buckets of water grew heavier each trip, but Grettir was as stern and as quick-tongued as ever. No matter how fast we went, she yelled at us to go faster.

Midday meal, usually the largest of the day, was pathetically small and hurried, and then Grettir rushed us back outside after only half a cup of beer apiece. I understood Grettir's fears; only half of their onions were planted, and without a full harvest, they wouldn't survive the winter. Still, it was hard to feel sympathy with her constantly barking at us like a tied-up dog. I felt miserably mistreated; after toiling for weeks on our farm, I was sent to do even more work in Garad's fields. I was doing twice as much work as anyone else in the village, probably in the whole world! Yet, although smaller, Garad worked incredibly fast, and planted almost twice as many onions as I did that first afternoon.

Garad fared no better than I under his mother's harsh tongue, and at the end of the day, Grettir ordered us both to the swimming hole to wash up, skin and clothes, without dawdling, and then come straight back to her house as quickly as we could, with only a few mumbled threats of what would happen if we weren't there when her cook-pot reached a boil.

Stumbling with weariness, we both fell into the icy water fully-clothed and splashed underneath. Under the relentless sun, the skin on our necks was red and hot, and the first sting of the cool water was followed by a chill numbness as the fire began to recede. Able to hold my breath a long time, I closed my eyes and sank face-first into the weeds on the bottom; it felt wonderful.

When I splashed up, gasping and sputtering, and wiping my eyes free of the water running from my hair, I found Garad laying on his back in the shallows, just the circle of his face visible above water.

"Thank the Gods you came," Garad sighed with exhaustion. "Mother's driving me harder every day. We're weeks behind, and she's so sore from working that she collapses right after dinner."

"You plant fast," I admitted.

"I have to," Garad mumbled. "I'm the man of our family. I have to do my work and Father's; Mother never lets me forget that."

I looked at Garad, whose eyes were closed and breaths still coming in small gasps. He appeared likely to die from exhaustion. He and Grettir had been hand-planting since before Father rented the horse and plow. But his reaction wasn't what I'd expected; it was too ... adult. Garad had always seemed so childish and excitable. He seemed to be two different people now; the laughing friend that I'd always known, and the sad child of a dead father.

"What about the thieves?" Garad asked.

I took a deep breath, preparing to recite exactly what Ingrid had told me to say.

"I told Ingrid, and she ..."

"You did what?!?" Garad shouted, trying to sit up so fast that his head tilted underwater and he splashed up frothing and spewing.

"I told Ingrid, and she said ..."

"You told me not to tell anyone!" Garad shouted. "You made me promise, and every day my mother goes off into danger ...!"

"Ingrid will help us!" I seethed, wanting to shout but fearful of any who might overhear, even out here in the woods. "Ingrid won't tell anyone, and she knows how to help!"

"How can a girl help against six armed thieves?"

I hesitated, determined to finish the sentence that Ingrid had made me memorize.

"Ingrid said there was a way – a dark, secret way – to drive off the thieves so they'll never come back."

"How?"

"Magic," I replied. "Dark, evil sorcery. Women stuff."

As the words left my mouth, I realized how stupid they sounded. I couldn't believe that I'd said them, and knew that Garad was only waiting until his disbelief ended before he laughed at me. Magic ... the old stories were full of magic, but the idea that Ingrid had any was ridiculous.

"Magic?" Garad asked incredulously.

I couldn't believe that Garad was swallowing the biggest lie that I'd ever told, but he could never fake his eyes-wide expression of surprise.

"Can she do it?" Garad asked.

"Yes," I replied, but then I thought better of it. "At least, I think so. She's older than we are ... and very wise. And she's a woman, which means that she has magic."

"Women have magic?"

I struggled for an answer to this. It took longer than I'd expected, but Garad seemed transfixed.

"Why would any man marry a woman unless she cast a spell on him?"

Sometimes, by the way that you ask a question, you know what the answer will be, even if it's wrong. Garad knew nothing about girls, even less than I did, and that was saying a lot. Yet he couldn't admit ignorance; Garad thought for a moment, and then bowed his head.

"I know girls use magic," he said defensively. "But will Ingrid use it for us?"

"I think so," I said finally. "Thieves would hurt her, too, if they attack after Father sails."

"What can she do?"

"I don't know," I answered. "But tomorrow night is the full moon, and she said that we'd do it then."

"How will we get out?"

"We'll have to wait until Mother, Father, and Grettir are asleep."

"Sneak out?!? What if we're caught?"

"Don't get caught. We'll meet you at the swimming hole when the moon is high. Don't be late ... or we'll do it without you."

In the distance we heard a banging; Grettir was using a wooden spoon on her iron pan.

"We'd better go," Garad said.

"So ...?" I asked. "Are you coming ... or not?"

Garad frowned but set his teeth as if unwilling to admit that he was afraid.

"Yes," he said resignedly.

* * * * * * * * *

Moonlight shone pale yellow and twinkled off the water as I tossed another pebble into the swimming hole just to watch its shimmer ripple across its surface. The night was clear with thin clouds shading shining stars, but a winter chill seemed to linger in the wind blowing in from the sea. Brine hung heavy in the air.

"Where is he?" Ingrid hissed.

A loud crunch and thrashing of leaves answered her. Someone had tripped and fallen; it had to be Garad; there was more than enough light for anyone else.

"About time!" Ingrid scolded.

"It was easy!" Garad whispered. "Mother was snoring, and I lifted off the brace and set it on my bed, and ..."

"Let's get started," Ingrid interrupted him.

"Is this really going to work?" asked Garad.

"Yes, but when we get near the thieves, then we'll have to be very quiet," she said. "In order for it to be as powerful as possible, we'll have to get very close to the thieves. This is very dangerous, for if they see us, they'll kill us."

"Kill us ...?" Garad gasped.

"Time to be brave," I said, but Garad looked very uncertain.

I fought to keep from smiling. Silencing Garad was easy, but Father and Grettir were still going off together every day, supposedly to look for thieves. What was I going to do about them mating? Anything that I said would only make things worse, or reveal what I knew, and what a disaster that would cause!

"Just do as I say," Ingrid said. "First we have to draw a circle in the dirt ... with my lantern in the very center."

Ingrid uncovered a lit lantern beside her basket, then lifted and held it up high.

"Frigg and Freyja, I call upon thee," she spoke to the stars overhead. "Sygn and Geffon, I invoke your holy names. Look down upon we three, and bless us now, and forever keep secret this magic spell of ours."

I glanced up at the stars, then back at her stern face. Ingrid sounded so serious that I was worried; she was using the names of the gods and goddesses: *their real names.* What if they listened? Would they make our spell real?

Ingrid placed her lantern gently upon the bent grasses and knelt before it.

"Draw the circle now," she ordered us. "Use a stick and scratch a circle in the dirt around us. Don't step outside the circle. Black magic attracts Dark Elves, and once they're here, they'll kill anyone not inside our circle."

Ingrid bowed to her glowing lantern, slowly and solemnly, and began speaking words in a tongue I'd never heard. Garad glanced at me, a look of unmasked fear on his face, and I returned his gaze silently. I knew that women were different than men, but I hadn't known how much. Ingrid was two years older than us, and wiser, but I'd never imagined the secrets she held. Was she faking? If so, then she faked with a skill that I wouldn't have believed possible. Mother's words echoed in my mind: women were the trainers of men. Father had said that Mother lied, but then, he was laying with Garad's mother. How much trust could I put in his words?

Gritting my teeth, I searched in the poor light for a stick to begin marking a circle around Ingrid. Garad quickly found a big stick and started marking the circle. I found one and helped before he finished, gouging out a curving line in the sandy dirt beside the swimming hole. Soon we all stood inside our circle, Ingrid still chanting in her mysterious tongue.

"Now we have to purify ourselves," Ingrid said, and she reached into her basket with both hands and pulled out a small clay jar and a bottle of Grandfather's mead.

"What're you doing with that?" I gasped. "If Father finds it missing ...!"

"He won't," Ingrid said. "I dug it up carefully so that he won't notice before he goes viking. When he returns, I'll tell him that Vespa opened it one night when Grettir was over, and he won't ever ask."

I bit my lip and said no more. Ingrid was right; Father would never talk about Grettir to Vespa, but fear shivered up my back, realizing the ease with which Ingrid could manipulate Father. *Wasn't manipulating the same as training?*

"First, we have to undress and purify our outsides," Ingrid said. "Then we have to drink the mead to purify our insides."

Undress? My mind reeled. *What was she up to?*

"Turn around, both of you," Ingrid said. "We all have to undress, but I don't want you watching me."

She started to lift her skirt up, then paused and gave us an evil glare. Garad and I instantly spun around, facing away from her. We glanced at each other, but what could we say? I'd watched Ingrid undress many times, but I couldn't say so in front of Garad. But Garad; *did Ingrid know that he'd always wanted to see her naked?*

"Well?" Ingrid demanded as we heard her rustle out of

her clothes. "We don't have all night. Get undressed!"

Gulping, I started pulling off my clothes. Garad slowly followed my example. I had to do whatever Ingrid said and tried not to focus on why. If this didn't work, if Vespa found out about Father and Grettir, then he'd sail south and I'd never see him again. I'd be like Garad, fatherless, alone with Mother on a farm that we couldn't maintain. I pulled off my clothes and tossed them onto the grass.

"Now turn around," Ingrid said. "We have to anoint ourselves with magic oil."

We all turned to face each other. In the glow of our lantern and the starlight, Ingrid was just as beautiful as I remembered, pale and tall, her round breasts hovering temptingly. Garad's eyes bulged; *never had he imagined what he was seeing this night!* I didn't like him looking at Ingrid; she was mine, but I couldn't say so in front of him.

Ingrid pulled the cork from a small jar and poured some oil onto her hand. Without warning or ceremony, she reached out and smeared some on Garad's forehead, then marked both of his cheeks beneath his eyes.

"Stand still," she ordered him, and then she continued down his body, touching him all over, even places where both Garad and I were shocked that she touched. She did it quickly, then ordered him to turn around, and began at his neck, dabbing more oil in places all down his arms, back, butt, and legs.

"Okay, you're finished," Ingrid said. "Thron, your turn."

Ingrid poured more oil onto her hand and began marking me in exactly the same way. From the top of my head to my feet, every few inches she touched my skin, leaving a spot of glistening oil. When she touched my manhood I felt it swell, but she ignored it and continued as if it was nothing more than a daily chore. She anointed me more heavily than she anointed Garad, and soon I felt the chill of the night wind across the patches of oil on my skin. I turned around when ordered, and she poked me all over my backside until I felt covered in oil.

"Now, Thron, hold out your hand," Ingrid said, and when I did, she poured oil all over my hand. "Okay, now you anoint me."

I swallowed hard. *Rub oil all over Ingrid's naked body?* She'd let me touch her before, but never in front of anyone else! I desperately wanted to, but I was afraid, uncertain.

"Look, I don't like this anymore than you do," Ingrid said, sounding irritated. "Just do it. Start with my forehead. Go on! Touch it."

I reached up and touched her forehead. The oil clung to her skin, reflecting the starlight as she moved.

"Hurry up," Ingrid said. "Now do my cheeks, and then the rest of me, just like I did to you two."

Touch her everywhere? I wanted to, but ...

"I'll do it!" Garad said excitedly.

"No," I said so quickly that my own words startled me. "I'll do it."

Quickly I brushed Ingrid's cheeks and chin, then her neck and shoulders. Then I kept going. I went fast, too fast to enjoy it, but it was exciting, exhilarating. Soon her front was covered in oil, and Ingrid turned around and exposed her delicious backside to me, and I touched her neck, and then dotted her all the way down to her heels.

"That's enough," she said suddenly, breaking me from my attentiveness, and she reached out a hand to each of us. "Now we all join hands and look up at the stars."

We clasped hands drenched with oil and glanced up at the

familiar night sky. The stars seemed unusually bright.

"Hail Odin, Alfather, look down upon we who beseech you!" Ingrid said aloud. "Come down to us and help us drive away our enemies!"

Enemies? Oh, yes; *the thieves.* So much had happened that I'd forgotten why we were here. Ingrid released our hands and reached down and picked up the bottle of Grandfather's mead. The cork was tight but she managed to pull it out, then raised it high.

"As we have anointed ourselves on the outside, so let this precious mead now anoint our insides," she said. "Thieves be gone!"

Ingrid took a swig on the bottle, then passed it to Garad. "Say *'thieves be gone'* and take a drink."

"Thieves be gone!" Garad said uncertainly, and he took a sip.

"Drink more," Ingrid insisted. "We have to finish this bottle."

Garad hesitated, then took a bigger drink.

"You have to say *'thieves be gone'* before you drink!" Ingrid scolded him.

Garad glanced nervously at me, then said "Thieves be gone!" and took another drink. Then Ingrid motioned for him to pass the bottle to me.

"Thieves be gone!" I said, and I took a big drink. The honey-wine was strong and thick in my mouth, far more potent than the beer that we drank every day. I frowned, a little concerned; if we drank this whole bottle then we'd be very drunk.

"Thieves be gone!" Ingrid said as I passed the bottle to her, and then she took a drink and passed it back to Garad.

'Thieves be gone!' became more fun to say as we drank,

and soon we were passing the bottle back and forth very quickly. Our voices became louder and more exuberant as we went, our gestures more exaggerated. Ingrid kept raising the bottle to Odin as she spoke the words, and watching the stars and lantern light shine off of her glistening skin was mesmerizing. It bothered me that Garad was obviously enjoying watching her, but soon I was too engrossed in the flashing lights and sights of her to think about him.

When Ingrid finally upturned the empty bottle, we all cheered, but she shushed us up quickly.

"Are you mad?" she seethed, suddenly angry. "Do you want your parents to find us like this? Or worse, the thieves? This won't work unless we finish the whole spell. Now join hands again and let's finish our chant."

We joined hands less easily; Garad was having trouble standing, and my head was spinning. Ingrid began to chant again, softly and slowly, in solemn tones, using that strange language that I'd never heard before. Garad and I stood in silence, listening to her, hearing her occasionally name Thor, Baulder, Loki, and all of the other great gods amid her arcane chant. I could feel the power of her spell surrounding us, like a tingling of senses I'd never known I possessed. *It really was working!* The thieves would be gone by morning!

Thieves ...? What was I thinking? There were no thieves! That was a stupid lie that I'd made up to silence Garad. But then ... what were we doing out here in the middle of the night? What was that tingling that felt like magical power?

I shook my clouded head, trying to think clearly. All of this was a show, wasn't it? All for Garad? Why did I feel so ... expectant? Was this really a magical ceremony? *Was Ingrid really casting a spell, only pretending to be faking?*

I glanced at Garad; he'd closed his eyes, as if praying, and looked as serious as I'd ever seen. Ingrid had her eyes closed and was mumbling magic words with equal seriousness. *Was I the one confused? What were we really doing?*

Eventually Ingrid finished her chant. Her hands released ours, and we all lowered our arms.

"It's time," she said, and she reached down and picked up her basket. In the bottom of it were sewing scraps, strips of old, plain cloth that I recognized from Ingrid's sewing kit, mixed with lengths of yarn no longer than a handspan. "Now we come to the dangerous part. We have to anoint these scraps with this oil, and then leave them all over the area where the thieves are. We have to be quiet so that the thieves don't hear; if they catch us, they'll burn us as witches. And we have to be quick. Leave your clothes here or they'll just get all oily, and then your mothers will know you've done black magic. Come, take a handful of these scraps, and let's get this over with."

We each took a third of the scraps, and then Ingrid poured oil all over them, and we had to work the oil into the cloth and yarn strips. Then Ingrid lowered her voice to a whisper.

"All right, Garad, you lead the way," she said. "Take us back to the area where you saw the thieves, as close as you dare, and then we have to tie these onto the branches and bushes all over that area. Don't speak or make any noise, or we're dead!"

Garad nodded, then turned and led the way down the familiar path. Despite my spinning head, I kept trying to focus, to concentrate, to figure out what we were doing. Why was Garad leading? I'd seen the thieves, not him! *Or did I ...?*

Before we reached the tree that I'd climbed, I felt slightly sick. We were close to the thieves, but I couldn't purge the image of Father's naked back bouncing up and down on top of Grettir. Then Ingrid slid past me on the narrow trail, our greasy bodies sliding against each other, and I quickly forgot about whatever was bothering me.

Ingrid tied a scrap of oily cloth around the branch of a bush. She motioned for us to do the same, and instantly we started. Ingrid nodded her head to Garad and sent him up the trail, and then motioned for me to follow him. She pushed deeper into the brush, continuing to tie tiny bits of oily cloth all over the bushes.

I followed Garad up the trail and found him tying a strand of yarn to the hanging branches of a tall willow tree. I nodded as he looked at me, and then began tying a strand to the branch of a small sapling. I dropped my bundle once and had to fumble for it in the dark. My stomach was churning; *I wasn't well.*

We ranged all over. It took forever to tie all those sticky, greasy scraps to the branches, but once we'd finished, Ingrid took off at a run back toward the swimming hole. Garad and I ran after her, although it wasn't easy; without her long skirt, Ingrid ran faster than I'd thought she could. Everything was spinning and I could barely keep from falling. If my feet hadn't known this trail so well that I could walk it blindfolded, I'd never have made it.

"It's done," Ingrid announced. "As soon as you can, you'll both have to go and inspect the area to make sure that the thieves are gone, but I know that it worked; I can feel it. Can you feel it, Garad?"

"Oh, yes!" Garad said instantly, although his voice was slurred and he seemed unusually happy.

"What about you, Thron?"

"Oh, of course," I answered quickly. "I could feel it the whole time."

"So could I," Ingrid said. "Now, we'd best wash off before we put our clothes back on. We can hardly expect to keep this a secret if our mothers wake us up tomorrow with oil smeared all over us."

Ingrid pulled out a tub of soap that she'd brought, and we piled beside the swimming hole to wash. The water was icy cold and the night wind chilled us to our bones, but we soaped and scrubbed all over. Ingrid washed our backs and then let me wash hers; I thoroughly enjoyed it, but Ingrid pulled away too soon. Then, with our bare hands, we wiped off the water as best we could and drug our dry night-clothes back over our damp skin.

"Now remember," Ingrid said seriously, "no one must ever know what we did out here. We'd be branded as witches and cast out of the village. We've saved our families from terrible thieves, and must remember: that's the only reward we'll ever get for what we've done tonight. Thron, are you satisfied that the thieves are gone, and promise that you'll never speak of this night to anyone?"

"Yes, I am ... I mean, I do," I stammered.

"Garad?"

"I swear!" he promised.

"Good," she said. "Now we must go back and get in our beds so no one ever knows that we were out here. We should go back separately. Garad, you go first. Be careful and quiet! If any of us get caught, we're all done for."

Garad nodded, then turned to run home. He hesitated and looked back, as if he wanted to say something else, but then he dashed off across his fields until he was just a shadow under the starlight.

Ingrid turned to me.

"I think that it worked," she smiled.

"What worked?"

She hesitated, then grinned widely.

"What was that?" I demanded. "I did feel ... something. What ...?"

Ingrid suddenly grabbed me, pulled me close, and kissed me hard. It was a long, passionate kiss.

"Next time," she smiled, "you can smear oil on me for as long as you want."

With a giggle, she snatched up her basket and lantern, and ran off towards home, up the starlit trail and across our fields. I wanted to run after her, to ply her with a hundred questions, but my stomach twisted and doubled me over; I fell onto the hard ground. I couldn't hold the powerful mead inside me any longer: I puked.

* * * * * * * * *

Chapter 10

* * * * * * * * *

The onion seedlings' stench made me want to vomit all the next day. Garad was as sick as I, and Grettir yelled at us as never before. We tried, but we couldn't go faster.

"What's wrong with you two?" she demanded.

"Berries," Garad gasped, looking like he was going to throw up. "We ate some berries yesterday, near the ... swimming hole."

"Strange berries ...?" Grettir shouted. "At this time of year? Well, don't expect sympathy if you choose to be stupid! I expect this whole field to be planted by dusk, and Odin help both of you if it's not done!"

"Yea, ma'am," we muttered, and we went back to planting the sickening onions.

"And never, ***NEVER,*** eat strange berries without showing them to me first!" Grettir scowled one last time, and then she carried her empty bucket back toward the well, and she took her almost-empty seedling basket as well. I glanced up at Garad, amazed. He'd successfully lied to his mother and saved our skin; *I'd not thought him capable of managing a deception.*

Although sick, I felt guilty. If Garad was old enough to deceive his mother, was it all a waste of time? Wouldn't we have been better off just telling him the truth about Father and Grettir? Yet I wouldn't undo last night for anything. Ingrid had seemed so ... powerful, so commanding. I didn't wish to be trained by any woman, but the memory of her soft, naked skin, touching her all over with oil, and watching the starlight flash off her glistening spots; *I couldn't wait to see her alone!*

"You lucky bastard," Garad said once his mother was out of earshot. "That was unbelievable! Ingrid is ... incredible! All these years of wanting to see her, and suddenly ... Wow!"

"I've seen her before," I said, trying not to show my feelings, but my stomach turned. I couldn't bear the thought of him watching her as I did, thinking the same thoughts that I enjoyed.

"You don't deserve to look at her all the time," Garad said. "I deserve that; a beautiful girl in my own house to look at whenever I please."

"Ingrid doesn't like me ... I mean, anyone ... to look at her while she dresses."

"I'd look anyway," Garad said. "Don't you?"

"I ... Ingrid ... we ...," I started, scrambling for words, but instantly I realized I was about to tell another lie. My last lie had caused me too much grief; I certainly didn't want to start the whole mess all over again. "I don't want to talk about it," I finished.

"Tell me!" Garad insisted.

I scooped out the last of the dirt, poured some water into

the hole, set the seedling inside, and buried it so that just the green tip of its stalk was sticking out of the ground.

"I thought that you liked Helsa," I said.

"Helsa's not built like Ingrid."

"Ingrid didn't have breasts when we bought her."

"Who says that I can't have both?" Garad laughed, and then he doubled over as if he were going to be sick and his stomach growled loudly.

Grettir came back soon, lugging her spashing bucket and her basket refilled with onion seedlings, and Garad went to refill his water bucket. Grettir yelled at us for not finishing more while she was gone, but I didn't care; *her interruption was just what I'd wanted.*

* * * * * * * * *

Garad was satisfied, but Father and Grettir were still going out almost every day, searching for the thieves. My stomach tightened to see them leave, knowing what they were doing. That I spent those miserable hours on my knees planting onion seedlings, while they were off mating, didn't make me any happier.

Coming back from Garad's one evening, I spied Ingrid standing just inside our barn, waving for me to join her. Glancing to be sure that no one was watching, I casually walked toward her. Inside, she gave me a long, hard kiss.

"We have to do something to stop Thorir and Grettir from seeing each other," she said. "Vespa asked me today if I knew where Thorir was really going. Soon Vespa will find out, and then we'll really be in trouble."

"We can't stop Father and Grettir without telling what we know," I said.

"That means we need to be more devious," Ingrid said. "Lies are always the weakest point in any tale. This story about there being thieves in the woods is the lie that lets them see each other. If there were no thieves, then Thorir would have no reason to sneak off during the day, so they'd have no opportunity to be alone."

"But we already know that there are no thieves in the woods," I reminded her.

"We know, but Vespa doesn't," Ingrid said. "Didn't you say that Clamsby invited you for a free drink at Tavern Hall?"

"Yes, at Rath's wedding ..."

"Good. You're going to get that drink. Tonight."

* * * * * * * * *

"That's enough, Thron," Grettir said, standing over me in the growing darkness as I stuffed another seedling into the ground. She stretched her back, rubbed her aching muscles, and groaned. She'd come back after only an hour's dalliance with Father, but she'd resumed planting the moment she returned. Now it was after dusk, the day's work done.

I poured the last of my water onto my last seedling and picked up my bag and bucket. I looked across the fields and saw Father headed home, carefully walking across our fields between the new rows. Mother would be home, with Ingrid, heating up the leftovers from our midday meal. I was hungry, but I was even more nervous. Father expected me to come home for supper. Tonight I wouldn't.

Grettir barely noticed as I walked toward her house, bucket in one hand and seedling-sack over my shoulder. She didn't seemed concerned that I was walking slowly, allowing her to get far ahead. Yet I was greatly concerned; I'd be punished severely when Father found out what I was about to do.

Ingrid had said that I had to be brave, as brave as any man. Tonight I'd prove, at least to her, that I was a man. Father would punish me either way, but this way Mother need never find out, and that made this the lesser punishment by far. If I pulled this off, Ingrid said, then she'd give me a special reward.

Father reached the house, gave a look across to Grettir, and then he disappeared inside. Grettir didn't appear to notice, just walked inside her house. I hesitated; there was still time to back out. But trouble would eventually come.

As I reached the door to Garad's house, I saw Garad bringing in more wood from their pile. Grettir was inside, cooking. I dropped my bucket and sack just outside of their door.

"I don't feel like an ale tonight," I announced.

"Fine," Grettir mumbled, not even turning to look at me.

Avoiding Garad, I walked around to the far side of their house, behind our barn, and then I leaped over the few rows planted near their house, jumped their fence, and ran toward town. It was dark and no one was watching, but I couldn't afford a single mistake.

Halfway to town, I stopped and gasped for breath. As Ingrid had instructed, I dusted myself off; I didn't want to look like a child or like I came straight from the fields. Then I headed for Tavern Hall.

Many people saw me as I walked nervously toward Clamsby's. A few waved or nodded, and I forced a smile at them, but I didn't wait to talk. Outside Tavern Hall I hesitated; the building loomed even larger, strangely oppressive, yet it was too late to back out now. I swallowed hard, clenched my teeth, and entered.

"Thron ...?" Clamsby asked as I closed the door behind me.

"Come for another swim?" asked one of the men near the fireplace. Several chortled at his rebuke.

"C-Clamsby invited me," I stammered, "for ... an ale."

Laughter filled the hall, and one man jokingly stood up and bowed to me, making his companions laugh even louder. I knew most of them, although I'd never spoken to any of them. They were village men, Father's friends, who went viking with him, even though some of them were very old.

"Well, Master Thron!" Clamsby laughed. "Glad you decided to join us! Where's your young friend, Grettir's boy? I thought that you'd come together."

"He's home," I said, "protecting his mother."

There was some scattered laughter at this.

"Protecting her from what?" one laughed.

"That's why I came," I said. "Father and Grettir have seen ... strange footprints ... near the back of our fields. Father thinks that it's a thief, and he goes out every day looking for him. Garad and I were supposed to be ... busy planting, but we ... we snuck off to the swimming hole a few days ago. That's where we saw ..."

"Saw what?" Clamsby asked, his deep voice serious.

"Footprints," I said. "In the mud, near the water. Large boots, several different pairs. Garad and I are afraid ... that there may be more than one thief. But we were ... supposed to be planting ..."

The silence of the men deafened me. Would they see through my lie, know I wasn't telling the truth? What would they do to me, and what would Father do when the truth was revealed?

"Come, have an ale," Clamsby said. "You did right, bringing this news to us. We'll help Thorir chase away these thieves, and we'll ... keep your visit to the swimming hole our little secret."

A flood of relief washed over me. I couldn't believe that it had worked. I started to relax; *it was finally over.*

Suddenly Clamsby poured an ale and held it out to me. As far as I was concerned, my mission was accomplished, and all that I wanted to do was bolt out of there.

"Take it, lad," Clamsby said. "By bringing this matter to us, you're proving how grown you are. Maturity deserves reward."

"Here, sit by the fire," said another.

I hesitantly stepped forward. Clamsby held out the foamy wooden mug and I took it. One of the men scooted over and made room on his bench for me to sit. Again I hesitated, but the man insisted, and I obediently sat down. I took a small sip and bit back a cough; Clamsby's ale was much stronger than what Ingrid brewed.

"How old are you, boy?" asked one of the men.

"No time for that," another man said. "We should send out word at once. Get Rath, Kampi, and the others. Tomorrow morning, we can all meet here, and then go out to Thorir's armed and ready."

"Damn thieves," said another. "Probably a whole gang of them waiting until we sail. They could raid the whole village, if there are enough of them, once most of us are gone."

"Happened in Odshire a few years ago," said another man. "Right after the men sailed, about twenty robbers who'd been living in the hills descended on their village. They killed seven men, two women, took every horse and cart, and drove their stolen wagons out of town filled with stolen goods.

Some of the women were raped."

"The villagers trailed those men for days, but the thieves made it to Oslo and vanished into the city," said one old man. "Some of the horses and carts were recovered, but no one ever found the thieves."

"We can't let that happen here."

"The hills behind Thorir's fields are rough and thick," Clamsby warned. "They climb up into the mountains, are crisscrossed with animal trails. There's lots of room for men to hide."

"Good thieves would keep their hideout well-concealed," said one man. "And they'll have scouts."

"They won't be easy to find," said another. "As soon as they see us, they'll hunker down in the brush."

"Kampi has those loud dogs," Clamsby said. "They could sniff out any man."

"I'll stop by at Kampi's and Læknir's on my way home."

The men continued talking while I drank my ale. I was terribly afraid: what if this didn't work? What would they say when they got back, having found no thieves at all?

Several of the men got up and left. Only two of the oldest remained. Clamsby took a vacated chair right across from them, near me.

"So, Thron, when did you see these tracks?"

"A few days ago," I replied uncomfortably. I didn't like lying; that's what got me into this mess, and Ingrid's magic ceremony wouldn't fool grownups.

"I see," Clamsby said. "Thorir should've brought us this news, but he's a mighty man, able to deal with his own problems. You're starting to take after him."

"Thank you, sir," I replied.

"You must be looking forward to the viking, eh?" said one

of the elders.

I looked down. "Not this year."

"No? Well, next year, certainly."

"That's right," Clamsby said. "There's more to going viking than just fighting. Avoiding trouble keeps you alive longest. The trick is knowing when to take risks ... and when the risks are too great."

"But you can't always hide from trouble," said the other man. "All hands must fight, and be ready to kill, or they're endangering the rest."

"You'd have dumped the wounded overboard," the first man accused.

"Fewer would've been wounded if we had," the other countered.

"Enough!" Clamsby interrupted. "Haven't we been all through this? Don't spoil Thron's first visit with an argument."

"Actually, I'd better go," I said meekly. "I'm supposed to be at supper."

"See what you've done?" Clamsby scolded the other men. "Alright, go on home, Thron, but come back soon!"

"I will," I promised, and I wasted no time escaping out the door.

* * * * * * * * *

"Where have you been?" Father demanded as I came inside. He was already sitting in his chair before the fire. Mother was still finishing her dinner while Ingrid had started washing the dishes.

I'd dreaded this moment. I'd missed dinner and left the farm without permission. A dozen lies came to mind instantly, all elaborately concocted on the path back home, but I hesitated: lies had gotten me into this. Father had lied to Mother. Ingrid and I had lied to Garad.

"Answer me!" Father shouted.

"I went to Tavern Hall to see Clamsby."

Father's expression changed to surprise. *"What ...?"*

"Clamsby invited me, at Rath's wedding, to come and visit him," I said confidently. My voice deepened and I spoke louder, knowing that not only was I telling the truth, but that Clamsby could verify it.

"So you chose to go off today, without any warning, leaving your mother here to worry ...?"

"I told them about the thieves in the woods."

Father looked aghast.

"Why did you ...!" he jumped up out of his chair, but then he froze and fell speechless.

I looked up at Father and saw something unexpected. Father was so big and strong; I'd never seen him fail at anything. Nothing existed on our farm that he couldn't lift, if he put his back into it. He was also very wise, probably the smartest man in the world. Standing beside his chair before the fire, in his old gray tunic, his head brushing the wooden rafters and his thick black beard hanging from his chin, he looked the same as always, yet entirely different. He didn't look like a warrior or a farmer. He looked ... smaller, almost afraid. He looked like I had so many times ... whenever I'd told a lie and gotten caught.

"What did they say?" Mother asked anxiously.

With great effort, I tried to tear my eyes away from Father, but I couldn't. He seemed shrunken. Slowly it dawned upon me: *I'd hurt Father.*

I loved Father. Or I did love him; I loved the man that he

was before I'd spied him sporting with Garad's mother in the middle of the day. I wanted him to be as I'd always known him, a giant, fiercer and stronger than any man alive, wiser than any mortal ever could be, noble, blessed by Odin, and favored by all of the gods. He sailed the summer seas and took treasures from weaker men because it was his right. He harvested and planted turnips twice as fast as I could. This ... *stranger* ... who lied, cheated, and dishonored Mother: *this man I'd never seen before.*

Guilt welled: I didn't want Father to be weak, small, or dishonored. I'd diminished him, the last man on Earth that I wanted diminished.

"Well ...?" Mother demanded.

"Huh?"

"What did Clamsby say about the thieves?"

"Oh," I stammered. "H-he said that he would ... come here ... tomorrow ... with Rath and some others ... and they'd help find the thieves."

"About time," Mother said.

Father said nothing, just stared at the floor.

"I ... I'd better make sure ... that things are ready for them ... when they get here," Father said, and suddenly he marched to the door and vanished outside.

"Thorir!" Mother shouted, but the door was already banging shut.

I bowed my head. Father had never once entered or left this house without having to duck under our low doorframe. This time, he left smaller than when he'd entered.

* * * * * * * * *

Chapter 11

* * * * * * * * *

I was just scooping the last of the turnip stew into my mouth when Ingrid's fingernails lightly scratched down my back. I froze, cast a quick glance at Mother, who was too engrossed in working her loom to notice. I hadn't seen Ingrid naked since she, Garad, and I had stripped to perform our magic spell.

Seeing Mother not looking, I cast a quick glance at Ingrid. Ingrid had finished all of the washing except for my bowl and spoon, and she walked around the table, putting her back to Mother so that her face couldn't be seen. Ingrid glanced briefly at Mother, then put her hands on her breasts, squeezed, and blew me a silent kiss.

I knew what she meant, but I wasn't elated. I'd done well and would be rewarded, but I didn't feel happy; my success had been the failure of Father. No reward, not even touching Ingrid, was worth that loss.

* * * * * * * * *

We heard the men approaching before they opened the gate; Kampi's barking dogs could awaken the dead. Squawks of our frightened chickens, squeals of our pigs, and the men's deep, rumbling voices combined with the clank of weapons and jingle of mail that seeped through our walls.

Mother and Ingrid took an iron pitcher of steaming ale off the fire hooks and filled all of our wooden cups. Father opened the door, and I ran out, as instructed, to open the gate for the men.

Clamsby and Rath led the rest, Clamsby with a stout spear that he was using as a cane, Rath in a shirt of heavy mail, his large axe over one shoulder. Kampi had a sword strapped across his back, but was otherwise dressed in a ragged, stained tunic, holding tight leashes on three eager dogs. Kal was jumping and skipping beside his father, as if on holiday. I understood his excitement; we seldom got together like this.

Derek walked behind Kampi, looking much bigger than he had the last time that I'd seen him. He also had an axe, although not as big as Rath's. I was relieved to see Halgrum; we hadn't spoken in ages.

Many other village men arrived. Old man Ranglátr ambled in the rear; he bore no weapon, just leaned on his carved, polished staff. None of the other boys came. Rath and Clamsby nodded to me as I opened the gate, but they didn't disrupt their conversation.

"Thorir!" Rath shouted gladly as they entered our gate. "Well met, old friend! It's been too long since we all got together."

"Welcome all," Father said. "I can't express my gratitude

enough, but I fear that you've come in vain. I've searched the hills thoroughly and found nothing."

"We assumed so," Clamsby said. "Otherwise their blood would've stained your sword. But the summer viking can't begin until we're all satisfied that no danger threatens our village, so let's search again ... together."

Mother and Ingrid came forward with serving boards laden with hot ales. Ingrid made sure, after all of the men had ales, that I was the first of the boys to be served, and she served Garad right after me. I'd not even seen Garad arrive, but I couldn't miss the glower that Derek gave us. The men broke into small clusters of conversations, but we boys stood silent, trying not to attract attention; any bad behavior now would ban us from the hunt.

"Your sword!" Ingrid whispered in my ear.

Realizing that all of the other boys were armed, that even Garad had my old walnut sword and the steel dagger that Father had given him, I chugged down my ale and dropped the empty mug onto Ingrid's serving board, and then slid back toward our door; I couldn't be the only boy unarmed, not when I had the best weapon of all.

I opened the door, trying to be quiet so that no one noticed that I'd forgotten my sword, and found Mother and Rath alone inside my house.

"...almost hate to go viking," Rath was saying. "Læknir's wonderful, generous, and far more prosperous than I'd ever guessed. Helsa's happy, learning her healing arts, and I get to do more visiting every month than I did all last year. We ..."

Our door creaked on its rusty hinges, and they both fell silent and looked at me. I blushed, reached for my sword, and slipped back outside.

* * * * * * * * *

"What in Loki's name is this?" Clamsby asked.

Everyone stopped, since Clamsby and Father were leading us, crammed together on the trail.

"What ...?" Rath asked.

Clamsby bent down and lifted up a thin, leafy branch bearing budding red flowers. Tied onto it was a short, greasy strand of yarn.

"Here's another!" Kampi said, and he drew out his sword and used it to lift up a low-hanging branch of a pine tree with a tiny scrap of cloth tied to it.

Pandemonium broke out and everyone started digging through the bushes on both sides of the trail. Clamsby pulled off the scrap of yarn and examined it closely. Father had the most-puzzled look on his face.

"Here's one!" Derek shouted, and soon others were going farther up the trail, finding many more.

"What are they?" Halgrum asked.

Garad opened his mouth to say something, but I quickly grabbed his arm and pulled him away.

"Let's search farther up the trail!" I suggested.

At once, the other boys agreed, but as we started running, Rath shouted.

"Hey, stop there! We need to search up there before you boys spoil the tracks."

"Back to the end, Thron," Father commanded, and he stared at us until, despite our numerous grumbled complaints, we all trooped back down the hill to the end of the line.

"I can't imagine what they're for," Clamsby said to Kampi. "A marker, a signal ...?"

"They're oiled: maybe someone meant to start a fire,"

Kampi shrugged. "Damndest thing I ever saw."

"Helsa used to tie white ribbons onto the holly bush in front of our house," Rath said. "Maybe it was kids ...?"

The men looked at us. I froze, terrified that it would all come out, but Halgrum shrugged back at Rath, waving his arms in confusion.

The men puzzled over the scraps for hours, slowly moving farther uphill, where the main trail branched out in many directions. They searched in small groups, and once we boys were finally left alone, we easily found an unsearched trail and ran up it. Once out of sight, the adults couldn't stop us from exploring.

Kal, Halgrum, and Derek argued constantly over the oily scraps' purpose. Garad and I spent the day in silence, following Halgrum and Derek as they wandered far up and down the hills, squeezing through deer trails too narrow for grown men. Only I knew that no thieves ever lived out here; Garad believed that Ingrid's magic spell had driven them away, and I stayed nearby to insure his silence. Romping through the woods, shouting at imaginary foes, and swinging our weapons to chop back the brush, made for a wonderful afternoon.

* * * * * * * * *

"No signs at all?" Mother asked.

"No," Father replied, collapsing into his chair. "Just those strange oily scraps. Rath thinks that it was a madman living wild. But he must've left; we searched the hills for ten miles ..."

"But some trace, campsite ... or footprints? There must've been something ..."

Mother's voice faded and Father didn't reply. I sat down, tired but relieved. It'd been a great day; Father couldn't sneak off to mate with Garad's mother anymore.

The sun dawned bright and clear the next day. I got up early, fed the animals, and collected the eggs for Ingrid, who smiled brightly at me for it; our plan had succeeded. After breakfast, I was sent to Garad's to help finish his planting.

But Grettir wasn't in their fields. Garad knelt alone before a planted sapling, crying. He looked up at me with an expression of absolute misery.

"She knows."

"Who knows?"

"Mother. She beat me. After I told her that we were searching for the thieves. She kept saying that I knew why. I swore that I didn't, but she made me tell ... about ... Ingrid's spell ... everything ..."

"Everything ...?" I asked.

Garad nodded.

My world collapsed into ruin. Not entirely; Garad didn't know what I knew. But his mother knew what was going on and probably assumed that Garad, Ingrid, and I knew.

* * * * * * * * *

Grettir came out shortly afterwards, but I didn't look at her. I focused on my planting. There were only a few rows left; soon we'd be finished. I feared that she might speak or drag me back to her house and force me to tell her everything.

Long moments passed, each worse than the previous. *Would she beat me, as she'd beaten Garad?* Her stare burned like a midday summer sun even though it was a cold morning. What would she do?

The waiting grew intolerable. I kept planting, trying to ignore her, not even looking at Garad, who was planting the next row. Eventually I'd run out of seedlings and water; how could I go back to the house without looking at her, facing the hate in her eyes?

Finally, footsteps walked away. I tried not to look but couldn't help myself: Grettir was storming back toward her house, having never said a word. I stopped planting and hung my head so low that my scalp rested on the ground.

* * * * * * * * *

"Do nothing," Ingrid said.

"But ...!"

"So what if Grettir knows? If she tries to punish us, then Vespa will learn about her and Thorir. All that we have to do is keep Garad silent. Here they come!"

We separated instantly. When the door opened, Ingrid was stirring our onion stew and I was examining a new plate that I'd spent the evening sanding. We weren't even looking at each other, but Mother eyed us suspiciously as she and Father came in.

Father went to the wash bucket and dipped his hands in, then washed the sweat off his face. The planting season was finished, the hard work done, but there were always chores on our farm.

"Garad will be eating with us today," Mother announced, mostly to Ingrid. "Do we have enough?"

"Yes," Ingrid said. "If anyone's still hungry afterwards, we could open that new cheese wheel."

"No one will be that hungry," Mother said flatly, and no

one dared dispute her. Mother, like everyone, knew that Ingrid loved fresh cheese, but her attitude toward Ingrid was colored by suspicions.

Garad showed up a few minutes later, but we didn't get to talk. Garad looked haggard, panting as if he'd just run a long race.

"Shoveling feed ... all morning," Garad explained. "A board broke ... last night, and our chickens gorged themselves. Their fighting woke Mother up, and ... this morning, Mother had me shovel out the whole bin so that she could fix it, then I had to ... refill ..."

"Good for you," Mother said. "Idle hands are trouble for young boys. What are you doing after lunch?"

Neither Garad nor I answered. I'd hoped to spend the day relaxing, which I badly needed after planting our fields and then Garad's. I'd been thinking fondly about the swimming hole, but I felt the hammer of Mother hovering over my head.

"No one's weeded my herb garden since planting started," she said. "There, now you boys have something to do."

Lunch was nothing special; Ingrid had finely diced some rabbit into the onion soup, but it had no spices and seemed watery. The bread was days old. Garad and I ate in silence, not wanting to have more chores piled upon us.

"Thorir, what're your plans for this afternoon?" Mother asked.

"Clamsby's," Father replied. "We made some tentative plans during the thief-hunt, but I need to know more. With all of this good weather, Branwulf may want to sail early. I'd better find out what's going on."

"You'd better have a good viking this year," Mother said. "Our pantry won't last to winter. Anything else?"

"Like what?"

"Were you planning on doing anything else today?"

"Not really. I may be at Clamsby's until late. I should stop in at Grettir's on my way, to see that she fixed that bin properly."

"I'm sure that she did," Mother said.

"Still," Father said, "it's the neighborly thing to do."

I knew why Father wanted to stop at Grettir's, and it had nothing to do with feed bins. I ground my teeth in silent frustration. I wasn't too worried; soon Father would leave on the viking. Branwulf wouldn't return until the fall, and hopefully Father's fascination with Grettir would be over by then.

Father said good-bye and departed while we were still at the table. He left his sword, but belted on Grandpa's large scramsax before he left. I bowed my head; this time there was nothing that I could do.

Suddenly Mother stood up. Silently she stepped to the door, opened it just a crack, and peered out. I froze, then glanced at Ingrid, but she was staring at Mother with an equally horrified expression, her face as white as a sheet.

Suddenly Mother pulled open the door and started to follow Father. *She'd find them together, Father and Grettir ...!*

"Mother, no!" I shouted.

Halfway out of the door, Mother stopped. She stepped back inside, closed the door, and fixed me with a terrible stare.

"What do you know?" Mother demanded.

I stood dumbfounded, trapped. I struggled to think of a lie, to say anything, but my horror of the truth drowned me in a sea of guilt. *The truth would kill her, kill Father, and kill everyone!*

Mother came at me, red eyes glaring under thin, angry brows. Her hand rose threateningly. I backed up against the pantry door.

The idea of defending myself never entered my mind. Mother struck hard and repeatedly. Barely was I aware of Ingrid's voice begging Mother to stop, then I heard a crash and a painful cry as Ingrid fell over the loom. The toe of Mother's shoe kicked hard into my ribs; more kicks came, and then fists pounded down on me.

Through an endless red haze, I realized that the beating had stopped. Slowly I forced open my wet eyes. Near the fireplace, Ingrid lay huddled on the floor amid a pile of broken pottery and an overturned bench. Sobbing hysterically, she'd curled up in a ball.

I pushed myself up and climbed over the tumbled furniture. Ingrid recoiled at my first touch, not recognizing me, but when her eyes opened, she flung herself into my embrace and wept against my shoulder. Mother was gone, and I'd no idea where ... *no: I knew, but the ramifications were too terrible to conceive.*

Listening carefully between Ingrid's sobs, I caught a distant sound; Mother screaming, cursing, pounding on Grettir's door. I heard Garad cry out ... and then only silence.

Our door burst open. Mother stormed in. She stopped, seeing Ingrid and I embraced, and the pure hatred of her glare tripled. Mother said nothing, but she walked straight toward us. I feared that she was going to hit us both, but she only reached over us, toward the fireplace. Mother's hand closed firmly upon the long handle of our axe, and she lifted it, and in one rushing movement, she vanished out of the door.

The next thing that I heard was the unmistakable chop of an axe.

* * * * * * * * *

Chapter 12

* * * * * * * * *

Tearstreaked, Mother came back shortly afterwards, dirty, her skirt torn, her hair disheveled and fallen about her face. Our axe was no longer in her hands. Ingrid and I were still holding each other, but Mother ignored us. She stumbled to her bed and collapsed upon it, barely stifling her sobs, not even trying to hide the trembling of her shoulders.

Father! Even as I clung to Ingrid, I thought of him, wondered where he was, what he was doing, and what had happened to our axe. I glanced at Ingrid, whose face was drenched with tears; she was still sobbing, holding onto me as if afraid that I might vanish forever.

I stood up. Ingrid's hands never let go, although she gripped me gently. Misery etched her face, her twisted expression forlorn and anguished. Pity swelled within me, but I couldn't stay; I had to find Father.

But did he want to see me? If Grettir told him, if he

suspected that I knew ... what would he do? *What would I do ... if he didn't want to see me again?*

I kissed Ingrid gently, and then I nodded toward Mother.

"Take care of her," I said softly. "I ... I'll be back."

Ingrid swept me into her strong embrace, but released me when I gently pushed away. I grabbed my sword and I ran outside.

* * * * * * * * *

Garad was crying, curled up outside his ruined door, which now had several deep axe cuts in it. His door was braced from the inside; its latch was shattered, otherwise Garad's weight would've pushed it open. From inside, I heard other sobs: *Grettir's.*

"Garad? Garad, where's Father?"

He didn't answer.

"Garad, where's my father?"

"I don't know!" he shouted so loudly that I heard a break in Grettir's sobs. I glanced at the door, wondering if Father was inside.

I left Garad and ran around his house. It was still early afternoon and the goats were all out in their pen. I jumped over the fence and ran inside their open barn door. Suddenly I was peering between the thin woven chicken-fence. Grettir was on her bed, crying, as Mother had been when I left. But Grettir was alone; *Father wasn't there.*

* * * * * * * * *

I searched everywhere, and asked everyone that I met, and no one had seen Father. I spent the whole day searching until long after sundown. I scoured the hills, the woods, the fields, farms, and every barn.

My starlit, plodding footsteps led me home. I was hungry, thirsty, tired, and had nowhere else to go. I didn't want to go home; *what was waiting for me there?*

One pig squealed loudly as I climbed our gate and staggered toward my door. Our door flew open wide as I approached. Mother stood in the doorway, looking somehow stern, angry, and frightened all at the same time. She glanced at me, then scanned our farm and the empty road.

"Hurry in," Mother said resignedly.

Ingrid was inside, but she looked as disheveled as Mother. Ingrid's eyes widened as I entered, but then she broke into tears. Ingrid was shaking, not even attempting to hide her tears. Her sleeve was torn, her hair wild and tangled, worse than I'd ever seen before. *Had Mother beaten her?*

Mother came back in and closed the door. She stood with her back to us, facing the door as if expecting it to open suddenly. Then, slowly, as if with great effort, Mother lifted the brace. She dropped it firmly into place; it fell loudly, landing in its brackets with a woody clunk, sounding exactly like the chop of an axe. Our door was now secured, sealed from entrance ... and Father was outside. Tears welled in my eyes; *Mother had just chopped Father out of my life.*

* * * * * * * * *

Father didn't return. Three days passed, each adding to the heavy weight pressing upon my chest. For as long as I could remember, Father had been my hero. He was huge and powerful, traits he drew from our giants' ancestry. Even Rath and the other men regarded him as a deep thinker and a formidable fighter, legendary in honor and reputation. I'd discovered his indiscretions with Grettir; I felt guilty. I could've said nothing. I could've acted differently, done otherwise, anything, but my foolish fumblings had caused him to be discovered.

Daylight became an endless string of chores. All of the work that Father had done before each noon seemed to be several days' labors. I was barely able to finish my chores before dusk. Mother and Ingrid also worked hard, but their friendship was over. No one spoke except when Mother assigned chores. Ingrid once tried to reassure Mother that he'd come back; Mother threw a wooden spoon at her and screamed that she was never, *never!* to speak his name again, or she'd throw her out of the house and brace the door behind her. I made the mistake of mentioning Garad and received much the same reaction, save that I was informed that Garad was no longer any concern of mine, and that I was never, *never!* to speak to him again.

After we'd eaten and Ingrid had washed the dishes, a soft knock rapped on our door. Mother froze, Ingrid stopped her spindle from twirling, and I dropped the half-carved ladle in my hand.

"Vespa?"

Læknir's voice filtered through our thick door. Mother hesitated, then pushed aside her loom and, with all apparent dignity, rose and stood before our door.

"Thron," she said, "open the door."

I glanced at Ingrid; her expression betrayed her fear and confusion, but she nodded for me to hurry. I quickly lifted the brace off and set it aside, glanced at Mother's expressionless face, and then pulled open our door.

Læknir stood, leaning on her cane, her slight, aged frame

filling our doorway, her gray dress, light and frail-looking, blowing gently in the night wind. Around her long neck lay a necklace of tiny seashells, and her fingers bore many rings. The walking stick that she braced on was intricately carved, polished, and chased with real silver. She'd been to our house before, many times, but only when someone was hurt or ill.

Beside Læknir stood Helsa, holding a brass candle lantern, illuminating them both. Helsa looked older; taller than I remembered, her bodice more full, her pale green dress crisp and new-looking in the flickering light. Helsa didn't look up as the door opened, but my eyes widened; Helsa had never looked more like a grown woman.

Heavy footsteps behind them and the snort of a horse made me look; Rath walked up from our gate where he'd tied Læknir's fancy lighted carriage.

"Good evening, Vespa," Læknir said softly. "May I come in?"

"You are always welcome here," Mother said after a noticeable pause.

Læknir bowed slightly and set her walking stick inside our door, then slowly followed it, shuffling across our threshold. Helsa followed her in, and Rath came last, ducking, his bulk filling our door.

"You honor my house," Mother said politely. "Ingrid, drinks for our guests."

Ingrid hesitated only a second, then she filled mugs from the keg, placing them on a serving board. No one spoke while Ingrid hurried, but tension hung like a choking fog. Mother and Læknir both stood silent, motionless, with infuriating, endless patience. Intently they stared at each other as if speaking only with their eyes.

"Thank you," Læknir said to Ingrid as she lifted the first mug off the serving board. I thought it strange that Ingrid served Læknir first; we rarely entertained guests, but when we did, the oldest man was always honored highest. Yet Rath said nothing, seeming not to notice, so I kept silent.

"Please, take my chair," Mother motioned to her chair beside the loom.

Læknir bowed slightly, then came forward and gracefully sat down on Mother's accustomed cushions. Rath stepped forward, and at Mother's polite gesture, he sat in Father's chair. Helsa remained standing by the door. She didn't blow out her candle despite the bright flames in our fireplace, but held her glowing lantern dangling from a leather thong. Rath thanked Ingrid heartily as he accepted his ale, and took a deep drink. Then Ingrid offered an ale to Mother. I couldn't help noticing the daggers in Mother's eye, the look of disapproval she cast at Ingrid, as she declined a mug. Then I saw Mother's evil glare mirrored on Ingrid's face as she offered a mug to Helsa.

I knew better than to speak; whatever Læknir had come for *(what could it be about but Father?),* my input wouldn't be asked for or welcomed. Whatever was going to happen, I wished that it would just come out in a rush and be done. Even the briefest moments of silence seemed an eternity. Given a choice, I'd gladly have escaped out the door; I wasn't made to endure women's talk.

Helsa lowered her eyes before Ingrid and declined the proffered mug with a slight wave. Seeing the two of them together, Ingrid was clearly taller, fuller, more womanly, and Helsa seemed to recognize it. But Ingrid was a servant and appeared painfully aware of that fact as she bowed slightly to Helsa, and then turned toward me.

I hadn't expected Ingrid to offer me a mug, but when I looked at the serving tray, there were three full mugs still on it: Ingrid had planned to serve me all along; *that's why Mother had glared at her!* I reached for a mug, but Ingrid's eyes flared. She obviously didn't want me to have one, but then, why had she poured it? It made no sense, but I dropped my empty hand back to my side. Ingrid nodded slightly to me, then performed a slight bow, as she had to Mother, only to me; I stood flabbergasted. Then Ingrid turned away, sat on her bed, and stared at Urd, who was now almost too big for her cradle.

"What beautiful work!" Læknir exclaimed suddenly, reaching out with one hand and tracing the pattern still on the loom. "You truly have a gift for weaving, Vespa."

"You are most gracious," Mother bowed slightly, accepting the compliment.

Læknir continued to admire the half-finished fabric for a long moment, then took another small sip of her ale.

"I hope that your health is excellent," Læknir said.

"Thank you, we are all well," Mother said.

Another long moment passed.

"We've come on behalf of the village," Læknir said, apparently not willing to continue with distractions. "Gossip is flying, but very little truth is known. Your family has been in this village for generations. There's much concern."

Mother paused before responding.

"My family is under this roof."

"That may be true, for now," Læknir said, "but what of tomorrow? Harvest? Winter?"

"We'll endure, as always."

Læknir paused, looking directly at Mother.

"Words are easier than deeds. I thought the same, but age

came upon me early, and last winter I was ready to quit my healings. Without my dear husband, I doubt if I would've had the strength to go on. But the village needs me, so Rath came to my aid. Though I had my doubts, he's proven a wonderful husband.

"Vespa, you're still young and proud, but someday you'll be in need. Who will come to you then? Men are scarce these days, and good husbands are always rare."

Læknir fell silent, waiting, but Mother didn't respond. Mother stood tall and stiff, and crossed her arms over her chest, sealing herself shut like she was putting a brace on her heart.

"A woman betrayed can never trust again," Læknir said. "I know. I've buried two husbands, both of whom betrayed me. If their bodies had been brought back, then I would've buried my sons beside them. In my heart, I've always wondered if my sons would've died, had their fathers stood beside them in battle. Uncertainty is a terrible doom."

"Disgrace is a terrible doom," Mother answered.

"Dooms abound," Læknir agreed. "In this evil world, there's no certainty. As a healer, I've sat beside the dying more than any; even great warriors don't witness the deaths I see."

Rath shifted in Father's chair as if he wanted to say something, but he held his tongue and took another long, slow drink. I wished that I'd taken a mug.

"You own the only turnip farm in these parts," Læknir said to Mother. "Most of the village gets its turnips from trading with you, and your income from traveling merchants helps support many. Our whole village would suffer if your farm failed. This year's planting may be finished, but who will help you harvest? Work from sunrise to long after dark?

Toiling in the fields is hard on a woman's back, and Thron's only beginning to grow into manhood."

"After harvest, I plan to sell Ingrid," Mother explained.

Læknir paused and looked at her mug as Ingrid choked, trembled, and finally jumped off her bed, ran past Helsa, banged open our door, and disappeared into the dark outside. I stood horrified. *Sell Ingrid? No, she couldn't!*

Angrily I started to speak up, but Rath turned and looked at me suddenly, his thick brows knit, his eyes full of threat. At first I startled, then I understood: he was warning me, not as a man to a boy, but as he'd warn Father or Clamsby: *nothing that I said would help.* Frustrated, I gnashed my teeth and remained silent.

"Your food will last longer, but the village will still suffer," Læknir said finally, breaking the silence. "You'll never finish your harvest with just yourself, a servant-girl, and a boy. Your crops will freeze, then rot in the ground. You'll have no income and no rewards from the viking."

Mother paused long before she answered.

"Those things are already gone."

"If you choose so, then they will be," Ingrid said. "Norse women aren't property like the women of England and France. We may own land, sign contracts, ... and divorce our husbands. You won't punish Thorir by setting him free; there'll be a line of wealthy widows from here to Oslo willing to take him in, and hundreds of young virgins with coy, tempting eyes. You'll doom yourself, your farm, and our village, all for nothing. Sell Ingrid ... and then what? Thron will go south soon; he already has a sword. Don't doom yourself to loneliness, Vespa; I've lived there too long. There's no doom worse than loneliness."

Læknir spoke slowly, her voice never rising, but she

emphasized each word to make its meaning echo hauntingly inside my head. Long after she finished speaking, I kept hearing her words in the silent air. I'd heard of divorce, but I couldn't remember what it meant. I'd go south soon; I knew what that meant. *But what of Father? How could I go viking without him?*

Rath rose suddenly, drained his mug completely, and turned and bowed to Mother.

"I'd best check on the carriage," Rath announced. "You women have much to discuss, and Læknir may need the freedom of words unheard by her husband. For my sake, let me say this: Perfection doesn't exist in this world; even the most excellent blade can break at the wrong moment. But few men exist of Thorir's metal. Even Branwulf isn't as respected among the fighters. If you trade steel for copper, then you ..."

Læknir exhaled softly, a gentle breath, barely audible, but her hiss drowned Rath's deep voice like a tiny coiled serpent startling a great horse.

"Your pardon," Rath bowed lightly, and in one turn he headed out the door. I was barely aware of his thick-muscled arm as it closed around my shoulders and swept me outside.

* * * * * * * * *

"Where's Father?"

Rath eyed me in the starlight.

"You're a bold lad, Thron. You have your father's blood in you."

Rath led the way to their carriage. Even in the starlight, it gleamed very impressive, still looking polished, although worn in some places, obviously not new. Two strong horses stood harnessed to it. Rath casually checked them with a cursory glance, then wandered up the road slowly, away from town. I followed, not knowing what to say.

"Thorir will be heading south soon. I'll be with him. The roads here are easy to travel in summer, and Helsa can already hitch the horses and drive the wagon."

"What're they talking about?" I nodded back toward my house.

"Us," Rath said. "Men. Whatever women say when we're not there. I've learned much that I was unaware of since I wedded Læknir. Healing isn't done only for the flesh; many wounds and sicknesses can't be healed. Læknir is more often called upon to counsel people against the inevitable, to heal their spirits, even to calm their anger. She's very good at it. Helsa's learning her craft; that's why she stayed behind. She won't speak, not a single word, but she'll listen and learn what to say, and what not to say, for the days when she's called upon to heal."

Rath paused as if he wanted to say something else, but he withheld it and continued walking.

"Thorir loves you very much. He wants to take you south as soon as you're old enough. But whether or not he returns depends not on you or I; Læknir will decide it. Her healing skills, plied on your mother, may turn Vespa from her pride. Then again, women's hearts are deep and hidden. What Vespa will decide may not be known for many months. Don't press her ... or ask her to choose. The harder you push, the less women bend."

Walking beside Rath I remained silent; if he wanted me to know something, then he'd say it. If not, I could never force him.

"You have this summer, Thron," Rath said. "When

Thorir first sees you, coming off the ship, he'll know if you've grown enough to sail on Branwulf's ship next year. Make good use of this time. Eat lots. Drink really hot tea and lots of strong ale. Work hard. Build up your muscles. Practice fighting, and be careful; if you break a leg, or cut your arm off with your own sword, then you'll stay here, next year for certain, possibly forever."

I grimaced and looked away. The scar under my hair warmed suddenly; I hadn't known that Rath knew of my mishap the morning of the funerals below Seal Ridge.

"I will," I promised.

"Good," Rath said. "So, what do you think of Helsa? Very pretty, isn't she? I want you to keep an eye on her, and Læknir, while I'm gone. Be ready to help them, if they need anything; that means defend them, if any need arises. You want to be considered a man? The only reason that we get to go south for the summer is because Clamsby and a few others remain here to defend our women and our town. Always be ready to fight beside them. Your father and I expect to find the village safe when we return."

"Yes, sir."

* * * * * * * * *

I wanted to search for Ingrid, yet how could I explain that to Rath? We sat long on the fence by the gate under the stars in unchallenged silence.

As our door opened, the streaming light silhouetted Mother's outline, and Rath sighed heavily and jumped off the fence. I followed him down onto the dirt, glad that I hadn't been forced to endure the women-talk, but curious about what had been said.

Læknir appeared as Mother stepped aside. Slowly she walked out our door, her cane stabbing the ground before her. Rath offered his arm and she accepted it readily. Rath thanked Mother politely for her hospitality, and Mother insisted that it was her honor, and that our house would always be open to them. I listened to their courtesies with anxious contempt; *what about Father?* What had they decided? *Why can't adults just say what's on their minds?*

As Rath led Læknir past me, she paused and looked down; Læknir ran her slender fingers through my hair, smiling at me in a piercing way.

"Take care of your mother, Thron, my dear," Læknir said, and then they walked past me.

Helsa followed Læknir, her face ashen, her expression horrified, and seeing me, her red eyes widened as if she were about to rain tears. Helsa instantly turned away, hiding her face, and hurried past me without a word. She followed Læknir into their carriage and Rath closed its door. Læknir leaned forward, around her tiny curtains, and waved at Mother as Rath climbed up onto their rig. Taking the reins, he shook the horse's bits and drove off, heading back toward town.

* * * * * * * * *

Ingrid burst into the barn suddenly, startling me so that I dropped the log that I'd just spilt. She swept me into her arms and kissed me hard and long. Surprised, I willingly yielded, reveling in her embrace; it'd been so long since we kissed that I'd feared we might never kiss again.

"Vespa's asleep at the loom," Ingrid whispered, through breaths heavy from our kiss, as she hugged me tighter. "You can't imagine how much I've wanted to talk to you."

In the last four days, Mother hadn't left us alone once, and conversation wasn't allowed. With Father gone and Garad forbidden, I'd no one left to talk to.

"I'm to be sold," Ingrid said bitterly. "Vespa would sell me today if she thought that she could get through harvest."

"Why?" I asked, confused.

Ingrid looked surprised.

"To keep me away from you," Ingrid said flatly. "*To keep you free ... to marry Helsa!*"

* * * * * * * * *

Chapter 13

* * * * * * * * *

Pigs always eat like pigs. When they started squealing, and many didn't greedily push forward to the newly-filled trough, I knew that something was wrong. Suddenly they all reacted strangely. Then an odd drumming reached my ears; a low, distant rumble, like an echo of thunder, growing, not fading. I stopped pouring the slop, and even those pigs whose unending hunger drove them forward complained and backed off; many seemed in a blind panic.

The thunder stung my ears, burned into my brain and charred my heart. *Hoofbeats:* many horses were rapidly approaching. Over the distant hills I spied a thin, rising cloud of dust as the pounding grew louder.

The riders crested the hill with a deafening noise. Twenty-some men, it was hard to count them all, poured into view, riding hard and fast. Mother and Ingrid burst outside to see, as did Grettir and Garad. The pigs went wild, so I jumped up and climbed to stand on the fence, which was shaking with the din of the rider's passage. A few darted glances at me; young faces, thick beards, shaven chins, light helmets, round shields, long swords, and leather armor. Their horses were huge and powerful, plowing their path with frightful speed.

Branwulf was coming.

"Thron!" Mother shouted as I jumped down and ran into the dust of their wake as they flew past our gate.

I paid her no heed. She'd punish me later, but I didn't care. *I had to find Father!*

"Thron, come back here!"

* * * * * * * * *

No one noticed as I entered Tavern Hall. Clamsby was busy pouring ales as fast as he could. Riders were pacing, stretching their legs. Everyone was talking. One of the riders had drawn his sword and was pantomiming some fierce sword fight with one hand, a frothing horn in his other, much to the amusement of his audience. All of the conversations were so loud that it was hard to hear any of them, but their meaning could clearly be picked up in snatches: Branwulf would be here shortly after dawn. The riders were only stopping for an ale, had already eaten on the road, and had other villages to alert.

I stumbled back as a rider, talking to Kampi, almost walked me down. I ducked around a table, dodged as Clamsby pushed past, and slid deeper into the hall. No fire lit the fireplace, but men were standing all around it, even Old man Ranglátr.

A hand gripped my arm and I jumped, but it was only Halgrum.

"I'm going viking!" Halgrum cried excitedly. *"Father just told me! I'm going viking!"*

"Where's Father?" I asked, but he didn't hear me, hopping up and down so exuberantly that he looked like a rooster about to crow. I grabbed him and pulled him toward me hard. " *Where is my Father?"*

Halgrum froze, as if suddenly aware, his exaggerated smile faltering as his joyous exuberance stumbled to anxious bewilderment.

"I don't know," Halgrum said solemnly, averting his eyes toward the ground. "I heard that he was with Rath. You might ask Rath."

"I tried," I growled, angrily clutching his arm, determined to get an answer. "Now I'm asking you."

"Have you tried Helsa?" Halgrum asked. "She'd know, if any of us kids do."

Kids: the word stung my ears. He still thought of himself as a kid, yet he was going south.

But his message entered my brain like a glowing torch in a dark cave.

Helsa would know! She had to!

* * * * * * * * *

After no answer at Rath's old house, I remembered that they weren't living there anymore. I dashed across the whole village, running to the far side. Læknir's house was nestled in a small clearing on the top of Seal Ridge, a long way up; a big house that I'd only seen from a distance. I ran along the familiar path, then turned off the main way and settled into a knee-pumping stride that carried me up the wagon-rutted path all the way to Læknir's house. My breathing grew labored;

gasping breaths strained my chest before I was halfway up the hill.

Goats and sheep wandered about inside the wide pen outside their house, and many chickens perched on their fence. They clucked, bleated, and baa-ed warningly as I approached; I couldn't understand why anyone would keep sheep: they stank, attracted swarms of flies, and their constant bleating drove me nuts, yet I ignored them and pushed to the front door, huffing and puffing as I knocked.

An eternity later, Helsa opened the door. A wave of relief washed over me; if she'd been away, helping Læknir on some errand, I didn't know what I'd have done.

Yet, as I tried to catch enough breath to ask, the expression on her face froze me. Undisguised dread widened her eyes and slackened her jaw. Helsa half-stepped behind her door, as if to shield herself.

"What do you want?" she hissed nastily, glancing behind to make sure that no one else could hear.

Her vehemence was icy and flaming at the same time. Helsa acted like I was a stranger, or worse, a threatening thief, and her words stabbed like daggers. Was I her mortal enemy? What had I done to elicit such fury?

"F - Father!" I sputtered out finally.

"What ...?" Helsa asked, no less surprised.

"Where's my father?"

Helsa's look of surprise doubled.

"You – you came here ... *looking for your father?"*

It was my turn to look surprised.

"Yes, why else ...?"

Helsa's eyes widened to the extreme; she looked as if she wanted to shout her nastiest curse. Instead, she gasped as if furious ... and slammed her door shut.

Baffled, I stood outside. *Why was Helsa acting so strange?* But I had no time for nonsense; Branwulf would be sailing tomorrow. I pounded my fist on her door again, hammering as I shouted.

"Helsa! Open up! I need to talk!"

Finally, my relentless banging was answered. I pushed forward as the door opened, determined to force Helsa to tell me where Father was. Instead, I walked face-first into Rath, who stood unmoving as I bounced off him and back out of his door.

"Thron ...?" Rath asked quizzically. "What do you want?"

Stunned but determined, I stared up at him.

"Where's Father?"

Rath frowned and his whole face darkened.

"If Thorir wanted you involved in these troubles then he'd have sent for you," Rath said. "Now run home. Don't knock here again unless somebody's hurt."

"No!" I shouted, trying to put on a brave face. "*He's my father! It's my right!"*

Angrily Rath came at me. He grabbed and roughly lifted me, his huge fist raised to punch.

"Rath? Who is it?"

Læknir's voice floated out of the open door like a godly reprieve.

"It's Thron, Thorir's boy," Rath answered, his deadly fist still poised.

"Thron? What a delightful surprise! Invite him in."

Slowly Rath's fist lowered, but he didn't release me.

"No man talks like that to me, let alone some boy!" Rath growled softly. *"Mind your tongue, or I'll beat the hide off you!"*

Rath pulled me inside and shoved me forward. Læknir

stood there, by a window that looked open although it wasn't, until I realized that it was paned with real, clear glass. Something else was strange about the house, leaving me disoriented; from outside, their house seemed huge. Inside, their house was tiny.

"Thron!" Læknir smiled brightly. "What a pleasure to have you visit! How are you?"

"I ... I'm fine."

"Wonderful," she beamed. "How is Vespa?"

"Fine."

"Excellent. Now, what brings you to visit on this exciting day?"

"Uh ...," I stammered, not knowing what to say. Rath was hovering behind me, judging my every word. "I was ... hoping ..."

"You want to see your father," Læknir said. "You saw the riders; you know that he'll be sailing tomorrow."

"Yes, ma'm."

"What a good boy you are, Thron," Læknir smiled. "After all that's happened, you don't want your father sailing off without saying good-bye."

I bowed my head.

"Dear," Læknir said to Rath, "could you give us a few moments alone?"

Rath nodded stiffly. "Do you want me to send Helsa in?"

"No," Læknir smiled. "Thron and I can manage."

Rath cast me a scathing glare, then exited through one of the two doors that I'd not entered through; beyond that door was another house. No, it had the same ceiling; the rafters matched. Læknir's house was divided by walls, walls inside their house, breaking it into separate rooms! Our house had a huge pantry, Garad's barn was attached to his house, but this other room was neither pantry or barn; it had a wide carpet on its floor, which only rich people owned, and I caught a glimpse of elegant chairs and a matching table before Rath closed the door behind him.

"Now, Thron, we can have a good talk," Læknir said, and I shivered slightly at her words; *I didn't want to talk to anyone but Father.* "Such a lovely view, don't you think?"

I looked out of their window, seeing our wide fjord, the tall, forested hills that enclosed it, and the sea beyond. It was impressive; I'd never been to the top of Seal Ridge before, and now I wished that I had. The world looked different from up here, the blue sky and white clouds somehow brighter, the hills more majestic. Any ship sailing up the coast could be seen through this window, as if it were a portal to the whole world. I had to force myself to remember that there was a pane of glass between me and the outside.

"It's ...," I stammered, unable to find proper words.

"Yes, it is," Læknir smiled. "I do love this old house. I'd hoped to leave it to my sons, but alas! The vikings took both of them, and two of my husbands. How I miss them!"

I slowly looked up at her. *Two husbands? And two sons?* All dead ... because of the vikings? Where was I? How could I not have known?

* * * * * * * * *

"Father?" I called softly. "Læknir said you were here."

I rapped my knuckles on the stout wooden door of Rath's old house by Tavern Hall. Eternities came and went, and finally I heard a familiar sound: a wooden brace being lifted.

Father didn't look surprised to see me, peering out of the door-crack. He glanced behind me, swept his eyes in every direction, and then opened the door fully. I rushed inside and threw my arms around him. I was so happy; *I'd been afraid that I'd never see him again.* Father reached down and hugged me in silence, then pulled me aside, closed the door, and reset the brace.

"I'm glad that you came," Father said, and he led me to the fireplace. A tiny flame danced about the glowing coals on the hearth. Inside, Rath's old house looked the same as always.

"How's Vespa doing?" Father asked carefully, trying to keep his voice casual, but there was an edge to it that I couldn't miss.

"We ... don't talk much," I said. "Dinners ... are quiet."

Father sat in Rath's chair, bowed his head, closed his eyes, and frowned deeply.

"She's a good woman, Thron," Father said softly. "She means well. But this ... *'training'* thing of hers ... she takes it too far."

Mother did like to control things; she always decided what we could and couldn't talk about at dinner, what belonged in the house, and what everyone should wear. But all mothers did that, didn't they? I hated most of her decisions; who cares what comes into the house? Why could some things be discussed in the barn but not at the table?

"The conquered never conquer," Father looked up at me. "Obey your mother, Thron. Listen to her. Learn from her. Vespa has much to teach that men need to know. But don't be trained; she's not a man. She can't teach you to be a man."

I nodded silently, a lump in my throat, but no tears wetted my eyes. I knew why Father was saying this; he was sailing away, leaving me behind, and we might never see each other again.

"Take me."

"I can't," Father sighed heavily. "Even if Branwulf allowed it, I wouldn't; boys taken too early get killed."

Silently I shook my head.

"You need proof," Father said slowly. "I'd hoped that I wouldn't have to do this, that you'd believe me, but you don't, and I don't want you jumping on some mercenary ship a week after I sail. Pretend that you're on viking. Pretend that I'm a Danish knight. If you don't kill me, or at least knock me out, then I'll ring the church bell and summon help. The door is the bell rope; if you can subdue me before I reach it, then I'll take you viking tomorrow."

Stop him? Subdue Father?

"I'm about to stand up ... unless you can stop me."

Father looked at me, then firmly grabbed the arms of Rath's big chair and leaned forward.

I swung my fists and hit hard. *I wasn't a child to be diapered and dismissed!* But Father didn't even flinch. I punched his face, shoulders, and chest. I kicked his shins. He never even reacted, as if I was no more than a mosquito buzzing about his head. Slowly he stood up.

Suddenly Father doubled over; I'd kneed him in the stomach: *I'd hurt Father! Perhaps ...*

I flew backwards, toppling over a bench into the fireplace, knocking aside the iron poker and tongs. My head crashed against the hearthstone, sending brilliant white sparks streaking across my vision. A broom handle fell atop me as I struggled for balance.

"Wounding an opponent isn't enough," Father's voice echoed distantly. "You have to kill them."

I glanced up at Father; his expression was pained, but he

was standing, tall and unbreachable, a towering giant of a man. Father was testing me again, not against a squealing pig, but against himself. And I was failing. *What could I do?* Father was bigger, infinitely stronger, a fierce fighter, descended from giants ...!

No! I said silently with a determination that I'd never known. *Father wouldn't leave me behind!* He wouldn't sail off on Branwulf's dragon, never to return, leaving me to farm turnips forever. Father would take me viking this summer: *all I had to do was kill him.*

I pushed myself up. I lifted my right hand; firmly clutched in my fist was Rath's hard iron fireplace poker. The blood of giants that flowed in Father's veins also flowed in mine: *Father wouldn't reach the door.*

Father smiled.

"Don't stop now," he whispered.

I charged Father, swinging the iron poker as hard as I could.

Pain exploded in my belly. The poker flew from my hand, clanging somewhere against the other side of Rath's house. I grabbed at my agonized stomach; my hands closed upon Father's clenched fist. Slowly I crumpled.

* * * * * * * * *

The wooden arm of Rath's chair started to hurt where it was pressed into my neck. I shifted and sat up; my whole body ached. My stomach was afire, but I pushed onto my knees and peered over the back of the chair.

Father was on his knees digging through a large chest. He looked back at me when I coughed, clutching my chest with one hand, my stomach with the other.

"I really wish you'd hurt me," Father said.

"Me, too," I groaned.

Father lifted up Grandpa's scramsax. Grandpa had died before I was born, but Father had seen him killed and had told me all about him. His knife was Father's most-prized possession. Father held out Grandpa's scramsax to me.

"This is for you now," Father said. "Grandpa's father passed it to him, he to me, and now it's yours."

Tears welled in my eyes.

"You're ... not coming back ...?"

"Who can say?" Father shrugged. "Every man who sailed last year meant to come back. Many didn't. But the smart ones, the lucky ones, left sons behind, a family to mourn them and continue after they were gone. Every year since I was fourteen I've taken this risk, the risk that I'd be one of those who didn't make it home. I married Vespa so that I'd have a family to return to. Now, this year, the way things are: I've never had less reason to return.

"You're a man now. You must make the decisions that'll keep our family together or break it apart. You must put food on our table, find more food, invent ways to make our stores last until harvest, and bring in all our crops, even if you must work day and night. You must keep your mother's temper from ruining everything. Don't challenge your mother, Thron; there's no victory to be won there, but don't let her, or any woman, *'train'* you. Be like your father, and my father, and his."

Inside, I trembled.

"Wh – what should I do?"

"Whatever needs doing," Father said, and he placed Grandpa's heavy scramsax in my hand. "A man doesn't need others to tell him what he should do; he knows and he does it.

"If I can, I'll come back before harvest. If I don't, don't try to find me; you're the only defender of our family. Learn to fight; if I do make it back, you'll still have to fight me, a year from today, and beat me, to ride on Branwulf's ship."

* * * * * * * * *

The next morning, Father and I awoke at the same instant. A horn was blowing, distant but clear. I lay pressed against Father, very hot from sleeping in my clothes, although the dark, unfamiliar house seemed unpleasantly chill. But it wasn't the dark or cold that frightened me; *the blowing horn was from Branwulf's ship.*

Father stirred, yawned deeply, and shook his head. He writhed under the blankets slowly; his joints popped softly, and then he pulled me tight against him and held me close. I snuggled against him, unwilling to let the moment end.

All too soon his arm lifted the blankets off us. He sat up, shook his head, and fumbled for his boots. I laid very still, hoping that he'd lie back down. I kept trying to think of something, some words, anything ... but nothing came. Father also said nothing. He glanced at me several times as he finished packing his chest and belted on his sword, and then he gently reached down and cuffed my boots. I slid off the bed; I'd slept fully dressed, so I was ready to go. Father motioned to his sea chest and I helped him lift it. We paused so that he could lift the brace off the door one-handed, and then we carried his chest outside.

Branwulf's ship had its sail lowered, oarsmen gently maneuvering it against our dock. A large crowd had already gathered. Mother wasn't there.

The docking dragonship was an impressive sight. The sail

was stowed, leaving the stout mast standing like a giant spear dangling ropes to the prow and stern. The dragon head looked as fierce as ever, but today it was only carved wood. I stood silent by Father as the dragon slid beside our dock and lines were tossed to Rath and Kampi. Many shouted glad greetings.

"Thorir!" Sammuel called, looking as thin and pale as ever, waving from the boat.

Father waved back at him. A great many others shouted, and husbands and sons hugged wives, daughters, and sisters. Rath stood in the center of everyone hugging Helsa, and then he glanced at his wife. Læknir bowed gently to her husband, but Rath laughed at her. Smiling, he drew her into his arms and kissed her like Father used to kiss Mother in front of the whole village, and many shocked or smirking townspeople instantly began whispering.

Surrounded by many of her kids, Beigaldi burst into tears, earnestly hugging Hal, Digr, and Brun in turn, although each was obviously embarrassed by the fuss that she was making. But Father and I stood silently, not even looking at each other, just standing side by side.

When the last of the line boarded, and the last call was shouted, Father turned to face me. I wanted desperately to say something, but my mouth was dry, my throat tight. He formally placed a hand on each of my shoulders.

"I'm proud of you, son," Father said softly, almost breaking into a smile, but never losing the seriousness in his gaze. "Now go home. You're the master of our house."

Father kissed both of my cheeks, then wrapped his arms tightly around me, squeezing me so hard that I feared I might break in his embrace. Then he released me and picked up his chest, heaved it onto one thick shoulder, and marched up our narrow dock.

Sammuel greeted him as he boarded the ship, but their words were lost in the clamor of the women's crying. Father set down his chest and turned to look at me. I returned his gaze. The rowers plied the oars as Branwulf shouted orders, and the great dragon set sail. I stared at Father until Branwulf's ship grew too distant to see clearly. Still, I kept watching until its oarsman rowed into the surf, around the bend, and out of sight.

Father was gone ... and I hadn't said a word.

* * * * * * * * *

Chapter 14

* * * * * * * * *

Mother screamed at me as I pushed open the door and entered the house.

"Where have you been! What do you mean by staying out all night? I've been ...!"

"Father's gone," I said.

Mother's eyes flew open. A thousand angry remarks struggled, trapped in her mouth, each fighting to be the first one out. Then she closed her eyes, and balled both fists; I thought that she was going to hit me.

"Help Ingrid finish your chores."

I nodded and went back outside. Ingrid was inside the barn scooping out slop for the pigs; I could tell from the way that the pigs were pushing against the empty trough.

"Ingrid!" Mother shouted. "Let Thron finish his chores. Come inside and paddle more wool."

I glared back at Mother, but she met my eyes with her own

determined stare. I wanted to challenge her, to declare my place as master of our house, but she was right; *I had chores to do.*

* * * * * * * * *

The swimming hole in the early daylight looked as inviting as ever, but I didn't throw off my clothes and splash in, as I always had. I'd swam here alone many times, but now, knowing that Garad and I would never play together again, the pond looked too still and quiet, as if it'd be a crime to disturb its peace. Swimming alone would only make me feel lonelier. I missed Garad. I missed Father. Ingrid was here, but Mother never left us alone, so I had no one to talk to.

Sighing, I hung my clothes on a low hanging branch before splashing into the water. It was very cold, tingling; these early spring melts came straight from the high-mountain ice-flows. The sting felt good, chillingly relaxing. I couldn't stay in long or I'd get the shivers. But I was dirty, my skin crusty and dry. Somehow I needed this bath to wash away more than dirt and sweat. Father could choose to never return, or worse, he could get killed. Tears didn't wet my eyes, but came so close that I wondered why I didn't cry.

Had I driven Father away?

The surrounding foliage suddenly coalesced into clarity: a rabbit, brownish-gray, too big to have been born this spring but not very old, was sitting in the tall grass under the big oak that shaded the swimming hole. He was frozen, as rabbits get when frightened, only his blinking eyes and twitching nose displaying any sign of life at all. It was no surprise; these hills were full of rabbits, and the village men hunted wolves to keep them so. Often we'd spent a fine spring afternoon playing with some newborn rabbit; the older rabbits were too fast and canny to catch. The few times that we'd caught a full-grown rabbit, Father or Holbarki had killed it and skinned it for dinner. Mother and Ingrid loved rabbit. This one was big enough to fill a stewpot.

I moved very slowly, gliding almost imperceptivity through the chill water. I knew not to make a sound or sudden gesture, or the rabbit would bolt. I slid toward him, carefully stepping on the familiar, uneven bottom of the pool. The rabbit never moved, but kept watching me. I approached it gently, neither too slowly nor too fast. I could see it trembling, its breath rapid, eyes wide. I had to be careful: rabbits bite hard and can move very quickly. Cautiously I reached out a hand and gently, barely touching, stroked its soft fur with my fingertips. I reached up and scratched between its long ears, which lay nervously pinned down against the sides of its head. This wasn't the smartest of rabbits; I slid my hand down its neck and slowly pinned it to the ground.

* * * * * * * * *

The rabbit was delicious. Mother and Ingrid complimented me on it several times, although all that I'd done was kill it and carry it back home. Ingrid had skinned and cleaned it, and Mother had chopped up some of her best spices to put in it. The taste alone wasn't the best thing; I was helping our family, sparing our turnips for the long wait until harvest. *I was doing what Father expected of me.*

It was our first midday meal with conversation since Mother had caught Father with Grettir. Not much was said, but anything was better than uncomfortable, abject silence;

Mother expressed her hopes that I'd catch many more rabbits, and Ingrid wholeheartedly agreed.

That evening, Mother pushed aside her loom and headed out to the privy. As soon as she exited, Ingrid's voice spoke in a barest whisper.

"Thron?" she asked pleadingly. "*Do you still ... want me?"*

She was sitting on her bed, spinning wool into yarn, her expression pleading, anxious. I didn't know what to say. *Was she asking ... what I hoped she was?*

"Want you ...?" I asked wonderingly.

Ingrid choked and started to cry.

"Don't ...!" I insisted, starting to get up. But Ingrid waved me back, glancing nervously at the door.

"I understand ...," Ingrid sobbed into her hands.

"It's ... been so long," I stammered, "since you ..., since we ..."

"I know. I wish it wasn't. I wish that we could ..."

"So do I."

"You do?"

"Yes! All the time!"

"But ..."

"I want you."

* * * * * * * * *

Something soft brushed against my cheek. I swatted blindly at it and pulled up my covers; I wasn't ready to wake up yet. Then I heard a soft hiss near my ear; not the sound of a buzzing insect. A finger touched my lips.

Ingrid stood over me. She held a candle lantern in one hand; my eyes winced at its glare in the darkness. Then my eyes widened fully.

Naked, Ingrid leaned over my bed. I couldn't see Mother, although I could hear soft snores coming from her bed; it wasn't morning but the middle of the night. Alarmed, my eyes widened; *what was Ingrid trying to do? What if Mother woke up ...?*

Ingrid bent over and kissed me, hard and demanding, and my whole body responded. I pushed back the covers, but she quickly pulled away and put one finger to her lips, blowing softly. I understood completely; *Mother would kill us.*

Ingrid caught my right hand and lifted it to her breast. She pressed my hand against her and I squeezed softly; Ingrid closed her eyes with a barely-audible intake of breath. I was thrilled by her reaction. She bent and kissed me again, and I gave myself over wholly to the hot sensations of her perfection and delight.

Slowly she drew back and blew a kiss at me. Ingrid stood tall and regal, lifted the glowing lantern up to her grinning face, and then slowly lowered it down to her thighs, highlighting every inch of her creamy white skin, the silent shadows of her breasts sliding intoxicatingly over her, and then she lifted the lantern high again, blew me one last kiss, and then blew out the candle.

* * * * * * * * *

Ingrid was gone.

Panic seized me. *Was she trying to tell me something last night, something that I hadn't understood?* I'd already lost Father and Garad; *I couldn't lose her, too!*

I glanced anxiously at Ingrid's empty bed illuminated by the pale light of morning glowing through our two thin windows. *Had Mother heard ... seen ... last night? How could she have cast Ingrid out without waking me?*

Then a strange sound reached my ears as I sat frozen in my bed; a soft voice, outside, singing: *Ingrid hadn't left.*

I pushed back my covers, jumped out of bed, and ran to the door. Ingrid was sitting on the fence with several grunting pigs at her feet, working with bloody fingers on some strange project, holding a knife in her teeth. She glanced up as I opened the door.

Suddenly Ingrid started to giggle. She took the knife from her mouth before she cut herself, then laughed. I was standing in the open doorway wearing only my nightshirt, and slowly it dawned upon me that Ingrid was laughing at me.

"I need fresh seawater," Ingrid said, "as soon as you can. Before you start your chores, take a bucket and go to the fjord. Bring back as much as you can carry."

I hesitated, unsure.

"You might want to get dressed first."

* * * * * * * * *

Ingrid barely noticed when I set the heavy bucket at her feet. Mother was standing inside our open door, grinding wheat in her mortar and pestle.

"Thank you," Ingrid said, never looking at me.

Blood covered her hands; Ingrid was cleaning the skin of the rabbit that I'd caught. She'd cut off its legs and head, and then cut a stout green willow branch which she'd bent in a circle and tied with thongs. Stretched inside of the circle was my rabbit-skin, tied inside the looped willow branch through tiny holes cut all around its edges. Ingrid was tightening the thongs, carefully stretching the skin wider.

"Thorir always cut up the skins and mixed them in the slop bucket for the pigs," Ingrid said. "He thought this was a waste, but I don't think so."

Ingrid tied off the last of the thongs, then jumped off the fence. Cupping her hand, she liberally ladled seawater from the bucket that I'd carried onto the skin, washing both sides vigorously. Then she took her knife and began using its curved edge to scrape across the underside of the skin.

"I'll need fresh seawater every day," she said to me. "This'll take weeks to finish properly."

"Thron, get started on your chores," Mother shouted from inside our house.

Ingrid risked a glance at me ... and I caught the faintest trace of a smile.

* * * * * * * * *

The sun was hot on my back as I pulled another weed. As always, there seemed to be more weeds this year. Mother and Ingrid kneeled nearby, pulling more newly-sprouted weeds. I kept hoping that they'd both quit so that I could sneak off to the swimming hole.

Garad was kneeling in his field, weeding, just like I was. I felt terrible, knowing that we couldn't speak. Occasionally I saw him looking at me from his field, but what could I say to him? *'So, can we still be friends now that Father and Grettir are no longer mating like pigs?'* or *'Now I know what it feels like to lose a father!'*.

The sun burned relentless. Tiny weeds poked up through the freshly-planted dirt, mocking me. Furious, I yanked them out.

* * * * * * * * *

I heard the splash before I saw the water. I hesitated, then approached slowly, trying to walk quietly over the fallen sticks and loose stones. Garad was alone in the water, splashing around the swimming hole. He didn't see or hear me; Garad was jumping high and landing on his back, splashing big waves all around. He looked like he was having fun, more than I remembered him having since his dead father had been carried off of Branwulf's ship.

Garad didn't notice as I walked to the edge of the pool. Then he caught a glimpse of me and almost fell over trying to suddenly turn around in water up to his waist. I wanted to smile at him, but I couldn't; when he recognized me, the expression on his face changed from the pure joy of play to his blackest glare of hate.

"You!" he shouted angrily, and instantly he slogged toward me, fists clenched.

I tried not to draw back; we'd been best friends all of our lives.

Garad kept coming, cursing me so fast that his shouts blustered unintelligibly. His rage flamed nearly palpable, and I deserved all the names, but surely Garad wouldn't try to fight me. I was bigger and a better fighter. Garad could never hope to beat me.

Garad splashed up out of the water snarling, wet and furious.

"... lied to me, used my mother, bastard-cheater ...!"

Incredulous, I stepped back as his fist flew, but then he jumped me. Punches came from all directions. I tried to defend myself, but Garad knocked me backwards, pummeled, and I could only feel his fists against my skin.

Then we toppled; I hit the thick grass, hard ground, and jagged rocks face-first, and still Garad punched.

I squirmed and struggled. *Garad was smaller than me!* I'd always pinned him before, but he struck faster, hit harder, and gripped stronger than ever. Every time that I thought I had his arm or ankle clutched tightly, Garad jerked it loose, pried it free, or bent my arm the wrong way until I had to let go. Dirt and branches scratched my face.

I pushed him off, but Garad sprang like a spider. I rolled us over, taking the advantageous top, and punched with all of my might.

Garad's foot kicked into my stomach; breath blasted from me. I tried to pin him, to grasp his arms and press him flat, but Garad kicked with both feet, punched with both fists, and sharp teeth bit my grasping fingers.

A deep fog rolled over my vision. I stopped throwing punches long before Garad did. The pain wasn't all-consuming, as when Father hit; Garad's pain was a hundred tiny blows, landing all over, and one blow greater than all the rest combined: *humiliation.* Garad was smaller than me. Garad was weaker than me. Garad was less than I in every way. I kept thinking, even as I lay helpless: *this couldn't be happening! This couldn't be ...!*

* * * * * * * * *

Garad was gone. Tears wet my face although I didn't remember crying. Blood trickled and welled inside my mouth. I ached all over.

I pushed up from the ground, tiny rocks pressed into my dirty face and twigs were tangled in my hair. I'd never guessed that Garad could fight so hard, so angrily. Garad must've been practicing, held rocks in his fists, or attacked me from behind; something, *anything* to spare me the humiliation of having been beaten to a pulp. I hung my head; *what would Father say?*

Father would've congratulated Garad and chastised me. *'You can never fight too well, only too poorly.'*

I didn't deserve to go viking. I wasn't worthy of Branwulf. *I shouldn't have lost to Garad.*

I brushed off and cleaned up at the pool as best I could before I walked back home. I didn't want anyone to know that I'd been fighting, especially not that I'd been beaten by Garad.

"What happened to you?" Mother shouted as I entered, and Ingrid froze, staring open-mouthed.

I glanced into the copper mirror on the wall; I was covered with large, dark bruises, a shiny smear under one eye, and several small cuts and scrapes, my whole face swollen.

"You've been fighting!" Mother affirmed as she grabbed my chin and turned my face to examine me. Her thumb pressed a sore spot on my jaw and I flinched, but I didn't draw back. I hurt everywhere, too much for any one spot to assume precedence.

"Who were you fighting?" Mother demanded.

Ingrid crowded close behind Mother, her face a mask of concern. I couldn't tell, couldn't let her know ...

"Who?" Mother grabbed my arm and shook me.

"Garad!" I blurted out suddenly, not knowing why, wanting only to lie down and die.

Mother hesitated and Ingrid looked shocked.

"Garad did this ...?" Mother asked.

"I didn't fight back," I lied, hoping that they wouldn't press me too hard.

"Why not?" Ingrid asked in disbelief.

"Garad found out ... everything," I stammered. "That I lied to him ... "

"You lied to your mother as well," Mother reminded in her most-acidic tone.

I pulled away at last, staggered over to my bed, collapsed upon it, and laid there like a dead thing.

"Ingrid, get the ointment," Mother said. "Thron can't do his chores if he gets infected."

Insult to injury, I mused silently.

* * * * * * * * *

I spied Garad weeding his fields the next day. I didn't look at him long or often. I tried to concentrate on pulling out the tiny weed-shoots, but my sore bruises tormented me. Our friendship was ruined; Garad would tell the other kids, and I'd be the laughing stock of the village. Even the grownups in Tavern Hall would repeat his story and laugh. By the time that Father returned, I'd be a joke.

Jokes never go viking.

I didn't speak to anyone for days. I worked hard and fast, in silence, and eventually finished weeding all of our fields and started over again, but I just couldn't bear pulling up another blade of grass or dandelion. I shook my weed-bag off my shoulder and dropped it between two rows of sprouting turnips. I glanced at Garad in his field, then angrily tromped off in the other direction.

I didn't go near the swimming hole; I might never go there again. The sun was high with puffy clouds; soon the dirt would become dry and dusty, but it was still spring. I walked to the farthest corner of our field and kept walking.

Long thorny branches had overgrown our old trail, leaving barbed tendricals that I had to dodge around, duck under, or gently hold aside as I slid past, fully aware of how deeply they could rake skin once they bit, and how their cuts itched for weeks afterwards. My trail led into the hills, to the base of what we called 'the cliff'. It wasn't a huge cliff, nor a sheer drop, but it was very steep. My trail snaked up it; a rough climb. Still, I felt the need to accomplish something.

I climbed to the top, and then looked down. Through the branches, I spied my house in the distance, but not clearly. All around me was deep forest. Many times Father and I'd come this way for firewood; we'd cut up the fallen trees and toss the logs over the cliff, and then carry them home.

I wondered where Father was, what he was doing, and if he was thinking about me. Was he fighting? Was he ... already dead ... and I just didn't know? Shivers slid down my spine.

Something caught my eye: smoke, a puffy steam of gray mist blew up from the distant treetops. It was far outside of our village, in the foothills below the mountains. I'd been there only a few times; nothing lived out there. Those woods were wild, rugged, small peaks divided by thorn-filled ravines. Yet a fire burned there.

Thieves? Real thieves? I wondered if I should go for help, but the idea of walking into Tavern Hall a second time and reporting unseen thieves was unthinkable. No, I had to be a man now, like Father had said: *I had to go alone.*

* * * * * * * * *

Afternoon was passing into evening as I quietly pushed

through the thick brush. The deer trails out here were barely visible, and I was forced to crawl in many places. There were no other trails here, just thick underbrush and animals that'd probably never seen a human. I spotted a lot of game; rabbits, fox, and beavers slid into the thick brush as I approached. I should come out here and hunt them; Ingrid and Mother would be pleased.

Smoke rose, clearly visible in the trees, but I no longer needed to see it. The wind was blowing straight toward me, carrying the unmistakable scent of roasting meat. I slowed my pace and became watchful; if these animals could sense my approach, then so could a thief.

Finally I found the fire. It blazed in a tiny glade, surrounded by maples, with a small stream of icy water flowing right through it. A strange, crude hut stood beside the stream between two trees; huge sections of peeled bark formed its roof. The snores of a fat old man leaning against a tree roared loudly.

I'd never seen anyone like him. His face was covered in rough red patches and he boasted a short, unkempt beard. He wore a long brown robe reaching to his leather sandals, a single plaited rope bound about his waist.

Over his fire hung a poorly-cleaned duck stuck on a sharpened stick. The flames were too high; the duck was burning, dripping grease into the flames, which made the fire sizzle and burn high, but the stranger was sleeping too deeply to notice.

Was he a thief? Probably, but what was I supposed to do about it? Run home like a good boy and tell Mother? No, Father wouldn't do that. Kill him? I didn't have my sword, not even Grandfather's sax, and he was big, even bigger around than Rath, though nowhere near as tall.

The scent of the roasting duck made my mouth water. I remembered what Father had said; *'Bring any food home to keep our stores from running out'.* If I was careful, I could slip in, snatch the cooked duck, and be home before sunset. Then we'd have extra food ... and nobody would ever again doubt my stories of thieves in the woods.

I crept forward carefully, cautiously, keeping my eyes on the sleeping thief. Tiny twigs cracked and pebbles ground under my feet and hands as I crawled forward; I froze as the sleeping man snorted suddenly, but he only wiggled his heavy brows, mumbled something unintelligible, and resumed snoring. Finally I reached the edge of his encampment; the thick bushes offered no more concealment.

I stood slowly, in plain view, fearing that my movement would wake him. The roasting duck hung only a few feet away; I slid toward it, carefully balancing on each foot as I stepped closer. I reached out and grasped the stout sharpened branch that the duck was stuck on; carefully I lifted it; the stout stick holding the burning duck slid silently free.

A deer path on the far side of the encampment led off into the forest. I decided to trust it; a path would let me escape with my prize most quietly, and once away, I could slip back into the woods. The man kept snoring; *I'd almost escaped!*

Excitement filled me as I slipped past the first trees and ran down the narrow trail: *I'd done it! I'd stolen the thief's dinner!*

A rope seized my ankle and yanked me high up into the branches.

* * * * * * * * *

Chapter 15

*　*　*　*　*　*　*　*　*

"Oh, God, my blessed lord!" the strange man cried as he rounded the bend. His hands trembling, he stared in horror as if I were some dreadful portent.

I was caught, hanging upside down, a crude rope tight around my ankle, the blackened, greasy stick holding his duck still in my hands. Defenseless, I shook off the roasted duck and aimed its sharp, greasy point at him, although my movements spun me around. His eyes followed his steaming, overcooked duck as it bounced and rolled into a tumble of weeds.

He said something in a language that I'd never heard before, and then looked up at me.

"You ... thief," he said.

"You're the thief!" I shouted.

"Me?" he asked. "*Friar James, a thief?* May God send a bolt of lightning to blast out your lying tongue!"

God? Lightning? Did he mean Thor, the Thunderer? I tried to keep the point of the stick aimed at the stranger as I slowly spun around on the rope.

"God is punishing you for stealing my dinner," Friar James said. "He put your foot in my trap."

Tired of spinning around, I swung the stick up, desperately trying to sever the rope biting into my ankle. I hit my own boot: *it hurt.*

Friar James cried out, something in his foreign tongue, and then slowly spoke through his thick accent. "Don't break my rope! I spent days making it."

While helplessly hanging, I snarled fiercely, but Friar James didn't seem impressed. He seemed more frightened by my presence than my sharpened stake.

"Does anyone else know that I'm here?" Friar James asked.

I maintained a stubborn silence, but the rope burned into my ankle; I couldn't wait forever.

"If you kill me, then my whole village will hunt you," I snarled.

"Kill you?" Friar James sounded shocked, then let loose a string of his own garbled language before he slowed down and addressed me again. "I don't kill. I'm a friar. Do you know what a friar is?"

The rope slowly turned me around, but I twisted, trying to stay facing him.

"You're a ... cook?"

"Poor pagan boy," Friar James said. "Doomed to the fires of Hell."

"Hel?" I asked, frustrated. "Niflhiem's Goddess of Death ...?"

"No, boy," Friar James said disgustedly. "Hell, the fiery pit of damned souls. Hasn't a Christian missionary ever visited your village?"

"A what?"

"A missionary," Friar James said. "I'm a missionary. I came here to teach your people the truth about religion."

"What's 'religion'?"

Friar James closed his eyes as if deeply pained.

"Throw down that stick, and promise that you won't tell anyone about me, and I'll help you down."

My fists clenched tightly around the hard stick. I was already trapped; I wouldn't disarm myself. Frowning, Friar James folded his arms over his chest.

"I can wait all day," he said.

We stared at each other until I couldn't stand the burn of the rope any longer; angrily I threw down his cooking-stick.

Friar James came cautiously forward and wrapped one arm around me, lifted, and tugged at the rope with his other hand. It took a few moments for him to loosen it, and then he slowly dropped me onto the ground.

Instantly I grabbed for the sharpened, pointed cooking stick, but his sandaled foot stepped on it just as I wrapped my fingers around it. I cried out, my fingers squeezed between his stick and the hard ground.

"Let me go!"

"Why? So you can tell your people about me?"

"I won't tell anyone!"

"Why should I believe a thief?"

"I'm not the thief!" I shouted. "I don't live alone in the woods!"

"Neither did I, until I decided to come to this cursed Sweden."

"This is Norway."

"Norway?" Friar James gasped, then he shook his head. "I never should've trusted those sailors! Threw me overboard; said that it was bad luck to sail through a storm with a priest on board. *Stupid heathens!* And to think that I hoped to save their souls! Ah, they'll all burn in Hell now, the filthy beasts."

"Hel?" I asked again. "Why do you keep mentioning her?"

Friar James rolled his eyes and looked up.

"Thank you, Lord," he seemed to be talking to the branches overhead. "My first pupil … and you send me the village idiot."

* * * * * * * * *

"There's only one God."

"No, there're many," I insisted. "Baulder, Thor, Vor, Vidar, …"

"Those are pagan gods!" Friar James shouted.

I licked my greasy fingers, tasting the last of the roasted duck. Friar James seemed exasperated and kept pacing in front of his crude hut.

"What's a pagan?"

"You are," Friar James sighed. "All of these gods that you worship are false gods. They're devils trying to trick you."

"What're devils?"

"Devils are fallen angels."

"Angels …?"

"Angels are servants of God."

"Devils and angels are servants of God?"

"No, I mean, they were. God created all of them. The angels are those that stayed faithful, and the devils are the ones that turned against God."

Friar James continued speaking long after I'd stopped listening to him. Friar James wasn't a thief, as I'd assumed; he was crazy. He lived alone in the woods, somehow catching plenty of food, and what seemed to worry him most were the bed-tales that Father told me as a child. He had his own stories, very different ones, but children's tales didn't interest me anymore.

"Are you paying attention?"

"Yes," I said, "well, no. I need to get home before dark."

"Well, you're welcome to come back," Friar James said. "If you could bring me a real knife, and a pint of beer, you'll be very welcome. Just don't tell anyone that I'm here."

* * * * * * * * *

"Where have you been?"

I looked at Mother through distrustful eyes. *What would she say if I told her of Friar James?* I didn't want to say anything that'd remind her that I'd already lied.

"Out."

"Out where?"

"In the hills."

Ingrid looked up expectantly. "Any rabbits?"

"Saw plenty, but didn't catch any." *That much was true.* "Almost got a duck."

I half-smiled; Friar James' duck had been delicious; how had he caught it? Then my smile faded: just when things had been going well I'd told another lie. I seemed to lie all of the time these days, whether I intended to or not. Why? There'd been no need!

"Better that you didn't," Mother said. "Any wild duck that

lets you get close enough to grab it is probably sick, and might've poisoned us."

Ingrid frowned; she'd have liked some roasted duck. I'd have to ask Friar James how he caught it.

"Thron, is something bothering you?" Mother asked.

"No," I snapped defensively, but then I forced myself to relax. "Why?"

"You look thoughtful," Mother said. "Sit and eat your dinner, then get busy on your new bowl. I broke a needle today and only have one good one left."

Should I tell them about Friar James? Probably, but I wasn't sure that I wanted anyone else to know my secret. It felt good, somehow powerful, to know something that they didn't. Yet I couldn't help but wonder what trouble would come of it.

* * * * * * * * *

"How can you ask that?" Friar James looked shocked.

"Ingr – I mean, my mother likes duck," I said.

"Yes, but ...?"

I gazed up at him uncomprehending.

"What happened to you yesterday ... when you tried to steal my duck?"

I stepped back. *Was he angry?*

"Think, boy! I was sleeping, you snuck into my camp, stole my duck, and ran down that trail ..."

"Yea ...?"

"You ran down that trail, then what happened?"

"I got caught by your rope ..."

"My trap, boy! You were caught by my trap. I'd hoped to catch a deer with that trap, but you stuck your foot in it, and it trapped you instead."

Friar James paused impatiently, as if expecting something else from me.

"Well ...?" he asked.

"Well ... what?"

"Traps! I caught the duck in a trap!"

"You mean that duck came running down your trail ..."

"No!" Friar James shouted, and he stared up at the tree branches again. "Lord, why did you do this to me? The trap on the trail was a deer trap! I caught the duck in a duck trap. Isn't that obvious?"

Slowly I glanced at the woods around me, which had suddenly grown dark and ominous.

"There're traps around here?"

Friar James slapped his palm against his forehead.

"Of course! How do you think that I eat?"

I paused, considering.

"Will you show me how to make traps?"

* * * * * * * * *

Three days later, I jumped with delight and Friar James laughed. Hanging from the old rope that I'd brought from home was a struggling beaver. He was huge, old, fat, and twisting in the wind. He seemed asleep until he heard us, and even then his struggles seemed minimal; he was exhausted. Friar James raised his fire-hardened spear and ended the beaver's terror with a quick, firm thrust.

Taking down the beaver wasn't as easy as I'd hoped. Friar James had me pull it down, then step on the rope before I took the loop off its ankle, but I got so excited that I let the rope slip, and it sprung up into the branches and off the high limb that supported it. I had to climb the tree again to reset the rope in just the right place, with Friar James holding the heavy log that was our counterweight over his head. Then I had to scramble back down and reset the trap before he could lower the heavy log.

The beaver was big, his fur thick.

"A fine catch," Friar James said. "This one's yours, Thron. Take it home to your family and show them what you've done. Your father will be very proud of you."

"Mother will be proud, and Ingrid," I said, still smiling. "Father sailed south with the viking."

"Viking?" Father James sounded shocked. "*Your father ... is one of those ... raiders?"*

"He goes viking every year," I said proudly.

"But ... they're thieves! Murderers! Your father is ... one of them?"

"Yea!"

"Vikings attack Christians!" Friar James shouted. "*They ravage churches and monasteries, murder innocents, rape and plunder ...!"*

Friar James broke into his strange language suddenly, muttering sounds totally incomprehensible. He looked up at the branches overhead and with his right hand touched both of his shoulders, then his forehead and chest. I'd seen him do that many times, but very quickly, never this slow. He always glanced up when he did it; I assumed that it had something to do with the trees.

"What's the matter?" I asked.

"What's the matter?" Friar James blustered and fumed. *"What's wrong with murder? What's wrong with rape? What's wrong with invasions and looting the very house of God?!?"*

Friar James glared at me with bulging eyes, as if desperately looking for some sign in my face. Obviously he didn't like the yearly vikings, but lots of people didn't like the summer raids; even Mother occasionally complained about them.

"Thron, your father kills people," Friar James said seriously.

"Many people," I agreed.

"No!" shouted Friar James. "You don't understand! *He murders men! Christian men!"*

"Yea ...?"

"That's wrong!" Friar James shouted.

"No, it isn't."

"Yes it is!"

"No, I know for a fact that he kills people. He kills people every year."

The thin wrinkles around Friar James' eyes stretched lengthwise as he glared at me, his speechless mouth hanging open as if dumbfounded.

"I know that he kills people!" Friar James shouted when his voice returned. "*I meant .... killing people is wrong! It's wrong to kill people!"*

"It is?"

"Yes!"

"Why?"

Friar James looked like he was going to explode like a sealed jug of fermenting ale.

"Would you want people to kill you?" Friar James demanded.

"Of course not," I said.

Friar James hesitated, impatient. "*Well ...?"*

"Well ..., what?"

"Why is it right for you to kill them, but wrong for them to kill you?"

I hesitated, trying to figure what he was raving about.

"Who said that it was wrong for them to kill me?"

"Do you want to die?" asked Friar James, looking exasperated.

"No," I answered. "That's why Father taught me to fight, so that I wouldn't die."

"Why fight at all?"

"For ... for my family."

"What?!?"

"For my family," I repeated. "Those people in the rich lands, they have their own families, and they fight to protect them and their property. Without their wealth, my family would starve, so we go viking, and the better fighter's family survives."

Friar James looked aghast. "Who told you that?"

"Father told me, but it's no secret. Everyone knows it."

"But what if there was a better way, a Christian way, a way where nobody had to kill anybody ...?"

That thought was very strange, but Friar James seemed to think that it was important, so I thought about it long and hard. No need to go viking ... *how could that be good?*

Friar James kept looking expectantly, as if hoping that I'd agree with him, but his Christian ways made no sense.

"Where would we get the treasures that we need?" I asked.

"You'll be rewarded with the treasures of Heaven," Friar James said.

"Oh! That would work."

Friar James smiled.

"There're no rewards greater than the treasures of

Heaven," Friar James said.

"Great!" I said. "So, instead of England, we sail to Heaven ... and fight those people."

Friar James closed his eyes and cried out.

* * * * * * * * *

Mother stood up and kissed me when she saw the dead beaver.

"Thron, I'm very proud of you," Mother said as she hugged me tightly.

I'd never felt as happy; *Father would be proud of me.*

The beaver was delicious. Mother and Ingrid cooked a whole quarter of it; the rest they sliced into thin steaks and hung them in the pantry. Ingrid stoked up the smoke in there thicker than usual to keep flies from infesting the meat, which meant that I had to go out three times the next day to get more green firewood and chop up a huge pile of chips, but it was worth it. The beaver tasted even better than the rabbit, and I liked having meat with every meal.

As days passed, I found fewer chances to escape. I told Mother that Halgrum and Derek showed me their traps; Mother didn't question this lie, and I quickly changed the subject. Mother was pleased, but then she insisted that more weeding had to be done.

I kept thinking about Friar James. The villagers wouldn't kill him, but every time I saw him, he made me promise not to tell anyone about him.

Why did he insist on living in secret?

* * * * * * * * *

I took Friar James an old, rusty knife that I'd found in Morgan's room, some turnips and an onion from our pantry, and a pitcher of beer, but from his reaction you would've thought I'd given him Mjollner and all the jewels of Asgard. Instantly Friar James took a deep drink of beer, then built up his fire, which was only a few smoldering embers, and prepared to cook the turnips.

"I can't tell you how much this means to me," Friar James said, smiling widely. "Next time, if you have a spare one, I need something to cook in - a pot or a little cauldron. Even a dished helmet would do. If you have one that won't be missed, please bring it.

"Now, how can I reward you for these wonderful gifts? I know; I'll tell you the story of the Garden of Eden."

"A story about a garden?" I frowned.

"This was a very special garden," Friar James said. "The Garden of Eden is God's garden, and in it was a very special tree: the Tree of Good and Evil."

"Good and evil?" I asked. "How can it be both?"

"You'll see," Friar James promised. "God made it that way for a reason."

"Which God?"

"There's only one God."

"No, there are ..."

"Those false idols aren't gods!"

"But yours is ...?"

"Yes ... I mean, God isn't a false idol. He's real; the one, true God."

"What's his name?"

"We call him God."

"Then, how do you tell him apart from all the other ...?"

"Do you want to hear this story or not?"

I swallowed my arguments; best to listen to his tale. Perhaps it'd be a good one.

"The Garden of Eden is one of the first stories from the Bible," Friar James began. "God created man there, the first man, and his name was Adam. The Garden of Eden was a wonderful place; every kind of food grew there, and all of the animals were tame, but God saw that Adam was lonely. So God created woman, the first woman, and her name was Eve."

Friar James paused as if tempting me to ask another question, but I merely nodded.

"In the Garden of Eden was one special tree, the Tree of Good and Evil. God gave everything in the Garden of Eden to Adam and Eve except this one tree, from which he forbade them to eat. But the devil came disguised as a serpent, and the devil tempted Eve into tasting fruit from the forbidden tree, and then Eve talked Adam into taking a bite. Suddenly, when they looked at themselves, they realized that they were naked ..."

"They were naked ...?"

"Yes, but until ..."

"Really naked? Both of them?"

"Thron, that's not the point ..."

"What about when it snowed?"

"It never got cold in the Garden of E..."

"Where is it?"

"Thron ..."

"Is it in the south? I hear that it's warmer in the ..."

"Enough!" Friar James shouted. "*This isn't about people being naked! It's about how mankind was cast out of paradise!"*

"How?"

"God cast them out."

"Why?"

"Because they disobeyed him by eating fruit from the Tree of Good and Evil."

I waited expectantly.

"That's it?"

"That's the story of how man was created."

"And then Heimdal came along?"

"Who's Heimdal?"

"Heimdal slept with the old people and bore the races of kings, peasants, and thralls."

"Where did you hear that?"

"Father."

"That's one of those false tales, isn't it? I told you; those stories aren't real."

"What do you mean *'real'*? It's a story, just like yours; somebody tells it, and ..."

"Mine aren't stories!" Friar James shouted. "*They come from the Bible!"*

"Where's that?"

"Where's what?"

"The Bible? Is it in England?"

"The Bible isn't a place! It's a book, a sacred book!"

A long moment I pondered this.

"Do people go naked in England?"

Friar James shouted and stomped. He raged, threatening that he would send me to Hel, or was it Hell? I couldn't keep it straight. His story was boring; no swordfights, no rapings, nobody stabbing spears through their body ... I could tell him some really exciting tales, but he seemed to prefer his own.

"You should tell your story to my mother," I told him. "She likes boring stuff ..."

"The word of God isn't boring!"

"You should come home with me."

Friar James looked exasperated, closed his eyes and took a deep breath.

"You're just a boy, Thron; you don't know what they'd do ..."

"They won't kill you."

"The last Norsemen that I trusted almost killed me; I don't think I'll ever be able to swim or sail again."

I shook my head: thrown overboard into a strange, cold, dark stormy sea; *what was frightening about that?*

* * * * * * * * *

Chapter 16

* * * * * * * * *

Traps were harder to make than I'd imagined. After weeding all morning, I headed out to the hills close to my house. Everywhere birds, squirrels, and all sorts of wildlife flew, crept, and scampered. I made three traps, two for small game and one for a deer. If I could catch a deer then I'd really be a hero.

Making three traps took all week. I had to find just the right location, logs that weighed enough to spring without breaking it, and cut green branches, of even thicknesses, and notch them so that they hung together but would release with the slightest pressure. The memory of all the praise that I'd received for bringing home the rabbit and beaver fueled me.

The next week, I made three more traps. I didn't tell anyone about them; if they didn't work, then I'd look like a fool, so I carefully kept my distance from Mother and Ingrid, speaking only when necessary. They kept asking me what was wrong, but I only muttered noncommittally at them and concentrated on my carvings.

Mother traded my bowl as soon as it was finished. She got three stout steel needles for it, which she praised as being as strong as sword blades. They looked like the same steel as my sword; shiny, not blackened at all. But I wasn't impressed with needles.

* * * * * * * * *

Hauling seawater back to Ingrid each morning was less than fun. I carried two buckets now; the rabbit skin was nearly finished and the beaver skin was curing nicely. Every morning and evening, Ingrid scrubbed both sides of both pelts with the fresh seawater. She started using a sanding rock to scrape the inside of the rabbit, but went back to the edge of the curved knife on the beaver. She worked hard but carefully, then hung them from branches to air out. She started brushing the fur on the rabbit. I didn't offer to help; Mother was watching us more closely than ever.

I checked my deer trap first; I kept hoping to find a deer hanging from the trees, but it always lay empty.

Garad and I hadn't spoken since our fight. I felt guilty: *I should've fought harder.* Sometimes I felt so angry that I wanted to run over and beat him three times as badly as he'd beaten me, but then ... I'd lied, tricked, and kept secrets from him.

Whenever I could stomach no more weeding, I headed out to check my traps. Friar James would check my first trap near his home, that he'd helped me make, but I had to check the six that I'd built myself.

My deer trap was sprung again, but empty. Whatever had

tripped it was long gone, but something had been there; the tiny pile of pig's slop that I used as bait was eaten. I felt dispirited; here was another example of my failure. I reset the trap, but I'd brought no more bait; *another failure.*

My second trap had caught something, but not for long. Its rope was chewed in half, hanging useless from the tree. I sighed heavily; I hadn't brought extra rope; *my failures were mounting.* I walked past the ruined trap without even touching it.

My eyes widened as I approached my third trap. A fat gray rabbit was hanging in the air, my noose tight around its foreleg. It twitched frantically as I jumped toward it. Luckily, I'd worn Grandpa's scramsax.

My fourth trap was ruined, chewed through like my second, but both of my last two had caught prey. The fifth had another rabbit, younger, almost pure white, and the last held a large badger, old, but still stewpot-worthy.

I carried home my trophies of war. Even Garad and Grettir stopped working in their field to stare at me as I carried the bloody carcasses toward my door. Ingrid spied me, dropped the broom from her hand, and screamed for Mother. When Mother saw me, my face barely visible behind the huge pile of fur, she started to jump up and down and squeal with delight.

* * * * * * * * *

Covered in blood, I expected Mother to send me to the swimming hole to wash, but she took me inside while Ingrid took my catches outside to the big basin. Mother stripped my clothes off and washed me with clean rags, then had me put on my other tunic while she set my blood-stained clothes in water to soak.

"Children are sent to wash," Mother said. "Men provide food for their families."

Mother poured an ale, and to my surprise, offered it to me.

"Sit," she said, indicating Father's chair.

I took the ale, but I hesitated; no one but Rath had sat in Father's chair since he'd left. Mother had her chair, I my stool, and Ingrid her bench.

"Sit down," Mother insisted.

Slowly I sat on Father's chair. It felt uncomfortable. I wanted this to stay Father's seat, to still be his when he came back.

If he came back ...

I didn't want to be Father's replacement. He belonged here, not me. This would never be my chair, not as long as I could help it. Slowly I stood up, holding my ale.

"No," I said. "It's Father's chair."

Mother's smile inverted abruptly.

"There's too much of your father in you."

"He'll come home," I insisted.

"That remains to be seen."

* * * * * * * * *

Garad's eyes flared as he saw me walking across his field toward him.

"Get off my land!" he shouted.

I walked up close enough to talk without shouting, but not close enough for either of us to hit the other without clear warning.

"Our parents are pigs," I said.

"Don't make me ...!"

I stood ready for him. I itched to revenge myself.

"What do you want?" Garad demanded.

"Men don't let their mothers decide their friends."

"We were never friends," Garad snarled.

"We've played together all our lives."

"You picked on me all of our lives," Garad shouted. "You just kept me around because you were bigger and needed someone to pick on."

"No ..."

"Get out of here! Never come here again!"

"Garad ..."

"Never speak my name!" Garad shouted, and he stepped forward threateningly.

Garad's face flaired scarlet, eyes glaring, fists clenched. *Was he mad?* We'd been friends since we were old enough to crawl to each other's house! Slowly, showing no fear, I turned away.

"And stay away from my mother!"

* * * * * * * * *

"Time," Friar James answered. "Your young friend is alone and angry. What else could he say?"

"How long will it take?"

"How long before he realizes that he's wrong, how long before he forgives you, or how long before he admits that he was wrong? When he grows up, I'd say. Your friend sounds very childish, but that's expected. Growing comes in increments; it doesn't happen all at once."

I stared into Friar James' tiny fire, watching the waves of heat engulf the steaming chunks of rabbit on our sticks, making them sizzle and drip.

"So there's nothing that I can do? To speed things up?"

"You can pray," Friar James said.

I glanced up at him questioningly. His foreign accent was so thick that it was often hard to make out his words.

"Pray ...?" I asked. "What's that?"

"A request for God's mercy," Friar James said.

"Oh, that," I sighed. I didn't know why I kept coming back here. All that he wanted to talk about was God, his god, whom he said was the only god. I liked his stories; they were new, but they weren't exciting. Father said the gods rewarded deeds, not words. Friar James' god must talk like Grettir.

"Yes, *'that',*" Friar James said. "Why, in England a boy would be severely punished for calling God *'oh, that'.* Such words are blasphemy; perhaps that's why you have so many problems. You can't expect His mercy when you speak ill of Him."

That made sense, I thought; it was the first thing that Friar James had said about his strange religion that made any sense at all. I wondered why it was so important to him.

"You're thinking," Friar James said. "I see it in your eyes. That's good, very good. Perhaps I'm having an effect on you after all."

"Your stories ... your god ... isn't as exciting as Odin," I said plainly. "Odin carries a magic spear, rides an eight-legged horse, and craves wisdom so badly that he once hung himself until he was dead, and then tore out his own eye, just for a few tidbits of knowledge."

"Those may be exciting stories, but they never happened," Friar James said.

"They're as real as your stories!"

"Your stories are just fireside tales passed down from your

fathers. My stories come from the Bible. *Alas!* The viking sailors threw my bible into the sea, may God forgive their heathen souls."

"Father told me about Odin," I said firmly, that being the only proof that I needed.

"Your father's raiding right now," Friar James said as if this supported his argument.

"So ...?"

"You still don't understand," Friar James said. "How could you? Raised in this backward, uncivilized land ..."

"Don't let my mother hear you say that."

Friar James smiled.

"I'm sure that she's an admirable woman..."

I nodded.

"Of course, but she's never been to England, has she? Never visited France or Italy? Never seen the cathedrals of Rome? There are levels of civilization, and civility, that can't be seen from the tallest mountain in Norway. Your people may be civilized compared to wild savages and beasts, but there's more to life than you've ever seen, more than you can even comprehend. Why, in England, we have towers so tall that you have to climb many flights of stairs ..."

"Flights of what ...?"

Friar James smiled.

"Stairs. You do know what stairs are, don't you?"

"Sure I do!" I insisted, but Friar James looked doubtful. Truthfully I wasn't sure if I did, but I'd seen many different birds: flights of sparrows, flights of pigeons, even the strange arrowhead flights of geese in the fall. I might not be able to tell a falcon from a hawk at a distance, but if there were any *'stairs'* flying around Norway then I was sure to have seen one.

"Do you have any buildings in your village with multiple

stories?" Friar James asked.

"Not that I know of," I answered hesitantly, wondering why he asked such a strange question. "There's a story about how Tavern Hall got built, and Father told me about building our barn ..."

Friar James smiled triumphantly.

"In England, there are buildings built on top of other buildings," he explained. "The roof of the lower building is the floor of the building above it."

"That's crazy," I said, but then I thought about it. "We have a loft in our barn over the horse stalls."

"Exactly," Friar James said.

"You climb a ladder to get up there."

"Well, a flight of stairs is like a wide ladder."

"How can a bird be like a ladder ...?"

Friar James closed his eyes and grunted.

* * * * * * * * *

My next trip to visit Friar James was more fun. A deer had stumbled into his trap, and we feasted on roasted venison. Friar James asked if I wanted to hear another story, but my grimace answered him.

"Tell you what," Friar James said. "Watch this."

Friar James smoothed out the dirt between us, then he took a small stick and scratched some lines in the dirt.

"There," Friar James said. "Guess what that is."

I shrugged.

"That's my name," Friar James said. "That's writing. I can teach you to write."

"Why would I want that?"

"Why, so you can write. Every boy should know how to

write."

"Why?"

"You'll find out," Friar James said. "Here, I'll teach you to write your name."

I saw no point to it, but it was better than listening to his stories. I spent the afternoon drawing runes, learning how each sounded, and Friar James wouldn't stop until I could write my name.

* * * * * * * * *

Suddenly rocks spilled from the cliff beneath my feet. I grabbed at the roots sticking out of the steep cliff-side trail, but they tore free. Despite my every effort, I roughly slid down the tall cliff's face and crashed through the thick underbrush into screams and blackness.

Shock faded to pain. Sharp thorns stabbed, my clothes and skin shredded. Tears burst; I tried to wipe my eyes to clear them, but the blood on my arm blinded me.

Slowly I tried to extricate myself. Long, thick, thorny branches pressed in on me from all sides, many thorns, their leaves painted with my blood. I gritted my teeth; more thorns stabbed every time that I moved, but staying still, lying atop thorns tearing apart my back, was no better. Moving slowly didn't help; the branches pressed in on me harder every time I moved.

My leg hurt terribly; I wondered if it was broken. I needed help, but home was far away; no one would hear me shout.

Something tugged at my belt: Grandfather's knife, its leather sheath snagged by thorns. I drew the scramsax. The sharp, gleaming blade was my only hope.

The thick vines were tough, and each movement drove the agonizing thorns in deeper, but one by one I cut, sawed, and hacked until I'd cleared a thorny prison around me. Then I had no choice: I pressed my torn hands into the thorns beneath me and tried to stand.

My right boot pressed deep between the thorny branches and found ground. I tried to support myself on my left leg, but it crumbled as I put my weight on it. I stabbed the tip of my knife through a thick branch and used it to balance myself. More spiny vines closed in upon me as I stood, my right leg seized in a barbed vise.

I looked up at the steep trail above me: its base was no more than four feet away. But four feet of thick, thorny vines: *I'd never make it out.* I stood shivering, although not cold.

Just above me hung birch leaves. Gingerly, wincing against the tearing claws, I reached up, closed my fingers on the closest leaves, and then pulled them gently toward me, hoping that they wouldn't break. The branch that they were on was thin, too weak to support my weight, but not hopeless; the branch above me connected to a thicker branch closer to its trunk. If I could just pull it close enough ...

The thin branch threatened to snap with every inch, but I drew it slowly closer, ignoring the cool, soft leaves that pressed against my face. It didn't matter that I doubted this would work; the thin branch would soon break, but I had no choice. It was this, or lie down and die. I slid Grandfather's knife back into its sheath as soon as the tension above me was strong enough to keep me from falling, and then I used both hands. The thicker branch bent closer.

Finally I touched it, and crawled my fingers spider-like around its top. I pulled on the branch as gently as I could; if it broke now then I'd drop back onto the deadly thorns. Yet it held, and finally I slid both hands up it, toward its trunk, feeling hope as the branch grew thicker under my fingers. I pulled with all of my strength until I felt my weight leave the ground, but my leg was still trapped, caught in a thorny death-grip. I pulled as hard as I could; there was no going back.

The branch held. My trousers ripped, taking much of my skin, which stayed behind with the countless shreds of my tunic; I pulled myself up into the tree and climbed hand over hand toward its trunk. When I hugged the trunk tightly, I started to cry; my left leg was on fire and no part of me felt better.

I slid to the ground, still surrounded by thorns, but these were smaller, thinner, meshed with other bushes. Hopping, I pushed through them easily and fell onto the trail. Sobbing, I started to crawl. Every movement was a nightmare of torment, but I kept going.

In the middle of our fields, torn and bleeding, I shouted again, and Mother and Ingrid ran out and saw me. With their screams in my ears, I surrendered to blackness.

* * * * * * * * *

Incoherent screams awoke me. I thrashed, flinching away from the burning agony even as I recognized that the screams were mine. I couldn't jump; pain wracked my whole body.

"Place your hand firmly on his chest," said a wheezing, familiar voice. "Hold him down, then continue the treatment."

I forced my eyes open. Helsa was leaning over me, looking uncomfortable. Her soft hand gently pressed me back down and then her other hand lowered a wet cloth onto my arm. Her hand, where she touched me, burned like a flaming brand.

"Owww!" I shouted, struggling to flinch again.

"Talk to the boy," said the same voice, which I recognized as Læknir. "Keep him distracted."

Helsa struggled internally, twisting up her face, but finally managed a few words.

"Hello, Thron," she said. "Hold still. I ... I have to clean your wounds."

She slid the cloth up my arm; I jumped so hard that I slammed into the wall.

"Don't slide the cloth over his cuts," Læknir admonished Helsa. "Lift it straight up, then put it back down gently in the next location. Dragging cloths over torn skin tears open wounds."

Helsa obeyed. The wet cloth stung like a hive of hornets, but I only gritted my teeth and growled.

"The water's hot," Ingrid said from a distance, dimly, as if far away.

"Good," Læknir said. "No, Helsa, keep cleaning out the wounds. Without that ale-bath, infection will enter, and then Thron could die. I'll make the chamomile tea."

I opened my eyes. Through blurring tears I spied Mother at the foot of my bed. Behind her stood Ingrid, who looked worried, and something more, but I couldn't make it out clearly. Helsa pressed the alcohol-soaked cloth against my wrist.

"Keep talking, Helsa," Læknir said.

Helsa frowned as if disgusted. "So ..., Thron, uh. ... how are ... uh..."

"Ask how he got injured," Læknir suggested.

"Oh," Helsa said, stammering as if it were very difficult to talk. "Uh, how ... did you get ... how did this happen?"

The burning cloth scalded my shoulder. The last thing that I needed was conversation.

"Answer her, Thron," Læknir ordered.

Through clenched teeth I let out a long hiss, then spat a few words.

"Fell. Cliff. Loose rocks."

"Keep him talking," said a strange voice. "Lie still, Thron, or we'll have to tie you down."

Someone patted the fire-cloth down my chest.

"Why were you climbing a ...?" Helsa's voice asked.

My mind reeled, my fists clenching and shaking, breaths coming in explosive gasps. Awareness grew; the room was spinning, voices strangely muted, as if echoing through thick walls. My sight blurred, focused suddenly, and then went black. A wracked throbbing was coming from my leg: I was hurt more than I'd realized.

The burning rag slowly dabbed down my left ribs, across my stomach, and back up the right side. Slowly I became aware that Mother had moved up to the head of my bed and was holding me down with both hands.

"The tea's ready," Læknir said finally, "Hold off and make him drink this. He'll need to be fully drugged before I start to work on his leg."

Hands lifted me and a hot wooden cup was pressed to my mouth. It was very hot, almost burning, and I coughed out the first mouthful.

"Drink, Thron," Mother ordered, and they poured.

I drank, hating it, but too tired to resist. I gulped, certain that it was burning my mouth, but unable to think anymore. The chamomile tasted thick, strong, more like gravy than tea.

As the single, distant point of light expanded to reveal my house, a burning incinerated the sole of my left foot, although

I knew there was no fire. I writhed, but Mother held me firmly.

"I need to roll him over," Helsa said.

"Finish this side first," Læknir said.

"But ...!" Helsa hesitated.

"You're a healer," Læknir said determinedly. "Such matters mean nothing to you."

Helsa took a deep breath.

Fire exploded on my most sensitive parts. I jumped up and pushed her hand away, overwhelmed by searing pain as I moved, but far more shocked to discover that I'd been lying naked on top of my covers all this time ... watched and tended by all four women.

"Control your patient!" Læknir shouted. "Talk to him. Don't let him move."

Helsa fumbled and Mother struggled, but suddenly a strong weight stiff-armed me in the chest and slammed me flat.

"Stay where you are!" Læknir shouted, leaning over my face and commanding me. "You're hurt, and wounds need to be tended. Lay still, or I'll make it worse!"

I fell back, agonized, sick, embarrassed, and humiliated. I wanted to fight, but something in Læknir's voice struck deeper than the rents in my flesh, and I was too weak to resist.

"Finish quickly, Helsa."

The alcohol burned into places where no cuts should ever be. An eternity later it was over, and someone's voice ordered me to roll over. Crying, I flopped face-down onto my pillow, exposing my naked backside to the torturous burning cloth and the stares of the women.

* * * * * * * * *

Chapter 17

*   *   *   *   *   *   *   *   *

"Oh, my poor baby!"

I tried to push Mother away, but through the dim fog I realized that it wasn't Mother. Ingrid was holding my head, lifting it off my pillow. *It hurt.*

"That horrible girl!" Ingrid hissed. "*Touching your ...! As if she ...!"*

The door opened, and Ingrid dropped my head; my crash onto my pillow was like another fall from the cliff. My throbbing swayed as dizziness swelled.

"I think he's waking up," Ingrid announced.

"Thron?" Mother's voice called from far away.

Someone else was standing there where Ingrid had been.

"Mothe...?"

"Don't talk. Læknir said that you'll only heal if you get lots of rest."

A cool hand pressed against my forehead. *It hurt.*

Everything hurt. I felt weaker than I'd ever imagined possible. I tried to lift my hand to brush the hair from my eyes, but my arm laid limp by my side and didn't even twitch.

"What were you thinking? Climbing cliffs all by yourself; you could've been killed. If I hadn't found you lying in the field then you'd have died."

I focused my eyes on our rafters, trying to clear my brain. *Mother found me?* What about my long crawl home? It was thanks to me that I wasn't dead! But something held me back from mentioning it; it wouldn't improve anything.

A cup of warm tea was held to my lips and a hand cupped the back of my head, tilting me forward. It wasn't very hot so I drank, but the tea was strangely bitter, and when I coughed the cup vanished.

"What - what's wrong with me?" I gasped.

"You sliced open your leg," Mother's voice said. "There's a lump on your head; you may have cracked your skull. You've more cuts than a diced turnip. You're lucky to be alive."

The thick tea was vile, but I was too weak to spit it out. Mother's face was grim, hard-set, as if she were trying to hide her worry. Ingrid's face momentarily appeared behind her, looking closely at me, her eyes flaring, her lips stretched anxiously thin.

Days passed like an unpleasant dream, foggy, floating, and incoherent. At times my leg ached terribly, at other times it felt numb. I was inexplicably sleepy, and every candle-flame blinded me. Noises were especially confusing; most sounded distant, some seemed to echo, and some tiny noises blasted loudly in my ears. Mother's chair, as it creaked under her weight, seemed to shake our whole house. The *clack-clack* of her loom thundered.

The horrible tea made me gag; my stomach churned with each swallow. My refusals were met with fierce determination to fill me with the despicable brew. The slightest effort drained me, and then fog cloaked everything until the universe became a rancid taste that made me want to vomit.

Father! Father would save me! In my mind, I saw him; a big bag of silver in one hand, his bloody sword clenched in the other, terrified Saxons fleeing before him, and countless bodies of warriors strewn around him. Sobbing women begged him to spare their lives, offering food, wealth, even their naked bodies, if only he'd let them live. Men jumped to get out of his way and then cowered in his wake. Branwulf consulted him constantly, knowing how many times he'd saved their whole ship.

* * * * * * * * *

My innumerable cuts scabbed over, and every movement pulled, tore, and broke them, making blood flow. Mother and Ingrid changed my blankets and the straw underneath: both were black with blood.

Læknir and Helsa arrived shortly before our midday meal. Mother greeted them exuberantly, praising their efforts on my behalf.

"Thron's very lucky," Læknir replied. "I've seen similar accidents go badly. But let me inspect his wounds; there's still a chance of infection despite the poultice of minced dandelion leaves."

Læknir reached down and grabbed my blanket. I seized it quickly, self-consciously; I was still naked under my blanket.

"I have to inspect you, Thron," Læknir said firmly, her tone allowing no challenge. "I'm sorry for your modesty, but

I'm a healer. Close your eyes."

I glared at her.

"Close your eyes," she repeated sternly.

If I fought, then I'd pass out; grimacing, I closed my eyes. The weight of my blanket lifted. I blushed as if I could feel the staring eyes of all four women.

Læknir's fingers prodded and probed, lifting my arms one at a time, examining every scratch. Then she moved lower, actually touching my manhood, lifting it and examining it on all sides.

I wanted to die. *Every boy in the village would laugh at me when they heard about this!* And to make it worse, Helsa, Ingrid, and Mother were watching! I prayed that death would take me. Things couldn't get worse!

"Helsa, come look at this," Læknir said, still holding my manhood.

'Hel, take me now!' It was blasphemy; warriors called for Odin or the Valkyrie to take them in battle, not to die in a bed with an old woman holding onto your most-important limb. Father would chastise me, if he knew.

"See this scratch, high inside the thigh? Touch it."

I squirmed, fighting to stay still. *Helsa touch me? There?*

Fingers pressed against me.

"Press firmly. Feel the blood pulsing?"

"Yes," Helsa's weak voice said.

"That scratch is right over a big blood vessel," Læknir said. "If there're any evil vapors in his blood, that's the first place that it'll show. You'll have to watch that scratch closely. If infection sets in, it's best to know of it as soon as possible."

I pried open one eye, then quickly shut it. My quick glimpse showed Læknir, stern and imperious, her white, lined face devoid of emotion as she held my delicateness, but Helsa was blushing almost scarlet, leaning over my naked body, her face full of emotion, looking as uncomfortable as I. As she leaned forward, the wide neckline of her dress draped open; my eye instinctively glanced at her slightly-exposed chest even though I could see only a little pale skin. I closed my eyes instantly; Mother and Ingrid were standing at the foot of my bed, watching intently. Having all four of the women watch me lay naked before them was bad enough; I didn't want them watching as I stared inside Helsa's blouse.

Not soon enough, Læknir instructed me to roll over. Moving hurt, but I rolled gladly. Then I got the same treatment as before, poking and prodding, with special attention to my left leg. Twisting slightly to look as they lifted off the bandage, I saw a long gash across the back of my calf just below the knee. It was thick with heavily-crusted blood: that explained why my leg hurt so much.

"We need to clean that out," Læknir said. "Helsa, soften it with rags soaked in hot water."

"Ingr...," Mother started.

"I'll put the pot on," Ingrid interrupted.

Læknir stood up and wiped her hands on a towel tucked into her apron.

"Soaking will take a while," she said.

"Would you care for some tea?" Mother asked.

"That would be delightful," Læknir smiled.

"Ingr..."

"On the way," Ingrid said.

"Your turnips seem to be growing well," Læknir said.

"Yes, the weather's been perfect," Mother replied. "My herb garden is especially beautiful this year."

"May I see it?"

"Of course."

I heard the door open and the older women exited, chatting politely as they went. I was glad that they'd left; now only two girls were staring at my naked backside. They didn't really count; Helsa used to go swimming with Garad and I at the swimming hole, and Ingrid ..., well, Ingrid could look at me in any way that she wanted.

I glanced at my calf again. The gash was horribly long and deep; it would probably leave a wicked scar. Kal's father Kampi had lots of great scars from his vikings; I'd always hoped to have a few scars like his.

Ingrid hung the small pot over our fire, and then sat rigidly before it, poking the logs with our blackened fire-stick. Helsa stood by the door, examining Mother's embroidered cloak hanging on its peg. Only their stiff backs faced each other.

I looked away, trying not to make a sound; better to be trapped by a thousand thorn bushes than stuck between two fighting girls. Fortunately, it couldn't last much longer.

"...a lovely idea," Læknir said as she and Mother came back inside. "We'd love to have lunch with you."

* * * * * * * * *

Læknir sat in Father's chair. Mother sat in her chair. I sat on my bed, covered from the waist down with a blanket: *a sadly small compensation.* Læknir had personally cleaned up my leg wound; I wasn't as hurt as they'd pretended.

Ingrid pulled thick beaver slices off the spit, divided them into five trenchers, each beside a wide wedge of white cheese and a hearty slice of black bread. She started to hand each out in turn, the first to Læknir, the second to Mother, and the third to me.

"Ingrid!" Mother scolded. "Serve our guests first!"

Only I saw the thin smile momentarily upturn Ingrid's lips. I glanced down at the plate that she held: it was the worst piece of meat, mostly gristle and fat, the thinnest wedge of cheese, and the smallest piece of bread. As her expression went void, Ingrid turned and presented it to Helsa.

"Why, this is delicious," Læknir said after her first bite.

"Thron caught it," Mother smiled brightly. "He's been trapping all summer, bringing home plenty of meat."

"I noticed the pelts curing outside," Læknir said, and she turned to me. "Very commendable."

I blanched at her complement.

"Ingrid is curing the pelts," I said quickly.

"Yes, but you brought them home," Mother instantly countered, then she turned back to Læknir. "Thron's modest, but he's a good farmer, and now a trapper as well. He began trapping on his own with no prompting; I have high hopes for him."

"As you should," Læknir replied. "It's rare and wonderful for a young man to show such early promise."

I took a bite of cheese, desperately wanting to change the subject.

"Next year I'll go viking," I said.

"Why would you want to go viking?" Læknir asked as if the very thought were appalling. "You've a fine farm, a new skill for trapping; you don't need to steal other people's wealth."

I gaped dumbfounded. *Not go viking?* It was the most horrible idea that I'd ever heard!

"Ah, these terrible times!" Læknir said. "All the boys want to go viking. Their fathers train them to want it, teach them to fight, and prepare them all of their lives. Small wonder why there're so few husbands available.

"When will it end? Men could earn more by tending their farms, not to mention their wives. More real sons and fewer bastards; that's what we need."

"Praise Freyja!" Mother agreed. "Men with sense: every year they throw their lives to the wind for a few trinkets."

"Stories to tell in the tavern; that's all that they care about," Læknir said. "As if bravery was the measure of manhood."

"Leaving their wives and children defenseless," Mother said.

"Drinking and whoring in foreign lands," Læknir said.

"Not just in foreign lands," Mother said.

Læknir stiffened and a moment of silence fell. I wished that I could crawl away unnoticed. Women think strangely; Mother's reference to Father mating with Grettir had stopped their tirade, but it wouldn't last. Farms are boring! Tales of the vikings: those are exciting!

"Vikings ruin good men," Læknir said finally. "Off on their own, living like beasts, no women to keep them civilized ... it's amazing that they don't come back with horns and tails!"

All of the women laughed, even Helsa and Ingrid, but Mother laughed the loudest.

"Wealth makes life easier, but gold can't buy wise, healthy sons," Læknir said. "Only wise sons can make strong families."

"And it takes wise daughters to train sons right," Mother said. "Helsa here; she's a beautiful young girl, *don't you think so, Thron?"*

"Uh ...," I fumbled, caught off-guard. *What was I to say?* Helsa, Ingrid, Mother, and Læknir all looked at me.

"Sure," I said noncommittally.

"You see?" Mother said to Læknir. "And Helsa is learning

healing; she'll make a strong, wise mother. You want to have a big family, don't you, Helsa?"

"Oh ... of ... of course," Helsa stammered.

"Big families require a lot of turnips," Mother warned Helsa.

Mother's words bent a shackle about to be riveted around my neck. *I was being trained!* I cast about desperately: I had to do something!

"Friar James taught me to make the traps!"

* * * * * * * * *

Clamsby's sword rattled against the side of Læknir's carriage. I tried to avoid his eyes; Clamsby stared distrustfully at me. From inside of the carriage, I caught occasional snatches of garbled conversation between Mother and Læknir, barely heard over the clop of the horse's hoofsteps. I knew what they were all thinking; I'd sent all of the men in our village out after imaginary thieves in the woods. Only Læknir's insistence had forced Clamsby out of his hall so early in the morning.

Finding Friar James' place from an unfamiliar direction was unlikely. *What if I couldn't find him?*

Just as our wheels splashed through another small stream, Clamsby slowed and halted the powerful horses. I started to speak but was silenced by a gesture; Clamsby was barely breathing, and the conversation inside the carriage had ceased.

"Is this the stream that he lives by?" Clamsby's deep voice growled.

"It could be," I mumbled.

"Are we there?" Læknir asked from within.

"I think so," Clamsby said, and I looked at him questioningly. "Smell."

I sniffed, but detected nothing unusual.

"Watch the hills," Clamsby said, and we both did.

"There," he pointed. "Just over that hill: smoke." He sniffed again. "I smell heady oils: cooked meat."

Clamsby climbed down off the carriage. I tried unsuccessfully to scramble down with my bad leg; his strong hands lifted me off. Mother and Læknir peered at us from the carriage window.

"Scream loud if you see anyone appear," Clamsby said to them. "Don't wait until they're close."

"Thank you for your concern," Læknir said.

Clamsby walked toward the woods. Mother and Læknir looked apprehensive; neither had really believed me. I followed Clamsby, my wounded leg limping worse than his.

With his sword, Clamsby hacked a wall of dead evergreen branches out of our way. I drew my sword, tiny compared to his, but I had nothing to do but stand by while he plowed a path big enough for him. The terrain forced us to turn right, then right again, and finally Clamsby chopped aside more branches, then turned to look at me.

"Chop down the bushes behind us; we still have to come back this way."

Suddenly he swiped at the tree, slicing away enough bark to display a bright bare spot.

"Make marks like this on the trees so that we can find this path again. And Thron: you did good this time."

I'd done good: Clamsby said so!

Most of the trails that we found were deer trails, narrow, but easy to push through. Soon Clamsby ordered me to walk ahead and call out for the stranger.

"Friar James!" I shouted, leading the way up the hill. The smell of cooking was so thick that the air tasted good.

"Thron ...!" Friar James shouted, and I followed the sound of his voice.

"What happened to you?" Friar James gasped as he saw me covered with scratches, my leg splinted. A moment later, he saw movement behind me.

"God help me!"

"No!" I shouted as Friar James turned to run. "No one's going to hurt you! This is Clamsby, our Tavern Master."

Friar James glared horrified as Clamsby strode forward, his heavy sword naked. The two stared silently at each other.

"No one's going to hurt you," I promised.

"Thron, what have you done?" Friar James' face was ashen.

"What he should have long ago," Clamsby growled. "Thron, douse that fire and make sure it's out. Use water from the stream. Stranger, come with me."

Friar James touched his forehead, chest, and shoulders.

* * * * * * * * *

Chapter 18

* * * * * * * * *

Looking terrified, Friar James wouldn't let me walk beside him, turning away every time that I tried. Clamsby's sharp sword didn't ease the situation. I didn't know what to make of Friar James; *a grown man ... scared like a rabbit?*

Like Clamsby, I kept my sword naked in my hand; I didn't need it, but I didn't want to look childish.

As we approached, Lælknir and Mother climbed out, but they waited for us beside the carriage as we pushed through the tall grass. I didn't know what was going to happen. Father had told me stories of Clamsby before he was wounded, claiming that he killed Saxons and Irishmen so fast that they never had time to scream. *What would I do if Clamsby decided to kill Friar James?*

Friar James stopped before he reached the road and bowed deeply before Mother and Lælknir. They stood looking at each other. *Why do adults do everything so slow?*

"You're Friar James?" Læknir asked finally.

"I am," he replied meekly.

"According to Thron, you washed up on the shore near here?"

"Yes," he pointed toward the sea. "Right over there."

"And you made yourself at home in our woods?"

"I didn't intend to trespass."

Læknir frowned and fell silent. Everyone looked at each other; eyes furtively darted back and forth. These weren't really our woods; they belonged to Branwulf. *Why would anyone care if a castaway built a refuge in it?*

"You told Thron not to tell us about you."

"Your people threw me overboard ... sacrificed to your sea god."

"His name is Njord." I interjected, but Mother shushed me.

"No one blames you for caution," Læknir said to Friar James. "Thrown overboard in the middle of a storm; it must have been dreadful."

"It was a miracle that I survived."

"But we can't allow strangers to live near us unless we know that they're safe."

"I'm a friar."

"Do you mean that you're a monk?"

"No, monks are ..., well yes. The difference between us is minor."

"Vikings have razed your homes, churches, and killed your people. Are we to believe that you want no revenge?"

"Vengeance is the province of God. We're teachers, missionaries ..."

"What does that mean?"

"Catholic means everybody," Friar James said. "Not just

vik .. I mean, not just Norwegians, but Saxons, Normans, Irishmen, and Germans. Everyone. We believe that all men are brothers, equals under God. We're a faith of peace. That's why I was sent here; to preach our faith to your people."

"Your *'men of peace'* kill plenty of Norsemen," Clamsby snarled.

"Even men of peace must defend themselves," Friar James said.

Clamsby scowled, but Læknir ignored him.

"Peace," Læknir said slowly, as if it were a strange word. "You mean ... you came here ... hoping to end the vikings?"

"Yes," Friar James said.

Clamsby snorted hard, startling Friar James, but he said nothing else. Clamsby's eyes flickered on me for a single moment; Clamsby wasn't impressed with Friar James and his talk of peace. But after an uncomfortable moment, Læknir turned and looked at Mother with a thin-lipped smile so plain that it horrified me. Friar James was useful to her, a tool that she could use to end the raids, to keep me trapped on our farm, to never to go viking at all.

I snorted as Clamsby had. I was nowhere as loud or deep as the Tavern Master's, and no one startled, but instantly Mother shot me a murderous glare. Then I glanced at Clamsby; he gave me the faintest nod.

"Thron says that you can read and write," Læknir said. "Is this true?"

"Yes."

"Could you teach others?"

"Oh, yes. That's part of why I came to Sweden ... I mean, Norway."

Clamsby frowned deeply, and so did I. Læknir was

speaking more freely now. Friar James wouldn't be hurt, but I never expected this; for them to plot together to keep me from viking.

"You can't stay here, a stranger, living wild so close to our village," Læknir said. "I have an empty house that you could use right next to Clamsby's, where he can keep an eye on you. Any thefts, threats, or violence against any of our people will be the death of you."

"I would never ...!"

"See that you don't. Even rumors of foul deeds mustn't follow you. All our men will be watching."

"I understand completely."

I went to pet the horses; their decision had already been made. It was even the decision that I'd hoped that they'd reach; I'd be credited for finding him, which would clear up the doubts that people had of my stories, and Friar James would be welcomed in our village.

But it didn't feel like a victory.

* * * * * * * * *

"Come with me, Thron," Clamsby said brusquely.

"Sir!" Friar James spoke directly to Clamsby.

Clamsby glared at Friar James, who was standing inside the doorway of Rath's old house.

"I ... will ... earn your trust," Friar James promised.

Clamsby held him in a silent gaze, then repeated:

"Come with me, Thron."

We walked toward Tavern Hall. Clamsby led, stomping his boots unusually hard. I hoped that he wasn't angry with me for finding Friar James.

"Thron!" Mother called. "Stay around town. Læknir and I

are going up to her house. We'll meet you inside Tavern Hall at dusk. Don't get into trouble."

Mother climbed up onto the driver's bench and shook the reins. The horses tugged the carriage forward and Læknir waved at me from the carriage window. I couldn't believe it: *Mother knew how to drive a carriage?*

"Thron!" Clamsby ordered.

Inside Tavern Hall, two large chairs sat directly before the fireplace, a small table snugged between them. Clamsby headed straight for the table, snatched up two empty mugs, and hurried behind his bar to fill them.

"Thank you, dear," said a thin, wheezy voice from the closest chair. "Did you find the friar?"

"Yes, exactly where Thron said he was," Clamsby answered. "Læknir put him up in Rath's house."

"I see," said the voice. "Where's this boy?"

"Right here," Clamsby said.

"Bring him around."

The bottom of my stomach felt queasy, as if it were about to drop out of my body, but Clamsby waved me forward. My eyes widened as I saw the occupants of the two chairs: Old man Ranglátr and Widow Væna, the oldest and most respected of our village elders.

"You are Thron, son of Thorir, son of Thrinn?" Widow Væna asked.

I swallowed hard, then nodded.

"Don't be afraid," Old man Ranglátr smiled. "We've known Thorir and Vespa since they were born."

They were the strangest-looking pair: both had bizarre, wiry hair colored like mushy snow mixed with fireplace ash. Their skin, wrinkled like rotten turnips, hung from their faces like their skulls were too small. Skin dangled loose under their chins and jiggled when they spoke; terrifying to see. Few people lived to be forty, but rumors said that these two had sealed dark pacts with Loki and Hel. *How else could they be over seventy and still alive?* They only had a few teeth in their mouths; *could that have been part of their bargain, like when Odin had torn out one of his eyes to throw into the Well of Mimir?*

Like all of the other children, I'd always avoided the elders. Adults spoke respectfully about them, but children could see through that: whenever the adults looked at them, a fear or jealousy made their voices quaver; it could only be magic. *Perhaps I should ask Ingrid ...*

"Tell us about this friar," Widow Væna said.

I stood there, afraid to say anything.

"Speak!" Clamsby ordered.

"Boy, start at the beginning," Old man Ranglátr said. "How did you meet him?"

"I ... I saw smoke," I stammered.

"Good. Then what?"

"I went to ... investigate."

"Keep going."

"I ... knew that I shouldn't, but ..."

"More *'thieves in the woods'?"*

"Yes."

"Understandable: no one wants to be called a liar twice."

"Why did you claim that there were thieves in the first place?" Widow Væna asked.

"Father ... and ... Grettir," I confessed.

"You knew?" she asked.

"We tried to stop them."

"We?"

I suddenly realized that I'd said too much.

"Garad and I," I lied, leaving Ingrid out of it.

Clamsby snorted in disgust, and Widow Væna and Old man Ranglátr exchanged glances.

"Quite impressive, actually, that you were able to pull it off," Old man Ranglátr said. "But we're not here to discuss your parent's infidelity. Tell us everything that you know about Friar James."

I spoke quickly, hoping to be dismissed. I told them about his hut, his traps, and his stories.

"And now he's in the village," Old man Ranglátr said. "Do you know what he wants to do, now that he's here?"

"He wants to tell his stories," I answered. "He wants us to believe in his sky-god."

"Why did Læknir bring him back to the village?"

"She wants to end the vikings," Clamsby interjected.

"Læknir," Widow Væna spoke her name with disgust. "She should've consulted us. She assumes too much ... she hopes to replace us."

"Someone has to, eventually," Old man Ranglátr said. "Who else can? Clamsby?"

"Læknir would refuse to treat anyone who drank here," Clamsby grumbled.

"Once Helsa's trained ...," Old man Ranglátr started.

"Thank you for telling us this, Thron," Widow Væna interrupted the men. "You've done very well. You can go now."

Needing no further prompting, I limped toward the door. For the first time, Tavern Hall was so stuffy that I thought I'd suffocate.

"Thron!" Clamsby shouted.

Fearfully I looked back.

"You've earned yourself another free ale," Clamsby said.

"Come and collect it soon. But don't think that I'll tolerate any more lies!"

I fled out the door.

* * * * * * * * *

"Ingrid!" I hissed as I rapped urgently on the door. "Let me in!"

I heard her remove the brace, then pushed inside, spied Urd asleep on her small new bed, and then glanced behind to make sure that no one had seen me enter. Then I paused to catch my breath.

"Thron ...?"

"I - I'm ... okay," I stammered. "Just ... leg hurts ... w-walked from the village. Took the back trails ... no one saw me."

"What happened?"

"Clamsby caught Friar James. Læknir put him up in Rath's old house. Then Clamsby drug me into Tavern Hall, and guess who was there? Widow Væna and Old man Ranglátr! They asked me about Friar James."

"What'd you tell them?"

"Everything. I don't think ... that they liked him, and the way that they ... spoke about Læknir ...!"

"Do you blame them?" Ingrid asked. "Widow Væna and Old man Ranglátr have been running our village for generations, and now Læknir's making decisions."

Ingrid stared at me as if I was supposed to understand this.

"Never mind," she said. "Then what?"

"Then ... nothing," I said. "I was alone in the village, wondering where I should go ... and I came here."

"Where's Vespa?"

"Drove Læknir home. She told me to stay around the village."

"So you came here?" Ingrid asked. "You could've gone anywhere ... and you came home?"

I hesitated, unsure; I hadn't thought about it. I could've gone to visit any of the other kids, Derek, Kal, or Halgrum – no, Halgrum went viking. Actually, the thought of visiting Derek or Kal wasn't very exciting.

"Move," Ingrid said, and she held up the brace.

Quizzically I moved aside. Ingrid set the brace on the door, barring it shut. Then she turned to me.

"You came to see me?"

"Y-yes ..."

"Out of everyone in the village ... you wanted to see me?"

"Of course."

"Then ... I guess I ... should let you see me."

Slowly Ingrid reached down and grabbed her skirt. In one steady motion, she lifted it up high, until it slid clean off her. Naked, she threw her dress over Mother's chair.

Ingrid was as beautiful as ever. She grinned as I drank in the sight of her. I hadn't thought of this; *we had all afternoon!* Mother was at Læknir's and would be going to Tavern Hall after that. *Ingrid and I could be alone, together, for hours...!*

Ingrid unbuckled my sword belt and dropped it beside us, then carefully lifted off my tunic. She never spoke a word, and I said nothing, afraid to break the delicate moment. Did she want to see all my scratches again? My bandage?

Hands fell on my trousers, untied its string, and then pulled them down. I felt a little uncertain; we dressed in front of each other every day. She'd stared at me after my accident. *Why did Ingrid want me naked?*

Ingrid pulled back my blanket and gently pushed me onto

my bed. Then she climbed atop and sat upon me, her knees straddling my chest. I didn't know what she was doing, but I didn't want it to stop; *the touch of her skin flamed my desires!* I floated in a dreamy fog, my heart pounding, my mouth dry, my breathing rapid.

"I belong to Vespa no more," Ingrid said softly, lowly, almost a whisper. "*Now I belong to you, my beautiful Thron ...!*"

* * * * * * * * *

Chapter 19

* * * * * * * * *

The whole village gathered at Tavern Hall. Widow Væna and Old man Ranglátr sat at the biggest table with several other elders, including Læknir. Room for several more chairs sat around the table, but no one dared assume a seat beside the elders. Even Mother stood, although looking very pleased. Clamsby was laughing and pouring ales as fast as he could. The roar of voices drowned out anyone not speaking directly into your ear; but they might as well have been chickens clucking around a feed-pail as I pushed through the door and strutted inside.

Never in my life had I understood what it meant to be a man, what it felt like, how it washed over you like a mighty wave. I was washed clean of childishness, scrubbed of immaturity: *Ingrid had made me a man!*

"Hey, where've you been?" Derek pushed through the crowd.

I smiled but didn't respond. I looked at Derek's bloated, boyish face; Derek was still taller than I, but not by much. I wondered if I could out-wrestle him, once I'd healed.

"You know this friar-guy?"

"I found him," I said proudly.

"So?" Derek demanded. "What's his story? Everybody's talking about him."

Suddenly Helsa came around Derek. Our eyes met and she quickly blushed and looked down.

"Hello, Helsa," I said.

"Hello. How are your ... how is your ... your leg?"

"Much better."

Derek glanced back and forth at us.

"What?" he demanded.

Neither of us spoke. I certainly didn't want to tell him that Helsa had touched me in places where no one touched each other. Well, actually, people did touch each other there: *Ingrid had touched me in all those places!*

"Helsa fixed my leg after I was injured," I said.

"Yea, I heard about that," Derek laughed. "You fell off a cliff!"

"The cliff-face crumbled while I was climbing it," I corrected him. "I was checking my traps. Did you hear about them? We've been eating nothing but beaver, ferret, and rabbit."

As I'd hoped, Derek's smile vanished. But then I looked at Helsa; she was looking straight at me, her eyes wide with surprise.

"Excuse me," Helsa said abruptly, and she pushed into the crowd.

"Trapping ...?" Derek asked after she left, but there was a definite disappointment in his voice.

"You should see the pelts," I bragged. "I've seven so far, and hope to have more soon. Three are cured and off their stretchers. I haven't gotten a deer yet, but I expect one soon."

Derek looked as if he'd eaten something foul.

"Never mind about that," he said. "What about this friar?"

Suddenly Mother appeared behind Derek.

"Thron, run next door and get Friar James," Mother said.

"Okay," I said, and I started to turn away, then I hesitated. "Derek, you want to come with me?"

"Let's go!" he said.

More people arrived, forcing their way into the crowded hall through the narrow door, but Derek and I pushed outside into the darkness. No stars shone tonight, only the glow of the hidden moon illuminating thick clouds, but our path was easy to see.

"Friar James! It's Thron!"

The door opened and Friar James smiled widely.

"Thron! My old friend! I can't thank you enough!"

Friar James grabbed and shook my hand. I hardly recognized him; he was wearing a new green-and-gray striped tunic and looked cleaner than I'd ever seen him.

"Læknir and your mother have been so kind to me! You were right all along; I should've trusted you the day that we met!"

"Mother told me to bring you ..."

"Yes, I know. Who's your friend?"

"Derek."

"Glad to meet you, son!" Friar James grabbed and shook Derek's hand. "Well, shall we go? We'd best not keep them waiting!"

Friar James motioned for us to precede him, which we did. But, as we entered Tavern hall, a loud crash hammered three times. The room fell instantly silent and all eyes turned to us.

Derek and I stood there, too shocked to move, and then Friar James' hands descended onto our shoulders and pushed us apart. Between us, Friar James walked into Tavern Hall before the eyes of the whole village, and suddenly he bowed.

"Friar James!" Læknir said, her weak, raspy voice filling the silent hall. "Come forward."

Friar James bowed again, and as he took his first step forward, the crowd parted, leaving an aisle for him alone. He walked slowly, his back straight, right up to their table. Læknir stood up as he approached, but none of the others did. As he reached the table, he stopped and bowed again.

"This is Friar James," Læknir said to the other elders, as loudly as she could. "He is a monk from England washed up on our shore. He wishes to remain in the village."

Friar James bowed again, and Læknir proceeded to introduce everyone at the table, but her frail voice faded as the aisle closed, people moving closer to hear.

Derek and I exchanged glances. Both of us wanted to push through the crowd, to get close enough to hear, but no adults would let us move in front of them. Personally, I wondered if I'd be missed if I slipped out the door and hurried back to Ingrid.

I could still feel, taste, and smell her. Ingrid was all that I could think about, an all-encompassing excitement muted by an unexpected, surreal calm. Just thinking about Ingrid deepened my breaths, yet I dared not open the door; everyone would notice. So I stood there, beside Derek, wondering what was being said.

"Thron!" Mother called my name, and people turned to look expectantly at me.

Taken by surprise, I didn't know what to do.

"Go!" Derek whispered.

Swallowing hard, I took a step forward, then another, and suddenly people moved aside for me. I approached Friar James. He patted my shoulder as I reached him, then faced the table.

"Thron, son of Thorir, you found Friar James by yourself, living alone in the woods," Læknir said. "Is that true?"

"Yes."

"He taught you how to make traps, a very useful skill that has served your family well," Læknir continued. "Is that true?"

"Yes."

"Friar James never hurt or threatened you, and your recent injuries weren't caused by him, were they?"

"Uh ..., no."

Læknir smiled. I momentarily hoped that my part was over and I could escape back to where Derek and I'd been, when suddenly Old man Ranglátr spoke up.

"That cliff that you fell from," Old man Ranglátr said loudly, "was that the first time that you ever climbed that particular cliff?"

"No."

"You climbed that cliff before? Many times?"

"Yes."

"You climbed that cliff even before you met Friar James, and never once fell before this recent incident?"

"Yes."

"Well ...?" Old man Ranglátr demanded. "Did it never occur to you why you fell, suddenly, from a cliff that you'd climbed many times? Did you never question why you fell only after meeting Friar James?"

"Uh ..., no."

"But why would that ...?" Læknir began.

"Did Friar James ever tell you stories?" Old man Ranglátr interrupted her.

"Uh, yes."

"Stories about foreign gods? Stories that refute the gods of Norway, the gods of our fathers?"

I fell silent, bewildered. *What was he talking about?* But Old man Ranglátr just went on, his voice rising angrily.

"And you listened, didn't you? You listened to this evil man blaspheme our gods, your gods, and suddenly you fell off a cliff ... and almost got killed! What greater sign were you waiting for?"

I froze, terror-stricken, but Old man Ranglátr kept ranting, focusing his angry red eyes upon me.

"He asked you to lie for him, didn't he? To keep his existence a secret, even from your own mother ...?"

I stared, confused.

"Didn't he?"

"Yes."

"He asked you to lie ... and you did! He taught you to lie, despite all that your father taught you! And you trusted him, this stranger, more than your own father!"

"No!" I shouted back.

"Be silent!" Old man Ranglátr commanded, glaring so angrily that his wrinkled face turned red. "Hold your tongue! You lied to your mother, to everyone, and threatened the safety of our whole village!"

"He's a boy!" Læknir shouted suddenly. "He didn't know ...!"

"You did ...!" Old man Ranglátr shouted at Læknir. "You knew that this foreign monk had poisoned and brought

disaster to this poor boy, and yet you invited him into our village! What will happen now? Will we all fall off cliffs ... or be trampled by horses? Will our crops fail, and winter come early? Will our whole village suffer because you brought this blasphemer into our midst?"

"You can't believe ...!" Læknir argued.

"I can't believe in our gods?" Old man Ranglátr roared. "I can't believe in the gods that have protected our village for generations beyond count, made our crops grow, and given us life and prosperity? You would have me abandon the faith of our fathers, the fathers and the mothers of every man, woman, and child in this village, for this stranger with his tales of a murdered god, who brings lies, poison, and disaster to everyone who listens to him?"

"Sir ...," Friar James began.

"Silence!" Old man Ranglátr bellowed. "How many folk of our peaceful town will you condemn to death?"

"Thron's wounds weren't caused ...!" Læknir insisted.

"How do you know? How can you be sure?"

I trembled; I'd never seen Old man Ranglátr angry before, hadn't even imagined that he could be enraged. I'd never heard him shout.

A nervous quiet fell over the hall. I almost felt the echoes of Old man Ranglátr's rant echo off the silent walls. Læknir looked horrified; Friar James was as white as a freshly-bleached sheet.

"This is madness ...!" Læknir said flatly.

"Enough," Widow Væna said, and she gestured for Old man Ranglátr to sit down. Then Widow Væna addressed Læknir. "You brought this stranger among us with no council save your own. You brought him into this village with only your unproven belief that he bore no danger to our people.

Have we not suffered enough? How could you bring this risk upon all of us?"

"I spoke to him before I brought him here," Læknir defended. "In front of Clamsby, I questioned him very thoroughly."

"And you believed him, despite that you knew that he'd instructed Thron to lie?" Old man Ranglátr asked.

"Every stranger is a threat," Widow Væna said. "You're very learned, Læknir, and I'd turn to no other to identify an illness, but surely an experienced warrior like Clamsby has more experience identifying enemies. Neither his presence nor his opinion seems to have affected your decision to bring this English monk into our village. Nor is it wise to tempt the anger of the gods by inviting with open arms one who openly speaks against them."

"Please ...!" Friar James interrupted. "I don't wish to stay where I'm not welcomed. I didn't intend to intrude. I will leave at once, if you want me gone."

"The damage has been done," Old man Ranglátr growled. "Those sailors lived because they wisely sacrificed you before their ship was lost. We can do no less."

I glanced up at him, wondering what he meant.

"This monk must die!"

Suddenly the room filled with one voice, a single loud, piercing cry; I was just as shocked as everyone else to discover that the lone cry had come from my mouth.

Tavern Hall fell silent as all eyes locked upon me. I didn't know what to do or say. An hour before, I'd felt so strong in Ingrid's arms, so powerful and determined; now I felt like a dead leaf blown helplessly about by every little wind. I wished that I was back in Ingrid's arms, but I stood self-conscious, every eye staring at me.

Unable to speak, I stepped forward toward the table, licked one finger, and drew a rune on the table's surface.

"That's a 'thorn'," I said, making the mark, and then I made another. "That's an "R". Then I drew a circle. "That's an 'O'." then I finished. "That's an 'N'. That's my name, right there. Thron. My name.

"Friar James taught me that. He taught me to make traps. He tells strange stories and talks to the sky ... and he doesn't like the vikings ... and that's crazy. But he's not an enemy. He ... he's my friend."

* * * * * * * * *

'This monk must die!'

While the adults argued, those words haunted my ears. I barely listened, and finally pushed back through the crowd, back to Derek. Derek looked at me with a furtive grin.

"You told them! You showed them all!"

I stood shaking, trembling, as if I'd just fallen off that crumbling cliff and landed on even sharper thorns. *Would they really kill Friar James? I'd betrayed him, promised that they wouldn't harm him ... this was my fault!*

I pushed past Derek and out the door; I didn't care if anyone noticed. It was dark outside, quiet, and suddenly I doubled over and vomited.

Long I stood there, purging, able to feel only my stomach churning, my head pounding ... and then ... *soft hands.*

Soft hands held me as I puked. They kept me from falling over. When I stood up, shock and surprise almost made me jump; Derek wasn't holding me: it was Helsa.

"Are you all right?" she asked.

I spat and wiped my face on my sleeve. I must've nodded

because Helsa nodded back.

"That was very brave, what you just did."

Suddenly Helsa leaned forward and kissed me on the cheek.

"Oh, and thank you ... for what you said earlier."

Helsa turned to leave, but she kept a hold on my arm.

"I have to go back," she said. "Are you sure you'll be all right?"

This time I nodded clearly. Helsa smiled, let go of my arm, and went back inside.

* * * * * * * * *

Friar James was allowed to live.

Mother hugged me twice on the walk back home, chattering praises about me and Læknir, and curses about Old man Ranglátr and Widow Væna. I tried not to listen; some of our chickens made more sense with their clucking than Mother raving about moralities.

Mother breezed inside without pausing or catching her breath. She seemed determined to repeat everything to Ingrid, who looked confused and tried to understand her rapid babbling.

Exhausted, I laid on my bed, wondering if I'd ever sleep again. I should be working on my new wooden bowl set, but I was too tired. So much had happened so fast: Mother, Ingrid, Læknir, Ranglátr, Væna, and Friar James. My head was spinning so hard that it hurt as badly as my leg.

Helsa: *she ... she'd kissed me! What had I said? The part about her being a good healer?* I hadn't really meant that, just said it to keep Derek from knowing where Helsa had touched me.

Helsa had kissed me ...!

*   *   *   *   *   *   *   *   *

Chapter 20

*   *   *   *   *   *   *   *   *

It'd been ages since I'd dreamed of Father's bedtime stories.

"You have one great purpose in life, my son: *impress the Valkyrie!*

"The Valkyrie are the choosers of slain warriors. They're beautiful women warriors, the handmaids of Odin, strong, fierce, and deadly. They wear golden armor and bear silver shields. Over every battlefield they ride, flying magical winged horses. You must learn their names, my son, and pray to them every day. You must learn their secrets and earn their praise; they alone can save your soul.

"The Valkyire hold the greatest gift of all: immortality. They survey each battle and choose, from all who die, the strongest and the bravest, those fierce enough to join them in glorious Valhalla.

"Valhalla is the only paradise for men like us, Thron.

Your grandfather, and mine, are there, waiting for us to join them. I'll go there, when my time comes, and I want you there with me, when it's your time, and all of your sons after you. You must train your sons, as I'll train you, as my father trained me, going back to the time when we were giants. Train your sons to know each Valkyrie by name, train them so well that their last breaths shall be a shout to one of the Valkyrie. Train your sons to die gloriously.

"Never forget this, Thron; it's the most important lesson that I'll ever teach you: *nothing is as important as getting into Valhalla!* Not your mother, not this farm, not anything. All the men of our family go to Valhalla. We'll stand together in the final battle under Odin's banner, and buy our immortality with the heads of our enemies!

"Be strong, my boy! Be fierce, and we'll be together forever!"

* * * * * * * * *

"I'm back," I grumbled, setting down both buckets of fresh seawater and rubbing my sore arms. I liked the pelts; Mother was sewing a rabbit skin onto the collar of a new tunic while Ingrid washed dishes. I needed the new tunic; the sleeves of my old one were halfway to my elbows.

"T'on!" Urd cried, giggling, and she ran toward me, almost fell over, then grabbed my mostly-healed leg, which made me flinch.

"You should begin harvesting today," Mother said. "The turnips are almost ripe, and you need to start early, if you want to finish on time."

"I was going out to set my traps today," I complained, picking up Urd and swinging her, which always made her laugh.

"Not on that leg," Mother said. "What if you fell again and hurt the other?"

"I'll be all right."

"No, start harvest."

"I'm the man!"

Mother froze, and Ingrid startled so badly that she almost dropped a dish. I set Urd onto my bed.

"I'm your mother!"

"I'm the man of the house," I repeated, but my voice wasn't as strong as I'd meant it to be.

"Then prove it," Mother said. "Do what needs to be done. Your father never waited."

"Father never started this early."

"Your father may not come back."

I winced. Mother hardly ever mentioned Father anymore. She was right, and that thought burned. *What would I do if he didn't return ...?*

The answer echoed from the back of my mind: I'd be the man of the house ... and do my chores without needing to be told. Suddenly I understood why: waiting to be told is for servants, not for men. If I waited to be told every time, then I'd be making myself Mother's servant.

But I didn't want to start harvesting. Day after day of pulling turnips; who wanted that? I hadn't been to the swimming hole for a month, almost the whole summer. Why did I have to start pulling turnips today?

"Not today," I said.

"When?"

"Tomorrow."

"Very well," Mother said, and she turned back to her sewing. "Rest today. Ingrid, since Thron's starting harvest, you'll have to start feeding the animals."

"Yes, 'mam," Ingrid said.

"Start today," Mother said. "Thron will need all his strength if he's going to harvest everything."

* * * * * * * * *

Garad was in his fields, his mother nearby. Both were on their knees; they'd already begun harvest. I shuddered, remembering my weeks of pulling onions. *How would they manage without me?*

Garad and I hadn't spoken since our fight. I still couldn't believe that Garad had beaten me up, but it seemed long ago; I wondered what he'd say if I walked over and tried to speak to him. Not that I dared: Grettir would have me pulling onions in an instant, if she could.

Ingrid came out, saw me, and smiled.

"Hurry up, Ingrid," Mother called from inside. "We've a lot to do today."

Ingrid glanced back momentarily, then blew me a kiss before proceeding into the barn. The chickens ignored her; they were used to being fed by me, but when she threw their grain, they ran to her. I watched her move: hips, breasts, and long golden hair swaying. I wanted to be alone and naked with her. *What good was having a day without chores when you can't spend it doing who you want?*

Suddenly we both turned: a horse was galloping up the road. I wondered why; nobody gallops horses unless there's an emergency: one broken leg and sometimes you'd have to kill the horse. *Was somebody sick or hurt?* But no, this horse was coming from the village; someone needing Læknir would be riding toward the village.

It was Derek. He slowed as he reached our house, but only excitedly shouted before riding on.

"Branwulf! Branwulf's back!"

Father ...!

* * * * * * * * *

The men waved as the dragonship sailed closer. Mother stood beside me holding Urd, who squirmed to get free. I didn't know if Mother wanted Father to come home or not ... but she was there.

We had to stand close together as the rest of the village crowded around us. Garad stood nearby wearing the knife that Father had given him, but Grettir wasn't there; Branwulf's return must have brought up painful memories of Holbarki ... *or was she hoping Father would return for her?* Kal stood there, waiting for Kampi, as was Widow Eardai, who'd lost her husband Gaceth many years before. Even Merta Hodkins, Derek's mother, waited in the crowd. Many others I knew awaited: Clamsby, Beigaldi, Læknir, and Helsa. I'd have loved to talk to Helsa, but at the same time, I didn't. I spied her looking at me several times, but each time that our eyes met, she quickly looked away.

Women: most of those watching Branwulf approach were women, far more than the number of our men who'd sailed. For the first time I realized how many more women than men lived in our village ... *women outnumbered us two to one.*

I couldn't wait to see Halgrum. He'd been so excited; I couldn't wait to hear his tales. But all that I really wanted to see was Father, to know that he was safe and alive.

One man on the ship, wearing a bright red tunic, stood up on the rail and waved. It was Rath; *Helsa's father had come home.* A loud cheer came from the crowd and bright smiles glowed on both Helsa and Læknir. But I couldn't see Father.

The dragonship sailed closer. Lines were cast. Men came off the ship. Still I couldn't see Father.

Someone stepped in front of me, looking at Mother. It was Sammuel, Father's tall friend from Finland. He towered over me, eclipsing the sun as I stood in his narrow shadow. He was still very thin, more sunburned than ever, and his beard still looked like a new broom with too few straws.

"Vespa, my dear," Sammuel said. "Thorir was separated from us in England. He was still alive when last I saw him. He might've made it onto one of the other boats; we joined up with a fleet and took several large towns, but we were dispersed, and then a storm hit. I'm sorry; I wish that I could tell you more. I just ... don't know."

No ...!

Father! He didn't ... *Father didn't come home!*

Sammuel looked down at me, then placed a hand on my shoulder.

"I'm sorry, Thron, but don't lose heart. Thorir told me how much he loved all of you. I'm sure he'll find a way back."

Father ...!!!

I couldn't breathe. My world collapsed. A giant hammer came down and crushed my soul: *Father hadn't returned.*

* * * * * * * * *

Tears blinded my eyes but I didn't care.

"Thron ...?"

Friar James' voice barely penetrated my darkness.

"Thron, can you hear me? Hold out your hands. Drink

this."

Something lifted my hands, pressed a cup into them, and then lifted it to my mouth. The ale tasted warm, bitter, and stale. I looked up, blinked, and recognized the ceiling through my tears' watery blur: Rath's old house.

"Don't give up hope, Thron," Friar James' voice echoed from nowhere. "Your father may still be alive ... somewhere."

Friar James sat down in Rath's old chair.

"I've some other bad news for you," he said. "There was another boy, from this village, who didn't make it back. Helsa said that you two were friends. I think that she called him ... Halgrum."

Slowly I focused on him.

"H-H-Halgrum ...?" my voice sounded weak and distant.

"He was killed ... by a Norman ... the first time he got off the boat."

Halgrum. My old friend. Halgrum was dead. Halgrum didn't come back.

Father!!

"I'm sorry," Friar James said. "Come, Thron, we have to get you home."

Friar James took the cup from my hands and pulled on my arm.

"Come on, Thron. Stand up; you're too big for me to carry."

Numbly I stood and stumbled forward as he led me to his door and outside.

"Thron!" Clamsby shouted.

"It's all right, I found him," Friar James said. "He was out back underneath the maple. I'll take him home."

"Very well," Clamsby said. "I sent his mother home an hour ago."

Clamsby placed a heavy hand on my shoulder.

"Thron, listen to me. I've been viking many times. These things happen. People get separated, driven apart. It doesn't mean that Thorir's dead ... or even hurt. I've known him all of my life, and it'd take more than a few Normans to hurt him. You buck up and go take care of Vespa. It may take Thorir a bit longer to get home, that's all."

Clamsby's words rung hollowly in my head. He didn't know if Father was alive. Even if he was, what good was that ... *if he never returned?*

Dead faces, terrible faces, floated before my eyes. Corpses stacked on the tables in Tavern Hall, Father holding me out, making me look. *The faces wouldn't go away!*

* * * * * * * * *

Ingrid's face was cloud-white. Mother was sitting in her chair as always, somewhat stiffly, a pair of knitting needles clicking noisily in her hands. Friar James patted me on the back and closed our door behind him.

"Brace the door," Mother said, her voice strained. "Get started on your bowl. You won't be able to finish it once harvest starts."

Whimpers came from Ingrid. She was rolling soft wax, making a new candle. I stood, not moving. *What were we going to do without Father ...?*

Mother had finished several new rows on Urd's blanket, and Ingrid had finished a thick candle and was tightly twisting a strip of cloth as a wick for a second. *How long had I stood there, doing nothing?*

My bowl: I sat down in Father's chair and picked it up. Father's chair seemed small. I used to be able to curl up in it;

now it almost fit me. I was the man of the family. Now I'd have to do the chores, harvest the turnips, do the trading, everything. Without me, our farm would fail. Mother and Ingrid would starve. Without me ...

I didn't want to be Father. I didn't want the responsibility: his burdens, his duties. I hated chores, and suddenly chores started to number beyond count, to pile up into a huge wall of endless work, teetering, collapsing, crashing on top of me.

* * * * * * * * *

I gripped my sword tight in my hand. Fog shrouded the world, glowing even as the morning rain drizzled down from the gray, hidden sky.

The pigs squealed hungrily and the chickens clucked and ran underfoot. I ignored them. I kicked off my shoes and climbed over the fence into the pen, felt the muck squish between my toes. We had thirteen new piglets this year; they ran about squealing the loudest while the others eyed me sleepily.

I surveyed the pigs and chose the biggest and meanest. He was awake, snorting and complaining. He wanted his breakfast. I lifted my sword.

One of us wasn't leaving this pen alive.

I took a slow, deep breath, fighting for control. I forced myself to look around at the other pigs; I didn't want my prey knowing that I was hunting him. I took a step forward slowly, trying to look casual. One of the pigs whined and I slowed; they knew that something was wrong, but I didn't stop. I reached down and petted one, then stepped to the side and petted another.

Slowly I made my way across the pen and came at my prey

from behind. The piglets were dashing about, often right across the tops of my feet, splashing my trousers with filth. I ignored them. My prey shook himself but didn't run off. He didn't know what was coming. I was doing it right.

I inverted my sword and gripped it in both hands. As I approached his backside, he snorted gruffly. I raised my blade. I kept my eyes focused on his neck, right behind the ears, the spot that I wanted to hit. If I did this right, then it'd kill him instantly. If not, he'd turn on me with sharp, biting teeth. He was much shorter than I, but we weighed about the same. If I missed, then I'd be in big trouble; *Father wasn't here to save me.*

I took my last step and moved in one quick, fluid motion, exactly as Father had taught me. My sword lifted high, I stabbed its point downward with all of my strength. I hit the spot that I wanted. The pig never knew what was coming; he brayed deafeningly, jerked away so hard that he almost pulled my sword from my grasp, and then it was over. He plopped down in the muck and moved no more.

No, I thought, horrified. *It can't be that easy.* I didn't want it to be easy. I wanted it to be hard and deadly dangerous, as it had last year when Father had me kill a pig under his watchful eyes.

But it wasn't. The pig was dead; it was all over. I'd killed him with no more effort than it would've taken to feed him. Pigs were no longer a match for me; killing them was just another chore.

Seized by wracking sobs, I fell to my knees in the muck, my hands still grasping my sword stuck in the pig.

"Drag it out of there," came Mother's voice.

Mother and Ingrid stood at the gate, staring at me, still in their gray nightgowns. I looked at the pig. I pulled out my sword; its blade was drenched in blood.

I'd have to clean it before I started pulling turnips.

* * * * * * * * *

A shadow fell over the turnip that I was about to pull. I startled; I hadn't heard anyone walk up behind me, and then I recognized the face: Garad stood over me.

We stared at each other in silence. Garad was taller, thinner, and looked very gaunt. His knees were covered with patches and very dirty. His hair was clean but uncombed, and had no oil smoothing it.

"I'm sorry," Garad said.

I didn't know what to say.

"It must be terrible, not knowing."

That I understood. Holbarki had been returned for burial; Garad got to see him dead. I didn't know if Father was dead. He hadn't even decided to not come home; he'd been forced into mystery.

I pulled up the shaded turnip, looked at it, and then dropped it upon the dirt. I stood up and looked at Garad. I was surprised to find that I was still taller than him; we'd both grown considerably.

"Where's Grettir?"

"Looking for me, probably."

We both talked slowly, with long uncomfortable pauses in between: adult pauses. I didn't want to be an adult.

"Too bad we can't run off to the swimming hole," Garad said, attempting a joke.

"I have turnips ..."

"I have onions ..."

We stood facing each other, neither knowing what to say.

"Garad …!" Grettir's distant shout was welcomed.

"I'm sorry."

"I know."

* * * * * * * * *

"Thron!" Ingrid called.

From our fields, I saw her wave for me to come in. I looked at my bag; it was almost full, so I would've had to go back soon anyway. I wondered what she wanted; it was late afternoon, but too early to stop.

I pulled a last turnip, stuffed it into my bag, and then stood up. The bag was heavy; I carried it back home.

As I approached, Ingrid looked strangely anxious. Her apron was dirty; she and Mother had been harvesting near the house while I worked the back fields.

"Læknir's here," Ingrid said. "Rath is with her, and so is … *Helsa."*

Helsa's name hissed between Ingrid's teeth. *Wisely I'd never told her about Helsa's kiss.*

"What do they want?"

"To see us," Ingrid said. "You and Vespa. They've been with Halgrum's parents since dawn. I guess they want to check on us."

"I don't have time for visits."

"You can't refuse Læknir."

I sighed; it didn't matter what I wanted. *Why did I ever wish to be an adult?*

"Thron? Do you still … want me?"

"I'm so tired that I don't know what I want."

Ingrid's expression paled.

"I just want to lie down and rest," I continued. "But I sure would like it ... if you were there, resting beside me."

*   *   *   *   *   *   *   *   *

Chapter 21

* * * * * * * * *

"I doubt if Thorir's dead," Rath said after he'd sent Ingrid inside. "He's a fierce fighter, but he's also smart; he knows when to run. There were ten different longships there, and he could've boarded any of them. In the confusion, he'd run to safety, no matter where it led. I know: that's what I did."

Rath's words echoed hollowly in my ears. I felt dead inside, like a candleholder whose candle had finally gone out, its wick burned and crisped, alone in an empty circle surrounded by the last small puddle of once-melted wax.

"He may yet come back," Rath said. "Or he may not; that doesn't mean that he's dead."

I almost couldn't blame Father for that; Mother and Grettir still hadn't spoken to each other.

"He loves you," Rath said.

Yes, but how much? *Enough to come home? Wasn't Rath talking to me the same way that Father had talked to*

Garad after Holbarki had died?

"I know," Rath said, as if he sensed my thoughts. "You don't want to talk. But part of being a healer means talking to people when they don't want to talk. Læknir wants to talk to you ... and I suspect that Helsa does, too. Go inside and let them have their say. Talk, even just a little. I won't let it last long."

Rath took my bag of turnips and emptied it onto my bed as I followed him inside. Læknir got up as I came in and held out her arms to me. Disgusted, I let her hug me, embarrassed to press my head against her aged, sagging chest, which wasn't nearly as big or firm as Ingrid's.

"My poor boy," Læknir said. "Don't give up hope. Thorir's a strong man. If he survived, he'll find a way home."

Læknir pushed me away, but she held me at arm's length.

"You've grown so much!" Læknir said. "On the outside, at least. Now tell me; how do you feel inside?"

"Okay," I muttered.

"Of course you do," Læknir said. "Strong, brave boy. Like your father. And I hear that you killed a pig, and started harvest, all by yourself?"

I nodded silently.

"Very impressive," Læknir said. "Commendable. Your father will be very proud of you when he gets back; I'll tell him myself."

"As will I," Rath said. "Thron, I'd like to buy you a drink at Clamsby's. Tonight; come right after sunset."

I nodded again.

Læknir asked a few more questions and hugged me again, then turned back to Mother. As the two of them started talking, I turned toward the door.

"Don't go yet, Thron," Læknir said. "I need to examine

your leg. And take off your shirt; I need to insure that your cuts didn't get infected."

I stopped, sighed, and slowly pulled off my shirt.

"Helsa, check his cuts for infection," Læknir said.

I gritted my teeth but said nothing. Helsa wasn't the last person that I wanted touching me, but not in front of Ingrid.

Helsa came up slowly, as if as reluctant as I. She tried not to look at my face but examined all of my cuts, most of which were tiny crusted scabs or just pale white scars on my skin. Helsa lifted my arms and looked all over my chest and back. A few places she probed momentarily, but then she moved on.

"Sit down," she directed, and as I sat on the bed, she knelt before me and, with a deep sigh, pulled up my pants' legs and examined my skin. I couldn't help but look at her while she examined me; Helsa had grown more than I'd realized. She wasn't as tall as I, about Garad's height, and she was still thin, but she looked older, more adult. Her hair was yellow as the sun, unlike Ingrid's, whose hair was gold like honey. She wasn't unattractive, but I quickly banished the thought; Ingrid couldn't read minds, but she was good at reading faces.

Læknir examined my leg, announced that it was healing very well, and gave me a short lecture on how lucky I was, and how I'd no business climbing cliffs, and about how badly Mother would feel if something dreadful happened to me.

"I'm sure that he's learned his lesson," Rath said suddenly, holding out my empty bag for me. "Those turnips aren't going to harvest themselves."

* * * * * * * * *

It was almost dark when Ingrid came out again.

"Mother says that it's time to come in," Ingrid said. "Dinner's ready, and she wants you to eat before you leave."

"Leave ...?" I asked.

"Clamsby's," Ingrid reminded. "Rath ...? Tonight ...? You promised to meet him at Tavern Hall ...?"

"Oh." I'd forgotten.

"Are you all right?"

"Huh? Why?"

"I ... while Helsa was touching you ... you ... smiled."

"Oh? Was I? I ... I was thinking about you."

"While she touched you?"

"Yes," I lied. "I was ... wishing that you were touching me."

"I wish that I could kiss you right now," Ingrid smiled.

I held out my arms.

"Your mother could be watching."

"Soon?"

"Soon."

* * * * * * * * *

I really didn't want to go to Tavern Hall. That struck me as odd; I used to dream about going into the village, sitting in the hall all night, drinking and laughing with the men.

Derek rode up as I was walking. Kampi was just coming down the trail with Kal leading.

"What's going on?" I asked.

"Rath said to be here," Derek said. "Looks like he said the same to everyone."

Derek and I entered the hall, which was strangely quiet. It was crowded, most of the men and many boys were there. Old man Ranglátr sat center, in the same place that he'd occupied when Friar James had been discussed. All of the tables were set up in a single row, as if they were one long table. Only Friar James was absent.

"Come in and sit down," Rath said, walking over to us and pointing us to a bench near one end of the table where Garad was already sitting.

We sat in silence and stared at each other as Kampi and Kal came in. Kal sat by us while his father was given a chair near the center, across from Old man Ranglátr. Clamsby came by shortly afterwards, setting wooden mugs in front of us.

"Don't drink too much," he warned. "We've a lot to talk about tonight."

An hour later, we were still sitting and drinking. Most of the men were talking softly, but we sat at the far end sipping our ales, fearing to speak.

"I think that we're all here," Rath said suddenly, speaking up so that all could hear. "First, of course, I wish to drink to the memory of our dearest companion, who should be with us tonight. Ralg, you have our deepest condolences for the loss of such a brave and manly son. He died in the greatest tradition that we have; we shall all honor him as deeply as we mourn his loss. Everyone, raise your ales high. Let us drink to our lost brother: *To Halgrum, son of Ralg!"*

We raised our mugs, but suddenly all of the men stood up, and we hurried to join them on our feet.

"To Halgrum, son of Ralg!" everyone chorused, and we joined in just in time to get the last word out. Then everyone drank, and we did, too. I took a sip, then noticed that all of the men were still drinking. I took another sip, holding the cup at my lips until I saw all of the adults turn their mugs upside down and set them, emptied, onto the table: they were drinking them dry. I hurried to do the same, noticing that

none of the other boys had known what was going on.

Kal finished last and set his cup down while still holding his last gulp in his mouth. Several of the men watched us but no one moved or spoke until the last mug was upside down.

"I hope that you'll forgive me, Ralg, if I must continue," Rath said. "You all know what's going on. This English monk has come, and we must decide what to do about it."

"I agree that we must discuss it," Kampi said, standing up. "But ... *do?* I won't agree to do anything until after we discuss it. If this Friar is a threat, then we must do something, but until then, until he represents some danger, we don't need to do anything. So I say, here and now, that all talk of *'doing'* should be postponed until after we discuss the problem."

Old man Ranglátr banged his fist on the table.

"I say he is a threat!" he said.

"Then you must convince me before I'll take action," Kampi replied.

"Very good," Rath said. "Discussion; that's what we're here for. But we aren't here to fight. We all have many points to argue, some in the friar's favor, some not. No one's asking anyone to agree with anybody. All I ask you to do is listen."

There was a great nodding of heads, some eagerly, others less so. Rath motioned to Old man Ranglátr.

"I will speak first and last!" Ranglátr said. "You all know why I'm here. I say that Friar James is a disaster to every family in this village! And I don't mean that Odin is going to slay us all with lightning bolts, but the result will be the same. What will happen to us once word gets out that we have an English monk living here? What will people say? What will Branwulf say? What will happen the next time that there's a great sickness, or if all the chickens in our district suddenly die? People will look for someone to blame! They'll look for someone, some village, some place that's done something different, something that makes them stand out. And what'll they see?

"You've all been south. You've seen churches and cathedrals topped with big white crosses. Do you think that people won't notice when one of those goes up in our village? Those churches have always been a summons to our people, a sign that says *'Come here! We're vulnerable!'.* Is that the sign that we want painted on our village?

"Look what we do to lands with churches! Do you want raiders landing here? Killing, raping your wives and daughters, burning Tavern Hall to the ground?

"What'll happen while we're away? Who'll guard our families? I don't question Ralg or Clamsby's worth; I remember what valiant fighters they were on their vikings, and have no doubt that they'd do so again, but how many could they stand against, and what would happen to our village if they fell?

"I don't like Friar James. I don't like what he teaches. I don't like his tales of peace. You start thinking like that and you become weak, and we all know what happens to weak men when they're confronted by the strong!

"The many brown rabbits will kill the one white hare. We can't afford to be different, not in these troubled times. What do we lose by killing him? Nothing, and there's no risk! I say that we do it now ... tonight! Who's with me?"

Several men shouted gladly. Old man Ranglátr bowed to them slightly, then sat down.

"Very wise words," Rath said. "But everyone here, even the boys, have the right to be heard. Who'd like to go next?"

"I will," Kampi said after a short pause where no one

jumped up to speak. "You all know me. I've already lost one son; I have two sons and three daughters left. If I thought that Friar James was a threat to them then we wouldn't be having this discussion: I'd have killed him already.

"But I see no threat. I see a ..."

"He is a threat!" Smiðr stood angrily.

"Peace!" Rath shouted. "We'll each get a turn to speak, but if we start arguing then we'll sound like a bunch of gossiping fishwives. Kampi, finish what you were saying, then Smiðr may speak."

Smiðr glared, but sat back down.

"I see no threat," Kampi continued. "I see a fat man with no weapons. I see a weakling who spends his life on his knees. I see a fool or a madman; I'm just not sure which. Even our boys could kill him. Such a man is no threat to me.

"But only days ago I saw a boy in this village do something that no one else could: Thron wrote his name. This monk knows the Futhark, the secret runes, their sounds and their meanings; Odin hung himself for knowledge such as this. To kill this monk would be throwing away valuable knowledge." Kampi fell silent and slowly glanced at all the faces around the table, his fingers combing through his long beard. "A wise man doesn't throw away advantages without considering their possible benefits. Before we slay this man, let's balance his small risk against our considerable gain."

Kampi nodded to Smiðr, then sat and drank from his ale.

"I've heard of this Futhark," Smiðr said, again standing up. "What good is it? When I want to say something, I say it. I don't need a bunch of symbols to speak for me. And if any of you have something to say to me, come and say it; I'd be insulted if somebody sent me a stick with marks burned onto it.

"Well, that's what I wanted to say."

Smiðr sat down as many nodded in agreement. Digr slowly stood and Rath signaled for him to speak.

"I wish I knew how to read runes," Digr said. "I hear that, in Oslo, everybody knows. Business agreements are written on lambskin so that no one can claim more than was bargained. That prevents feuds, and we all know how devastating those can be. Runes are used for everything. Wives send messages to their husbands carved on split sticks; what they need and when to come home."

"I don't want my wife doing that!" Smiðr said, and all the adults laughed.

"I don't either," Digr said. "But think of their value! We have laws, but only a few old jarls can recite them all. If they were written down, then everyone could know them. Most feuds start over disagreements; with promises recorded in runes, there'd be no feuds. The Futhark are symbols of power ... power that we could have!"

"The Futhark are more than symbols," Gandr warned when Digr sat down. "They're magic. Do we dare unleash it? What will its evil do to our village?"

"Superstition," Kampi answered.

"Thron learned runes and almost got killed!" Old man Ranglátr interjected.

"Accidents happened before Friar James came to Norway," Kampi said. "You, Rath, fight well with axe or sword, but how well do you pull a bow? I was never a swordsman, but I'm an excellent archer. A man who is both a swordsman and an archer possesses two valuable skills. Runes are another skill. It may not do me any good, but when my sons go viking, I want them armed with every bit of knowledge and craft they can have."

"You can't kill an enemy with runes!" Old man Ranglátr argued.

"You can kill whole armies with runes," Hal spoke up. "Using runes on arrows to send messages, you can ambush enemies in coordinated attacks; the French do it."

Old man Ranglátr scowled.

"And not all wealth comes from fighting," Kampi continued. "We all know the importance of knowing when to flee. Intercepting messages from your enemies is useless if you can't read them. And there are other ways, such as Digr said: business is commerce, wealth that places like Oslo has. Writing could lift the shadow of ignorance from our village."

"Then what?" Old man Ranglátr asked. "We learn to read; do we become Christians? I've seen Oslo. There're churches in Oslo, churches with big crosses on them; already the faith of our enemies has invaded our lands! You've all killed Christians. Would you become them? And if you do, what'll become of the vikings? What'll happen to our gods, to our way of life?"

A silence fell in the hall.

"You can't slide halfway down a slippery slope," Old man Ranglátr warned. "Once you start, you go all the way."

"He's right," Gandr said. "We're deciding the future of our village, the future that your kids will inherit. I lost my future when I lost my arm. Now you want me to turn away from the gods of my fathers. I won't! I can't!"

"You know my business," Smiðr said. "What happens to me if you all become Christians? Every fireplace in this village has my hooks in it, my pots, and your barns are full of my hoes and plows; I can't live repairing tools. Swords put food on my table.

"Christians don't go viking against each other. Once you

become Christians, who'll you go viking against? Or is it your intention to give up the vikings?"

Smiðr said nothing more and no one challenged him. Garad and Derek looked as nervous as I. Rath had said that we'd get to speak, but did he mean it?

"The vikings are about more than profit," Rath said. "How'll you get to Valhalla without the vikings? The vikings are our heritage, the way of our gods. The vikings keep us strong, feared by our enemies.

"But they're dangerous. One dead this year, another lost, six dead last year, and three the year before that; what'll happen to our village when no more of us are left?

"We were a larger village in my father's time. When I was a kid, there were dozens of other kids; now only twelve in the whole village. This hall wouldn't hold our whole village then; now we fit in here with ease. Who'll be left to father the next generation, protect our women, and plow our fields?"

"The Scots, the Danes, the English, and Irish are growing stronger every year," Brún said. "Coastal towns are fortified. I've been wounded six years in a row. How much longer before I die, and for what?"

"Too much change," Old man Ranglátr said. "My father remembered when stirrups were new. He always called them silly: *'I never fell off a horse before stirrups and I'll be damned if I'm going to stick my feet in rings just because some fool can't ride'*. I'm warning you: change leads to chaos."

"Everything changes," Hal said. "Back in my grandfather's day, every hill in these parts was capped with ice in mid-summer, but now only the high mountains wear ice all year round. That's change, and I don't hear anybody complaining that our lands are warmer.

"My father worked for Kampi's father, but he died a'viking. I worked for Thorir, and he's missing. Now I work for Digr. I've worked in other men's fields all my life; my back is all that I have. Learning to read and write would give me another skill, one that I might need if I get hurt and can't plant or harvest."

"The vikings themselves are change," Kampi said. "Our people were once bound to these shores, scraping a living out of a hostile, frozen land. Then we discovered how to make dragonships; that changed us."

"I don't want to quit the vikings; I'd have to spend all summer with the wife," Rath said, and everyone laughed. "My best skill is wielding an axe, and my father's last words were *'I'll expect you in Valhalla'*. I won't disappoint him, but I admit: my reasons for going viking grow less each year. Our enemies defend themselves better with each season. Every year, the booty grows less.

"Our village is dying right before our eyes. We're half the size that we once were. Our daughters can't wait to get married because most of our sons don't survive their first viking. Almost every wife in the village is a widow, and some women've never married because there're no men left.

"Will killing Friar James help our village ... or doom it?"

"Oslo has Christians," Hal said. "I've heard that the king himself has monks in his employ. What if all of Norway becomes Christian except us? If Norway's becoming Christian, do we want to join early ... or late? Dare we ...?"

"Do none of you fear our gods?" Gandr shouted. "What will Odin say if he sees us burning his idols and putting crosses on our roofs? *We're risking being cursed!"*

"Yes, we are," Digr said, "but we risk the same no matter what we do. There's not a man in this room who doesn't wish that he had more wealth. Well, if you want to go from poor to rich, then you're asking for change. And every change risks the wrath of the gods. But who knows what the gods want? Who can say which path will anger them?

"If we're doomed either way, then we might as well pick the best path that we can, the one that leads to wealth and security ..."

"Security ...?" Gandr shouted. "*You sound like a woman!"*

"How dare you!" Digr shouted, and suddenly all of the men jumped up and started shouting at once. I jumped up, mostly to see, and so did the other boys.

"Enough!" Clamsby shouted angrily, and he repeated his shout until everyone fell silent. "This is my hall, and anyone who draws blood in it has *me* to answer to! I've kept silent all this time. Now I'll have my say."

No one spoke, but everyone settled angrily into their chairs.

"We've all killed our share of Christians. When I was young, there were no Christians in Norway. Now there are many, so many that even a village as small as ours has finally got one. Is Norway becoming Christian? It looks like it will, eventually. I don't like it, but Brún's right; our enemies are growing stronger every year. And they're Christians. And we're growing fewer ... and weaker.

"What happens when we grow too few? When all of Europe is Christian except us, then they'll swat us like flies. We may have to become Christian, unless we want all of Norway to look like some village we plundered and burned. Men killed, women raped, animals stolen; is that what it'll cost to hold on to our gods, when the Danes no longer sacrifice to their Great Bird? The Irish no longer homage their Blue

Snake? When the Saxons no longer pray to their Horse god? They've all given up their old ways, and I see no curse coming down on them!"

"I do," Old man Ranglátr said. "I see us. We're their curse, coming down from the north to plunder at will."

"Curses die out," Clamsby said. "We're dying out. That's why I didn't kill Friar James the day I met him. I could've. Anyone here could do it right now; he's next door, in Rath's house, without a single weapon. He has no family to avenge him. But that doesn't mean that his killer can't be outlawed; anyone here can ride to Law Rock and claim an injury ..."

"How?" Smiðr demanded.

"I could," Kampi said, "and I will."

Many men gasped.

"Are you declaring Friar James under your protection?" Rath asked.

"No," Kampi said. "He's not a member of my house, and I won't fight to save him. But his knowledge is valuable. I want my sons to learn runes, to learn everything that they can, because someday it may mean the difference between wealth and poverty, life or death. If any man kills Friar James, then I will ride to Law Rock and demand restitution. At the very least, I'll demand enough to hire a teacher from Oslo to come here and teach my sons."

"Unfair!" Smiðr shouted. "What does it matter who teaches the Futhark? If anybody here learns it, then we're changed!"

"Thron knows it," Kampi said, "and Thron and his family are the bedrock of this village. We're all poor, only a bad harvest away from starvation, and we're weakened by our losses. I say that it's time for a change."

"Here, here!" Digr shouted.

"But what about the vikings?" Old man Ranglátr demanded.

"We keep going viking!" Derek shouted.

I startled, turning my gaze to Derek, who seemed surprised that he'd spoken so loud. A few of the men turned and looked at us, and some chuckled.

"I want to go to Valhalla," Derek said. "I want to go viking."

"So do I," I said.

"And me!" Garad said.

"Me, too!" Kal said, looking down so not to meet his father's eyes.

"And so do I," Old man Ranglátr said loudly, and no one spoke after him.

* * * * * * * * *

Chapter 22

* * * * * * * * *

Day after day, turnip after turnip, I pulled until pain looked purple-white and came out of the ground dirty. My hands hurt, my knees hurt, my back hurt. Chilled when it rained, baked when sunny, and miserable always, I filled my bag, carried it to the house, emptied it, and came back for more.

Why was I doing this? What good would it do to survive the winter? How was I going to plant these fields alone, all by myself, without a horse? Even if I could plant everything, what then? Would Mother let me go viking without Father? Would I ever get to go viking, or would I remain here, trapped forever on this farm, beaten by endless chores until I died from pure heartache?

I hated turnips. I could barely gag them down. Every third day I went to check on my traps; I caught two more skinny ferrets and a weasel, but nothing else. No deer. My leg still bothered me after the long hikes there and back, but I didn't dare mention it; it saved us from having no meat.

Friar James was still alive, I assumed; someone would've brought news if somebody'd killed him. He was still living in Rath's old house, but the men were going viking next year; we'd all agreed to that.

But would I get to sail with them ...?

* * * * * * * * *

Weeks passed. Eternities. Pain unending. Sadness and anguish. Mindless drudgery ... repetition.

I hate turnips ...

I hate turnips ...

I hate turnips ...

* * * * * * * * *

"Thron!" Ingrid screamed.

I glanced up from my mindless stupor. The sun was hot today, but the wind was strong and cold; the weather had turned decidedly wintery, and I wasn't feeling well. Everyday, Mother woke me when the roosters crowed, and it was after nightfall before I got to sleep; the difference between awake and asleep was measured only by gloom.

"Thron!"

Ingrid ran fast; numbly I wondered why. She sounded excited, and for an instant I wondered if another problem had developed, but no fear tinged her voice.

I stood up as she came closer, running faster than I'd ever seen. Her eyes blazed wide and she fought to smile and breathe at the same time.

"Come!" she exhaled through heavy gasps, her breath lost, and she grabbed my arm.

"What is it?"

"Come!"

She pulled hard. I tried to pick up the half-full sack of turnips, but she pushed it from my hands to spill upon the dirt. The next thing that I knew we were running, her frantically pulling my arm.

As we reached home, I discerned laughter between her gasps. She stopped as we reached our door. A strange horse stood by our gate. Mother stood beside it, kissing ...

Father!

* * * * * * * * *

Father was home!

I hugged him so hard that Father grunted.

"Who's this? Who's this strong man? Where's my little boy that I left here in the spring?"

Something felt strange. I was pressed against metal; tiny sharp points poked me; Father was wearing a shirt of steel rings.

"Like it?" Father smiled. "Armor; mail, real steel links."

My eyes blazed. Steel rings strung in woven rows, like knitting but without yarn, stretched across his chest. I slid my fingers over it; rough but very strong. Could a sword even cut it?

"Come here!" Father shouted joyously, and he pulled Mother, I, and even Ingrid, into a big hug. "I'm so glad to be home!"

An hour later, we were laughing around our table. Father had put the horse in one of our barn's stalls and given him hay and water. I'd never seen a horse in our barn before; *we had a horse!* But Father had only laughed at my questions and hugged me as we walked back to the house. He held Urd up to the ceiling, then kissed her, and sat down in his chair, cradling her to his chest. Urd cried; she didn't remember him, but Father held her until dinner was ready.

"It was a good viking," Father said. "Took longer to get underway, but finally we sailed into great weather with a strong southerly wind. We sailed toward Ireland, but diverted to chase some ships; they turned out to be from Sweden; Jarl Oakney's ships. Branwulf met with him, and after much discussion, we joined his fleet. Branwulf promised that we'd take his right flank on attacking, and Oakney swore that he'd repay us from the center-spoils.

"Except for Halgrum, everything on our first raid went fine. Hjálmun tried to stop Halgrum, but he fearlessly charged the first Norman that he saw, a stranger hiding in a shadowy alcove. The Norman had a spear, and Halgrum never saw it until too late; he ran right onto it, according to Hjálmun. Hjálmun avenged Halgrum, but afterwards he blamed himself. He didn't say so, of course; Hjálmun never talks unless he has to, but you could tell. Hjálmun looked ashamed as he told us what'd happened."

"Poor Halgrum!" Mother said. "So young! Poor Ralg! He's been crying every night, they say."

Father and I frowned: *Ralg wouldn't ever cry in public.*

"What about Hjálmun?" I asked.

"Who knows?" Father said. "He's a great young fighter. Doesn't make trouble, always eager to man an oar."

"He's a good boy," Mother said. "He needs a good wife."

"What would Igrár say to ...?" Ingrid suddenly stopped, as if she'd said too much. Mother's eyes flared, but Father smiled.

"Igrár ...? Really ...?" Father asked.

"Just gossip," Mother said quickly.

"Well, good for both of them, if it's true," Father laughed.

"Igrár's old," Mother said. "Our village needs young mothers. Hjálmun would make a good father if he'd take a wife of his own age. It's not like we've a shortage of virgins." Mother glanced quickly at Ingrid, but she pretended not to notice.

"Anyway," Father continued, "the whole summer went pretty much the same. Oakney chose a landing spot, and we sailed in on his right. We had six fully-manned ships, so we went after large towns. Branwulf often landed first, but we had little time for plundering; we guarded the roads and alleys so that the others could do the plundering, but after every retreat, Branwulf climbed over to Oakney's ship and came back laden with spoils. But it was the kind that we usually got; sheets, candleholders, stuff that we didn't need. Oakney kept all of the gold and silver; Branwulf wasn't happy about that.

"Trouble came in a hamlet that we suspected was too small to put up a fight. Saxon cavalry suddenly charged us, riding right down the street, only their galloping horses giving us any warning. Armed only with swords and bows to fight villagers, not spears to defend against horsemen, we fled into the shadows, through burning houses and down alleys too narrow for horses. I fled with two men; both were killed, Saxon lances pierced them as they ran. I only survived because I ran faster.

"I didn't see any of my shipmates again. I thought I saw Sammuel running away, down another street, but I didn't dare shout his name. I don't even know if ..."

"Sammuel came off Branwulf's ship and told us that you'd

gotten separated," Mother said.

"Thank the gods," Father said, and he took a deep breath, then he sighed slowly as if it'd bothered him greatly.

"So what happened?" I asked anxiously.

"Everything happened. Oakney's ship was the only one still there when I made it back to the docks, and I had to run to the edge of the pier and jump to get onto his ship before it sailed off. Oakney welcomed me aboard, but in the end it didn't matter; a nasty storm struck, lasted for days, and blew us all over. We tacked up and down the coast, found a few survivors from one of Oakney's ships that'd been tossed onto a reef. We never saw Branwulf again.

"Oakney knew how to viking. We attacked several more villages, a couple of churches, and pirated some merchant vessels. I actually found a silver jewelry box full of brightly gemmed necklaces, bracelets, and rings ..." He paused, looking at his hands as if reliving the moment. "I'd only heard of such treasures. Jarl Oakney took it, of course."

We sat silent. Suddenly I noticed: *Father had brought nothing home.* I'd been so glad to see him that I'd not noticed that he had no chests or bags. He had the horse, but I didn't want him to sell that; I'd always wanted a horse. But what would Father trade if he had no plunder? *How would we survive next summer until harvest?*

"The rest of the viking was great, but I was glad when Oakney ordered his men to sail home. We docked in Sweden; that's why it took me so long to get home. I've been riding for three weeks."

"We ... were worried," Mother said.

"Yes," Ingrid agreed.

Father glanced at Mother, took another bite of food, and sat smiling strangely. He reached out and touched Urd's nose, and Urd startled and tried to hide under the table.

"So, Thron, how do you like the horse?" Father asked.

"Can we keep him?" I asked eagerly.

"You'd better ask his owner, not me," Father said, grinning.

"I ... I thought that he was yours ...," I said, realizing that it wasn't as great as I'd hoped.

"No, I just rode him here," Father said. "He's your horse, son; my present: I'm giving him to you."

My horse? My eyes nearly burst out of my head, and then I was hugging Father so fast that I couldn't recall standing up.

"Thorir!" Mother gasped. "I mean, Thron certainly deserves it ... after all he's done, but ... how can we afford...?"

Father waved her silent, then pushed me back. He reached into his mail shirt and pulled out two pouches. One jingled as he shook it, and finally, smiling widely, he opened it, and poured its contents out onto the table.

Coins! All shapes, sizes, and colors, some copper, some brass, and three silver. Lots of them. Mother screamed, and Ingrid's mouth fell open in soundless surprise.

I'd never seen such wealth. Father folded his arms across his chest, leaned back, and grinned proudly. Mother reached out and touched the coins as if afraid that they were some beautiful dream that would fade the instant that she touched them. She ran her fingers through them; there must've been twenty coins, at least, and the music of them clinking together filled our home.

"Praise Odin!" Ingrid gasped.

"And that's not all," Father said proudly. Slowly he held up the last pouch. "Not even Oakney knows that I stole this. I took this off a ten year old girl that I found hiding in a closet; I almost ran her through, but she was cowering, tears running down her face. Then I saw the glint in the candlelight; I pulled back her collar ... and when I saw what she wore, I nearly shouted. But I kept my tongue, lifted it off her head, and closed the door behind me. I didn't kill her; she'd made us rich."

Father carefully opened the tiny pouch. Gingerly he slipped his fingers inside and slowly drew out a thin, tiny necklace, a delicate thing made of pale brass beads with a little cross hanging from it. I wasn't impressed, but Mother and Ingrid froze.

"Is that ...?" Mother gasped.

"Mothers of Baulder!" Ingrid whispered.

Father held it up.

"I'd trade our whole farm for this, house and all," Father said.

"Is it real?" asked Mother.

"Hold out your hand," Father said to her.

Mother's hand trembled as she held her palm out flat. Father lifted the necklace up high, then slowly lowered it onto her hand.

"*It's beautiful,"* Ingrid breathed.

"What is it?" I asked.

"Gold!" Father grinned. "*Real gold!"*

* * * * * * * * *

"Ingrid, take Thron out and sleep in the barn," Father smiled, pulling Mother into an embrace.

Mother suddenly stiffened, then looked at both of us.

"What's wrong?" Father asked.

"N... nothing," Mother said hesitantly, although her expression said otherwise. "Ingrid, do as he says."

Ingrid looked shocked, glanced at me, and then back to Mother. I didn't know what to say; *spend the night in the barn with Ingrid, just the two of us, alone?* My dreams had come true, but ... Mother? *She'd never ...!*

"Hurry up," Mother ordered us. "But don't get *too comfortable!* I'll be out there soon to bring you back inside."

Father looked confused, but said nothing. Ingrid stood up slowly, then went to the door and lifted off the brace.

"Come ... Thron," Ingrid said.

* * * * * * * * *

"Start the fire," Ingrid said.

I smiled, dumped the red, glowing coals from the iron scoop into the tiny, cold fireplace, grabbed some kindling, and threw it atop the coals. Then I turned, grabbed Ingrid, and pulled her close.

"No, Thron!" Ingrid hissed through clenched teeth.

"Hey, easy!" I whispered, wrapping my arms around her.

"Thron, stop!"

"What ...?"

"Vespa knows that we're here!" Ingrid insisted. "She could be just outside right now, listening to us! She won't just come pushing inside; she'll check to see what we're doing first!"

"So ...?"

"So no touching! No kissing! No looking!"

"But ...!"

"You don't own me anymore," Ingrid said. "I ... I didn't think ... that Thorir was coming back. After Grettir ... and Vespa ..."

I stood staring, not knowing what she meant.

"If Thorir hadn't ... come back, then you'd be the man of

the house. You'd own everything. You'd own me. But Thorir's your father; the farm belongs to him. I belong to him. He ... he can still throw me out!"

"He won't ...!"

"What if I become pregnant? What'll he do then?"

"What ...?"

"Pregnant! You can't hide that!"

"Don't become pregnant."

"Thron! We mated! You ... inside me!"

"So?"

Ingrid stared at me.

"You still ... don't know ...?"

"Know what?"

"Thron, I could be pregnant right now!"

"Well, stop it!"

"What?!?"

"What are you talking about?"

Ingrid looked exasperated. "Thron, sit down."

I hesitated, then sat on the edge of the bed. Ingrid bent low over the fire to blow on the coals, then added more kindling on the tiny flames, and used a stick to edge the fire further underneath the charred logs. Dead coals glowed again, and the shadows fell back as flickers rose. Then Ingrid sat apart from me, on the far edge of the bed, by the headboard.

"Thron, women are ... different," Ingrid said. "My mother explained it when I was young. We ... women ... are born with seeds inside us, inside our bellies: baby seeds. They're planted in a special soil, deep inside us. When men ... water them, sometimes they miss the seeds, and the water just wets the soil. But sometimes men hit a seed; when a man waters that seed, then the seed grows. Women become pregnant, like Vespa did, and then she bore Urd."

Ingrid paused, and looked at me for a moment.

"Thron, do you understand what I'm saying?"

"Baby seeds," I said. "Watering them."

"Mating!" Ingrid said. "We mated! You watered me!"

"I did ...?"

"Thron, if I'm pregnant, it's your son!"

"What? No!"

"Yes! We mated! Men water women every time that they mate. If you watered one of my seeds, then I'm already pregnant! And Vespa will know! She'll tell Thorir, and he'll throw me out!"

I tried to comprehend what she was saying, but it was too much. Was this magic, like we did in the woods with Garad? *I didn't want a son!* A little ... squalling infant ... like Urd ... inside Ingrid? *Was this the blackest magic of all?*

"You ... are ... preg...?"

"I don't know," Ingrid started to sob. "It's ... too early to tell. But I could be. If Thorir hadn't come back, and I was ..., then you and I ... Vespa wouldn't be able to throw me out. You and I could've ... been together ... as often as you wanted ... every day ... every night. But now ..."

"You're saying ... we can't ...?"

"We can't!"

My mind reeled. *Never again? But I wanted her so badly!*

Ingrid started to cry. I didn't know what to do. I sat there, trembling, numb; what did it mean? Would Ingrid get fat like Mother did before Urd was born? If one of Ingrid's ... seeds ... got watered, then Mother would know that we mated!

"We could ... tell Mother it wasn't me," I suggested.

"It was you!" Ingrid shouted, and then she quieted, listening for sounds outside. "Never say that again; Vespa

would throw me out for sure if I slept with someone outside of our family. I'd never ... I've never ... given myself to a man before, not freely, of my own will."

"What do you mean, *'not freely'?"*

Ingrid started to cry harder.

"That doesn't matter..."

"What'd you mean?"

"Grow up, Thron!" Ingrid seethed, casting a black look at me. "What'd you think happened? You were locked in a trunk ...!"

I struggled to recall.

"Those ... thieves?" I asked. "From Lapland?"

"They held us down, forced us to mate ...!" Ingrid sobbed.

"Us ...?"

"Vespa, too. They swore that they'd kill you and Urd if we didn't, if we screamed or fought back ..."

Dim, almost-forgotten memories bubbled to the surface. Mother and Ingrid crying all day, every day, nonstop for weeks, until I thought them both mad. Læknir coming to visit eight days in a row, sending me out to the swimming hole with Garad to play while she and Grettir stayed with Mother and Ingrid; *it'd never made sense before.*

"We were lucky," Ingrid sobbed. "They didn't hit any seeds. But they could've. And Vespa was still sore from birthing Urd; she was in agony for days."

A long silence ensued.

"I'm sorry," I said softly.

Ingrid continued to sob. I sat there, not knowing what to do.

"You were just a boy," Ingrid whispered. "You didn't know."

She was right, even though it'd occurred right under my nose. I'd thought that Mother was sad because they took her amber necklace; I'd never known why Ingrid was sad.

How could I be so blind? Was I stupid? All this stuff happening around me; how much was happening right now that I didn't understand?

Ingrid curled up against Morgan's headboard and sobbed into a straw pillow; what was going on inside her mind? *How many people knew that women had baby seeds inside them?* Did Father know? Did Garad know? Derek ...? Clamsby ...? *Was I the only one who didn't know these things?*

Mated; they mated with the thieves. Ingrid had let them inside her, like I'd been inside of her. But Ingrid had never said a word. What could she say? That she and Mother had mated to ....

"You saved my life," I mumbled.

"What?"

"You saved my life," I repeated, "and Urd's life."

Ingrid hesitated. "I ... I guess so."

Suddenly Ingrid grabbed and pulled me tight against her, sobbing hysterically. I had no idea why, what I'd said, or what it'd meant to her, but I must've said something right.

* * * * * * * * *

Chapter 23

* * * * * * * * *

Sleeping beside Ingrid, even fully-clothed, gave me happy dreams.

"Close your eyes, Thron, and I'll tell you about Heimdal, the cursed god. Of all the Asier, Heimdal was the only god who never had a father. Heimdal was born of the dreams and wishes of the goddesses; nine they sat together, naming every virtue that they desired of a son, not only strength, courage, and wisdom, but nobility, beauty, and courtliness. So powerful were their loving designs that Heimdal came into being right before them, and all nine of those powerful goddesses claim to be his mother.

"Heimdal was chosen by Odin, for the goddesses had gifted him with the greatest eyesight and hearing; he could see to the ends of Yggdrassil and hear the squeaks of every mouse on all nine worlds. Someone had to keep watch upon the giants, to always keep an eye open for the coming of

Ragnarrock, so that the gods would know the instant that the great, final battle approached.

"Thus was Heimdal doomed. Never can he sleep, not even for a second, and eternal weariness he must suffer for being regarded as the best.

"Being best is every man's goal, but don't brag loudly about your superiority. Let others compliment you rarely; times come when the best are chosen to be sacrificed. Be the best, but be the best quietly; don't let yourself be chosen!"

* * * * * * * * *

A cold, strong hand pulled on my shoulder, prying me from perfect warmth.

"Come, Thron, time to get up," Father said.

Ingrid awoke with a startled, stifled scream.

"You, too, Ingrid. Vespa's getting dressed. Go make breakfast."

Suddenly I realized where I was: on Morgan's bed, cuddled against Ingrid ... with Father standing over us. Daylight peeked in; it was morning. Ingrid hurriedly pulled back the quilts and pushed against me until I was half standing, my bare feet on the cold floor. Then she pushed past us and rushed outside.

"Sleep well?" Father asked me.

I feared to say anything. I was still dizzy, floating in my transition from dreams to awakening. It'd been a wonderful dream; one of Father's bed stories.

"Vespa says that you've been hard at work each day, harvesting early. She also says that you've become a trapper, and that ferret last night was your catch. And about this Friar, and how you got injured: you've had a busy summer."

I bitterly recalled the fight that I'd lost to Garad: I hoped that he hadn't heard about that.

"I'm very proud of you, son."

Slowly I looked up into Father's eyes, trying to say nothing.

"I hardly recognized you, you've grown so much."

I tried to smile and hoped that he couldn't read the shame in my eyes.

"Next year," Father promised, "we go viking together."

My eyes opened wide as his words rattled inside my sleepy ears, and suddenly I was wide awake.

"Really ...?"

"Really," Father said. "You've grown into a man. After breakfast, we're going out into the fields so that you can show me what you've done, and then we'll talk some more."

I wrapped my arms around him and clung tight, bouncing with excitement.

"Thank you! Thank you! Thank you!"

"And Thron," Father said, "we need to talk about you and Ingrid."

I stopped bouncing.

"After breakfast," Father said sternly, and my jubilation lessened, although it didn't fully vanish.

I was going viking!

* * * * * * * * *

"You've harvested more than thrice what Vespa and Ingrid have," Father smiled, surveying the fields. "It won't take us long to finish at this rate."

"I've been out here every day when I wasn't checking my traps," I said.

"How far away are your traps?"

"Not far. I can leave at dawn, check them all, and be back while the sun is high."

"I'd like to see them."

"You would?"

Father dropped his empty turnip bag on the dirt.

"Let's go."

Father said nothing all morning as we walked from trap to trap. Three sat untouched. One had been sprung, but it was empty, the bait eaten. One had caught something, but it'd chewed through the cord, and I didn't bring any replacement. I'd also forgotten to bring some slop to bait the traps, but Father only laughed when I mentioned it. One trap had caught a fat squirrel.

"Not bad," Father said. "Good traps. You say that this friar taught you to make them?"

"Yes."

"I'll have to meet him."

Father and Friar James: *I'd not thought of that.* I wondered what they'd say to each other.

"Thron, are you sleeping with Ingrid?"

"Ummm ..., well, last night ..."

"I don't mean sleeping," Father said, and he used a word that I didn't know.

"What?"

"Mating."

"Oh."

"I'm not angry if you have," Father said. "It's just more proof of how fast you're growing. But you do know, I assume, that Ingrid may have more reasons than love."

I glanced at Father, but turned away before he caught my eye. Yet I couldn't refuse to listen, so I stood there, holding my dead squirrel.

"Ingrid isn't property," Father said, "not according to our laws. She's an indentured servant, owing her obedience to me. She can leave at any time, but only if she takes nothing that she didn't have when she was bought, which consisted of a dress that she outgrew years ago. Otherwise she'd be outlawed. Do you know what *'outlawed'* means?"

"She'd have to leave," I mumbled.

"No, she wouldn't," Father said. "Many people think that, but that's not how our laws work. Outlawed means she loses all legal standing, retaining no legal existence at all. Anyone could kill her, rape her, enslave and torture her, and no one could stop them. Even if she had powerful relatives, which Ingrid doesn't, they couldn't avenge her, because she'd have no legal essence. If they tried, their claim would be ignored, and Ingrid's whole family could be fined or outlawed by the Althing for attacking Ingrid's killer.

"That's why people who are outlawed usually leave, to protect themselves. So Ingrid's choices are to leave naked and penniless ... or be outlawed. That's why Ingrid has no choice but to stay: Ingrid is trapped.

"Ingrid has two chances of escaping her station: find someone who'll purchase her ... or marry. She's too old to purchase; buyers prefer children; they eat less, are more obedient, and live longer. Brothels would take her, but she'd be worse off there. Some old men prefer young wives, but they'd have to purchase her first, and there's plenty of free, wealthy young widows these days.

"You are Ingrid's best hope. If she marries you, then she won't need to be purchased; you're already in the family. But what would you gain from marrying her? You'd get to mate with her? You're doing that already, aren't you?"

I said nothing, feeling sheepish.

"Aren't you?" Father raised his voice.

"Yes."

"Don't tell anyone else, not Vespa, not your friends, no one," Father said. "Even if you keep sleeping with her, tell no one."

At that I glanced up, and saw Father's frown change to a smile.

"Marriage is about more than getting to mate with a woman. Marriage is like ... like the course that you set for the ship of your family. How you marry will decide what your whole family's life will be like, and the future your descendants will inherit.

"If you marry Ingrid then nothing will change. We'll go on as always, poor turnip farmers, until we die. But there are other women, Thron, and all of them get naked and lay on their backs. Many of those wealthy widows would love to marry a young husband like you, and then what would you have? Our farm and theirs; you could double our wealth overnight with the right marriage.

"And there's Helsa, isn't there? You like her, don't you? And she's very pretty. She'll be rich someday; she'll inherit her father's house and her step-mother's mansion. Have you ever been inside of Læknir's home? It's a palace compared to ours. She has a sweat-lodge in back, a small shack with thick walls and a big rocky fireplace where the steam is so thick that just sitting in it is like taking a hot bath. Helsa will inherit all; Læknir's sons are dead, her daughters married off. Healers make a lot from people's sufferings; if you married Helsa, then you'd be richer than Digr, and he's the richest peasant in Branwulf's county."

* * * * * * * * *

"Can I ride him?"

"Of course," Father said. "He's your horse. Tomorrow we'll have to work hard in the fields to make up for today."

"What's his name?" I asked as Father carefully positioned the blanket on his back.

"I never asked," Father said. "Why don't you name him? But first, notice how I place the blanket and saddle high across his shoulders."

Father instructed me as he saddled the horse and tightened down the big strap, then put the steel bar into the horse's mouth and affixed straps around its head. I watched fascinated, anxious to mount him. *I couldn't wait to show him to Derek!*

My horse was tall and muscular, mostly black, but not pure; a darkish-charred color with ashen-gray patches dotting him all over.

"Slepinir," I said.

"That's Odin's horse," Father said. "It's a good name, but I thought that you wanted your own horse. Don't try to name him right away; get to know him first."

What to name him? Something big and powerful, like Lightning or Thunder? Something deadly, like Deathwind or Killer?

"He's ready."

Excitement surged through me. Father stood back and held out the reins. The leather straps felt hot in my hand. I stepped forward and tried to put my foot in the stirrup, but at my slightest touch, the hanging stirrup swung away from my boot. I tried again, but to no avail. Father stood watching me with a silent frown. Suddenly I felt as if I'd just let the pig escape from its pen; I tried to focus, but eventually had to reach down and hold the stirrup still with my fingers while I slipped my boot into it and put some weight on it.

Abruptly the horse stepped away. I shouted and tried to stay against it, but I only clung to its saddle and hopped forward.

"Stupid horse!" I shouted, and I pulled to hold him still, but all of my strength proved nothing against his; the harder that I pulled, the more easily he stepped away. I tried to shift my weight forward, to pull myself up by the saddle, but just as I managed to get my other foot lifted off the ground, the horse suddenly shook like a wet dog, and I crashed hard onto the dirt.

Father was holding his reins when I looked up.

"Watch, son," he said.

Father kept the reins in his hands, gripped the saddle firmly, pressed right up against the horse, and then suddenly he stepped right into the stirrup and stood up on it, flung his other leg over the horse's back, and sat on the saddle. He dismounted with equal ease.

"I wanted you to fail," Father said to me. "I always do. Do you know why?"

I looked at him uncomprehending; *he wanted me to fail?*

"Failing has a cost," Father said. "You need to know what that cost is so that you appreciate how important it is to succeed.

"Someday your own son will need to learn something, to harvest turnips, to ride a horse, or to kill a pig. Just because you tell him how to do something, even if he manages it, doesn't mean that he understands it. To truly know something, you have to learn more than just how to do it; you have to learn how to teach it. If I only teach you how I do things, without teaching you how to teach them, then all of my knowledge dies with you.

"Now try again."

I stood up and brushed off the dirt.

"Look at the stirrup," Father said. "Watch it, ready yourself, and then mount fast."

What must Father think of me? That I'm an idiot ... but I brushed away that thought. I had to concentrate, to prove myself, and do it right for once. I timed my breaths, then took my chance.

The saddle slammed against my butt ... and I sat looking down at Father. For a moment I felt disoriented, and then the realization hit me: *I'd done it! I was riding my horse!*

No. Actually, I was sitting on my horse. It wasn't moving anywhere. But Father was smiling.

"Do you see what I mean by teaching through failure?" Father asked.

I glanced at him questioningly.

"You're not going to ride him overtop our fields, are you?" Father asked. "You'll crush our turnips before we get them out of the ground."

I looked around frantically; *what was I forgetting?*

"Wouldn't it be easier to get him onto the road ... if you opened the gate?"

I hesitated; I didn't want to look like a fool in front of Father ... again, but ....

"I'll do it," Father laughed, "this time. Go on, get the feel of him, and have fun. Tomorrow we have to harvest. But remember what I said: be careful and go slow. Stay on the main roads and don't let him eat too much grass. See that he drinks lots of fresh, clean water. If he gets sick or hurt, then I'll take him back."

Father opened the gate. I took a deep breath and pulled

the reins to direct my horse toward the gate; the horse turned his head, but otherwise, he didn't move.

"Give him some encouragement," Father said.

I lightly kicked my heels against his ribs ... and still he didn't move. I pulled and kicked a little harder. Nothing. I increased my pull ....

Suddenly the horse whinnied in complaint, snorted fiercely, and finally took a step. I felt a little intimidated, but I didn't dare show it in front of Father. The horse walked slowly, rocking me from side to side on his back. I gently urged him on.

"Don't push him," Father said as I rode out the gate, "but make sure that he knows who the boss is. Just don't make him angry; he's bigger than you."

* * * * * * * * *

I could've walked to town faster, but never had I arrived with such style. People were used to seeing Derek on young ponies, since training and exercising them was what he did for his family's ranch. Everyone who saw me stared; a new horse being ridden by a boy who'd never owned a horse before was a spectacle.

At first I waved at everyone, but it felt foolish because my horse walked so slowly. I had to keep a firm grip on him and keep him in the center of the path, away from the tall grasses. Once he ignored me and stopped in front of some grass growing beside a fencepost; it took a lot of kicking and pulling to get him to walk away from it, and he snorted meanly; I tried not to be scared.

I kept petting him and talking to him; he liked the sound of my voice. He walked easily, lazily; I wanted him to go faster, but my fear and Father's warnings held me back. It'd take me a while to get used to riding him, but after harvest, I'd ride him every day. Ideas popped into my mind; on horseback, I could explore much farther than I ever had on foot. I could ride to neighboring villages, down the coast, even up into the snowy mountains. The whole world was open to me.

"Thron!" Friar James shouted as I rode into town.

I couldn't have asked for better: Friar James was standing outside of Rath's house beside Derek, Kal, Sjóna, Skratui, and Helsa.

"Where'd you get him?" Kal asked.

"Nice stallion!" Derek said at the same time.

"Well, look at you!" Friar James didn't raise his deep voice but easily overspoke the children. "What a handsome beast, and you look very grown-up on top of him. Is he yours?"

"Father gave him to me," I answered proudly.

Derek and Kal rushed forward to pet him and my horse stopped, seemingly enjoying the attention. The sisters Sjóna and Skratui stayed back, looking nervous and saying nothing, but Helsa stared open-mouthed.

"Thorir must trust you a great deal to give you your own horse," Friar James said. "Are you going to start lessons soon?"

"Lessons?"

"Rune lessons," Friar James said. "We began this morning; open to anyone who wants to come."

"Got to finish harvest," I said. "Maybe afterwards."

"Of course," Friar James said. "We're just covering the basics now ... you already know it. We won't start fully until all the crops are in."

"I'll come," I promised; it sounded better than sitting

around the house all winter.

"Well, we might as well end it here," Friar James said to the kids. "Be sure to be back by mid-morning tomorrow; that means before noon, Derek. Bring a small, sharp stick, and you'll each be getting a pad of clay to write on." Friar James stepped forward and patted my horse's head. "Good to see you again, Thron. Maybe you'll let me ride him someday?"

"Sure," I said, althouth I wasn't ready to let other people ride him just yet.

"Let me ride him!" Kal shouted.

"I'm the best rider!" Derek insisted.

"Nobody rides him until I say so!"

Friar James nodded approvingly, then he walked back inside Rath's house.

"What's his name?" Derek asked.

"I haven't given him one yet," I said.

"What about 'Champion'?" Kal suggested. "Or 'Warrior'? Or ...."

"Father said that I should take my time."

"That's smart," Derek said. "Some horses don't fit their names, and wrong names make them look stupid. How about a ride home? He can carry us both."

"Good idea," I smiled. "Helsa, would you like a ride home?"

Derek looked offended and Kal seemed confused. Sjóna blushed pink while Skratui giggled.

"I'd love to," Helsa said.

I held my hand down to her. We gripped wrists, but I couldn't pull her all the way up.

"Here," Derek said, and he laced his fingers and bent over in front of her.

A moment later, Helsa was sitting behind me, her arms

tight around my waist. I pulled my horse's reins to one side and kicked him gently. At first he didn't move, seeming offended by the extra weight, but Derek grabbed his bridle and pulled him a few steps, and the horse didn't object. I didn't thank Derek but noted it; Derek rode lots of horses: I could learn a lot from him.

"No kissing!" Derek taunted as we rode away.

* * * * * * * * *

Chapter 24

* * * * * * * * *

The horse was laboring; the first part of the hill was steep, and he was carrying two of us. I let him rest; he was strong enough to carry us non-stop to the top at a gallop, but I didn't want to press him on our first day.

"He's a magnificent horse."

Helsa's voice almost startled me; I was never as aware of anything as I was of her arms around my waist, her chest occasionally bumping against my back as the horse jostled us back and forth. He stopped, breathing, and I let him rest for a moment.

"Yea, he's great," I agreed.

"You're quite surprising," Helsa said. "Farmer, trapper, scholar, and now horse-owner."

"Scholar ...?"

"You're the only one in the village who knows how to write."

"Friar James knows."

"Friar James isn't of the village."

"Everyone will be able to write soon."

"Yes, but you're the first. You're changing our village."

"No, I'm not!"

"Yes, you are," Helsa insisted, and she gave a little tug, pulling me against her.

"You're changing the village: you're becoming a healer."

"The village has always had a healer; I'm just the next in line."

I didn't know what to say ... and we sat in silence.

"Do you want me to walk the rest of the way?" Helsa asked.

"What? No, I'm sorry; I was just thinking."

"What were you thinking?"

"Just thinking."

"Well, that's more than most boys do."

I prodded the horse onward. He seemed tired of standing still and began climbing at once. Helsa held tight to me; I could feel her small breasts pressed against my back.

"Thank you for the ride," Helsa smiled sweetly as I reined in before her house, and then she took my hand. I held her arm tightly as she slid down to the ground. But when I let go of her grip, I found my hand firmly grasped.

Helsa blushed, and then she let go of my hand and slowly walked toward her front door. I sat there unmoving, watching her swaying walk ... until her door closed.

* * * * * * * * *

No feeling in the world matches riding your own horse.

The farther I rode, the farther I wanted to ride. I only wished that I could take him viking so that I could ride him into battle.

I'd been so excited about having my own horse that I'd forgot to tell the guys my even-better news: *I was going viking next summer!* I definitely had to tell Garad!

I couldn't wait to go viking. Nothing would frighten me, despite countless dangers. Father would see how fearless I was, and I'd be rich from the booty I stole. Then, having gone viking, having killed innumerable Saxons and Danes, and watched the Irish and Scots run like cowards before me, I'd come home rich beyond my wildest dreams, to my house, to my farm, and to my own horse. I'd buy servants to harvest for me, spend every day riding ... and every night with Ingrid.

Ingrid; I couldn't wait to take her riding. What could Mother say? Maybe I should take Mother riding first so that she wouldn't be suspicious, and then I could take Ingrid on a warm, sunny day up into the hills, just the two of us. We could ride so far away that no one would ever find us, and we could do anything, everything, with no one to ever know.

The sun was almost set, so I reluctantly steered back toward our house. It'd be fully dark before I reached home.

Taking off the saddle was a lot simpler than putting it on. The blanket under the saddle was wet with sweat, so I hung it over the door to his pen before I brushed him down, as I'd done the few times that I'd gone riding with Derek.

"How was it?" Father asked.

"Wonderful," I said.

"Ingrid, put his dinner back on the fire," Mother said. "Thron, try this on."

Mother held up the new tunic that she'd been working on. It was bright red with a rabbit-fur collar: one of my first catches. It fit great, and the fur collar was warm and fuzzy around my neck. I felt like a whole new person. The red wool was thick and warm, and the sleeves actually stretched past my wrists.

“Put your belt on so that we can see it properly,” Mother said.

“Put your sword on,” Father said.

Soon I slid my scabbard into my belt and turned to face them.

“Very nice,” Mother said.

“Nice?” Father said. “Look at him! I’m glad that he wasn’t dressed like this the day that I got home; I wouldn’t have recognized him.”

“Very handsome,” Ingrid smiled.

Mother shot her a glare, and Ingrid instantly stopped smiling.

“I’m sure that Helsa will think so,” Mother said harshly.

Ingrid frowned, hung the cook-pot, with the last of the stew, and then swung it back over the flames.

“Now take it off,” Mother said to me. “No point wearing it around the house.”

“No, leave it on,” Father said. “I waved to Clamsby as I rode past him yesterday, and I promised him that I’d come to Tavern Hall and tell him how I survived. Tomorrow I’ll be too tired, so I’d best go tonight. Thron should come with me.”

“Can I ride ...?”

“No, horses need rest, too,” Father said. “Eat quickly, then we’ll walk into town.”

“Take it off while you eat,” Mother said. “That took forever to weave; no point spilling on it before anyone sees it.”

* * * * * * * * *

Cheers rang out as Father entered Tavern Hall. Clamsby held out a beer mug for Father, welcoming him to sit by the fire. Kampi was there, and Rath, Smiðr, Brún, Trandill, Gandr, and Hjálmun.

"Welcome back!" Rath shouted, and he seized Father in a strong, crushing hug.

"You had us worried!" Kampi said. "We wanted to wait, but ..."

"I never would've made it back to our ship," Father said. "Saxon knights chased me through five houses ... and almost caught me twice."

"Start at the beginning," Gandr urged.

"Can I drink first?"

I stood watching, proud of Father, but also a little annoyed; I was wearing my new tunic with the rabbit fur collar that I'd trapped myself, my sword in my belt, and no one had even noticed. Then I looked to the far end of Tavern Hall; sitting alone at a table in the corner was Derek, drinking all alone, staring fixedly at the empty table before him. He startled as I walked close.

"Oh! I thought you were a grown-up."

"We both are," I reminded him.

"Yea, right," he slurred his words, then took another drink.

"What's wrong?"

"My father," Derek said.

I hesitated; Derek's father was buried under a mound below Seal Ridge.

"He was a terrible father," Derek said. "He beat us. I had a sister, did you know? She was just a baby, but she wouldn't stop crying; Father hit her to make her quiet. She died a few days later. Father said that she just stopped breathing; Mother never believed him, but she was so terrified of him that she worshiped him. Can you believe that? He beat her most of all ... and she always stood up for him.

"But Father would've let me go viking."

"What ...?" I asked, and I sat down on the bench across from him. "You should've gone viking this year! You aren't going next year?"

"How can I? Horses and cows have to be fed, watered, milked, trained, moved from field to field. Mother can't do it; she's too old. We'd be starving right now if I hadn't taken over the ranch, but now what? If I go viking, then all of my animals will die."

"What're you going to do?"

"Sometimes I think that I should just throw it all away, jump on Branwulf's ship, and never come back," Derek said. "I'm a great fighter, better than you or Garad. I don't need this backwater village. I ought to ..."

Derek fell silent as a shadow fell over us; Clamsby had come up behind me with a pitcher of ale and an empty mug. He glanced at us as Derek stopped talking, then reached over and filled Derek's cup.

"Well, Thron, you look very grown up tonight. New tunic? I like the collar."

"Thanks."

"One of your catches?"

"Yes."

"Very impressive. Well, what would you like? Ale?"

"Please."

"And how will you pay for it?"

I froze, eyes wide.

"Thorir drinks for free tonight," Clamsby said. "It's my gift to him for making it back alive. I don't usually give ale away for free."

"I don't have any ..."

"Do you have anything for trade?" Clamsby asked. "That's a nice looking sword ..."

My hand fell protectively over my scabbard.

"I didn't think so. What else have you got?"

I thought hard, and finally it hit me.

"I have another rabbit-skin pelt."

"A plain rabbit-pelt is worthless to me," Clamsby said. "Of course, rabbit-pelts can be made into useful things. I could use a new rabbit-skin pouch. Could you make me one?"

"I ... I guess so."

"Fine," Clamsby said, and he set an empty mug in front of me and filled it with ale. "You drink tonight and you owe me one rabbit-skin pouch. I'll expect it by Saturn's Day."

"Okay," I replied, and he smiled, then wandered back to the men.

A rabbit-skin pouch? How was I going to make that?

"You should've bartered with him," Derek said. "A really good rabbit-skin pouch would be worth two night's drinking."

I shrugged my shoulders; I had no idea how I was going to make a pouch.

"I've got a bunch of new pelts," I said.

"Oh, yea, you're a trapper," Derek said. "You're probably going to go viking, too."

"Father said so today," I said. "Next summer."

"Lucky bastard."

"There has to be a way to get you viking," I said. "Maybe you could buy someone?"

"I can't."

"Why not?"

Derek hissed, as if building up enough pressure to explode.

"My mom's an idiot," he said. "She wants ... she wants another husband."

"What ...?"

"She wants to get married again."

"So?"

"I can't let her."

"Why not? Then you'd be able to go viking ..."

"I'd lose everything."

"What ...?"

"I'm my dad's sole heir. Right now I own the ranch; if she marries, then her new husband could claim the ranch, throw me out, and mom wouldn't say a word against him."

"Then you could go viking."

"And come back to what? Branwulf doesn't take on warriors year-round, only during the summer. Either my animals will die, or mom will marry the first man that comes along."

Derek took another swig, then nodded to the men laughing by the fire.

"Look at them, Brún and Trandill," Derek said. "There's two ripe prospects; a young cow, or a couple of old horses, and they could buy their freedom from Digr and set themselves up in my chair. And Gandr; could you imagine having him for a father? My whole house would stink like rotting seaweed."

"How can you stop her?"

"Mom's at home," Derek said. "I moved her in with Ingmar, her old servant. They're not allowed to open the door for anyone but me, nor to talk to anyone."

"How long can you keep that up?"

"Forever, if I must."

"But that means ... *you can't ever let her out, never let her leave the ranch!"*

"What other choice do I have?"

I couldn't believe my ears: Derek's mom was a prisoner. Mother would never live like that, and would beat me if I even suggested such a thing.

Looking at me, Derek cursed softly into his cup.

"You got the right idea," Derek scoffed. "You're marrying Helsa."

"What?!?" I shouted so loudly that the adults fell silent and stared at us, and we spent a moment wishing that we were elsewhere.

"I'm not marrying Helsa!" I hissed softly after the men resumed talking.

"Oh?" Derek smiled evilly. "You didn't give me a ride home. Did you snuggle and kiss on top of your horse, or stop on the ...?"

"Shut up!"

Derek pursed his lips and made kissing sounds.

"You marry her!" I snapped.

"Helsa ...?" Derek laughed. "I've thought about it; she's going to be worth some real coins someday, but she talks too much, and thinks too much, for a woman. Never marry a woman who talks back; Father warned me of that so often that I hear it in my sleep."

My insides crawled. *Marry Helsa ...?*

* * * * * * * * *

"A pouch?" Ingrid asked. "Easy. I can make it tonight."

"Why do you need a pouch?" Mother asked.

"It's not for me," I said. "It's for Clamsby, for his ale. We ... made a trade."

"A waste of a good rabbit-skin!" Mother made her disgusted sound. "You could've traded him some of your new cups when they're finished. Wood's more plentiful than rabbits."

"I think ...," Ingrid began, but Mother suddenly glared at her and she quieted.

I stared at the two of them, wondering what'd happened. Father and I had stayed out late last night, drunk too much, and my head felt like Smiðr's anvil.

"Come, Thron," Father said. "We have to make up for yesterday."

I wanted to ask Ingrid what was going on, but Mother was listening, so I followed Father outside.

Harvest; the thought sent shudders up my spine. The twenty rows closest to the back fence were already pulled; I'd done them during the weeks before Father came back. We only had about sixty more rows to go. Father started where I'd left off, and I started on the row next to his. We always harvested the farthest-back acres first; turnip thieves were less inclined to pull ripe turnips from the center of your fields. Arriving in the pantry first, they'd be piled on the bottom, and fully ripe by the time that our turnip supplies ran low.

Mother and Ingrid helped harvest, of course, after their other chores were done; we saw them hard at it as we carried our sacks back to be emptied. They harvested near the house, around the barn, and worked their way toward us. But they had to make sure that Father and I weren't distracted so that we could spend all our energy harvesting.

Father harvested very fast, probably to teach me some

lesson, but this year I didn't fall behind. This year I was bigger, stronger, and could yank turnips out of the ground just as fast.

Garad was already carrying a full bag of onions back toward his house; they must've started very early, and still they'd done less than I'd expected. Father had said that he'd take Garad and I viking, when the time was right, but I didn't think that he was speaking to Grettir anymore; Mother wouldn't allow it. So what would happen to Garad? Would he, like Derek, be forced to stay home all summer? *Would Garad ever get to go viking?*

Father pulled ahead of me while I was watching Garad, but I didn't want Father to think that I couldn't keep up with him, so I focused on harvesting. Father was starting to see me as a man; *I needed that to continue.*

* * * * * * * * *

Mother and Ingrid had done another three rows, but close to the house, so they were half the length of the full rows. Father and I had done four rows each, but we were stumbling with exhaustion as we carried our last heavy bags back in the growing starlight. We heard Grettir's distant shouts at Garad, but we were too far away to hear her words, and it was too dark to see them clearly. Yet we both knew that they were still pulling onions at this late hour, and after a momentary guilty glance, we stopped looking at anything but the ground before our feet. Neither of us could suggest helping them; Mother would have a fit.

Father pushed against the door only to find it braced.

"Vespa! Ingrid!"

Almost at once, we heard the brace being lifted, and the

door opened.

"Why ...?"

"Strangers on the road," Mother said.

"Merchants headed toward Market," Ingrid said.

"A bit early, isn't it?" Father asked. "Still, keep bracing the door. If any strangers knock, send them out to Thron and I."

My ears perked; *did Father just include me?*

Ingrid took the heavy bag from Father and carried it to the smoky pantry. I followed. We stepped inside together, and then closed the pantry door behind us all but a crack. Ingrid gave me a quick kiss, very quietly, then started stacking turnips on the small pile already there. I wanted another kiss, but suddenly the door flew open.

"What's going on ...?" Mother demanded.

"Uh, just putting away ...," Ingrid started.

"Thron, come out of there; Ingrid can stack turnips without your help."

With a deep sigh, I stepped out of the thick air, and Mother closed the door all but a crack.

"Don't dawdle, Ingrid; the house is filling with smoke."

My eyes met Father's as I stepped away from the pantry door; he wasn't pleased, but saying anything would only make it worse. But I was getting mad; Mother was treating Ingrid worse every day.

I sat on my stool by the fire, Father in his big chair. Mother brought us bowls of mashed turnips speckled with tiny cubes of meat.

"Good squirrel," Father said after his first bite.

I nodded appreciatively, but kept eating. Something was gnawing on my mind, something that I'd almost forgotten.

"Father, could we go to Market this year?"

Father paused, mouth full, and took his time before

answering.

"It wouldn't be easy," Father said. "We couldn't take more than a dozen bushels. We don't have a cart, and it would cost more to buy one than going to Market would make. But we do have a horse ... and I'd like to see Branwulf again..."

I edged forward on my stool. *Was he saying yes?*

"I'll think about it."

*　*　*　*　*　*　*　*　*

Chapter 25

* * * * * * * * *

"No traps today," Father said. "The sooner that we finish harvest, the more likely we'll go to Market."

Father's words fueled me. Ever since Ingrid had told me of it, going to Market seemed thrilling, like a magical adventure. The next day, I hurriedly repaired, reset, and rebaited my traps, and then hurried home to help pull turnips ... with a big new rabbit.

On Saturn's Day, Mother went into town. She took the rabbit-skin pouch that Ingrid had made; I'd complimented her so much that Ingrid promised to make one for both Father and I. Mother reported only that Clamsby had been satisfied; I felt certain that he'd said more, but Mother wouldn't repeat their conversation.

All too soon my excitement faded. Harvest was everything that it'd always been: exhausting drudgery. I hurt from scalp to toes, and just carrying endless bags of turnips back home seemed worse than being burned alive. I tried to think about going viking or being alone with Ingrid, but the sheer, dull tediousness of pulling turnips by the hundreds blanked my mind of everything except the shooting pains that increasingly cut through my constant agony.

My suffering was nothing compared to Garad's. He and Grettir were out before dawn, pulling stinky onions, and were still there long after we quit. But I didn't dare mention it in front of Mother.

* * * * * * * * *

Finally, the last turnip was wrenched from the ground. Father gave a sarcastic cheer and I dropped it in the sack, picked up the bag, and we walked back to our house together.

It was a great harvest. The pantry was stacked to the ceiling, and six baskets by the wash-basins were overflowing with turnips as we staggered inside and set the last of our burdens on the floor. Mother came up and hugged Father and I, and Ingrid smiled as she sliced, fresh turnips for dinner.

"Are you really going to Market?" Mother asked.

"Why not?" Father laughed. "We'll only be gone a few days, and turnips fetch a better price there."

"What if you have trouble?"

"Thron and I can handle it."

I should've kept my mouth shut. I should've said nothing, especially not in front of Mother, but I was exhausted and had just finished seven weeks of mind-numbing harvest.

"Ingrid grew up there ...," I said.

"You're not taking Ingrid!" Mother shouted.

* * * * * * * * *

"Taking Ingrid would leave Vespa alone with Urd," Father said as we stood by my horse in the barn. "One woman and a baby, alone on a farm in a house by the main road; that's asking for trouble."

"She wants to find her mother, sister, and brothers," I explained.

"You can look for her," Father said.

"Really ...?"

"Ingrid's part of our family," Father said. "But I hope that you've thought about what I said ..."

"I have."

"Good, but don't mention looking for Ingrid's mother in front of Vespa. I'll get Vespa out of the way to give you a few minutes alone; you can ask Ingrid where to look for her family."

* * * * * * * * *

"Bless you!" Ingrid shouted, and before I could shush her, she threw her arms around me and kissed me.

"Mother will be back any second," I warned her. "Where do I look for them?"

She blurted out directions, still holding me pressed against her, and then she took my hand and pressed it against her breast.

"I want you so bad ... atop me, inside me ...!"

I squeezed her breast; *it felt so good!*

Father coughed suddenly, right outside the door, and Ingrid shoved me away just as the door pushed open. Mother stormed inside, and glanced at us standing far apart.

"It's crazy," she said to Father. "Digr grows wheat, more than we could hope to grow. We raise turnips; why divide our fields when we can just trade? What do we know about raising wheat?"

"It was just an idea," Father insisted, and he winked at me.

* * * * * * * * *

Father carefully selected young, tall trees with slender trunks and not too many branches. We cut down eight of them, stripped their branches, and hauled them back home. Father tied the eight long, thin trunks together carefully in two bundles, four in each, at their thinnest ends, and then he tied the two bundles together with three lengths of rope, each about three feet long. He hung these over the fence, then tied all eight of the thicker ends together, each with a wide handspan of rope holding them apart. Then he laid wide strips of bark over the branches.

"It won't be easy," Father said. "We'll have to lift, while the horse pulls, all the way, but we should be able to drag it to Market."

"How does it work?"

"Like a sledge," Father said. "The two thin ends go on each side of the horse. One rope goes across his chest, the other two across his back. We bag our turnips, stack them on the sledge, and tie them down. If we go carefully, our sledge should survive all the way to Market."

* * * * * * * * *

The next morning, Father took five of our best baskets and left. I slept in about an hour, and then went out and saddled my horse. He didn't seem happy to be roused so early; the mornings were growing chilly, and I could see my breath if I blew slowly.

I was riding toward town when I met Father walking back. He'd traded our baskets for large bags big enough to haul lots of turnips. He made me dismount so that he could ride back home. He handled the horse masterfully; the horse never even tried to pull to the side of the road.

Father dismounted at the gate and let me start out again while he took the sacks inside. I rode off, but again I only made it halfway to town before I reined in again. Rath was driving Læknir's cart toward me; I moved out of his way, but shouted to him as he passed.

"Where you going?"

"Grettir's," Rath shouted without slowing down.

Læknir peered out at me from inside her carriage, and I caught a glimpse of Helsa's sun-bright hair as they sped past.

My horse slowly edged to the side of the road to chew on some long grass while I sat still, watching the wagon roll up the road. I wondered what was going on, but I wouldn't be welcomed there.

Eventually I tore my horse away from his snack and urged him back into the center of the road. Almost nobody in town was awake. Smiðr's hammer pounded rhythmically, but he didn't like kids hanging around his shop. Every farm had people out in their fields. Father and I'd worked hard, finished early, and tomorrow we were leaving. I'd hoped to see one of the kids, to brag about going to Market, but no one was wandering around town save for Beigaldi, with several very small children in tow, as she carried a basket of oats toward Tavern Hall, her youngest daughter, Sygn, in her arms.

I rode past town, out where the trail thinned and cut across Digr's lands. I spied Hal and some others working in Digr's fields, but they were busy and too far away to see clearly, so I rode on.

A group of riders with a wagon appeared on the road coming toward me; merchants headed to Market. I couldn't wait to see it, especially with Father. *Would tomorrow never come?*

I smiled as they approached: a rickety cart pulled by two horses with one driver, and a wagon filled so high that its tarp, stretched tightly over it, seemed to be holding whatever they were carrying from spilling out on all sides. Three riders led the cart, two men and a greasy-looking boy, seeming only slightly older than I.

"Hi!" I said.

"Nice horse," the boy said. "Want to trade him?"

"Not a chance," I replied.

The trail wasn't very wide; I'd ridden slightly aside so that their cart could pass. The greasy-looking boy rode right up beside me.

Suddenly he jumped me. An arm closed around my throat, and a dagger appeared in his hand. Our horses collided; I almost fell off, but he gripped me tightly.

"Karg!" shouted the driver. "Are you mad? These backwater villages hang you for killing!"

Karg, the boy holding the knife at my face, twisted around to glare at the driver.

"You can't take stolen horses to Market, especially not one whose rider was killed!" shouted the driver. "Save that for the ride home!"

With a grunt of disgust, Karg pushed me so hard that I fell off my horse and toppled to the ground. I kicked to free my right shoe from its stirrup, and rolled to keep from getting stepped on by my horse's hard hooves.

"See you around, boy!" Karg sneered at me.

* * * * * * * * *

"Father? Can you ... come outside?"

Father, Mother, and Ingrid all stopped stuffing turnips into sacks and looked up; something in my voice must have belied my distress. I turned away; I didn't want to face them.

Læknir's wagon was still outside Grettir's house, and Rath and Garad were sitting out on their fence, both looking uncomfortable. Grettir must be sick or hurt, with Læknir and Helsa inside for so long, but I didn't have time to worry about them.

"Thron ...?" Father asked, coming out the door behind me.

I gnashed my teeth. I didn't want to tell him, but we were going to Market ... and they were going to Market ....

"Karg," I hissed between clenched teeth. *"They said his name was Karg."*

Father grabbed my arm and turned me to face him.

"Who's Karg?"

His face paled as I told him. His expression grew grave. Only twice had I seen him so resolute; as he was carrying dead men off Branwulf's ship, and as he said goodbye to me, not knowing if he'd return.

"I'm sorry," I said after I'd answered all of his questions.

"For what?"

"I ... should've ... shouldn't ..."

"You shouldn't have been so trusting," Father said. "If this Karg had been coming from Market, instead of going to it, then you'd be dead, and Karg would have your horse, and we might never have learned where they came from."

"You taught me to fight ..."

"Not when there's a dagger pointed at your face," Father said. "Not when it's four-to-one on a deserted road. There's a time for courage, son, and a time for wisdom."

"I'm ... I'm ..."

Father caught me up in his arms as I started to weep. I tried not to, didn't want to, but ...

"It's all right, son. This won't go unpunished. I have friends at Market."

* * * * * * * * *

"Wake up, Thron. Time to go."

My brain throbbed. I wanted to sleep.

"Hurry, Thron."

I crawled farther underneath my blanket.

"Thron!"

At Father's yell, I pushed back my covers. Candles lit our house, and I peered painfully through half-closed eyes. Mother was pouring something into a pot. Father and Ingrid were almost dressed.

"Get your clothes on; it's cold out there."

I looked at our tiny slit of a window; it was black.

"It's still night!"

"We need to get going if we want to be at Market tonight."

Minutes later, I was dressed and hauling heavy bags of turnips outside, where the air was misty and chill. We stacked the sealed bags on the bark slats; Father carefully arranged each bag. Then I stood back and watched while he tied ropes all over the sledge, strapping down our produce. Ingrid went back inside and retrieved our packs, which were full of food and our best clothes.

Mother came out with a bowl and spoon in each hand; mashed turnips in fresh goat-milk, all warm and soft. Father and I ate quickly while Mother harangued us about being safe, keeping clean and dry, and coming back as soon as possible. Ingrid brought out our cloaks and swords, and presented both of us with rabbit-skin pouches that she'd made, identical to the one that she'd made for Clamsby. Father complimented her greatly; Ingrid grinned widely while Mother scowled.

Finally it was time to go. Father took two ropes and wrapped them around his neck; one was a thick rope tied to the base of the sledge, and the other was a thin rope tied to the horse so that he could steer from the back.

"Put this on, Thron," Father said, and he lifted up a thick rope identical to the one that he'd looped over his neck.

The rope was too short; once it was looped over my neck, I could barely stand up. The weight of the sledge, burdened by our turnips, was staggering.

"Ingrid, get the horse started," Father instructed. "Take its halter and pull it out onto the road. He'll resist; don't be afraid to pull hard."

Ingrid pulled, and the horse started forward, but the weight of the sledge held him fast.

"Harder!" Father shouted, shaking his long reins. "Now, Thron, lift and pull! Let's get this sledge moving!"

Its weight was enormous, so much that I doubted if we'd even make it out of our gate. I strained and grunted, and just when I was about to suggest that we take fewer turnips, the horse pulled hard and the sledge slid forward six inches.

"That's it!" Father shouted. "Keep going!"

It was horrible, back-breaking; we might as well have tried

to lift Thor's hammer, but we managed to drag the sledge slowly out of the gate and onto the trail. Ingrid pulled the horse with all of her weight; it snorted and hissed and tossed its mane in protest, but she kept pulling, and finally he got the idea.

Mother shouted good-bye from the gate, but we couldn't reply. I struggled to lift the sledge off the rough dirt to help it slide smoother, but to little avail.

Finally Father made Ingrid let go; the horse stopped, and we had to start all over again. It took three times before he got the idea and proceeded on with Father steering from the rear.

"Go ... back ... home!" Father grunted to Ingrid. "Stay ... inside ... both ... of ... you!"

I kept pulling and lifting on my side, while Father did the same on his side. Slowly we made our way up the trail. It was still dark, the few dim stars peaking through the clouds barely lit our trail, making footing treacherous.

About mid-morning, we heard shouts; a merchant with three wagons, each pulled by two horses, was slowing down right behind us.

"Get that crappy thing off the trail!" he shouted. "Move aside!"

About half an hour later, we were laying on the grass, exhausted. We'd pulled off the road and stopped for a rest. Father watered the horse and passed me a flask of watery-ale, then collapsed beside me. We were still breathing hard when he announced that we had to keep going. Fortunately, another merchant was approaching, with his whole family, aboard wagons piled high with goods, and they laughed at us as they rode past.

The entire day passed in a black memory of endless

torment. By noon, the back of my neck was rubbed raw, so I switched to my right shoulder, and by mid-afternoon I switched to my left shoulder, but after that the thick rope had rubbed me raw everywhere that it touched, even on the palms of my hands. Several times we had to pull aside to let laughing merchants pass, and once, where there were ditches on both sides and we couldn't let him pass, one merchant cracked his whip over our heads. Father dropped his ropes and drew his sword while I was still flinching from the sound of the crack, and the frightened merchant subsided.

Twice the ropes underneath our sledge broke and we were forced to stop, but Father had brought plenty of spare rope. Our ropes were rubbed in half, cut by countless sharp rocks, and often they got caught on tough tree roots, which forced us to back up and try again. I'd never ached so much. We were too tired to eat, but we drank a lot and refilled our empty flasks at every stream.

The sun set quickly, and still we struggled. I was exhausted, but Father kept shouting encouraging words at me, compliments of my strength and endurance, and somehow I managed. We strove to the foot of a great hill and rested there as the sky grew dark overhead, and then pushed on. The rise seemed impossible; afoot, without the sledge, I'd have barely noticed the rise. Lifting and dragging the sledge, every slope was a mountain.

Around midnight, I began complaining ... and still Father refused to stop. He explained, between grunts, that we'd fall asleep, and both of our throats would be cut before we woke up.

The sky was growing light, the dawn approaching, before we spied the fires. We'd just crested another hill, and below us, in a wide, distant field, were many rows of encampments, some lit with fires, torches, and lanterns. We actually cheered.

But it was a weak cheer; *a thousand harvests would be easier than this!*

* * * * * * * * *

Chapter 26

* * * * * * * * *

"Thron, wake up!" Father said, shaking my arm.

"Wha...?"

"I know," Father said. "I hurt, too. But we made it. We're here."

I lifted my head. The bright sun was high in the sky. I lay wrapped in my cloak, leaning against the sledge. Father was yawning beside me.

"Did ... did you sleep?"

"A little," Father said. "Come; I need you awake."

Father handed me our flask and I drank a little, then he gave me some bread and cheese. The raw sores on my neck and shoulders ached.

"Time to change," Father said. "We need to look our best here."

We pulled off our sweat-soaked, dirt-stained tunics, and put on our newest garb. I put on my new tunic, grimacing as the stitching grated across my swollen, tender shoulders. But the soft rabbit fur around my neck felt infinitely better than that cursed thick rope.

We'd dragged our sledge into a space next to a rickety cart filled with woven tree-bark carpets and fine white woolen linens. The cart had poles on each corner which held up a shade over the cart, in which two old women were sitting, both of whom were calling out to the many passersby, inviting them to examine the quality of their cloths and woven carpets. They had two young daughters and a boy almost my age, who had a bow in his hands, a noched arrow, and looked distrustfully at me.

"Stay with the sledge and the horse," Father ordered. "I need to walk about and see what prices turnips are getting. Don't leave the sledge for any reason! Dig a hole and crap in it, if you must go before I get back. Crap under your cloak to keep from being seen, but don't lose sight of the sledge, not for an instant. If someone throws rocks at you, don't chase them more than a few paces. If someone says that I'm hurt and need help, don't believe them. Stay with the sledge!"

"I will," I promised.

"Go ahead and dig the hole," Father said. "Keep the dirt in a pile so that we can bury it after we fill it up. I'll be back in a few hours. Remember: horse and turnips! Never stop watching them!"

"When do I get to see Market?"

"You will," Father said. "Before we leave here, you'll see everything, more than you'd believe right now. Stay awake! Keep your sword in your scabbard, but don't hesitate to draw it if you're attacked. But if they flee, don't chase them out of sight of the sledge. Just shout *'guards!'* as loud as you can."

Father patted my arm, then walked down the lane and

disappeared into the crowd.

I yawned loudly, glanced at the little boy next door, who was eyeing me suspiciously, and I waved at him. He scowled in a manner that would've been funny if he hadn't been armed. One of the old ladies there smiled at me, then turned her attention back to the crowd.

"The finest weave in all Norway! The purest white! Smooth as silk!"

I stood up and looked around. I was still aching, but I was here, at Market. People that I'd never seen before walked past, the strangest-looking people that I'd ever seen. Some men were fatter than Digr, so fat that I was amazed that they could walk down the lane. Others were very tall, or very short, and there were women in just as many shapes and sizes, each so different from our village that I couldn't believe the variety. Everybody seemed so unusual that I found myself just staring at them. Some had pale white skin, like Ingrid, but others looked so brown that I wondered if they were born that way, and one woman had hair so thick and black that each strand looked like hard iron wire heavily-oiled and blackened in a fire.

"What's in the bags?" I was asked several times.

"Turnips."

"First time at Market?" one man asked me before he continued walking down the lane. "Don't be ashamed. You should open a bag and show them off."

"Turnips ...?" asked one boy not much older than I was. "That's what we came here to buy! My father's out shopping for turnips right now."

"Really?" I asked. "Well, my father should be back soon. Maybe they'll make a trade."

"I don't know," the boy said. "We're camped on the other

side, and my father's too old to walk very far. Let me see your turnips; then I can tell him about them."

I'd been thinking about opening a bag, but hesitant until this opportunity arrived. Gladly I opened one bag; what could it hurt? The sooner that Father sold our turnips, the sooner I could explore Market.

"Those are big turnips," the boy said. "Biggest that I've seen this year. Tell you what: you give me just one to take back to my father, and when I show it to him, he'll be sure to come by tomorrow. What do you say?"

"Sure!" I said eagerly, and I gave him a good sized turnip, hoping that it would impress his father.

"Thanks!" said the boy. "See you tomorrow!"

I grinned as he quickly walked off down the lane.

"Ha!" laughed the boy with the bow and arrow. "Mother, did you see that? He just gave that boy a turnip for free and let him walk away!"

"Now, Lagor, I'm sure that he just felt sorry for the boy," the old woman said. "It's good to help the poor."

"He's not poor," I corrected her. "He's going to show it to his father."

The old woman raised one eyebrow.

"Is he going to bring the turnip back if his father doesn't buy your whole crop?"

I stammered, but no answer came.

"Don't be quick to believe anyone here, son, not unless you've known them all your life," she said.

Her boy laughed hysterically.

Chagrinned, I grabbed the hilt of my sword and jumped out into the middle of the lane, but the thief was gone ... with my turnip. Then I remembered: what was I going to do? Abandon our whole crop just to chase down one turnip?

Even my horse would be gone before I got back!

Cursing, I kicked up a clod of dirt and sat back down against the sledge.

That afternoon, another wagon pulled up beside me, a big wagon filled with large barrels. An old man drove it, and he had two big, loudly-barking dogs riding on top of his barrels. I reached out to pet one and it snapped its teeth at me.

"Don't!" shouted the old man. "They're not friendly! Try to pet them and you'll lose your whole arm."

He got down off his rig.

"Irgwin's the name, boy," he said, and he looked at my opened bag. "Good looking turnips you got there. Make a good dinner, I'll bet. I got plenty of wheat in my barrels. What say we trade, a handful of wheat for a good-sized turnip?"

"My father will be back soon," I said, not wanting to be robbed again.

"Let me know when he returns," Irgwin said.

* * * * * * * * *

"Stupid guards!" Father cursed. "I tried to see Branwulf but couldn't get inside."

"Branwulf's here ...?" I asked.

"Of course Branwulf's here!" Father said. "Where else would he be?"

"With ... with his ship ...?"

"His ship's down there," Father pointed, "in the fjord. His house is just over that hill. Branwulf runs Market; these are his fields."

Ingrid was right: *I'd no clue what was going on.*

"When can we ...?"

"I left a message," Father said. "We'll see if he gets it."

"What do you mean?"

"You'll see," Father smiled. "Meanwhile, let's eat something, and then I can stay with the sledge while you walk around Market."

"Really …?"

* * * * * * * * *

After an endless lecture on safety, Father gave me a single copper coin and let me go off on my own. I instantly stepped away from the sledge, then stopped, not knowing which way to go. Father smiled at me; I grinned back, then headed off down the path all by myself. *Finally, I was going to see something!*

At first, Market seemed smaller than I'd expected. I wanted to hurry, but each merchant had something new, and I wanted to see everything. I was surprised when I came to the end of the row rather abruptly, then I followed the crowd around to the next row and began making my way up it. The people were just as fascinating as their wares; I'd seen plenty of oats and celery, although never in these quantities, but I'd never seen so many strange people or so many colorful tunics and dresses. Some people seemed bothered by my stares, and one woman, who was knitting in front of her cart, was so beautiful that I just stopped and stared at her. She had gleaming brown hair, dark eyes, and looked like a goddess descended from Asgard, but suddenly a big man stepped in front of me, glared menacingly, and I moved on.

I made my way up and down four rows before I topped the rise, and then I stopped and stared.

Market was huge, far bigger than I'd expected. The slope

of the next valley was hidden by countless tents and carts, flowing as far as I could see down to a group of buildings so large that I stood stunned. Every building was bigger than Tavern Hall, and more merchant-tents stood on the other side of the buildings, leading up the hill past them. In the water, in the fjord, floated countless boats, and in the center of all of them was Branwulf's dragonship, docked as if it belonged there.

I couldn't believe my eyes. So many people, such huge buildings; *who could've imagined it?*

The day passed in a mesmerized blur of faces, colors, and trinkets, pottery and weavers, tailors, smiths, and farmers. Several sword-makers and armorers were there as well, some with hot forges set up, and I pressed against the other boys watching them beat iron into steel and shape them into swords. Everybody wanted to sell me something, to trade for my sword, my tunic, even my boots, but I refused them all, keeping my hands on my sword and my single copper.

I began to hurry as the sky darkened; I still hadn't seen everything, but I'd promised Father that I'd be back before sunset. I made it to the buildings as the sun touched the sky; they were huge, mostly barns filled with cattle and horses, but they had ropes across their entrances with guards to warn people away. The biggest house had wooden steps out front, leading up to its door, and I stared at them; these must be the stairs that Friar James had told me of. No house in our village had stairs. I walked up and down them twice before a guard ordered me off.

I went to look at Branwulf's ship; *I was finally going to sail on it in the spring!* But I'd seen it before, so I just wandered around the water's edge, looking at all the other strange boats. Yet, when the sun was halfway below the sea, I hurried back to Father. If I wasn't there by sunset then I wouldn't get to explore tomorrow.

* * * * * * * * *

"So you didn't buy a thing?"

"No," I complained. "I saw a lot of great daggers, but they wanted five coppers for even the smallest."

"Well, that's what they cost," Father said. "Don't worry; it'll all still be here tomorrow."

"That's true," Irgwin said. "Everyone here'll be glad to take your money ... as long as they can give you less than its worth."

I ate more of my boiled turnip. Irgwin was a strange old man with cookware, fresh water, and firewood, and Father agreed to let him cook our meal in exchange for sharing our turnips. I'd have preferred something else; Market boasted fruits that I'd never seen and meats from dragons, musk ox, and reindeer. But Father seemed content, and Irgwin wasn't nearly as threatening as his dogs, one of which was tied to the center of his wagon, the other staked out under his horse.

"Can I go out again?" I asked Father eagerly.

"Not at night," Father said. "It's too dangerous."

"It is," Irgwin agreed. "You won't see me leave my dogs while the stars are out. Last year, a gang of thugs surrounded a guy standing alone; they cut his throat and robbed him, in the middle of a huge crowd, and nobody heard anything until someone stumbled over his corpse."

All evening, I watched the dark strangers walk past our sledge with suspicion and regret. They were definitely different than they'd been during the day: more sinister. Everyone was drinking, dancing, laughing, and even singing as they walked past. I saw three beautiful young girls, about the same age as Ingrid, skip past our fire singing a strange song, and dancing with their arms around each other and bottles in each hand. I would've loved to meet them, to ask them why they were so happy, but they were gone in an instant, vanishing around a group of men coming from the other way, who were laughing their heads off, and so drunk that they staggered, almost falling down; people jumped aside to avoid colliding with them.

Everyone seemed to be having a great time ... and nobody seemed to be getting hurt.

"No!" Father said flatly as I looked imploringly at him.

"Can't blame the boy," Irgwin said. "First Market, first day off the farm, young and eager; I'd be wanting to go off and have some fun. But alone? That's crazy!"

"Some people are alone," I argued.

"Some people are crazy," Irgwin said.

* * * * * * * * *

Guards, more than I'd seen in one group, stopped in front of the old ladies' cart. Guards were easy to recognize; they all wore red and black striped tunics, the same design as all of the flags around the center of Market, the main house, and the docks. I'd been watching the crowd for hours, even after Irgwin had washed his pots and gone to bed. Father lay nodding beside me, leaning against the sledge.

"He's got to be here somewhere!" shouted a deep voice. *"Thorir!* Where in Niflhiem are you? *Thorir!"*

"Branwulf ...?" Father asked, and then he shouted *"Branwulf!"*

Father jumped up as the guards lifted their torches and

surveyed us. Branwulf jumped out of the middle of them wearing a gold-colored tunic and a bright red cloak.

"Thorir!" Branwulf shouted, and he embraced Father tightly. "You fox! I thought you were dead!"

"So did I, more than once," Father replied.

"Couldn't believe it when they told me that you were here," Branwulf said. "Come to the manor! We've drinking to do!"

"Got turnips here, a quarter of my tradable crop," Father said.

"Serg, post a guard here," Branwulf said to one of his men.

"Branwulf, this is my son, Thron."

"Good size," Branwulf smiled as he looked at me. "Can he fight?"

"We'll find out," Father grinned. "He's coming with us next year."

"Excellent!" Branwulf smiled. "Welcome aboard, son! If you can fight, drink, and wench half as good as your old man, then you'll always be welcome on my ship!"

* * * * * * * * *

"Sammuel!" Father cried as we walked up the magnificent wooden steps, and through a huge front door, carved with ravens and war-hammers, into a hall that was so big that I couldn't believe my eyes, which was filled with cheering people, standing in small groups or laying about against long, short, stubby tables.

"Thorir!" Sammuel shouted, and he and Father rushed to embrace. Sammuel looked nothing like I remembered, now wearing a red and black guard's tunic; still tall, pale, and very thin, with his thin beard now oiled and twisted to a point.

"What're you doing here?" Father asked, amazed.

"Me?" Sammuel laughed. "We thought you were killed!"

"You live here?"

"Had to leave Finland; bad story, tell you later. How'd you escape the Saxons?"

"Made it to Jarl Oakney's ship just as he set sail," Father explained. "Almost got speared by his own men; mistook me for a Saxon knight."

"We sailed for days looking for you!"

"We looked for you, but then turned south."

"Enough of this!" Branwulf said. "To the tables, before you tell every tale you know!"

I stared at everything, completely overwhelmed. The vast hall was mostly dark despite many bright torches, one of which would've illuminated our whole house. Two tall fireplaces blazed on opposite walls and candles shined on every table, but it still wasn't enough to brighten the huge hall. Father walked right into the center and Sammuel went with him and, to my surprise, Branwulf grabbed me by the arm and pulled me along.

"Don't be surprised, boy!" Branwulf said loudly. "Everyone who vikings with me is welcome in my hall!"

I gasped and gaped. *Had my whole life just changed?*

A loud cheering erupted as Father and Sammuel approached the center table. Several men got up and hugged or shook hands with Father, including one that I recognized.

"Hjálmun!" I gasped.

Hjálmun turned at looked at me, glanced back at Father questioningly, then offered me his hand.

"Thron," he said quietly.

I shook his hand, astounded. Hjálmun had never spoken to me before; I didn't think he knew my name. As Hjálmun directed, I sat on one side of Father, Sammuel on the other. Our table was the longest that I'd ever seen; at least sixty people crowded around it. Hjálmun sat next to me and drank from a painted horn.

The noise was deafening. Everybody talked far more than listened, and most laughed the whole time. Even Hjálmun seemed amused. Father retold of his escape from the Saxons, how he'd sailed the rest of the summer with Jarl Oakney, and of all the treasures that he saw the Jarl collect; Branwulf scowled at that.

In the distance, from outside the hall, came a thunder of loud drumming, and several people lifted up their heads.

"I hate when they do that!" Sammuel said, frowning. "I can't sleep with that noise."

"It makes them happy," Branwulf said. "Young girls like to dance and men like to watch 'em. Drummers draw a big crowd, all in one place, so the guards can watch them more easily."

More food appeared on our already crowded table, set there by smiling servant girls. Several men at our table obviously knew the girls well, and took liberties whenever they came near. One man apparently went too far; a serving girl poured a tankard of ale over his head, but he only laughed aloud.

I could die happy here!

* * * * * * * * *

I'd eaten a great deal, and drunk even more, when Father pulled me up. I tried to ask where we were going, but the hall was too loud. He led me out of the main hall, down a long corridor to a small room with a large fireplace, many chairs along three of the walls, and one huge table. The room was warm and richly furnished with bright tapestries, banners, and cruel-looking spears. I wanted to examine the spears closely, but my attention was stolen by the strangest object I'd ever seen.

Over the fireplace, a big rectangle of ornately-carven wood was mounted, and in the middle of it was a man, very tall and old, wearing thick robes, who seemed to be staring at me. But it wasn't a man, it was a colorful picture of a man, yet like none I'd ever seen. It wasn't a drawing or a mosaic, but made of many different colors: it seemed to be ... painted on cloth.

"Don't touch anything, Thron," Father warned.

Branwulf stood inside, talking to a strange man in whispers, and then the man nodded and walked out. At a signal from Branwulf, the guard followed the stranger.

"What is it, Thorir?"

"I've something for sale."

"I hope that you don't expect me to buy it. Do you know how much it costs to host Market?"

"Yes, but the vikings ..."

"Damn the viking! Damn Jarl Oakney!"

"What'd he do?"

"You saw his treasure."

"Part of it, yes. Your agreement ..."

"One seventh, and I should have bargained more carefully!"

"But didn't you get ...?"

"A seventh, aye, and more, but of what? One seventh of the gold? One seventh of the silver? No, I got a seventh of the stolen horns and blankets and women's dresses! What am I going to do with a hundred women's dresses?"

Branwulf pushed angrily at the papers on his table.

"Sell them?" Father suggested.

"Want to buy a dress?" Branwulf sneered nastily, and Father looked down. "No one does. I have merchants selling them for coppers. I lost money this year. And the vikings were barely paying for themselves."

"We need to find less protected lands," Father said.

"Show me where!" Branwulf shouted, waving at a large map on his table, and then he subsided. "There aren't any. If there were, we raided them long ago, and now they have nothing." Father glanced at me, but I said nothing. "My steward can help you sell your turnips, but he'll take a portion, perhaps more than it's worth. You might make a better deal by yourself."

"You're welcome to take a portion ... if you can help me with something else."

Branwulf glanced at Father, who lifted his hands to his throat and pulled out a tiny pouch on a leather cord around his neck.

"Jarl Oakney kills men who withhold from him," Branwulf said.

"You don't sound like a friend of Jarl Oakney," Father said. "I never swore a sailing oath to him."

"What'd you steal?"

Father opened the tiny pouch and drew from it the golden rosary. Branwulf came forward and took it from his hands.

"Well done!" he grinned. "You could get four gold coins for this in Oslo."

"I don't know anybody in Oslo, not that I'd trust with this," Father said. "I'll give it to you for three and your promise of silence. But not in gold; I can't spend gold back home. Silver and coppers ..."

Branwulf shook his head.

"A gold coin just to sell it ...?"

"I would if I could," Branwulf said. "But who would I sell it to? What if I can't sell it right away? I don't have enough coppers or silver to trade for what this is worth." Branwulf sighed heavily. "I can trade land or goods, but gold? You alone had a better viking than I."

* * * * * * * * *

Chapter 27

* * * * * * * * *

All day I sat in front of our sledge. Father brought three men by to look at our turnips, but they offered pitiful prices, and finally walked away. Each time Father cursed a little louder, paused to calm down, and then went out to look for more customers.

Little happened during the day. Several strangers tried to talk me into giving them a turnip for free, some promising to pay later, others just begging. I sent them all away empty-handed, even the beggars, some of whom I suspected were not as old, sick, or feeble as they appeared.

Irgwin and the old women spent the day calling to everyone who passed by. The old weaver-women, whose young son still carried a bow fitted with an arrow, were much louder and more vocal than Irgwin. Many people stopped by or waved to him as they passed, but while he greeted everyone, he didn't even try to show them his grain; he didn't seem excited about selling his wheat.

"Nobody wants to buy this early," Irgwin explained. "Everybody wants to make an outrageous deal. No one will, of course, but they all hope to, so day after day they run around like headless chickens trying to cluck through missing beaks. Most deals are done in the last few days, when people have to settle on what things really cost, and then they go home grumbling. I could do the same, but why? I'll stay to the end and, mark my words, boy: someone'll come up to me moments before they have to leave needing wheat. I'll offer a fair price, much less than the ones who raise their prices on the last day, hoping to snare a desperate buyer. They'll buy my barrels for the same price that I'd sell them for today."

"They waste Market …?" I asked.

"No, not waste," Irgwin said. "That's what makes Market, why all these people are here, not because they have to, but because they want to. Coming to Market is the highlight of their year. If they sell all of their goods and buy all that they need on their first day, what reason have they to stay? Look at them, boy! Tell me what you see!"

The crowd passed by: a woman with a squawking baby in each arm, a boy who looked so lost that I doubted if he'd ever be found, a guard who looked as bored as I, and fat man in a fancy maroon tunic with big pointy shoes who stormed past with a furious look on his face. I glanced at Irgwin; suddenly we both laughed.

The day passed much brighter after that. Occasionally we'd point to someone in a terrible hurry and make up some reason why they were so rushed.

"Look how he walks!" Irgwin said. "He's been so busy that he hasn't crapped for three days!"

"Look at all those braids!" I laughed. "If she twists one

more, her head's going to pull itself into a knot!"

Then a beautiful girl walked by; we both grinned widely.

* * * * * * * * *

"Not many can buy turnips," Father said. "Most want to trade for them, but what good's that? We'd have to drag whatever we trade for back home, and I don't think our sledge'll make it."

"What about Ingrid?" I asked. "When are we going to look for her Mother?"

"I've asked a few people," Father said. "Her house is in the village just north of here, but nobody that I talked with knew her. We'll go searching once we sell our turnips."

"Irgwin says that most deals are done on the last day of Market," I said.

"Yes, but every day that we spend here, Vespa and Ingrid are home, unprotected," Father said. "Things get worse when Market ends; strangers riding right past our house for days. I don't like leaving them alone, and I hope that you don't, either."

I glanced down, hoping to avoid the subject.

"Have you given any thought to what I said about Helsa?"

I hesitated, then shrugged, hoping that it would suffice.

"One bad harvest," Father warned. "One early freeze, one late snowfall after the planting, one summer where it rains every day; then what'll we eat? What'll you pass on to your sons?"

* * * * * * * * *

Market was chaotic and noisy, everyone rushing about,

and everything changing fast, but it looked different today. I walked about; Father let me go wandering, as long as I came back before mid-sun.

Suddenly a frightfully-familiar voice seized my spine, and I glanced through the crowd at a wagon I'd not seen before. The merchant who'd caught me riding alone on the road was calling to passers-by, and sitting by him, asleep, was Karg, the boy who'd held a knife to my throat, and threatened to kill me and steal my horse.

I had to tell Father!

* * * * * * * * *

"What did you expect?" Father asked. "You knew that he was coming here."

"What if he sees me?"

"Avoid him. Run from him, if you must. Until we sell our turnips I don't want him to know that we're here."

"Well, what do you know?" Irgwin laughed, suddenly coming up to talk. "I sold my wheat! An old friend came by and liked my grain, bought it all, and I didn't have to do anything! I might've gotten a little more, but friends are more valuable than anything else, wouldn't you agree?"

"What'd you get?" Father asked.

"Turnips," he beamed, grinning widely. "Your turnips."

Father and I exchanged confused looks.

"I live alone on my farm," he said. "What good are coins to me? I need food, not coppers, and your turnips are mighty tasty. Here." Irgwin held out both his hands to Father, his palms full of coppers. "This is for your turnips, if you'll take it. You might be able to hold out for more, if you want to, but that'll take a while, and you need to get home. So I called in a favor, and an old friend bought my wheat this morning."

Father took the coins and smiled at Irgwin.

"Done," Father said.

"Thron, you're a good boy," Irgwin said. "I could've gotten more food for those coins, but instead, I hope that I've made friends of you and Thorir. Friends are what really counts in this world. Friends are what I come to Market to make. I could sell my grain whenever I wanted to because I make friends every time that I come here. I'll be able to sit here with your turnips in my wagon and trade half of them for other things from now until Market closes ... because of friends."

"You're a friend for life," Father said. "Our farm's a day's ride south of here; just ask for us. We'd love to have you stay for dinner."

"I'd love to," smiled Irgwin, "but my home's three days north of here. My buyer's sending his boys with a cart to unload my barrels; I'll have to mind my dogs while they do. Once it's empty, if Thron here will load your turnips into my wagon, then we'll have a done deal."

I smiled. It was work, but I'd be glad to do it ... *for my friend.*

"Of course, I'd be very grateful if you, an obviously important man, would introduce me to Branwulf," Irgwin said. "I've always wanted to be a friend of his."

"We'll go straight there," Father promised him.

* * * * * * * * *

"There he is," I said to Sammuel. "Brown tunic, the ugly one with the greasy hair. See? He's drinking from that horn."

"We'll get him," Sammuel said to Father, Irgwin, and I. "Wait here."

Four guards pushed through the crowd, seized Karg, and wrestled him to the ground. Karg shouted curses and struggled, but the guards hit and kicked him until he subsided.

I led the way back to Branwulf's house, two of the guards half-carrying Karg as he stumbled between them. Sammuel and another guard didn't come with us. Everyone in Branwulf's hall stopped talking as Karg was drug inside and thrown to the floor in front of Branwulf.

"Stay down!" Branwulf commanded.

Karg glared up at him, then climbed to his feet.

"Impudent fool!" Branwulf shouted. "Do you know who I am? Get back on your knees, or I'll have my guards teach you respect!"

Karg stood, glared, and said nothing.

"Teach."

Eight guards came forward, smiling and clenching their fists.

"Not fair! You can't …! Stay back!"

The fool tried to fight back. The guards had little difficulty pinning him, and they punched until he stopped resisting.

"Had enough …?" Branwulf asked, motioning the guards back.

Karg was lying on the floor, bloody, beaten, and bruised, and in Branwulf's hand was a smoking, red-hot poker.

"Thron, come forward," Branwulf said.

Father laid a hand on my shoulder and gently pushed me forward. I went as directed, and Father stayed right behind me.

"I understand that you met Thron before," Branwulf said to Karg, his angry voice almost a growl. "Pulled a knife on him, and threatened to kill him and steal his horse. Is that right?"

Karg looked up as I approached, and fear crossed his eyes as he recognized me. But, badly beaten, he barely moved.

"He ... he's a liar," Karg snarled.

"Is he?" Branwulf asked. "Here, Thron." Branwulf handed me the red-hot poker. "Why don't you ask Karg if you're a liar?"

I stood there, holding the glowing, smoking poker. *Did Branwulf really want me to burn Karg with it?* Not that I'd have minded seeing it, but to do it myself ...

"Don't burn him!" Father whispered in my ear. *"Just make him think you're going to hurt him! Scare him!"*

I grinned wickedly; *that I could do!*

Karg looked defiant as I approached him, but despite his beating, he managed to crawl away as I held out the red-hot poker. The crowd suddenly came alive.

"Burn him!! Burn!!"

Karg struggled to stand, and suddenly someone threw a gnawed-bone at him, then a piece of bread, and someone hit him in the face with a half-eaten apple. Karg cursed them all, then scrambled to his feet and faced me. His hand reached into his trousers and pulled out a knife.

Two guards grabbed the end of the carpet that he was standing on and jerked it out from under him, then jumped on top of him, and moments later Karg lay weaponless, pinned between the two big guards.

"Burn him!!!" chanted the crowd.

I came slowly forward. Karg squirmed and cried out, his expression twisted with horror, but the strong guards held him fast. I lowered the poker, edged it toward his face, closer and closer. I leered and tried to look mean. It wasn't difficult;

he'd tried to steal my horse!

"No!" cried a deep, frantic voice, and Father's hand closed on my shoulder and pulled me back.

It was the old merchant whom Karg traveled with, the one that I'd assumed was his father. Sammuel and another guard were holding him back.

"Get away from him!" he shouted. "*Get away from my boy!"*

"Enough!" Branwulf shouted, and the whole hall fell silent. Branwulf turned to face Karg's father. "I understand that you met this boy, the son of my friend, on the way to Market," Branwulf said to the frantic merchant.

"Never saw him before," the merchant said.

"Perhaps not," Branwulf said. "Perhaps so. Why should I believe the word of your son over the son of my trusted friend?"

"You have no proof ..."

"I don't need proof!" Branwulf bellowed. "You're on my land! This is my Market! These are my friends!"

"The boy's not dead!" argued the merchant. "He's wasn't even hurt!"

"So ... you did see him," Branwulf said darkly.

The two men stared at each other.

"My boy was just playing," the merchant finally said.

"That's all we're doing," Branwulf grinned wickedly. "Playing ... *playing with your son."*

"He's got a brand ...!"

Branwulf seized the red-hot poker from my hand and brandished it at the old merchant, and the merchant fell to his knees.

"You said that you never saw him, and then admitted that you did! You lied to me, Branwulf, lord and owner of all these lands! I should sheathe this down your throat!"

"Mercy!" he cried.

"For lying to me, you're now suspect," Branwulf said. "If anything bad happens at Market, any thefts, injuries, or murders, then I'll hold you to blame."

"But this is Market!" the old merchant whined. "There're always ...!"

"Then I suggest you leave before anything bad happens," Branwulf said. "Sammuel, help these thieves off my lands!"

Roughly Karg and his father were dragged from the hall. The crowd laughed uproariously, and Father and Branwulf shook hands.

* * * * * * * * *

"Yes?" came a voice through the gray, cracked door. "Who is it?"

"Two friends," Father answered. "We're looking for Carrin, who had a daughter named Ingrid."

"There's no one here named that."

"This would've been seven years ago. She lived in this house."

"I bought this house two years ago. Go away!"

"Please, do you know ...?"

"Go away!"

"Who're you looking for?" asked a youthful voice.

We turned to find a young boy, about nine years old, standing in the street.

"Carrin," Father said. "She used to live here. She'd be an old woman by now."

"Are you from Market?"

"Yes. Is your mother home?"

The boy's mother feared us at first, but after we explained our search, she helped as best she could. She'd never heard of Carrin, but she took us up and down the street, knocking on many doors, and letting us ask her neighbors. Many remembered Carrin, but no one knew where she went, or what happened to her children. Some asked about Ingrid, how she was, and recalled her as a child playing with her older brother in the street, but no one had ever known what happened to her. Many delighted to hear that Ingrid was well, and told us all about the other residents of her house, which had been sold four times since Carrin had moved out.

Far past sunset, Father and I gave up. All that we'd learned was that Carrin had left the village suddenly, about a year after she'd sold Ingrid to Father. She'd left willingly, pulling a hand-cart piled with all of her belongings and two small children; it wasn't the news that I'd hoped to give Ingrid.

* * * * * * * * *

Market at night was fascinating. Father and I wandered through the crowd; I'd never guessed that so many people existed, let alone gathered together. Even in the daytime, when I could see more people, it didn't look so full, so vast, with dark, mysterious strangers emerging from every shadow.

We watched several magicians do things that I couldn't believe; they worked real magic right in front of packed crowds, and some people walked past without a sideways glance. *Was magic so common here that people were bored by it?*

I saw amazing jugglers, acrobats, and beautiful girls that danced before a bright fire surrounded by a ring of drummers and crowds of smiling men. But Father only let me watch for a few minutes at each place, then pulled me toward Branwulf's hall.

Suddenly I slammed into someone in the dark.

"Excuse me...!" I said, and I looked up; it was a beautiful woman.

"No problem!" she laughed. "You can bump into me all night!"

Suddenly her arms wrapped around me and she squeezed herself against me.

"Sorry!" Father laughed, grabbing my arm. "He's in a hurry."

"But he's so handsome!" smiled the woman. "I'll bet he'd like a nice warm bed for the night. How about you? I can do two, if you like ..."

"Tempting, but we haven't sold our crops yet," Father lied. "Of course, if you'd let us pay you later ..."

She laughed at Father, and he laughed back; no one here was going to trust anyone. Suddenly she kissed my cheek.

"You sell those crops, then come find me, eh?"

She pushed off into the crowd, and a moment later, another man just happened to stumble into her, and she wrapped her arms around him.

* * * * * * * * *

Branwulf was deep in conversation with Irgwin when we entered, but both waved to us as we found a vacant spot at the table. Father and I spent the night in Branwulf's hall; there was lots of food and drink, people laughing, and as the candles slowly died, people curled up and slept in their cloaks. Father joined the snoring crowd early, but I stayed awake, listening to men talk of old vikings, spying couples mating in the shadows, and listening to the drumming and revelry still going on outside.

I reached into my rabbit-skin pouch; the copper coin that Father had given me was still there. I was loathe to leave Market with my first copper unspent.

* * * * * * * * *

Outside, Market was dark and exciting. I set off quickly, nodding at the door guards standing under torches, drinking from their horns.

I headed for the drummers; the dancing girls were jumping over the flames, each time to an encouraging cheer from the men. I liked watching the girls, and wondered if Ingrid would dance like that for me. Their drums looked like bottomless buckets with shaved animal hides stretched tight across one end: I could make one of those.

I stood among the cheering men, my head spinning, and then I stepped back from the fire; there was more to Market, and I wanted to see it. I reached into my pouch and pulled out my one copper; I wanted something to remember Market by.

"You!" gasped an old woman.

Suddenly she seized my shoulders and spun me around. I found a deeply wrinkled face almost touching my own, and tried to draw back.

"Stand still!" she snapped gruffly. *"I must examine you!"*

Frozen, uncertain, she examined every inch of my face, then pulled open my palm, the one with the copper in it. I started to cry out when she plucked the copper from my hand, but she stared at my empty hand as if it held something very tiny, and then she pressed my copper back into my grip, and seized my head in her hands.

"The bump must be here, I know it!"

Quickly she ran her fingers through my hair in every direction, messing it up, but then she fixated on a spot on the back of my head.

"It's you!" she gasped wheezily, her eyes wide, delighted. "You're him! The Champion!"

"The ... *what?"* I asked.

"The Champion of the North!" she grinned. "The Avenger, foretold by legend; I knew it was you! You're going viking next year, aren't you? Sailing south to find your fortune?"

"Yes."

"It's as the legend foretold," she said. "You have all the marks."

"What marks?" I asked. "What legend?"

She glanced nervously about.

"I can't say, not here," she said. "It's too dangerous. Perhaps you won't find the gold or claim your kingdom."

"Gold ...?"

"Shhh!" she shushed me, and then she glanced suspiciously about. "Come, come with me. I'll tell you everything."

She led me through the crowd to a tent behind two stalls. Without hesitation, she pulled me inside. Skulls hung from its canvas ceiling; human skulls, animal, all kinds, some with horns or fangs. The flickering red candles illuminated an incredible scene; treasures and jewels lay everywhere. Many things were hanging beside the skulls; strings of beads and snakes that seemed alive, but weren't, and strangely-colored tapestries and scarves. On a round table was a chest of large gleaming gems and chunks of gold piled so high that they spilled out onto the table. Many other things gleamed, but my eyes hadn't adjusted to the light before she snatched up a glass jar and shoved it in my face.

"Look!" she cried. "Look! Behold the eye of Odin!"

I gasped and stumbled backward. Inside the glass jar, floating in some liquid, was a giant eyeball.

"You see, don't you?" the old woman laughed wildly. "You recognize it, don't you? Those destined to enter Valhalla could never fail to recognize the eye of Odin! You're a warrior; destined to enter Valhalla!"

"Uh ... I, um ..."

"Only the true Avenger, the Champion of the North, could see so clearly," she insisted. "The Gods of Asgard have smiled on you. You're destined to sail south this spring on a mighty dragon, just as the legend foretold."

"What legend ...?"

"The Champion of the North," the old woman said. "He'll walk ignored, but his greatness shall manifest. The evil serpent Jorgamund will rise from the deep, and even the bravest sailor shall quail before him. But the wise Avenger shall know that only gold appeases the first son of Loki, and he shall hurl a lump of pure gold into the monster's mouth. Then the monster will sink beneath the waves, and the Champion of the North shall be acclaimed the bravest and wisest of all. For sacrificing his only gold, Odin shall rain wealth and glory upon him, and before he returns home, he'll conquer all of Wales!"

I stared incredulously at her, her wild expression, the intensity of her eyes.

"Aim well when you throw your gold, boy!" she cried. "Aim well, and the entire world will be yours!"

I stammered, trying to say something, but my mind was

spinning.

"Where is it?" she demanded. "Please, let me see it! Show me your gold!"

I shook my head.

"Show me your gold!"

"I don't have any gold!"

"No gold ...?" she gasped. "How will you appease the Midgard Serpent?"

I had no idea what she was talking about.

Slowly she reached out and took my arm in one hand, and with her other hand, she reached out to the priceless chest of wealth on the table. Carefully she selected a large chunk of gold.

"This golden nugget is worth twenty silver coins," she said. "Do you have twenty silver coins?"

I shook my head.

"Can you get twenty silver coins?" she asked. "Without this gold nugget, you and all who sail with you will be devoured by Jorgamund. Do you want to die and kill all of Branwulf's men?"

"No, but ..."

"How much do you have?" she asked, and then she seized my hand that I still had clenched around my coin. Slowly I opened it and looked at my one copper.

"Ahh, you would ask me to sell this huge gold nugget for a single copper?" she scolded me. "You must think me mad. But you're the Champion of the North; someday wealth such as no man has ever dreamed of shall flow through your hands. Would you promise me, if I give you this priceless gold nugget, that you'll return here and pay me back the remainder of what this golden nugget is worth?"

I nodded; *was she really offering ...?*

She removed the coin from my hand, and slowly, firmly placed in my palm the shining golden nugget worth twenty silver coins.

"You've chosen wisely, Avenger."

* * * * * * * * *

Chapter 28

* * * * * * * * *

"It's gold, Father; twenty silver coins worth of gold!"

Father put down his spoon and took the nugget. He held it up to his eyes.

"I told you not to go out alone."

"But Father ...!"

"Thron, this isn't gold," Father said. "It's a shiny yellow rock."

"No, it's ..."

Laughter erupted from the table. I glanced from face to face; *they were wrong, they had to be ...!*

By the time that we'd eaten breakfast, the joke had spread all over the hall, and Branwulf himself bowed to me, mockingly calling me the *'Champion of the North'.*

* * * * * * * * *

"Vespa!" Ingrid cried. "Thorir's back!"

Mother came out and watched us approach. Father was riding my horse; I'd walked all day without complaint. After hauling our sledge, walking home from Market was a pleasure.

Mother looked happier than I ever remembered, but as we drew near, Ingrid fled back into the house.

"How did it go?" Mother asked.

"We sold the turnips," Father said. "Unfortunately, we didn't sell everything."

"So you still have it?"

"Let's talk about it inside."

* * * * * * * * *

Father and I took turns interrupting each other as we told all about our trip to Market, what it was like, and about all the strange people. Mother seemed fascinated, but Ingrid barely listened; I tried to catch her eye a few times, but not once did she look at me, and she left the table early to begin washing dishes.

My old bed was a welcomed joy as I sank onto its soft straw and curled up under my familiar blanket. Mother added a quilt; the nights were getting cold. I slept warm and happy, contented for the first time in days.

* * * * * * * * *

The next morning Ingrid still wouldn't look at me. She'd taken the news of her lost mother as if it didn't matter at all, yet looked as if she were about to cry.

Finally, when Ingrid got back with the sea water and then

went out to feed the chickens, I announced that I wanted to check my traps, and slipped out the door while Mother and Father were again discussing the golden rosary.

"Ingrid, what's wrong?"

Ingrid tried to push past me without answering, but I blocked her easily. I was almost as tall as Ingrid now; she couldn't out-wrestle me as she used to. She pushed, but I pushed back.

"Why don't you go ask Helsa ...?" Ingrid finally shouted at me.

"Helsa?" I asked. "Wh...?"

"Yes, Helsa!" Ingrid shouted. "*You're going to marry her, aren't you?"*

* * * * * * * * *

I'm going to kill Derek! Kill him and stuff his big, blathering mouth with pig-dung!

Why did he have to gossip with Ingrid? Dark thoughts raced through my mind as I wandered through the woods, collecting one very old rabbit who looked like he died of fright the instant that my snare closed around his leg. I spent the morning repairing my traps, and considering various painful deaths I'd like to subject Derek to, and finally I realized that I'd gotten caught, just like Father had, and how lucky I was that Helsa and I hadn't ...!

What was I thinking? Helsa was beautiful, smart, going to be rich; having not slept with her was hardly lucky! But then, if I had, Ingrid would've been twice as mad at me. Mother had tried to hack through Grettir's door with an axe; *would Ingrid have gone after Helsa?* I shut off the image of what could've happened while I was at Market; *feuds between women were someplace that no man wanted to go.*

I took my time; no hurry, now that harvest was over. I even gathered some flowers for Mother, and tucked one inside my tunic for Ingrid. But what could I say? I couldn't announce that I intended to marry Ingrid after the viking; Mother would send her away and I'd never see her again. Nor did I feel ready for marriage: *viking before marriage or you'll never get to go.* As much as I liked Ingrid ... and Helsa, the viking came first.

Mother was thrilled to get the flowers, and as I gave Ingrid the dead rabbit, I pulled out the flower that I'd picked for her.

Ingrid crushed the flower in her hand and tossed it into the fire.

* * * * * * * * *

My eyes flew open, but all that I could see were our rafters above me, barely illuminated by the glow of our dying fire. It was the middle of the night and everything seemed peaceful, but something was wrong.

Suddenly I heard it again: a high, whining cry, a distant shout.

"Father!" I shouted as I jumped out of bed. "Wake up! Father!"

"What ...? Wha ...?"

"Listen!" I said.

Mother and Ingrid startled awake. Urd mumbled and rolled over. Father sat up, listening, as I stood frozen by my bed, and then the cry came again.

"What was that?" Mother asked as Father jumped up.

I ran to the door and pulled off the brace. The cold wind blew strongly, but I stuck my head out and listened.

"It's Garad!"

"Something's wrong," Father said, and he reached for his sword. "Get your cloak."

I grabbed my cloak and, while Father flung on his, I got my sword as well.

"Where're you going?" Mother demanded.

Father turned to face her.

"Someone's hurt, or in trouble," Father said firmly. "I'm going to find out who."

"I'm coming with you," Mother said. "Ingrid, stay here."

Moments later, we were outside, cloaks over our nightgowns, racing toward Garad's. We could hear him clearly now, unless a gust of wind whistled too loudly past our ears; the cries came from his fields, not from Garad's house. In the cloudy night, we followed the wind-blown sound of his voice, and didn't see him until we almost stumbled over him. Garad was on his knees, his back toward us.

"Garad ...!" Father cried.

Garad looked up, his face twisted with grief. Tears poured down his cheeks. On the ground behind him, still holding a half-filled bag of onions, lay Grettir. She was staring blankly ... and there was frost on her eyelashes.

"Oh, gods!" Father cried. "*Odin, no!*"

"Sh.. She sent me in ... to get warm!" Garad sobbed. "I was waiting for her ... I fell asleep...!"

Grettir's frozen face told her full story: Grettir had been out late again, harvesting onions, as she'd been doing since before we went to Market. She'd fallen, exhausted, sick, trying to bring in their harvest before the snows started, with just her and Garad. Too tired to stand, Grettir had slowly frozen on the cold ground.

Grettir was dead.

Mother sobbed. Father took off his cloak and reverently laid it over her. I watched stunned, uncomprehending. *How could this have happened? Why hadn't they finished harvest by now? They did last year ...!*

Then I remembered: *I helped them harvest last year.* But I hadn't helped them this year, and the two of them couldn't do it alone.

Because I hadn't helped ... Grettir was dead.

* * * * * * * * *

Half-frozen, my teeth chattering so loudly that I could hear nothing else, I numbly opened our door. I remembered running away, despite Father calling my name, and I didn't stop running until I was leaning against the marker-post at the farthest corner of our fields. There I'd crumpled onto the ground. My best friend had lost his mother, after losing his father, and now Garad was orphaned. *If only I'd helped him ...!*

"Thron!" Mother cried, and she pulled me inside, closed our door, and made me sit in her chair before the fire.

My eyes flew open as I saw Garad, wrapped in a blanket, sitting still as stone in Father's chair. Father wasn't there.

"Warm ale!" Mother called to Ingrid. "Are you crazy, Thron? You could freeze ... Ingrid!"

"Here!" Ingrid said.

A warm wooden cup was pressed into my frozen hands.

"Drink slowly," Mother said.

Suddenly I heard horses and Rath's voice outside.

"Læknir's here," Ingrid said, peering out the door.

"Praise Freyja," Mother said. "Thron, go sit on your bed."

Ingrid opened the door just long enough to let Læknir in.

I heard Father and Rath outside, tending the horses that pulled Læknir's carriage.

Suddenly there was a pounding on the door. Læknir looked back, surprised. Reluctantly, Ingrid opened the door again.

Helsa stepped inside, giving Ingrid a dirty look, but Ingrid glared right back. For a moment, I thought that they were going to fight, but then Helsa stepped away from the door, and Ingrid slammed it shut.

"Garad," Læknir said. "What a terrible night! What a tragic loss!"

Læknir leaned over, kissed Garad, and sat down on the chair that I'd just vacated.

"Finish your drink and put on your tunic overtop your nightshirt," Mother whispered in my ear. "Then go out and help your father."

* * * * * * * * *

Father and Rath were carrying Grettir's frozen body toward her house as I arrived; I opened the door for them. They laid Grettir on her bed still covered in Father's cloak.

"Ugh!" Rath complained. "What a stink!"

"They haven't shoveled out their pen in weeks," Father said. "Too busy harvesting."

"Garad needed her more than an extra bushel of onions," Rath said.

Holbarki had strung an old fishing net in their rafters; that was where they stored their onions. Their whole ceiling was heavy with onions.

"I should've helped her," Father cursed.

"Vespa would've thrown your sword at you," Rath said.

"Grettir knew her limits; she chose this risk."

"For her only son," Father argued. "Those onions were their life."

"They were her life," Rath agreed.

"Thron, muck the pens," Father said. "Others will be by soon to pay their respects; no need to make them hold their noses."

I didn't complain at all, glad for something to do. I opened the door to their barn, pushed the goats and chickens back enough to close it behind me, and then found their biggest shovel and started to work; it was the least that I could do.

So ... Father blamed himself for Grettir's death. Surely Mother was really to blame, but then, Father could've come over whether Mother wanted him to or not, and I could've helped, too. Grettir bore her share of the blame as well. *The only person who was really blameless was Garad ... and he was suffering the most.*

Father had once told me that evil existed first, and evil was stronger than good; of that I had no doubt.

* * * * * * * * *

Many words were spoken over the next few days, but little was said. Mother cried a lot; she probably felt as if she'd personally held Grettir down while the cold ground sapped the heat from her body.

We held Grettir's funeral two days later. Her brother and some cousins arrived from a nearby village, so Garad wasn't standing alone before his Mother's bier. Garad did throw the first handful of dirt over her, and he burst into tears as he did.

* * * * * * * * *

We gathered in Tavern Hall afterwards, since it was so cold. Derek arrived late, and I reminded myself that I meant to kill him. All of the other kids were there, and many new, very young children that I barely knew, fidgeting and being ordered to stand still: we weren't the little kids anymore.

"It's an outrage!" Rath spoke over the hushed voices, but then he fell silent, as if he hadn't meant to speak so loudly.

Something was going on; I edged closer to hear.

"Garad's too young to run a farm," Grettir's brother said. "He's never been viking, so he has no legal rights as a man. I'm Garad's uncle; I'll take over for him."

"So take over!" Rath hissed quietly. "Run the farm until he's old enough!"

"I don't have the resources," he said. "Look, I appreciate your concern for my nephew, but he's my responsibility ..."

"Garad's a member of this village," Father said.

"And we have to live next to whomever you sell his farm to!" Rath argued.

"Garad's too young to inherit," Garad's uncle said, and his cousins all nodded their heads in agreement. "Grettir's farm, and her son, go to me."

"Just let the farm lie fallow," Father said. "It'll be good for the soil. Garad can come back when he's old enough ..."

"He'll have other duties then."

"What are you going to do, make him a servant?"

"That's my concern."

"What's next?" Rath hissed "Are you going to sell him?"

"That's my concern!"

Rath looked as if he were going to tear Grettir's brother in two. The cousins looked grim, as if expecting a fight.

Everyone was wearing their finery for the funeral, including weapons; if a fight started, then it'd get bloody.

"No," Father said, loudly enough for everyone to hear. "I won't let you sell Garad into slavery."

Conversation in the hall stopped abruptly. Mouths gaped open in surprise.

"I'm within my legal rights," Grettir's brother insisted.

"So am I," Father said. "Rath, Clamsby, Hal, Digr; don't let them leave. I'll be back."

Father stormed out of the hall, slamming the door shut behind him. It boomed loudly in the silence.

Slowly, conversations began again as the minutes passed: fifteen, then twenty. Clamsby refilled everyone's ale, including Grettir's brother's and his cousins', before the door opened again. Father stomped into the center of the hall and stared at Grettir's brother. Slowly he held up one finger; dangling from it was the golden rosary.

Slowly Grettir's brother took the rosary and looked at it closely.

"For the farm ...?" he asked.

"And the boy," Father said. "No deal without the boy."

"Not worth it," he said.

"It will be," Father said. "No one buys a farm without checking out the neighbors. I promise that anyone that you bring out to look over that farm will be hated by everyone here." A murmur of assent mumbled through the crowd. "We'll curse them the instant that we see them, throw rocks at them, and make them hate this village." Another murmur of agreement, louder. "No one will buy that farm, not this year, not next, not during our lifetimes."

The whole village chorused their agreement.

"You just want to sell the boy yourself ...!"

"Garad will never be sold!" Father shouted. "I'll take him as my second son, and he and his farm will become part of my family. I'll be his step-father and take him viking. Take the rosary and leave ... or fight your way out of here."

"Nobody orders me!" Grettir's brother shouted.

"Fine," Father said, and as he drew his sword, a dozen other swords slid from scabbards all around the hall. I pulled out mine and held it up so that everyone could see. Even some of the women, Mother, Læknir, and even Widow Væna pulled tiny daggers out of hidden sheaths.

"Enough!" said one of Grettir's cousins. *"This deal is done!"*

Father nodded, and not a single word was spoken as Grettir's brother and all of his cousins filed out the door, mounted their horses, and rode off into the night.

Suddenly everyone cheered.

* * * * * * * * *

"From this day on you're part of our family," Father said to Garad.

"What about my farm?" Garad asked.

"Our family has only one farm," Father said. "We have two houses, and we grow onions and turnips. You're my younger son, Thron's brother. Planting won't be done until both crops are in; harvest won't be done until both crops are out. It'll be difficult, but not as bad as you think; I spoke with Digr before we left Tavern Hall last night. He's willing to let Hal come back to us, and Hal will live with Garad."

Garad and I both brightened at this statement, and Mother and Father smiled widely.

"Even with Hal, we'll be hard-pressed," Father warned.

"Hal cost me every coin I made viking and at Market.

"And I have other news; I didn't have enough money to cover what Digr's wife paid for Hal, so Digr sold Hal to me with an agreement; Hal isn't coming back as a hired hand. He's coming back as a free man, as he should've been all along."

"Thorir!" Mother shouted.

"I'm the head of this family!" Father's voice boomed deeply. "We lost Morgan, and I can't bring him back, or I would. We lost Holbarki, my best friend, and now Grettir: I'll lose no more! I'm the father. Vespa is the mother, and she deserves every ounce of respect you boys can give her. Thron's our eldest son. Garad's our youngest son. Hal was here the day that Thron was born; he'll be an uncle to both you boys. And Ingrid ..."

Mother froze, shaking her head desperately.

"Ingrid is my daughter, and anybody who says otherwise will answer to me. We've a big farm now, with two crops. Someday we may have to hire people, but right now what we need is family, a big family. That's what I want, that's what we are: family!"

A dish rag and a bowl fell from Ingrid's stunned hands.

"I ... I'm free?" she stammered. "*You... you're setting me free?"*

"Never!" Father said. "You're my daughter, and like all of my children, you'll do what I say. But you're no longer an indentured servant. Come and hug ... your father."

Ingrid stood frozen, too stunned to move.

"I said come here!"

Slowly, disbelieving, Ingrid staggered forward, and Father hugged her. Mother's brows knit with disapproval, but she kept her trembling lips tight. My thoughts were flying too quickly to make sense. Garad looked as confused as Urd, and Ingrid was loudly weeping. Father was the only one who looked truly, undeniably happy.

* * * * * * * * *

Chapter 29

* * * * * * * * *

Life changes every day; *had it always been so, but like so many other things, I'd failed to notice?*

Father led us outside at early dawn with only a sip of warm ale and a crust of old bread. Hal was already out in Garad's fields, *now our fields*, pulling onions, and smiling wider than I'd ever seen. He hugged each one of us the moment that we joined him. Ingrid and Mother came out later with a basket of fresh bread and mugs of hot ale; it seemed like a party.

With all four of us working, we finished harvesting all of the onions shortly after sunset the next day, but we didn't cheer when it was done: had we done so only a few days before, Grettir would still be alive.

I suspected that Garad was angry; Father had saved Garad, but he wasn't the owner of his farm anymore. Garad was also grieving the loss of his last parent, so he was probably blaming everyone that he saw or thought about.

My brother: *I had a brother.* Garad and I'd always been friends, despite our many fights over the years, but to think of him as a brother; *how was I supposed to do that?*

Having Hal back was great. I'd missed him, and he seemed so happy that everyone who saw him smiled.

Ingrid still wouldn't look at me. A week had passed since Derek had told her that Helsa and I were getting married, and my attempts to correct him were ignored and disbelieved. Ingrid stayed close to Mother all week so that we were never alone long enough to talk, and she walked away from me whenever I stepped close enough to whisper.

Why was she determined to believe a lie?

It rained the next day, but we went out anyway, Father, Hal, Garad, and I, armed with axes instead of swords, and we carried lots of string, rope, and pig-slop for bait. We visited each of my traps, and I showed them all how they worked, how to fix them, and how to build new traps. My deer trap was completely destroyed, and all of the deer tracks around it showed how; it was built to catch a deer, but it looked like it had tried and failed. We had to rebuild it from scratch, and even with all four of us working, it took over two hours. Still, Garad and Hal were both impressed, and Father said that he was very proud. We did get a small fox and a squirrel, and Hal insisted on carrying them back.

* * * * * * * * *

"I'm not going to marry Helsa!" I shouted through the privy door.

"How dare you? Get out of here!" Ingrid's voice shouted back.

"No, you're going to listen to me!"

"Go away!"

"I'm not going anywhere until you listen!"

"I'll call for Vespa!"

"Go ahead. Scream. Shout. Bring everyone out here. Let everyone hear. You're not a servant anymore; Father won't send you away, and Mother can't. Let's tell everyone what ..."

"Leave me alone!"

"No!"

"You kissed Helsa! You gave her a ride home and you kissed her! You want to marry her!"

"According to who? Derek? He's dumber than his cows! Why'd you believe him?"

Ingrid didn't respond. Moments passed, but I stood there in the rain, getting soaked, until the water was streaming off my nose.

"You have to listen to ...!"

The door opened suddenly. Ingrid stormed out and pushed past me, her eyes glaring, her jaw set. I grabbed her arm, but she pulled away and ran for the house. I chased after, determined not to let her reach its safety. I tackled her hard, and we went down fighting. She thrashed to get free, but I gripped with all the strength of pulling a sledge. The splashing mud made her arms slick as ice, and soon we were both numb from the cold and soaked to the skin.

Finally I closed my hands tight around her wrists, sat on her waist, and pressed her against the ground. Ingrid grunted and strained and hammered her knees into my back, but it barely hurt. Finally she subsided and glared at me.

I looked at her and a chill deeper than any cold froze me: Ingrid was caked with mud; there wasn't a clean inch anywhere on her body, and I looked the same. We couldn't go inside, dripping mud, and explain how we got this way. Ingrid's expression changed from hate to horror; she realized it, too.

Suddenly she pushed with renewed fury, struggling to push me off, and I was amazed how easily I held her; the last time that we'd wrestled she'd tossed me around at will. Now I could hold her pinned all day.

"How are you gonna explain ...?" Ingrid demanded.

I paused, considering. How could we walk inside, caked with mud, and admit that we'd been rolling like pigs in slop?

"Do you trust me?" I asked.

"Of course not!"

* * * * * * * * *

The swimming hole was low for this time of year but the rain was filling it fast.

"That water's cold!" Ingrid complained.

"Do you have a better idea?"

Angrily she kicked off her caked slippers and splashed them in the water. I pulled off my boots and did the same.

"You don't have to stand so close!"

"I'm not going to marry Helsa!"

"Why not? She's pretty, isn't she? She's rich, isn't she? You kissed her, didn't you?"

"No!"

"Derek said ..."

"How would Derek know?" I demanded. "It was my first day riding my horse, and they were at Tavern Hall, and I gave Helsa a ride home. We didn't stop. We hardly talked. Derek talks 'cause he's got a big mouth and likes to cause trouble!"

"So you never kissed Helsa?"

I took a deep breath.

"She kissed my cheek, once, long ago," I said. "Outside Tavern Hall, the night that they almost killed Friar James. I'd told Kal and Garad that she was a good healer, that she'd fixed my leg, and Helsa said 'thank you'. But that's it; nothing else happened. The only reason that she came out then was because I was so upset about Friar James that I puked in the bushes."

Ingrid glared at me, searching my face as if evidence of any lie would be apparent on it.

"Have you and Helsa ever ... *mated?*"

" *What?!?* Of course not! I ... *only with you!*"

"Swear it!" Ingrid insisted, looking right into my eyes. "If I ever find out that you've mated with another woman ...!"

"Only with you," I promised. "Only you."

* * * * * * * * *

I banged my fist against the door until it opened.

"Thron ...?" Friar James exclaimed. "Wha ... you're soaked! Get in here! What're you trying to do, catch your death of cold?"

"T-t-thank y-y-y-you," I stammered, teeth chattering, and I pushed inside, pulling Ingrid with me.

Friar James pulled two old, ragged quilts from his bed and gave them to us.

"Riding on a day like this? You look like you were swimming."

"We were," I replied.

"W-we have to g-g-get out of these w-w-w-wet clothes," Ingrid said.

"Go ahead," Friar James said. "I'll boil some water for tea."

Ingrid and I started to peel off our clothes, which seemed glued to our frozen skins.

"Oh, Friar James, this is Ingrid ..."

"Later," he said, and he put more wood on his small fire and filled his pot with water.

Soon we were mostly dry, huddled before the fire, wrapped in damp quilts. Friar James handed us steaming mugs of weak tea, then wrung out our wet clothes and hung them over the rafters.

"Warm enough?" he asked, pulling up a stool. Ingrid tried to give him his chair, but he refused.

"Now, Thron, you can introduce us properly."

"Huh? Oh! Friar James, this is Ingrid."

"A pleasure to meet you, young lady," he said. "Are you from this village?"

"Yes," Ingrid said, "I'm Thron's servant ... I mean, sister ... I mean ..."

Friar James glanced questioningly at her, then looked at me.

"I don't know, either," I said.

"Well, this is a mystery," Friar James said. "Sister and servant ...? Forgive me if I don't know the local customs."

"She was a servant," I explained. "Father bought her when she was eight. But now he's freed her; he says that she's his daughter ..."

"Which makes her your sister; makes sense, except for the swimming part."

"We had to wash up in the creek," I said. "We got ... dirty."

"I see."

"Are you a real friar?" Ingrid asked suddenly.

"Why, yes, I ..."

"Can ... I mean ... can't friars marry people?"

Friar James' eyebrows rose.

"Yes, we can ..."

"Could you ...?"

"No," Friar James cut her off. "Ranglátr and Smiðr hate me. Clamsby wants to kill me; I'm afraid to go into Tavern Hall. I can't antagonize Thorir by marrying his kids."

"But we aren't really brother and sister!"

"I'll wager that Thorir knew what he was doing when he announced that you were siblings."

I sat silent, too shocked to talk. *Get married? Here? Now? What would I have done if Friar James had said yes?*

* * * * * * * * *

"Where've you been?!?" Mother screamed.

"To see Friar James," I answered.

Mother's face suddenly paled.

"Why did you go there?" Father asked, his voice deep and grave.

"To ask about lessons," I replied. "Harvest is over, and Friar James wants to start writing lessons soon. I missed the first lesson; I didn't want to miss any more."

"Why'd you take Ingrid?"

"She'd never gotten to ride a horse before," I replied, "and now that she's my sister ..."

"In the rain ...?" Mother demanded.

I shrugged.

"Vespa and I have been talking," Father said very slowly. "We think that you two are spending too much time together.

We've two houses now and each house needs a ... woman's touch. From now on, Ingrid will be sleeping in our other house with Garad and Hal." Father turned to face Ingrid and spoke directly to her. "Take your things over there. Vespa will call you when its time to start supper."

I glanced at Ingrid, who looked shocked, as if she were about to cry. Instead, she meekly picked up her small clothes chest and walked to the door.

"Thron, open the door for your sister," Father said.

Ingrid was crying loudly before I closed it behind her. I turned to face Father.

"That was mean," I said defiantly.

Mother stepped forward, her face so angry that I knew what was coming. She drew back her hand and slapped my face as hard as she could. I didn't even flinch; I rocked back on my heels, then leaned forward, daring her to do it again. Mother stepped back, holding her right hand as if her slap had hurt her more than me.

"'Mean' is riding off in the middle of a rainstorm without letting anyone know you're going," Father said.

I inhaled deeply before answering.

"We were fighting."

"On the horse?"

"No."

"Are you married?" Mother asked.

"Not before I go viking," I said bluntly. *"Nobody trains me."*

Mother looked as if she wanted to hit me again, but I stared at her, defiant. Father smirked, and then he sat down in his chair.

"Vespa, will you get me an ale?" he asked softly, "and ... one for Thron ...?"

* * * * * * * * *

"Quiet down!" Friar James shouted. "Now, you all have boards, your clay pads, and your writing sticks; from here on we'll call them quills. We're going to begin with the first letter." He lifted his board, and on his flattened clay he scratched a rune. "This is the letter 'A'. I want each of you to draw this rune on your clay, exactly as I have."

We all copied his rune into into clay. I tried to match his rune exactly; since I'd already shown that I could write my name I didn't want to be the only one who couldn't get it right. Actually, I wasn't sure that I could write my name anymore; even as I was drawing my name with my finger on the table in Tavern Hall, I hadn't been sure that I'd been drawing it right.

Garad sat beside me, slowly scrawling his rune. Kal was on the bench beside him, and Derek was on the other side of the table beside Helsa, Sjóna, and Skratui. Kampi sat at the adult table beside Katla; Hal, Brún, and Trandill sat across from them.

Watching closely, Læknir stood smiling back by Clamsby, who seemed very unhappy. Clamsby was wiping down his kegs with an oiled rag, making them gleam chestnut brown, a snarl on his lips and a look of disgust that deepend every time that he glanced at Friar James. Læknir seemed undisturbed by his occasional grunts.

Ingrid had wanted to attend classes, but Father said that we could barely afford to send both Garad and I. Hal bargained with Father to let him come, promising an additional year's service. Technically, since he was no longer an indentured servant, he could marry one of the widows and become the master of his own household, but Hal didn't seem inclined. For setting him free, he'd promised Father a year's service, and had hinted that, even if he did marry, he'd remain with our household, part of our family. But Friar James was charging each of his students food in exchange for lessons; I had to bring him two large turnips every week, and Garad had to bring him two large onions. Hal bargained to hunt for his lessons, and Friar James quickly agreed; Friar James was afraid to go into the woods, fearful that Clamsby or Smiðr might follow him.

I'd hoped that Hjálmun would be there, but he wasn't; I'd not seen him since Branwulf's, but I assumed that he was back at Igrár's. I seldom saw Igrár and barely knew anything about her, save that Farmaðr, her long-dead husband, had been a good friend of Father's. I wasn't surprised that Old man Ranglátr and Widow Væna weren't there, and was downright glad that Gandr had avoided our company.

"Very good," Friar James said at last, after looking at everyone's clay. "Now let's discuss this letter, what it means, and how to pronounce it properly."

* * * * * * * * *

I kept expecting class to get better, but it didn't. Katla and Trandill quit coming after a few days; neither could draw their letters, and Friar James had to explain everything to them two or three times before he'd shake his head and continue.

The best part of learning to read was walking home with Garad and Hal. Both seemed about as happy as they could be; while still upset about losing Grettir, Garad's mood quickly improved when Ingrid had moved in with him.

The weather grew worse and snow began to fall. Soon we

were walking single file in yesterday's tracks, Hal plowing our path. It snowed for four days without stopping, and then only a day passed before it began snowing again. But Hal was fun, and talked constantly about the vikings, frequently reciting the ancient quotes.

"Kill a beast, take everything it owns," Hal said. "Kill a man: no difference. Property belongs to the last man standing."

"Better a corpse than a coward."

"The conquered never conquer."

Once per week Garad, Hal, Father, and I would check our traps, but with winter approaching, our catches became fewer. We brought back heavy loads of firewood, preparing for the worst; Garad and I spent days chopping and splitting.

Cold seeped inside our house, even when the fire was lit, so much that Mother and Ingrid stuffed rags around the door and filled the window-slot. Soon the day came when Mother announced that it was too dangerous trying to go into town. The farthest that I got to go was Garad's house, inside which we'd stabled my horse and our pigs with all of Garad's animals, using our barn to store firewood for both houses. Everyday I groomed my horse, but it was too cold for riding.

Urd walked and talked nonstop, though she was often hard to understand. Playing with her was the only fun that any of us had; we'd pass her around each night, taking turns teaching her words while the others worked. I made a matched set of tall mugs with handles to trade Clamsby for ale.

Winter passed quietly, fixed in a dull routine. Hal, Garad, and I practiced our writing, and Mother and Ingrid watched us closely. Soon we were all drawing both alphabets: Futhark and Latin. By the end of winter, we'd made games of who could read or write the fastest.

Mother stayed aware of my every movement. When Ingrid was in the privy, I wasn't allowed to go out, and every day Mother went and got her when she needed her, or sent Garad rather than me. All winter, Ingrid and I never got to talk, not once, but our eyes longed for each other. Once or twice I silently pursed my lips, as if blowing her a kiss, but Ingrid only looked terrified.

But even my desire for Ingrid paled before the twinge of excitement that warmed me even on the coldest nights: *I was going viking ... and Garad was going with me!*

* * * * * * * * *

Chapter 30

* * * * * * * * *

Spring was a celebration. The snow began to melt, Friar James started classes again, and it was a pleasure beyond description to see other faces. Helsa was several inches taller, but so were we all. Little Kal was little no more; he was easily as tall as I and looked like he might match his father's towering height. Lingering snowdrifts lasted into late March, and then a sudden warm spell melted everything so quickly that lakes appeared in the lowlands.

Helsa seemed especially cheerful. She sat by me every day, laughed often, and excelled at writing runes. She'd been practicing more than we, and had written all of the recipes for Læknir's secret medicines and tonics on lambskin with real ink. Often I copied what she wrote, although she scolded me with a mirthful glare and moved her clay board away whenever she caught me. Friar James would give us a word, and we'd have to write it in both alphabets, and then he'd walk around and inspect how we spelled it; Helsa always got it right.

I liked sitting next to Helsa. She complained that her walk home was very strenuous, hinting that she wanted another ride. I wished that I could give her another ride home, or better yet, across the countryside, and several times I found myself just watching her, the sunlight yellow of her hair and the creaminess of her skin, which looked as soft as melted butter, her beautiful bright blue eyes, coy smile, and the tightness of her dress across her chest, the curve of her mysterious breasts, which seemed larger, but remained hidden by just a few layers of fabric. Then Friar James would shout at me to pay attention and often gave me a word to write, all by myself, and then he'd show my mistakes to the rest of the class. I tried to avoid staring at Helsa, but I couldn't manage it; Helsa was truly beautiful.

We only had eight weeks of classes before the the ground unfroze enough to begin plowing.

My horse wasn't a plow horse, but Father gave Garad and I heavy picks and sent us out to break up as much of the cold ground as we could before Hal came behind us, leading my horse, and Father maneuvered the plow in his wake. We started too early; the ground was so hard that Garad and I had to swing really hard just to plant our picks into the cold dirt, and then their long points would be stuck and we'd to lever them out.

When it came, planting was a relief. Blisters from the picks covered Garad's and my hands, and we often got splinters despite waxing our pick-hafts, but Father was well-pleased; we'd both grown two inches taller during the winter, and between wrestling and pick-swinging, our arms were thick with muscles.

* * * * * * * * *

One day Rath showed up, riding a horse, late in the evening, just as we were coming in from the fields.

"Thorir!" Rath shouted from atop his horse.

"Welcome!" Father shouted back. "What news?"

"Big news, and lots of it," Rath said. "Brekka had her baby!"

"Healthy?"

"Very," Rath said. "A large baby, and Brekka's doing fine."

"Boy or girl?"

"Girl, with a full head of blonde hair," Rath said. "Smiðr named her Valka. He said that his daughter's destined to be one of Odin's maids."

"What's the other news?" Hal asked.

"There's going to be a wedding!"

"Who?"

"Derek and Sjóna," Rath said, and we all gaped, especially Mother and Ingrid.

"He'll never go viking now," Hal laughed.

"No, but he had little chance of sailing anyway," Rath said.

"It's a boy's choice," Hal scowled. "Men's hands are stained by the blood of their enemies."

"He has no choice," Rath said. "Sjóna's expecting."

"No!" Mother gasped.

"She hid it as long as she could, but Beigaldi forced the truth from her. Apparently she and Derek've been secretly seeing each other since last summer."

"Come inside and tell us about it," Mother said.

"Can't," Rath said. "I have to invite everyone in the village.

Ranglátr and Væna forced Derek to admit it and demanded that they get married at Clamsby's tomorrow night."

"We'll be there," Father promised.

* * * * * * * * *

Ingrid came with us to Tavern Hall, despite Mother's protests. Hal offered to stay home with Urd, although Mother insisted that, as a free man, he should take every opportunity to socialize with the widows. Hal only laughed and said he wasn't ready to be fawned over yet.

Everyone arrived for Derek and Sjóna's wedding, even strangers from nearby villages. Sjóna was dressed in bright green, with her hair pinned in braids and covered with flowers, but her belly was round and made her look funny because the rest of her was so skinny; she looked like a slender green snake that'd just eaten a fat mouse.

I couldn't picture her mating with Derek; he was big and loud, and I barely knew her voice because she spoke so seldom. Still, Sjóna was a better match for Derek than Helsa; Helsa would never have tolerated how Derek would treat her. I wondered if I'd ever see Sjóna again, if Derek would lock her up on his ranch like he'd done to his mother, who was apparently there only to see her son married, and didn't seem happy.

Old man Ranglátr and Widow Væna performed the nuptials, as they had at Rath's wedding. The whole village cheered as Derek and Sjóna jumped high over the broom, and then everyone pushed forward to congratulate the new couple. Ingrid loved it; she'd not gotten to attend a wedding since before Morgan had died. Yet, when Helsa walked up and gave me a mug of Clamsby's ale, Ingrid's smile failed.

She insisted on talking alone to Skratui, Sjóna's oldest sister, who was also bedecked with flowers in her hair, and a dress so clean that it looked like it'd never been worn before. Skratui was also no longer a child; she looked like Helsa had a few years ago, only much taller, and I couldn't help but notice that everyone was starting to look older. Skratui was loudly predicting that Sjóna was bearing the first of seven sons, one of whom would become a king in foreign lands, and I walked away shaking my head.

Much later, pushing through the press of people, I slid past Ingrid, who was moving in the other direction.

"I love you," I whispered in her ear as we passed.

Ingrid's eyes flew open as she stopped, appearing shocked, but I only smiled and kept moving. Moments later, I looked back to find that Ingrid hadn't moved or changed her expression.

Late that evening I was feeling a little sick; I'd drunk way too much, and suddenly Ingrid's voice whispered in my ear.

"Meet me in the back."

* * * * * * * * *

"Did you mean it?"

"Mean what?"

"That you love me!"

"Of course I do! You know that!"

"You never said it before."

"I didn't?"

"Not like that."

"Well ... why should I? You know how I feel!"

"It's nice to hear it once in a while."

"When have I had the chance?"

"You're going viking soon; will you be coming back ... to me? For me?"

"Where else would I go?"

Ingrid smiled as if that pleased her.

"Garad wants me," she said suddenly.

"What ...?!?"

"He hasn't said so, but I can tell," Ingrid said. "Hal likes me too, but I think that he just likes to look at me."

"What ...!?!"

"Shhhhhh!" Ingrid shushed me. "Don't worry; I don't like Garad, and I make them look away while I dress."

"I'd like to watch you dress again," I said.

"I'd rather you watch me undress," Ingrid smiled, "and you can watch me undress every night when you come back from viking. You can touch me and sleep beside me and do anything you want. I'll wait for you, Thron."

I was too drunk to care what she was talking about, but I kissed her long and passionately.

Suddenly we heard whispered voices and running feet. Kal and Skratui dashed out of the narrow space between Tavern Hall and Friar James' house. Kal's eyes opened wide when he saw us, as if he'd been caught doing something wrong, but Skratui only laughed.

"By Odin's ravens, what's going on here?" Skratui asked.

"Tell on us and we'll tell on you," Ingrid said, and Skrauti smiled wickedly.

* * * * * * * * *

"Draw your sword," Father said to me.

I obediently bared my blade. As I did, Hal came forward, took my scabbard, and then went back and stood by Garad, who was holding our biggest axe. Father drew his sword and set his scabbard against the fence. Mother and Ingrid fell silent, standing by the house.

"Don't hold back," Father said. "You'll be facing real foes soon, grown men trying to kill you, and I don't want you to learn to fight while swords impale you. Defend yourself!"

Father stood waiting. I faced him, my sword tight in my grip; *I'd never felt so nervous.*

Suddenly Father yelled furiously and charged me. He seemed so angry that I threw up my sword and closed my eyes.

A loud *'clang'* rang in my ears as my sword was painfully ripped from my hand. Pain exploded throughout me; everything went black as yellow lightning flashed before my eyes. Dirt pressed against my face.

"Get up," Father's voice was angry. "Get up!"

Pain! My ribs felt caved in; *Father had kicked me!*

"Get up!" Father shouted.

I staggered up onto shaky feet. Father looked furious.

"You can't go viking," Father said flatly.

His words struck like an avalanche. *Not go viking ...?*

"Come, Garad, let's see if you have what it takes to go viking."

Garad looked horrified as Father raised his sword.

"Attack me, and if you can't at least draw blood, then you're staying home, too."

Garad glanced at me, then nervously raised his axe. I glanced disbelieving at Hal; he met my eyes, then shook his head; *Hal agreed with Father.*

"Pain never stops men," Hal said darkly.

Suddenly, unexpectedly, Father screamed and charged at Garad. At first, I thought he was going to cut Garad's head off, but he simply countered Garad's weak swing and slammed his forearm into Garad's head. Garad started to fall, but before he hit the dirt, Father swung his sword and deftly struck the underside of Garad's axe; the axe flew from Garad's hands, and Father caught it even as Garad bounced upon the dirt.

"What do you think?" Father asked Hal.

Hal frowned deeply.

"They're boys," Hal said. "They'll die ... like Halgrum ... in their first fight."

Father glared angrily. I winced under his glare, my head and ribs still throbbing.

"What a pair of disappointments!" Father said.

* * * * * * * * *

Not going viking!

Never going viking!

We wouldn't cry; Father would beat us if he saw, but we felt like weeping.

... Disappointments ...?!?

Garad jumped to his feet, then faltered, holding his head suddenly as if to stop it from spinning, and then seemed to find his balance; Father must've really struck him hard. With a furious glare, Garad stomped away; I watched him go, stomp by stomp, out the gate and up the road, away from town. He seemed to be walking slowly, but he quickly dwindled in the distance.

Suddenly I stomped crosswise over Garad's fields, kicking hard at the clumps left over from plowing.

* * * * * * * * *

The night gusted, stabbing me with a thousand needles. My breath exhaled in streams of white mist that vanished instantly, dragged off by the wind in a straight line from my mouth. I wasn't wearing my cloak: I was freezing.

I couldn't go home. *What was left for me there?* I'd lost Father's respect. I couldn't meet his eyes, couldn't face his shame at having me for a son.

I could never go back. I could never go anywhere. No matter where I went, faces would stare at me, could see that I'd never gone viking.

Faces floated before me: Mother's delight, Ingrid's embarrassment, Derek's scorning laughter: all mocked, all branded me a coward.

I'd never go to Valhalla, never join my grandfather in Odin's hall. I'd never see Odin, Thor, or even Loki; *I was a disgrace to my ancestors ...!*

The spring night was chill, ignorant of summer's warmth, until I couldn't suffer it any longer. Freezing, I jumped up and ran home.

* * * * * * * * *

Mother shoved a wooden mug of hot ale into my hands, and then she picked up the brace, sealed our door, and picked up her knitting. She was already wearing her sleeping gown. She never once looked at me.

I sat down on the foot of my bed, shivering with cold, sipping the hot ale as if it were Odin's golden mead. It was warmer beside our tiny fire, but Father was sitting in his chair, and I couldn't bear his disgusted glower.

I deserved to be hated.

* * * * * * * * *

Father was in the barn, fastening straps to my horse. I walked up behind him, but he said nothing. I stood there, waiting. He couldn't just sail off and leave me behind, not again! *I had to go!*

"What are you waiting for?" Father barked. "Get your pick and start digging."

It was still very dark; we'd never before gotten up before the cocks crowed or started before the sun broke the horizon. It was also very cold, but I seized the better pick and stood there watching Father harness my horse. I was tempted to swing the pick at him, to bury it in his back; *he couldn't say that I wasn't a warrior if I killed him!* But I knew better; all methods of killing an enemy are good, but a cowardly attack on a kinsman was an unforgivable crime. Not only would Branwulf never let me on his ship, I'd be outlawed and lose everything.

I stormed out to Garad's field. I reached the first row and drove my pick deep into the cold ground; it stuck so hard that I strained to pull it out, which only made me madder.

Father came out soon, the horse fully harnessed, and led him to the end of the row where the plow still stood. As he hitched it up, I kept hammering my pick in too hard, but I was so angry that it felt good to drive the spike in deep.

It wasn't fair! Father hadn't yelled like that when he'd attacked us before! I'd been momentarily surprised, and so had Garad! To bar us from Branwulf's ship forever was unreasonable! *We were Norsemen, too!*

Garad worked faster than I; before Mother and Ingrid came out with breakfast, he was almost caught up with me.

He seemed to be digging his holes more shallowly than I was, as if in a hurry to finish. But we both quit as Mother held out her tray of onion bread and cheese, and Ingrid stood beside her with a tray of steaming ales.

As Father and Hal came closer, I picked up my slices of bread and cheese, but I couldn't eat. I stared at them, certain that I'd choke if I tried to force them down my gullet. Finally I threw both bread and cheese onto the dirt.

"I have to go!" I shouted.

Father hesitated, surprised, as he reached for his ale. Then he picked up his mug and spoke softly.

"No."

"You can't make me stay here!"

Father stopped in mid-drink and put his mug back on Ingrid's tray.

"I'll do what I like," Father raised his voice threateningly. "You'll do as I say ..."

"No!" I shouted, and Father came at me.

I jumped back, knowing that I couldn't out-wrestle him, but I was too angry to run. Father paced off the distance, glaring, and I glared back.

Suddenly my foot touched a weapon: my pick, a stout, four-foot wooden handle with an iron foot-long curved spike pointing in both directions. I snatched it up and raised it warningly.

Father stopped and backed off. I pressed him; *this time I wouldn't stop.*

Slowly, never taking his eyes off me, Father bent low and picked something up from the ground beside him. Terror seized me: Father raised Garad's pick and faced me with a weapon matching my own.

I hesitated; these were deadly weapons. One landed blow

would kill anyone, but I couldn't back down: Father would never speak to me again. *To earn his respect I had to kill him.*

Mother started to shout something, but Hal silenced her. I didn't look to see how; all my attention was focused on Father.

"I'll do it," I warned, my voice almost a growl.

"Try," Father challenged.

I charged, swinging high. I put all of my weight into it, swinging harder than I'd ever swung a pick before, hard enough to pierce through Father even if he'd been wearing his mail. I screamed as I ran at him, determined to kill.

Father threw his pick up high, his hands tight around its handle, spread wide apart. He caught my swing but grunted, stunned by the force of my blow.

I pulled hard, trying to tear his pick from his hands, but Father was too strong, so I shoved it at him, determined to hit him in any way that I could. The blunt top of my pick hammered into his face.

Both Mother and Ingrid screamed, but Father only pushed my pick aside. He spun suddenly and his shoulder crashed into mine, knocking me backwards so hard that I rolled over several unplanted rows. Then he charged me, screaming, his pick high over his head. I spread my hands on my handle, ready to block his swing, but I doubted if I could stop his blow while lying on my back. Scrambling, desperate to get away, I kicked hard with both feet.

One foot connected into his groin. Father's eyes bulged, his swing went wild, and he tripped over me, stumbled a few paces, and sank to his knees, gritting his teeth. I jumped up, took a deep breath, and charged.

Father saw me coming. He lurched up and met me on his

feet. I swung high and hard again, as I had before, but this time Father blocked my blow more deftly than before, and then kicked his knee into my stomach, and flashes of lightning blinded my whole universe. I stumbled backwards and felt my pick jerked out of my hands. I couldn't see or hear, only feel the intense, overwhelming agony of my stomach crushed against my spine.

A rock-hard fist slammed into my face.

Moments lasting eternities passed. Finally I took my hands off my face enough to see. The first thing that I saw was blood, lots of it, covering my hands. Father was standing beside Mother, Garad's pick still in one hand, his other holding a cloth to his bloody face.

I'd hurt him! I'd hurt Father!

But he'd done far worse to me. He'd beaten me, and losing a real fight was unforgivable. *He still wouldn't let me go viking.*

Grunting, straining against overwhelming pain, I reached out and felt the ground beside me. My fingers closed on the cold iron point of my pick, and I drug it toward me. Father stopped pressing the now-bloody cloth to his face, a look of surprise in his expression. Despite my pain, I staggered to my feet, and slowly raised my pick.

"No!" Mother shouted, but Father jerked free of her, and Hal pulled Mother back.

Ingrid and Garad watched horrorstricken. Father stepped toward me and hefted his pick in both of his huge hands.

"You can't win," he said.

"Then you'll have to kill me," I snarled. *"I won't be left behind!"*

This time I didn't swing; I shoved the iron top of the pick at him, struck his haft, and shoved hard again. He blocked me, and I threw my shoulder at him and then swung with all of my might.

Suddenly my pick was knocked from my hands. Father's haft, the butt end, slammed into my chest. Then his iron point hammered over my far shoulder as he caught me in the crook of his pick, around the back of my neck. He pulled hard: I stumbled forward, trapped, helpless. He flung his pick, me with it, and suddenly I was rolling head over heels onto the dirt. I felt dizzy and sick, battered as never before. I landed on my back, but my head was spinning.

A boot kicked my thigh, and as I tried to sit up, suddenly Father knelt right on top of me with all of his weight. He sat hard on my chest, knocking the wind from my gasping lungs, and pinned my arms at my sides beneath him. I struggled, helpless, as his thick hand reached down and closed on my throat. Then he raised his pick over his head. This was it: *Father was going to kill me!*

I didn't care; *better dead than left behind!* Father held me as helpless as a kitten in a basket; I looked up and spat at him.

Father's pick hammered down hard and fast. The crunch sickened me, but not painfully; the iron point of his pick buried deep into the ground beside my head. Father was breathing heavily, blood pouring from his nose.

"Well done, Thron," Father gasped, his chest heaving as he struggled for enough breath to speak. "Welcome aboard. You did it."

* * * * * * * * *

Chapter 31

*   *   *   *   *   *   *   *   *

Was I really going viking?

"What about this one?" Hal inquired, motioning to Garad.

"He's yours," Father gasped.

"I'd rather use swords," Hal said.

"Tonight, then," Father said. "Garad, you saw what Thron did. Despite being hurt, he refused to quit. That's what I expect to see from you."

"Don't think that I'll go easy on you," Hal warned Garad seriously. "You saw Thron did: if you can't hurt me, or if you can't take it, then you'll stay behind; I won't risk my life defending a weakling."

Garad looked shocked and nervous, but slowly nodded his head.

"Congratulations, Thron," Hal said to me as Mother pressed her bloody cloth back to Father's bleeding nose.

Ingrid cheered, and suddenly she ran forward and threw

her arms around me. I staggered; she almost knocked me over, swept up in joy; she caught me as I was about to fall, thinking that I was returning her hug. She was jumping up and down so hard that I feared she was going to kill me.

"Ingrid!" Mother shouted. *"Let go of ...!"*

"No!" Father's voice boomed deep and commanding. "*No one tells a warrior who he can't kiss!"*

I stared at Father, my shocked expression mirroring the disbelief on Ingrid's face. Mother looked horrified, but I didn't care. I looked at Ingrid, and she at me, and suddenly we kissed.

To be honest, my face was so bruised, my lip split and bleeding, that I couldn't bear the press of her lips for more than a second. But Ingrid's expression as she pulled away, my blood smearing on her lips, was exuberant.

Mother shook with anger, which needed an outlet.

"You could have killed him!" Mother shouted at Father.

"On the viking, men will try to kill him," Father said. "Not until now did I know that he's prepared to face them."

* * * * * * * * *

"You can do it," I said. "Just don't give up."

"You heard Hal," Garad groaned. "He's going to hurt me."

"You've been hurt before, and you're not going to spend the rest of your life never being hurt again; this time you just ... know about it beforehand."

"Usually that's when I avoid getting hurt!"

"You can do that now."

"How?"

"Kill Hal."

Garad looked at me as if I'd just asked him to pick up Tavern Hall and toss it over his head. He could beat Hal ... if all of the gods and goddesses chose to favor him at the same moment. I suspected that he was going to end up like I felt, so sore and battered that my whole day plowing had been endless torment. Garad was lucky; Garad could go to bed after his beating.

Hal held his huge scramsax. He hefted it as if it weighed nothing, as if his fight against Garad was a simple chore barely worth his effort. Garad trembled, holding my steel blade as if it were a poisonous snake.

"Begin," Father said.

Garad didn't move.

"I'll tell you all about the viking when I get back," I teased.

Garad shot me an evil glance, then faced Hal. I stepped back.

Hal stood impatiently.

"I'm not going to chase you," Hal said. "Either kill me, or stay behind."

Garad took a deep breath, then took a step forward. Father walked over and stood by me as Garad advanced by inches.

"Never fear ... not even me," Hal said to Garad. "Impress Odin before you die ... if you would be honored."

"Watch closely," Father whispered to me. "Some things about fighting you can only learn by watching real fights."

Hal didn't seem concerned as Garad approached, but raised his sax casually. I wondered what Garad was planning.

"The longer that you take the worse it'll be," Hal said.

Suddenly Garad screamed and charged, sword high, swinging hard. Hal moved to block, but Garad suddenly pulled in early and stabbed. Even Hal seemed surprised by the sudden change, but he only jumped aside as Garad lunged past him, a loud clang as Hal blocked Garad's blade.

"Good move," Father whispered to me.

Garad's momentum carried him out of range, but he instantly spun and faced Hal. Hal seemed a little more wary now; he leaned forward, his feet farther apart, his attention fixed on Garad.

They clanged blades a few times, almost out of range, as if Garad was testing Hal, trying to determine his reaction. Then suddenly Hal snapped his sax forward and spun. His blow knocked Garad's blade aside and his spin brought him chest to chest against Garad with Hal's sax between them. Hal body-slammed Garad back, and Mother and Ingrid cried out.

"Be quiet!" Father ordered. "Garad needs this!"

Garad must have felt it at the same time that I saw it; his empty hand reached to his chest, then to his right shoulder; Garad's tunic was slashed open. He was bleeding from a long scratch; blood was staining his gray tunic in a line from shoulder-tip to sternum; Hal had slit him good. Garad stepped back, shocked.

"You can quit anytime," Father said said to Garad.

Garad didn't lower his sword. He kept his eyes wide, on Hal, gulped, and came at him again.

Garad screamed and charged, but this time he stepped into range and threw several fast blows; Hal blocked them easily. Hal's sax was thick and heavy while Garad's blade, my sword, was light and fast, yet Hal seemed at no disadvantage. They wove in and out twice, switched places, and then Garad reached his empty hand behind him, as if he were scratching his back. Suddenly he lunged at Hal, sword swinging, and the knife that Father had given him flashed in his left hand.

Hal jumped back instantly, but not fast enough; a splotch of red suddenly darkened his ribs. *Garad had stabbed Hal!* Hal shouted angrily, but Garad pressed him, giving him no quarter.

I started forward; *pulling a knife wasn't fair!* But Father grabbed and held me even as he yelled at the screaming women.

Hal suddenly swung his sax high, but Garad wasn't daunted; he came on, two thin blades raised to defend himself. But he only stepped forward once; Hal kicked out his right boot and caught Garad's groin unprotected; hard, on purpose, and on target. Garad collapsed onto his chest, screaming, but Hal didn't back off: he stepped on Garad's knife hand, laid his sword across the back of his forearm, and slowly drew his sharp blade across. Garad screamed as the sharp sax sliced. Ingrid turned away sobbing, unable to watch, while Vespa screamed angrily. Hal raised his sax to stab into Garad's back, and then turned to look at Mother, as if finally hearing her near-hysterical commands.

"Nobody stabs me!" Hal shouted angrily at Garad. "*Get up! Get up and fight! Up ...!"*

Garad laid there writhing. No one moved or spoke, the only sounds were Mother's screams, Ingrid's sobs, and Garad's gasps of pain. Hal glared down at Garad and finally cursed him, and turned toward Father.

"Did you see what he did?" Hal cried. "*He could've killed me!"*

Father nodded grimly.

"Well ...?" Hal demanded.

"What if he'd pulled a hidden weapon on a Saxon?" Father asked Hal.

"I'm not a Saxon!"

"Thron, help Garad up, but don't bring him in the house until after he vomits."

"He's coming?" I asked.

Father nodded.

"Come on, Hal. Let's see how deeply he cut you."

* * * * * * * * *

Hal wasn't cut as deeply as it looked, but it took him days to recover enough to steer the plow. Garad's wounds were very shallow, mostly scratches; Hal had known what he was doing enough to keep from really hurting him; the thorns that I'd fallen on had cut me deeper.

Garad and I quickly regretted our wounds; Father pressed us harder, while Hal rested. The frozen ground still had to be broken up before the plow could cut furrows, and my hands were soon covered in blisters despite their hard, leathery texture. Yet the dull, constant pain quickly became routine as the dreary endlessness of plowing fell into place. These days were doubled, since we now had two fields to plow, but even after all of the plowing was finished, the pain didn't lessen. After plowing came planting, first endless rows of turnips, then uncountable stinky onions. Everyone in the house worked from early dawn until long after dusk, and every conversation consisted mostly of pained expressions, muttered grunts, and exhausted groans.

Mother's commands to Ingrid often hissed through clenched teeth, or barked out commandingly. Ingrid wasn't happy, but she seemed content, as if her new station, as a free woman, shielded her from Mother's ire. Father sharply reprimanded Mother, and soon Mother was careful not to speak cruelly to Ingrid when Father could hear.

Ingrid occasionally blew me a silent kiss, but we were both too tired to do anything else. All the while, I felt secretly excited; soon I was going south, sailing on Branwulf's ship, away from women-problems.

* * * * * * * * *

Father wanted one last night alone with Mother. Garad's house stank of onions, and animals don't sleep quietly, although not as noisily as Hal's snores. I pushed back my covers and crept over to Ingrid's bed.

Ingrid was sound asleep; I leaned over her, breathing a soft, low hiss into her ear, and I gently kissed her cheek. I pressed a finger to her lips as she startled, and then she smiled. Together we went to the door, slowly lifted the heavy brace off its brackets, and placed it on the floor without making a sound.

The starlit morning was still chill, but not too bad. We went to Morgan's old room in our barn.

"Promise ...," Ingrid breathed softly as we kissed. "Promise that you'll come back to me."

"I will."

"I'll love you forever."

"I love you."

* * * * * * * * *

Waiting beside the dock, Mother insisted on hugging Garad and I every few minutes, and she wouldn't step more than a few paces from Father. Hal walked off with Trandill and Brún; both were still indentured to Digr. Gandr was talking with Eardai in front of the crowd. Breigaldi was holding young Sygn in her arms and chatting with Katla, whose apron was smeared with clay-stains. Rath was holding up his new axe for everyone to see, Smiðr standing proudly behind him. Kampi stood in the background, Kal beside him; Kampi had decided not to go viking this year, as Kal was too young.

Garad cheered as Branwulf's great dragon sailed into the fjord. My whole body tingled. Garad was jumping up and down excitedly, looking like a child beside Father.

"Thorir ...!" Sammuel shouted, raising his open hand as they sailed closer.

Rath and Digr grabbed the lines cast from the ship, and Branwulf himself greeted them. Clamsby held a tall, steaming mug of ale, and Branwulf gratefully accepted it, drank deeply, and then passed it around to his men while he gave Clamsby a big hug; I wondered if Branwulf would ever consider me that close a friend.

A line formed on our narrow dock and Hal, Trandill, and Brún got into it. Bregaldi ran up to them and hugged and kissed each of them in turn, and then did the same to several others.

"Shameless," Mother hissed nastily.

"She's got to feed her kids," Father said, but then he looked at me. "As long as none of her kids are related to us; *that would be shameful.*"

"As if she knows who their fathers are," Mother sneered as Bregaldi stepped back into the crowd and put one arm around Gandr.

As Hal stepped up onto the dock, Father turned to Mother.

"Are you sure you'll be alright?" he asked.

"I'll be fine," Mother said. "Ingrid and I will be careful.

Besides, we can't ask Hal to stay now that he's free."

"Tell Clamsby or Kampi, if you have any problems."

"Protect our boys."

Mother and Father hugged very hard, kissed, and then Father stepped back. Mother wrapped her arms around me and held me embarrassingly long.

"Keep your head down! Don't get chilled! Eat every ..."

"Vespa," Father finally said, "he's a man, not a boy."

Mother hesitated and a shudder ran through her.

"Fight wisely!" Mother said, and then she released me. She was crying, my face wet with her tears.

Mother hugged Garad just as long, but without the prattle of warnings that I got, and then she pushed him back beside Father and I.

"My three men ...!" Mother whimpered.

"Garad, get our bag. Thron, my shield."

"Thron ...!" Helsa shouted, suddenly running out of the crowd, but she stopped a few paces from me. "Ummm ... good luck!"

I hesitated; many people smiled.

"Uhh ..., thanks," I said.

"Bring me back something!" Helsa said, and then she ran back to Læknir.

"Lucky bastard," Garad mumbled. "Does she know about you kissing Ingrid?"

Just then, Father grabbed and pulled Garad up in front of him, and suddenly we stopped; I was waiting in line to board Branwulf's dragon: *I was going viking!*

I looked back ... and found the whole village staring at me.

"No stopping!" barked Digr, standing behind me.

I quickly stepped up onto the wooden rail, felt it tilt beneath my weight, and looked down at the inside of the busy ship. Men were jostling, moving things, trying to get out of each other's way or find a place to sit. I was here; *I was finally a man.*

"Stop daydreaming!" Digr shouted.

"Thron!" Father barked. "Stay behind me!"

I hurriedly stepped down into the rocking ship, and Digr climbed aboard and pushed past me.

"Here, Thron," Hal said, and he took Father's shield and wedged it into place on the side of the ship.

"Garad, put the bag down here," Father said. "No, not there! Against the rail; it's going to get more crowded than this. Sit against the rail and stay out of everyone's way."

"Man the oars!" Branwulf shouted. "Prepare to cast off!"

Heavy oars were lifted from their rests, the paddle-ends tossed out to splash in the water while the narrower ends were fitted through the worn, leather-padded ports. An older man pulled out a small drum and beat on it with a stick, pounding a rhythm.

"Alright, you flea-food!" Branwulf shouted. "On ... the ... mark ... Row!"

As one, the rowers dipped their oars and pulled. The ship lurched forward slightly, increasing speed as the oars dipped for their second stroke.

"Wave to your mother!" Father said to Garad and I, and both he and Sammuel raised a hand off the oar momentarily, joining many other hands that waved.

"Goodbye!" Garad shouted as we both waved.

Mother waved at us, one hand holding Urd, who was crying so loudly that she could easily be heard over all the noise. Helsa's sun-bright hair caught my eye; Helsa ran out to the end of the dock.

"Fight well, Thron!"

Several of the men laughed.

"Thron, we're going to have a long talk," Rath said loudly, and more men laughed.

"Row!" Branwulf shouted.

We sailed around the bend, out of sight of the village; *my boyish life was over.*

* * * * * * * * *

Chapter 32

* * * * * * * * *

"What're these girls doing on my ship?" Branwulf demanded.

I glanced about; I hadn't seen any girls get aboard. Suddenly I realized that he was talking about Garad and I; several men laughed.

"Whose girls are these?"

"Mine," Father said.

"Set a weak oar!" Branwulf ordered. "I'll have no girls on my ship!"

Father, Sammuel, and another man raised their oar and got up.

"Sit!" Father ordered us, motioning for us to take their places. "No, center! Center means not next to the rail, Garad! Thron, you sit here!"

We took the places they indicated.

"Well?" Father demanded. "Do you expect us to hold

your oar all day?"

Garad and I both grabbed the oar firmly, then Father glanced at the other men, and they all let go at the same time.

The thick, heavy wooden oar instantly flew up above our heads, out of our hands. Its other end splashed into the water; it'd have killed us if Father hadn't caught it. Our long paddle crashed into the oars of the rowers sitting in front of us, and they cursed us.

"Row!" Father ordered. "With the beat: up and down!"

Garad and I grabbed the massive oar, and Father held it as we struggled to push it down and pull it up.

"You'd better stop rowing like girls!" Father warned seriously.

"What's going on here?" Branwulf shouted behind him. "Why isn't this oar rowing?"

"Girls rowing, Captain," Father replied.

"Girls ...?" Branwulf sounded appalled. "They'd better be boys within the hour ... or they'll be shark-bait!"

Our oar fought against us, and our paddle kept fouling the rowers both before and behind. Many shouts rose to *'throw the girls overboard'*. The oar was more powerful than I'd ever imagined: when it dipped into the water, it stuck there as if the sea seized and held it.

"What's the matter with this oar?" Branwulf yelled the next time he came by, although he had a half-smile, and everyone around us was smiling, too. "If I don't see some boys soon, then I'll make girls out of them!"

"Stop rowing so hard!" Garad whispered to me after Branwulf passed by. "*Just make it go up and down!"*

It worked well enough, but then Father noticed.

"Put your backs into it! Do you think this is a pleasure trip?"

* * * * * * * * *

The hot sun burned the sweaty back of my neck, but I kept rowing. An hour later, I was exhausted, hungry, and the few meager swallows of water that Father had allowed me hadn't quenched my thirst. Yet I didn't voice a single complaint, even when I noticed that every other oar had three grown men on it.

Suddenly Father and Sammuel came and pressed down on our oar, levering it high out of the water.

"We're stopping for more men," Father said. "Take a rest."

We moved aside, and they took our places. Masterfully Father and Sammuel matched the others' stroke with their first pull.

"Hard port!" Branwulf shouted, and suddenly Father, Sammuel, and every man rowing on our side stopped their oar in mid-stroke, holding their oar as deep as it would go, while the other side kept rowing as if nothing had happened. The ship lurched and turned suddenly, faster than I'd thought possible. *Wasn't that what the rudder was for?*

"Stroke!" Branwulf shouted, and all the rowers fell in unison.

This fjord was very long, narrow, and shallow; Garad and I could easily see the mossy bottom even at its deepest point, and there were many large boulders under the water that the rowers had to avoid. Not far inside, the fjord turned sharply to the left, and ended before a rickety wooden dock; around the dock stood a crowd of villagers carrying spears and shields. Their village was different than ours, closely surrounded by terraced hillsides, all freshly planted, with a lot more buildings, but nothing like Tavern Hall.

"Don't even think about disembarking," Father said.

A large group of children ran along the shore beside the ship, waving and laughing, and they followed us all the way to the dock. Only Branwulf went ashore, where he was presented with another huge flagon, from which he drank greedily before he passed it aboard. A line of men stood waiting, and they boarded, greeted by many already aboard.

The dragon was too big to turn around, so the rowers had to row us backwards to get out of the narrow fjord.

"This the weak oar?" a bald man asked after the rowers had turned the ship back around outside the fjord, his hand on the shoulder of a boy about our age.

"Yep," Father smiled, and with a glance at Sammuel, they pushed and held down their oar; it was our turn to row again.

"This is Frej," the bald man said. "Put him on center. He needs it."

A minute later Father, released the oar, then caught it before it smacked Frej in the face. Garad and I had leaned back as far as we could.

"Are you waiting on the oar to row itself?" the bald man barked at Frej.

Frej rowed as badly as us, and I quickly realized how much the rowing of each oar depended on the man sitting center-side, who had the longest reach and therefore the hardest job. Garad and I tried to compensate, but Frej kept pulling or pushing at the wrong time, and we kept hitting the other oars.

"What's going on here?" Branwulf shouted angrily, and then he looked at Frej. "Who let these girls aboard my ship?"

"I'm not a girl!" Frej shouted back at him, and he dropped the oar so suddenly that it wrenched out of our hands.

Suddenly the bald man jumped forward and started hitting Frej.

"Never talk back to your captain!" he shouted. "*Never talk back to anyone!"*

"On our first raid, grab some women's dresses," Branwulf said to Sammuel. "The next *girl* who talks back *will wear those dresses for the rest of the viking!"*

* * * * * * * * *

Rowing reminded me of planting and harvest: my arms ached, my back ached, and rocking back and forth while sitting on a hard, low bench did my backside no good. Some of the men had thick blankets atop sturdy sea chests to sit on. Frej hadn't spoken since his beating; he was about our age, but very big, somewhat like Derek, but with Karg's long, greasy black hair.

"Why don't they use the sail?" Garad leaned close and whispered.

Shocked, I looked up; I hadn't thought of that. The sail was neatly rolled up and tied, running half the length of the ship, right down the center. *Why were we breaking our backs when we could be sailing?*

"Maybe you should ask," I suggested.

"You ask," Garad shook his head.

We made two more stops; we were replaced for each landing. The ship became heavily-manned; soon there was no room at all. Some of the oars were being manned by four or five rowers. Not ours; Frej, Garad, and I were left alone.

Hjálmun pushed and crawled his way through the men and finally stepped over us, dropped his large, mostly empty bag next to Garad, and sat on the rail.

"Hi," I said.

"Hello, Thron, Garad," Hjálmun replied. "Who's your friend?"

"Frej," I answered. Frej looked up, but he said nothing.

"How many vikings is this for you?" Garad asked.

"Seven," Hjálmun said.

"Where're we going?" Garad asked.

Hjálmun smiled the widest grin I'd ever seen.

"Paradise!"

"What ...?" Garad asked.

"You'll find out," Hjálmun said. "For now, you need to focus on learning to row."

"We are rowing ...," Garad began.

"Not well," Hjálmun said. "When all of our lives are on the line you'd better row better than this ... or we'll all be dead."

"What're we doing wrong?" I asked.

"Fine points later," Hjálmun said. "Right now, just row harder. Build up your rowing muscles and work on your timing. Focus. If any of your fathers see you talking to me, then you'll all be in trouble."

* * * * * * * * *

Rath, Brún, and two other men that I didn't know relieved us long after dark; never had I been so exhausted. Ahead of us twinkled many lights; we seemed to be approaching a village larger than any village that I'd ever seen, even bigger than Market. Yet we sailed right past it without stopping, I glanced questioningly at Garad, but he looked even more questioningly at me.

As we rounded a bend, the sight staggered us. Lights,

more than I could imagine, flared, glimmering off the black water. One huge village, stretching as far as I could see in both directions, lay directly ahead of us. Miles of shoreline it covered, as if a hundred Markets had gathered together.

"Another ship!" Garad said, pointing, and I looked, amazed. It was another huge dragon, and behind it ...!

"A fleet!" I cried. "A fleet of dragonships!"

At least twelve dragons raced off our bow, rowing toward the city through black waters. None had their sails spread, and bright starlight glinted off the foamy splashes of their oars as they paddled.

"Faster!" Branwulf shouted, and our rowers dramatically quickened their pace.

We bounced over the choppy water, holding on to keep from being tossed overboard as the mighty dragonship lurched forward with every oar-stroke. We seemed to be racing the fleet; most of their dragons slowly fell behind us, but two of them kept up, the nearest seeming to pull ahead.

"Harder!" Branwulf cried.

The darkness hid all but a few dozen of our rowers, but they grunted, sweated, and rowed as hard and fast as they could. I understood Hjálmun now: Garad, Frej, and I could've never rowed this fast.

"Do you want to starve?" Branwulf shouted angrily. *"Rob hen-houses all summer? Pull! Pull for your lives!"*

For almost an hour, we raced, neck and neck with their lead ship, but never managed to move ahead. Their second ship sped close behind us, but the others fell back. The bright city lights grew closer and closer; if we didn't stop soon, then both of our ships would drive up onto the shore.

Suddenly a horn blew from the other ship, and someone blew a similar note from our ship.

"Oars up!" Branwulf shouted, and all of the men pressed down on their oars, lifted them out of the water, and sighed. Sweat poured.

The other ship had also stopped rowing, and the tiller-men sailed our ships side-by-side. I spied their sweating rowers easily now, hard, determined expressions on their faces.

"Well met!" cried a voice from the other ship.

"Well met!" Branwulf shouted back.

"I'm Captain Knarff. Fast ship you got there! We could use another fast ship in our fleet."

"I'm Captain Branwulf. Let's share an ale and talk it out."

"I'll be at Minerva's Pantry on the south shore."

"I'll come myself!"

Branwulf walked to the tail of the ship, men scrambling to make room for him to pass while the ships drifted apart. In the rear, he turned and faced all of the rowers.

"Well done!" Branwulf congratulated us.

Garad, Frej, and I joined in the cheering, but our confused expressions admitted that we had no idea what had just happened.

* * * * * * * * *

"Stay on the boat," Father said, coming over to talk to us with the older man who'd beaten the drum. "This is Larg. Do exactly as he says without question."

"Yes, Father," Garad and I chorused.

"You, too, Frej," the bald man said. "No back talk."

Larg looked grim, thin whisps of black hair on an otherwise bald head, one side of his face badly scarred, wearing a ragged tunic and a long sword.

"Got your weapons?" he asked.

I displayed my sword. Frej put his hands on two very large daggers that he wore on his belt. Garad fumbled under his bag for his axe, and Larg frowned at us uncomfortably the whole time. Both Father and the bald man both looked disgusted. Finally Garad pulled out his axe.

"Very well," Larg said. "Draw and raise your weapons."

I hesitated only an instant before I drew my sword, but too late: Larg's sword flashed out, caught Garad's axe as he tried to lift it, and pulled it from his hands. An instant later, Larg's sword-edge, near the cross-guard, rested under my chin, the tip of his sword rested under Frej's chin, and Larg had caught Garad's falling axe in his other hand.

"Is this how you protect your ship?" Larg shouted furiously, and he withdrew his blade and thrust Garad's axe back into his hands. "When I call upon you, then you'd better be ready to fight for your lives, instantly, or I'll flay your bones and toss you overboard!"

I looked up into Father's eyes, then wished I hadn't: Father looked ashamed.

"Put those away!" Larg shouted at us. "No, idiot! Don't put your axe down there! How are going to get it when you need it?"

"In your belt, Garad," Father said.

Garad looked embarrassed, then slid his axe-handle into his belt while we sheathed our weapons.

"Not good at guarding, I see," Larg said disgustedly. "Well, that's man's work. Fortunately, there's always women's work ...!"

Frej's eyes glared, as if he were about to say something, but he glanced at his father and subsided.

"To the rear, boys, if you are boys," Larg snarled. "There's cleaning rags aplenty; I want this ship gleaming by dawn!"

* * * * * * * * *

Garad, being the smallest, got the best job. To Garad's belt, Larg tied a rope that went up to the pulley on the mast, and Frej and I had to slowly haul Garad up and down while he polished the mast with oily rags. Larg shouted at him the whole time, and when done, inspected it by lantern light, and finally hit Garad for doing such a terrible job. Then we were all given oily rags and forced to rub every inch of wood on the outer hull all the way to the waterline.

Hjálmun was one of the few men who remained aboard ship. He gave us some large hunks of bread and mouthfuls of ale when Larg wasn't watching, or busy yelling at someone on the far side of the ship, but he warned us to face the sea and not let Larg catch us eating.

My arms and back ached from rowing all day. My only consolation was that the oil on the rags soothed my swollen hands. I kept yawning, carefully looking away each time; Larg caught Frej yawning ... and chewed him out.

Only a handful of retainers remained aboard; most were close to Hjálmun's age. Hjálmun and his friends sat around a large burning brazier near the front of the ship describing past viking adventures.

"I want armor this year," said one. "Too many get killed who would've lived if only they'd had a good helm and mail!"

"Anchors to weigh you down," laughed another. "Running's your best defense."

"Well, I ...," Hjálmun began.

"What're you doing?" Larg screamed in my ear. "Listening to men? Woman's work is what you do! Rub harder! If I can't see my face in that rail by morning, then I'll

fish with your eyeballs!"

* * * * * * * * *

The raucous cries of seagulls awoke me near midday. Garad was still asleep, leaning against me, his feet under the edge of Frej's cloak. Frej was snoring softly.

A group of older men sat around the brazier now. Hjálmun and his friends were gone; in their places sat Hal, Digr, Trandill, and two others that I'd not met. I pushed up, out of my cloak.

"Morning, Thron," Hal said, his voice was low, almost a whisper. "Here, have some cheese." He turned to the two men I'd never met. "Thron's like my nephew; I've known him since he was a toddler."

"Hjalti," one man said, nodding to me.

"I'm called Kappi," the other said. "That means *Champion.* Do you know why they call me that?"

"Uh ... no," I replied nervously.

"Then you'd better not challenge me, eh?" Kappi grinned, and the others laughed.

"Shhhh!" Digr scolded them. "Do you want to wake Larg?"

"Ah, Larg don't wake this early," Trandill scoffed. "Not as much as he drinks."

"Let strange boots hit this deck and you'll see how fast he wakes," Digr warned.

The others laughed as if Digr had told a joke, but I noticed that they all lowered their voices.

"Actually, it's time that Larg woke up anyway," Hjalti said. "Boy, go over and wake him."

Me ...? Wake Larg ...?

“I told you: he’s my nephew!” Hal complained. “Thron, sit down and drink some ale.”

Thank Odin for Hal!

* * * * * * * * *

Chapter 33

* * * * * * * * *

I spent the day watching: each dock had at least two dragonships tied to it, and every empty space hosted guards with long spears holding berths open for ships yet to arrive. All were getting ready to sail south. It was glorious, but I was confused; *Father had never mentioned this place.*

Larg left the moment that he woke, ordering Digr to make sure that Garad, Frej, and I worked all day, but Digr told us to drop our rags after Larg left, and we all sat by the brazier passing around bottles of mead. The men told unbelievable stories and talked about how exciting this year's viking would be; I couldn't have been happier.

Late that afternoon, Father showed up with Rath and Sammuel.

"Thron! Garad! Come with us!"

Garad and I ran to the rail and leapt onto the dock.

"Keep your eyes on us," Father said sternly. "Oslo's

dangerous; we seldom walk with less than four in the day ... and six at night."

"Rath counts as two," Sammuel chuckled.

Garad and I stayed inches from Father as he, Sammuel, and Rath led the way through crowded streets filled with shops of all kinds. These weren't canvas-covered carts and tents, like at Market, but small wooden houses.

"Early evening?" asked a strange woman with red hair who stopped right in front of Rath. I stared at her; she had paint on her face, blue above her eyes and red on her cheeks, quite obvious on her pale, chalky skin.

"Catch me on the way home," Rath laughed, and he grabbed her behind with his massive hand. The girl shrilly laughed.

"Just two coppers!" she giggled. "Surely you have two coppers ...!"

"I'm so good that I should charge two coppers!" Rath said aloud, and everyone laughed, even people just passing by.

"We're berthed at þur's," Sammuel said.

"Oh, you like Tungu!" the girl laughed. "We're old friends! She won't mind!"

"Then come by tonight!" Rath laughed, extricating himself from her arms. "I'll do you and Tungu ... both for free!"

"Not if þur has anything to say about it," Sammuel grinned at us behind Rath's back.

Soon we left the street, entering a door with no sign over it, into a large room surrounded by curtains. Kegs were stacked in the center of four long, low tables set in a square. The tables lay covered with food and surrounded by men from our ship and *... naked women.*

"Who's this?" demanded a deep voice.

The deep voice belonged to a tall, massive woman glaring

down at us. She wore a worn, faded purple gown of foreign design, with a high collar, which made her look even more menacing.

"Þur, these are my sons, Thron and Garad," Father said.

"Oh, new boys!" she grinned. "We'll make men out of them. Gjallandi! Inn! Fresh meat!"

Many heads looked up, most laughing, but two women got up and came forward; neither was wearing a stitch of clothes.

"Make men out of these boys!" Þur said, and both women giggled.

One girl, the taller of the two, whose hair was so curly that it bunched around her head and made her look even taller, stepped forward and took Garad by the hand. The other, who had brilliant yellow hair like Helsa's, took my hand and pulled me forward toward the curtains. I glanced back at Father, but he frowned and motioned for me to do as I was told. Everyone in the room laughed.

"What's your name, boy?" mine asked as she pulled me into a tiny room surrounded by curtains.

"Uh ..., I'm Thron."

"I'm Inn Danski," she said. "I'm a Dane. Have you ever been with a woman, Thron?"

"Ummm ..., yes ..."

"Good," she smiled. "Let's see what you know."

She started unbuckling my belt. I stood stock-still, not knowing what to do. *What would Ingrid say? She'd skin me alive!* Yet how could I go back to Father, in front of all those people, and tell him I didn't want this strange woman?

"Ummm, I - I'm sorry," I stammered, "b-but I ... p-p-promised ..."

"Oh, how sweet!" Inn laughed. "You made a promise to your young lover back home! How you must love her! But you're in Oslo now, and about to go viking, are you not?"

I nodded as she dropped my belt to the floor and began pulling up my tunic, fumbling with my drawstring.

"Well, what if you get killed this summer?" Inn asked. "You might never make it back to your lover. Besides, what you do here doesn't count. Most of the men who viking are married ... and they sleep with Inn. You're not married, are you?"

"No."

"Then just relax," Inn smiled, and she pulled down my trousers and began fondling me. "That feels good, doesn't it? Here, lie down, and Inn will take care of you."

I glanced askance at the worn, stained mattress, but Inn pulled me down gently and I didn't offer much resistance. Her fingers were hot as fire where she touched me, and I was starting to breathe heavily, my mind going blank. But thoughts kept nagging me: Father was just outside these curtains! *What if he came in and caught me?* But then, he'd sent me in here with this naked woman; he must've known what we'd be doing! But soon even those fears faded away; Inn pulled me on top of her, and soon I had no thoughts at all.

Suddenly gasping screams, barely stifled, erupted from nearby.

"Don't be alarmed!" Inn whispered, smiling, pressing her firm breasts against my chest as she kissed my ear. "Gjallandi's noisy; sometimes she screams very loud."

She was already screaming loud, I thought, and then I realized that Gjallandi had been the curly, brown-haired girl who'd taken Garad behind the curtain right next to us. I turned to look at the curtain; *I could hear Garad's rapid breaths!*

"Nothing you need to worry about in there!" Inn whispered. "You have enough to keep your attention on here!"

* * * * * * * * *

The whole room applauded Inn and I as we emerged. I blushed, but Inn kissed me in front of everyone; they laughed louder. I scanned the crowd and saw Father laughing the loudest. Sammuel was patting him on the back and Rath was howling.

They all patted my back as I sat beside them, but suddenly Garad and Gjallandi appeared from behind their curtain, and the attention of the room left me. Garad blushed scarlet, and Gjallandi moved to hug him. Unfortunately for Garad, she was considerably taller, and as his face wedged between her huge breasts, she pinned him there, despite his efforts to free himself. Men roared with guffaws.

Garad pushed free and ran over to us, sitting down next to me. Father handed each of us a mug of ale passed to him by an old woman with long gray braids wearing a sleeveless, rose-colored dress, sitting on a stool in the center of the tables.

"Eat something," Father ordered us, and we both scanned the remains of the feast. There was plenty of meat still on the cold chicken bones, beside grapes and cheese and many loaves of bread and bowls of honey-butter. At once, Garad reached for some grapes.

"My turn," Sammuel said, and he got up and grabbed Inn Danski.

"You again ...?" she laughed.

"I love Danish women," Sammuel laughed, "as often as I can!"

As they disappeared behind the curtains, I sat drinking ale, glad that finally no one was looking at me. *How would I explain this to Ingrid?*

* * * * * * * * *

Garad couldn't stop grinning. I couldn't stop frowning. Inn and Gjallandi weren't the only girls working for þur, although they seemed to be the only ones who never wore clothes. Old Gyðja, with the long gray braids, worked inside the tables pouring ale, but Spákona was just as old, and she kept making predictions whenever she met someone, just like Skratui did. Apparently Hal had the mark of death upon him, while Rath would settle happily in Ireland, and Father would find wealth and glory in Wales. She told Garad that his life would be dark and stormy, while I'd be poisoned by the one person I trusted most.

Bekkjarbót, who wore only a green skirt and an unbuttoned vest, displaying huge breasts, scolded Spákona for trying to frighten us, and gave both of us big wet kisses, and promises that we'd both become rich and famous and return home to marry the girls that we loved. But Bekkjarbót was as fat as Spákona was old, and neither Garad nor I felt comforted by her predictions of happy marriage. Eyverska was neither fat nor old, but she wasn't pretty; she wore a faded blue silk dress that clung tightly to her skin, revealing her every curve, but her face looked like that of a tired old horse, and she had strange red bumps all over her cheeks. But Father must've seen the look in my eyes, for when all the women were elsewhere, he spoke to Garad and I in whispers.

"Branwulf paid for these women for us, and all this food and ale. Don't you dare make him look bad by refusing anything. If Þur herself wants to sleep with you, you do it, and not a word of complaint! Garad, you're doing fine. Thron, at least look like you're enjoying it."

"Can we ... can I ... do it again?" Garad asked hopefully.

"As much as you want, but not with the same woman," Father said. "Don't insult the other girls by not asking. Þur makes everyone sleep with Inn or Gjallandi their first time so that her fame spreads. Sleep with each woman in turn, even the old ones, and other women will be here later."

"No problem!" Garad smiled widely.

"Thron, what's your problem?" Father asked.

"It's ...," I stammered, "Ingrid. And Helsa. I promised ..."

"Are you trained already?"

"No!"

"Ingrid and Helsa aren't here," Father said. "They'll never be here. They'll never know about here. You'll never tell them about here, or every man in our village will make you regret being born. I'll make up a story about where we went on the first week, and you'll swear that it happened exactly as I say."

I looked up into Father's face questioningly.

"Do you think that Vespa knows about this place? Do you think that Rath tells Læknir? Branwulf's out gathering news, learning where all of the other ships are going; think what a mess it'd be if every ship here arrived at some tiny hamlet that could barely support one raid! No one goes home and tells their wives about this place. You'll keep this secret to your grave."

"Yes, Father," I promised.

Make up a story about where we went? All those stories that he'd told Mother ... they were the same stories that he'd told Ingrid and me! How many of them were just made up? All those tales of Father's bravery and strength: *had Father lied?*

* * * * * * * * *

Hjálmun came out from behind the curtains with a short, plump woman that I'd never seen before, who was holding him close. Unsurprisingly, no one laughed as he emerged. Hjálmun led her over to the tables, flopped onto an empty spot, and reached for a mug of ale. The woman that he was with said something that I couldn't hear, then slowly walked around the tables, smiling at all of the men.

"That's Tungu!" Father whispered to Garad and I.

Tungu immediately struck me as strange; she was short and plump and sort of dressed; she was covered in thin scarves, veils, and jewelry, enough that it covered most of her, but it often dislodged as she moved, displaying large nipples and wide hips. Her hair was cut short, barely off of her shoulders, and so gray that it was almost white, although she looked young. Yet I didn't stare at her long; a man whose name I didn't know jumped up, and Tungu led him behind the curtains.

I was pulling some white meat off a chicken carcass when Eyverska came by. Garad was staring at her, smiling, and when she held out her hand, Garad almost fell over himself jumping up, and then he practically pulled her behind the curtains. Rath, Sammuel, and Father all laughed as he vanished with her.

More women showed up that evening, and some men began playing musical instruments. Father picked up a small drum with numerous tiny brass bells hanging from it by colorful ribbons, held it up, and began to tap it to the rhythm of the music, but seeing me watching him, he handed me the drum, and made me hold it up and slowly hit it with my hand. It was easy, and so much fun that I wondered why we didn't have musical instruments at home. Everyone seemed to enjoy the music, and several of the girls, even some of the men, got up to dance. I loved watching; I'd seen girls dance at Market, but they'd been clothed ...

Inn and Gjallandi danced spectacularly, often blatantly shaking their breasts, which made their watchers howl with delight. Bekkjarbót danced between two men, and she was so large that, when she bounced against them, she knocked them aside, but they kept coming back for more. Eyverska didn't dance, but cheered her sisters on. Even old Spákona slowly waved her arms and walked back and forth, and Gyðja held up her long gray braids and rocked back and forth to the music behind the tables. Tongu rushed out from the curtains to a chorus of applause, spinning around and around so that her veils flung out in all directions, and then she began dancing very energetically, moving from man to man all the way around the table.

I pounded harder on my drum as the music played louder, and the dancing became more frenzied. Then, suddenly the music died; Branwulf entered with a group of heavily-armed men.

"What news ...?" Larg asked in the sudden silence.

"Good news!" Branwulf announced to everyone. "Not with Captain Knarff, though; he offered us a place in his fleet, but his terms were sheer piracy. But word of our rowing spread; I've had offers to join three other fleets! I haven't made a deal yet because no one wants to commit to where they're sailing so early, but I just wanted to tell you how well your efforts paid off, and that our prospects have never been higher!"

Everyone cheered, many jumped up, and soon we were all on our feet, chanting.

"Branwulf! Branwulf! Branwulf!"

I shouted Branwulf's name as loudly as I could. I'd never guessed what a great captain he was, or what it meant for a ship to have a captain like Branwulf. My excitement only grew as I dreamed of the treasures that I'd soon take home.

* * * * * * * * *

"There's Frej!" Garad said.

The bald man had brought Frej in with a group of others.

"Skalla!" Sammuel called, and the bald man waved back, but he waited until the other men had greeted þur before introducing Frej to her. Þur seemed delighted and hugged Frej, who looked about as uncomfortable as a boy could get. Þur called over Tungu, Gjallandi, and Inn Danski, but the newly-arrived men had escorted them behind the curtains. Frej got Bekkjarbót, who laughed and pulled him behind her as she headed for the curtains; Frej looked horror-struck, but obediently went with her.

No one paid much attention to Frej as he emerged a while later. Music was still playing, and I had my drum back; I'd let Garad beat it, but he had abandoned it and gone off with a cute new girl, with bright copper hair, whose name I didn't know. There were still a few people dancing, and suddenly a strange black-haired girl nearly Mother's age started dancing in front of me to the beat of my drum. I tried not to look at her face, but suddenly she grabbed my arm and pulled me to my feet, and before I knew it, I was behind the curtains again.

We never spoke or introduced ourselves. I did as I had to, but I wished with all my heart that she was Ingrid, and that the two of us were alone in our barn, naked and pressed together tightly, wrapped in each other's arms.

Father, Rath, and Sammuel were gone when I got back to the table. Garad was there, dancing while beating the drum, very drunk and exceedingly happy.

I leaned back against the table, and suddenly a hand touched my arm. It was Gyðja, reaching from inside the tables, holding out a fresh mug of ale. She was smiling, her eyes bright amid a hundred wrinkles. Though short and squat, she looked even older than Widow Væna.

"You don't look happy!" she squeaked in a high, creaky voice. "Why you look so sad? I never seen a boy look sad in here."

"I'm okay," I told her.

She smiled widely and didn't let go of my mug of ale even after I grabbed it.

"You got a sweetheart!" Gyðja grinned, pulling the lines on her face horizontal. "You can tell old Gyðja; I won't tell anyone. Or, maybe, you want me to tell the girls to leave you alone, that you want only your sweetheart, eh?"

"No," I said half-heartedly.

"Your eyes say *'yes'.*"

"My father ..."

"Ah, you must prove what a man you are!" Gyðja nodded. "I know; I've been here since Branwulf sailed on his first viking. Ahh, what a tireless lover he was! But I've seen many young boys; only the best ones pine for their sweethearts. You come with old Gyðja, eh? We'll make your father proud!"

I was instantly revolted, then terrified as Gyðja stepped

onto the low table and climbed over it. She took my hand, and Father's words pounded in my brain, no matter how much I wanted to refuse them. Gyðja weakly pulled me to my feet, still clutching my mug of ale, and she took me to the curtains.

Disgusted, I followed, but Gyðja didn't stop in the first room. She pulled me through many curtains, and finally into a small kitchen with an older, very-pregnant lady that I'd never seen before, who was stirring several cauldrons in a huge fireplace. A small table, piled with dirty dishes, lay in the back, and Gyðja sat me on a stool before it, then heavily lowered herself onto a nearby bench. She took a deep drink from my mug, and then handed it back to me.

"Now, tell Gyðja about your sweetheart."

* * * * * * * * *

Gyðja was very nice, offering me fresh herring hot off the fire, and a stew better than anything that I could recall. I told her about Ingrid, which delighted her more than anything. She laughed and smiled, and the pregnant woman joined us. They'd both been born in þur's; their mothers had worked here, and Gyðja explained that Tongu was one of þur's daughters. I asked about Inn Danski; they said that she, like many others, hadn't been born a whore: she'd been a little girl, the daughter of a wealthy Dane, stolen by a viking raider, and raped all the way back to Norway. Released when they reached Oslo, Inn had no where to go, no way to get home, and eventually starvation forced her to work at þur's.

Back at the tables, Gyðja put her hand on Father's shoulder, and said loud enough for Rath and Sammuel to hear:

"This must be your son, eh, Thorir? I thought my old heart was going to give out under him! Oh, what a man he is!"

Father never looked prouder.

Suddenly Tungu pushed out from behind the curtains, dragging Garad with her. His eyes were frozen, his expression stunned. People laughed, and Tungu encouraged their laughter, rubbing her hands all over Garad right in front of them, even squeezing his crotch and licking him on both cheeks, but despite their howls of laughter, Garad never moved or even blushed.

"We have to get going," Father said.

Rath, Sammuel, and Father waited for Tungu to finish exhibiting Garad, then pulled him away from her, leading us to the door. Only the moon lit Oslo.

"Take him, Thron," Father said, shoving Garad at me. "It's our night to guard the ship. Stay close."

I grabbed Garad by the arm and pulled him as Rath led the way. We were almost to the ship before Garad noticed the questioning look on my face.

"Y-y-you wouldn't b-believe me if I told you," Garad stammered.

* * * * * * * * *

Garad and I spent the night, the whole next day, and the next night aboard ship. Father, Hal, Digr, Smiðr, and Brún went back into Oslo the next day, but they never told us where they were going. Larg kept us busy polishing and repolishing everything; he even had us polish the paddles of the oars, but whenever he went ashore, we sat and rested, ate sausages and cheese, watched all of the strange men and ships, and listened to the stories of the crew sitting around the brazier.

Frej joined us, and he and Garad compared notes about the whores at Þur's. I put in a few comments, but mostly just listened to their endless chatter; *what they said about Tungu was hard to believe!*

The whores were great, especially Inn Danski, but I missed Ingrid. I missed Mother. Something was wrong with me: I was on my first viking, beginning the first adventure of my lifetime, and I was missing my old bed and the swimming hole back home. *Was I mad?*

Suddenly a shadow fell on me.

"Boys, go up stern," said Rath's deep voice, which seemed to boom like thunder even when he was talking softly. "I want to talk to Thron."

Garad and Frej obeyed at once. Rath nodded to the very rear of the ship, and I followed as he walked there.

"Thron, do you know what duty is?"

"Sure," I said. "Duty is ... duty."

"Duty is honor," Rath said. "Duty is obligation. You don't do your duty because you enjoy it; you do it to be proud of yourself, the pride that can only come from the respect of your peers. Do you know what respect means, Thron?"

I nodded silently.

"I thought so. Your father's a good man. Everyone respects him. He does his duty. Are you like your father?"

I swallowed hard. *Had I done something wrong?*

"We all have duties," Rath said. "I'm doing mine. I didn't want to go viking this year, but I couldn't abandon my friends. I don't have to sail anymore. I enjoy sitting at home by the fire all night, drinking the best mead, listening to Helsa sing, or driving our wagon wherever Læknir's skills are needed.

It's good to be the healer's husband: everybody welcomes me into their house, and I'm treated like an honored guest." Rath paused and chuckled at that. "A far cry from the man that I was after Ormstunga died. That was very hard, coming back to find that they'd already buried her. But I did my duty: family is the greatest duty of all."

I felt extremely uncomfortable.

"I hear that you're sleeping with your servant," Rath said. "Ingrid, isn't it? Pretty young thing; can't say that I haven't admired her. But she's not family, Thron, whether your father frees her or not. Even Garad's not your family. Your unborn children are your family; your grandchildren, and all their descendants yet to come, are. You've a duty to each one of them, Thron; a duty that you must perform.

"Digr sleeps with his servants, did you know? His wife hates it, but he has three young serving girls that never leave his house, and at least two of them are pregnant all of the time. He also goes over to Beigaldi's now and then, and I suspect that at least one of her bastards is his.

"My point is, just because you sleep with Ingrid is no reason to shirk your duty. Your father now owns the second largest farm in our village. He'll never own Digr's lands; with all those kids of Digr's, they'll be farming that land for a hundred years. But you need kids now, not bastards; real, honest heirs to take on your duties after you die, to insure that your family stays strong.

"Helsa likes you, Thron. I'd support you, if you asked to marry her. Helsa has my blood in her, and would bear you strong, healthy sons. You'd like being the husband of the healer; you get to travel all over, and gain an importance that even Digr can't claim. And you'd never be poor again, even when harvest is bad. Healing is the art of arts; when it's needed, no other help will suffice. Helsa's young, pretty, talented, and she can cook and sew – you've seen how good she is at that.

"Well, I've said enough," Rath sighed after an expectant wait. "Just remember, when you decide, to think back to the poor times when your family didn't have enough food to last until harvest. Do you want to ever look at your wife and admit that you're not man enough to put bread on her table every day? It's a terrible feeling, Thron, disappointing those you love."

* * * * * * * * *

Chapter 34

* * * * * * * * *

I don't know what Gyðja told the other women at Þur's, but I wished that she hadn't. Þur herself was nowhere to be seen, but Bekkjarbót came running up to me, squealing and giggling, as I walked in, and she hugged me hard, almost smothering me against her huge soft breasts. She kissed the top of my head, called me her little man, and took me off behind the curtains at once.

I like mating; nothing feels as good, but Bekkjarbót made it as uncomfortable as possible. She kept holding me pressed against her and whispering things like *'my responsible man'* and *'my little husband'*. When we finally finished, I was relieved in more ways than one.

Gjallandi's shrill cries and breathy gasps came from a nearby curtain as we exited, and Þur herself pushed out from behind another curtain as we emerged. Þur frowned at Bekkjarbót when she saw her clinging to me, and sent her off.

Bekkjarbót seemed offended, as if it were her right to have me, but finally she went back to the tables. Þur bowed slightly to me before talking.

"My girls have all the men that they need," Þur said. "You can politely refuse them, if you want."

Spákona sat behind the tables today, and she poured a mug of ale and handed it directly to me as I sat down next to Sammuel, who was holding Eyverska in his arms, his hands inside her blouse. Eyverska smiled very warmly, then softly reached out and squeezed my arm, as if offering comfort and reassurance.

Not all of the girls seemed happy to see me. Gjallandi's eyes shot daggers at me, but her expression told me that she wasn't angry; I'd have sworn that she was about to cry. Tungu wouldn't even look at me, no matter how many times she walked past, not even when Sammuel tried to introduce us. She pulled Eyverska out of Sammuel's arms and took him behind the curtains instead, and I couldn't help thinking that she did it to keep from having to meet me.

"Come with me," Eyverska said softly.

With no choice, I got up and followed as she led me behind the curtains, but like Gyðja had, Eyverska didn't motion me to an old mattress, but led me through several curtains. We didn't go to the kitchen, as I expected, but through a closed door.

Inside was a nursery, filled with kids of all sizes, although none older than ten. Laughing and playing, or sitting and whimpering, they all looked up as I entered. There were two other women in there that I didn't know, both pregnant, one nursing two infants. The third was Gyðja.

"Thron!" Gyðja shouted merrily.

Smiling widely and putting down the child that she was

tending, Gyðja hugged me tightly. A little girl ran up, demanding Gyðja's attention, but Eyverska scooped up the child and held it.

We had another great time, sitting around and talking while the noisy kids played. It felt good here, with no one pressuring me, and I finally told Gyðja about Helsa and what Rath had said to me.

"You must choose," Eyverska interjected. "You can't marry Helsa and keep Ingrid. As free women, either can leave."

"Yes, but either choice is evil," Gyðja said wisely. "You have an obligation to your family, and Helsa can fulfill those in ways that Ingrid never could. Helsa will make you rich and powerful, but will she ever fill your heart so much that no trace of Ingrid remains?"

No, she won't, I thought, but I couldn't say so. I looked down. Finished nursing, the other woman came over and gave me a comforting hug.

"We all pray to meet a man like you," she said, and tears shook her voice. She hugged me like she'd never let me go.

Eventually we had to go out. Eyverska mussed up her hair and we emerged arm-in-arm into the main hall, her hand on her chest and gasping for breath. I caught Father's eye just before he vanished behind the curtains with Þur, and he grinned approvingly. Frej was there, begging Inn Danski to go with him.

"You just had me!" Inn teased, and she pushed him back playfully and took the waiting hand of an older man.

Frej flopped down as if he didn't care, looking about to see which other women were available. Several that I didn't know walked past, but they only nodded courteously to me. One took Frej, who seemed so excited that he was about to burst.

I yawned sleepily, but I didn't close my eyes. I laid back, and Spákona saw to it that I got the hottest foods and all of the ale that I wanted. Some of the men complained that Spákona was giving me all of her best, and she informed them that my prowess behind the curtains had earned me special attention.

Late that evening, Frej and Garad both jumped up, shouting to be chosen, but Inn Danski stepped between them and reached down to me. Garad and Frej complained loudly before the adult's glares silenced them.

We didn't go to the kitchen or the nursery. Inn Danski pulled me down onto the first mattress that we reached.

"Just hold me," she whispered, "the way that you'd hold her."

"I wouldn't just hold her," I whispered back.

"That'd be nice, too," Inn smiled.

It was very nice.

* * * * * * * * *

"I swear now my life and allegiance to Captain Branwulf, that I'll obey his orders without question, and sacrifice my life, if asked to, for my ship and crew, and to reveal and share all profits that I steal from this day forth, until death takes me, or I return to my homeland."

I spoke loudly and proudly as Captain Branwulf watched. The roar of a hundred voices droned over the light waves splashing against the pylons. The words of the oath burned into my brain. *Once you return from your first viking, no one can ever call you a boy again!*

"Grab an oar near the front," Sammuel told Father. "Branwulf plans to fill 'er to the brim."

"How can he afford it?" Father whispered to Sammuel.

"He can't," Sammuel whispered back. "If we don't make a big haul, then we won't be able to sail at all next year; Branwulf may have to sell his ship."

* * * * * * * * *

"Shove off!" Larg shouted.

Garad and I sat against the rail beside Father, Rath, and Hjálmun, who filled the bench. Hal, Digr, and Smiðr manned the bench in front of us, Brún and Trandill on the rail. The ship had more men on it than I'd imagined it would hold; men near the mast were standing because there was no room.

"Ready oars!" Larg shouted.

"I want our departure as impressive as our arrival!" Branwulf added.

A drum sounded, beating a rapid beat, a beat that I knew well.

"Row!" Larg shouted. "Row! Row! Row!"

The dragonship strained, and the rowers heaved and grunted. We were much heavier now, the waterline so close to the oar ports that any wave splashed inside.

"Move this ship!" Larg cried. *"Move it! What's wrong with you? Where's my whip?"*

Crack!

Larg did have a whip, and many men ducked as he cracked it in the air. *Would he really whip us?*

We weren't the only ship sailing out of the harbor. One, much smaller, and not overbrimming with men, sped past us as if we were moving backwards, and Larg took great offence at this. He ordered men in the aisle to kneel beside the rowers and help, and soon four or five men worked every oar.

Garad and I reached down to help, but Hjálmun shouted us back.

"Hands clear!" he shouted. "Never reach near an oar port! Lean back and give us as much room as you can."

Hjálmun pulled hard on the oar, and we skimmed over the waves. We overtook and passed three large ships, one with its sail spread and no oars in the water at all, and still Larg shouted. By the time that we reached the mouth of the bay, and sailed out into the North Sea, Larg was red-faced.

"Lazy, worthless scum!" he cried. *"What, did we leave the men behind ... and let whores man our oars?"*

"Enough!" Branwulf ordered.

"Oars up!" Larg shouted. "Oars in the rear, stay! Oars in front, rest!"

Ten minutes later, two ships pulled alongside ours. Lines were cast near the front, and as we pulled closer, more ships arrived. Nine ships, including ours, gathered; nine mighty dragonheads staring into each other's snarling wooden faces.

"Welcome all!" cried a voice from another ship. "I'm Captain Jarl Flöskuskegg, commander of this fleet. First, I want to welcome Captain Branwulf and his crew, who rowed so well that they beat all of us here. Second, I want to promise that a single infraction, a moment of slowness to obey my orders, shall be rewarded with a very slow and painful death. If you doubt what I do to those who defy me, ask my brother in Niflhiem, who disobeyed me only once. Third, I want to tell you of our first target: we're going deep into the heart of our enemy, up the Rother River to a place called Rye Harbor in Sussex, England. It'll be very dangerous, but my spies tell me that a baron there named Cosset has been collecting heavy taxes all winter, and they consider themselves too far inland to be worried about raiders. Our goals are three: the treasury of Lord Cosset, every ship we can get, and anything that you men can carry. My plan is to send in a small group of scouts on foot. Then we'll sail up the Rother River in the middle of the night, right into Rye Harbor. Lord Cosset has a huge wooden house, not even a castle, and we'll storm it the instant that we land. Once his treasury is in my hands, I'll give you free reign! Anything that you find, you can keep, as much as you can carry! But we depart before dawn, so the faster that we capture his house, the more plunder you'll have. By dawn, we must be back in open sea. Any sea-worthy ships in the harbor or on the river that we pass, I want taken! They'll become our supply ships for the rest of the viking.

"That's my plan. We'll meet again just north of Der Helder on the westernmost Frisian Island. I've a friend there, a land-owner, and he'll let us disembark on his island; extra rewards to the ship that arrives first!

"You've all sworn oaths to your captains. Your captains have sworn oaths to me. Obey well, and you'll find me generous. No man who follows me goes unrewarded!"

* * * * * * * * *

We put on our cloaks as soon as we were underway, taking turns so no more than one pair of hands lifted from any oar at the same time. Rain fell harder. Many pulled their hoods low; you didn't need to see to row.

Jarl Flöskuskegg's ship took the lead, and his oars splashed in perfect unison as they rowed.

"Stay with the beat!" Larg shouted as he pushed his way up and down the aisle, banging his drum. "The more that Jarl Flöskuskegg sees us, the more reward Branwulf can demand.

Stay with the beat!"

"Can I row?" Garad asked.

"Take my place," Rath said.

"Thron, there's room for you as well," Father said.

Rowing was more fun than not rowing; I put my back into it.

Hours later, rowing didn't seem so fun.

"Father, why don't we use the sail?"

"Do you want to arrive in England ready to fight enemies ... or weak from days of resting?"

After noon, I smelled smoke, and something made my thirsty mouth water.

"Raise the sail!" Branwulf cried out.

"Raise sail!" Larg shouted, and men jumped to comply.

The great striped sail rose by men pulling on the ropes attached to the pulley on the mast. It billowed out strong and full, and our ship rocked when it caught the wind.

"Oars up!" Larg shouted. "Oars rest!"

Men pushed the oars through the ports, then set them in their rests.

"About time," Rath grumbled.

"Enough of that," Digr said seriously. "Start grumbling on the first day and everyone'll be surly for the rest of the voyage."

"I'm starving!" Rath complained.

"Wealth has made you soft," Father laughed.

"He said marrying Læknir would ruin him!" Hal chuckled.

"Thron, get out our bowls and spoons," Father said.

"It's going to take forever to get food way up here," Smiðr scowled, looking at the press of men.

"Let's start early," Brún whispered, and he and Trandill grinned.

"What've you got?" Rath demanded.

"Bread," Trandill smiled.

"Mead," Brún grinned. "Picked them up at Þurs."

"Ah, praise you both!" Hal whispered. "May the eyes of the Valkyrie always shine upon you!"

Finally, the men in the aisle near us were pushed aside by two of Branwulf's men, one being Sammuel, who was holding a large steaming cauldron. Another, whom I didn't know, was ladling out soup into the bowls. When our turn came, he splashed a meager single ladle of soup into my bowl, then moved on.

"Eat while it's hot," Father said to Garad and I, "and be grateful."

"Vikings aren't for eating," Digr laughed. "That's what þur's was for."

Rath poked Digr gently in his large stomach.

"If we have to run, you take rearguard," Rath grinned. "You're most likely to get stuck in doorways!"

"Those doors'll be plenty wide after I go through them!" Digr smiled.

Everybody laughed. I sat amazed: the adults were joking ... not somber or silent. They seemed ... like ... *kids.*

* * * * * * * * *

"Ready oars!" Larg shouted.

"Wash our bowls," Father said to Garad and I, and I stood there wondering how.

"I'll do it," Hjálmun said, who was sitting beside Garad.

"Watch, boys; you'll do this from now on ... for all of us."

Hjálmun took each bowl, one at a time, and shoved it overboard, down into the sea. Then he scrubbed it with his other hand and shoved it back underwater for a final rinse.

"We're falling behind," Rath noted, looking at the other ships, few of which had their sails spread.

"Oars out!" Larg shouted.

Hal, Trandill, and Hjálmun pulled out our oars, tossed out the paddles, and fitted them through the ports.

"Thron, Garad, sit beside Hjálmun," Father said, waving Smiðr back. "The boys need more practice."

Gladly Garad and I took seats by Hjálmun, Rath and Father both struggling to move in the limited space.

"Row!" Larg shouted.

They didn't take the sail down; they steered the ship to catch more of the wind and we began speeding along. Angry shouts rose from one ship as we cut a path across its bow.

Eventually Larg shouted to lower the sail, and we turned to port. Only four ships were ahead of us, but we could see land straight ahead, and veered straight south to avoid it. Bored, Rath pulled out a thick pouch with a flask of oil and a rag, and one at a time, everyone not rowing drew their weapons and lightly wiped them down.

Hours passed, and slowly the fun of rowing evaporated. My back started to hurt, as at harvest, and I was sore all over. Beside me, Garad looked exhausted, as if he were holding our oar rather than rowing it. By contrast, Hjálmun looked grimly determined. Sweat was pouring from him; he was rowing hard to make up for Garad and I.

I rowed harder.

* * * * * * * * *

"Sleep," Father ordered.

Larg had ordered the sail to be raised, and soon afterwards, all oars were lifted and stored. I ached. More soup was slowly ladled out to everyone, and then Garad and I washed everyone's dishes. We laid our heads by the rail, our feet pressed against the men sleeping in the aisle, and squeezed against each other, everyone wrapped in their cloak. Hal had an extra blanket which he spread over all of our feet; I wasn't comfortable, but I fell asleep almost instantly.

* * * * * * * * *

I awoke damp; pools of rainwater had collected in the folds of all our cloaks. One spot on my arm was wet, and my trousers were soaked from the knees down.

"Ready oars!" Larg shouted.

The sun was still hidden below the straight, flat horizon. No land poked above the waves, and a ceiling of gray clouds promised another day of rain. I sighed heavily, shivering.

"Cold?" Father asked, yawning. "A few hours at oar will cure that."

I was set to oar to row between Smiðr and Digr. Garad rowed between Rath and Hal. We rowed for about an hour, then Hjálmun relieved Smiðr, Brún relieved Digr, Father relieved Rath, and Brún relieved Hal.

"My turn," Trandill tapped my shoulder.

"I can do it," I replied, trying to sound strong.

"Thron!" Father barked.

"We take turns in the morning," Trandill explained as I got up, "especially when it's cold and rainy; rowing warms you up."

"Thron, come sit between Garad and I," Father said. "There's room on this oar for four, and you boys need bigger arms."

* * * * * * * * *

The gray clouds fell behind us after mid-morning, when more soup was ladled. Garad and I rowed whenever oars touched water. Our hands were raw and red, swollen huge, our butts stung from sitting too long, and our legs cramped from not having enough room to stretch. Some men stood while rowing; no one said anything when we tried it. When rowing with the wind, we managed incredible speeds, but when we had to row into the wind, our great square sail was furled.

"How long will it take us to get to England?" I asked.

"We're sailing toward the Netherlands, to the Frisian Isles," Father said. "How long it takes depends on the wind, the tide, and how well we row. Normally we could make it in a week, maybe a few days more, but we're hugging the coast, not cutting across open sea, because we're overloaded. We should make it in less than two weeks, unless there's a storm."

"Two weeks!" Garad exclaimed shrilly.

Father frowned at him. "Tired of rowing already?"

"No, never!" Garad replied quickly.

"Then what's the problem?"

"I – I ...," Garad stammered, "I ... just wanted to ... kill some Saxons!"

The men all laughed.

"Mind your oar," Father said. "Build up your arms; that's the best thing that you can do to kill Saxons."

Captain Branwulf came by at least once every day.

"What happened to those girls?" Branwulf asked.

"They're boys now, Captain," Father grinned.

"Good!" Branwulf said. "By the return voyage, maybe they'll be men!"

"They will," Father promised, "if I have to beat the *'boy'* out of them!"

Branwulf took Father and Rath back to the rear of the ship. I glanced questioningly at Digr.

"Branwulf wants to confer with them," Digr explained. "They're two of his best fighters; all my money can't buy that respect."

Fishing ships abounded, but most usually just waved or sailed away when they saw us. One day, we spied a lone dragonship being pursued closely by two large ships, but Captain Flöskuskegg's ship turned toward them, and the pursuing ships quickly fled. Captain Flöskuskegg had a long conversation with the captain of the lone dragonship, and when the horn sounded to get underway again, the lone dragonship fell into line behind us.

Now we were a fleet of ten.

* * * * * * * * *

Chapter 35

*　*　*　*　*　*　*　*　*

"Hail the Frisian Isles!"

At Branwulf's command, one of his younger retainers, only a few years older than Garad and I, climbed up onto the wooden dragon's head for a better look.

"There's a long chain of islands straight ahead," the youth reported. "We're about in the middle."

"Oars up! Oars rest!" Larg shouted, and the rowers pulled and stored their oars as quickly as they could. "Hoist sail!"

"Nobody rows here unless they have to," Hal leaned over and whispered to us. "Nobody minds a dragon at sail; it means that we're just passing by. But when a dragon's under oars, then they assume it's attacking."

We turned west following the chain of islands. Big farms, many houses, and strange trees, the like of which I'd never seen before, dotted the isles. We sailed for hours as the sun lowered toward the horizon, and finally Captain Flöskuskegg's ship turned toward a wide inlet on the largest island.

"What about the reward?" I asked. "The reward for arriving first ...?"

"There was never any reward," Trandill grinned. "Captain Flöskuskegg's ship has to land first, or it'd be a grave insult. He'd kill the captain of any ship that insulted him."

"So he gets the reward?" I asked.

"Captain Flöskuskegg decides which captain gets rewarded," Trandill said. "He keeps more than he gives, I assure you; every fleet commander does."

"Stay close to Captain Flöskuskegg!" Branwulf shouted, interrupting us. "Once we know where we're going, we want to land as quickly as possible."

Other ships crowded in. We sailed into the wide inlet jostling for position.

Someone on Captain Flöskuskegg's ship blew a horn, and many people came out of a house not far from the beach. One strange man in a white and purple dress came out onto the sand. Captain Flöskuskegg's ship sailed right up onto the beach near him.

"Man the rudder," Captain Branwulf ordered Larg. "Beach us as close to Flöskuskegg as you can. Don't leave us out on the wings."

"Aye, Captain," Larg said as he hurried past us.

Several boats tried to cut us off on the way in, but only one succeeded. Larg cut off a whole group of others so badly that they cursed us. Finally, sand scraped against our hull: a loud, long grinding-scratch. Several cheered, including Rath, and some men jumped overboard and waded ashore, pulling on stout ropes.

"Over the side!" Branwulf shouted. "Beach this dragon!"

Holding our weapons high, Garad and I excitedly jumped

behind Hjálmun as he leaped over the edge and ran to help those pulling the rope. The cold water felt good, and we splashed toward the white sandy beach, anxious to stand on dry land again.

We managed a spot two ships away from Captain Flöskuskegg's ship, which seemed to suit Branwulf; he smiled as men pulled the dragon almost to the edge of the water. Captain Branwulf and Larg finally jumped off as the dragon came to rest.

"Sammuel!" Branwulf cried. "Scavenge for driftwood. Get a fire started. The rest of you: stay by the ship. Larg, Bjarki, Hvamm, Drumb, Rath, and Thorir; come with me."

"Thron! Garad! Frej!" Sammuel called, pointing. "Run up the coast that way. Gather all of the driftwood that you can find. Hurry, before the other ships get it!"

Behind us, Sammuel sent others. There wasn't a lot of wood, but we gathered all that we could. Hal, Brún, and Trandill followed and helped lift the big pieces. Our boots splashed, full of seawater, but we didn't care; after weeks aboard a cramped ship, rowing every day, room to run felt good. We each gathered an armful of wood, but Hal ordered us to wait for armed escort before we went back; men from other ships looked at our scavenged driftwood enviously.

* * * * * * * * *

"Anyway," Kappi said aloud, rapt faces listening to his tale, "there I was, coming downstairs, and what do I see? Half of the town shouting and looking angry. Well, I've seen what happens to strangers in bad situations, and here I am, marooned in Greece, no way home, and I barely speak the language. It was too late to sneak back upstairs, so what'd I do? I put on my best look of confusion ..." Kappi masked his face with a goofy expression and his listeners laughed, "... and I asked the closest person to me what had happened. Apparently this wealthy girl, the daughter of somebody important, was with child: it was the very girl that I'd spent the night with!"

The crowd around the fire laughed and gasped appropriately.

"So here I am, thinking that these people are going to stone me, when suddenly this big man, wearing many gold rings, jumps up and shouts *'there's a satyr in the woods'!* 'A satyr?' I ask, *'what's a satyr?'* Well, it turns out that a satyr is some kind of wicked, randy spirit of the forest, half-man and half-goat. Well, you can imagine how surprised I was, but I knew better than to laugh out loud; this wasn't the time or place to draw unwanted attention. Several other faces in the crowd looked equally dubious, but this rich man started yelling and cursing about a satyr, and soon several others joined in, and ... you won't believe this! They pulled out their swords and stormed off to the woods after this satyr!

"I couldn't believe it myself ... I mean, these were grown men! Anyway, I told them that I needed my shield, then ran to my room and grabbed everything that I owned. I wasn't going to stay in a crazy town where people believed in goat-men! As soon as they didn't find any satyrs, that mob would start looking for someone to blame, and I didn't want to be the only stranger in town when they returned.

"I snuck back downstairs, after they'd left, and there's the pretty girl, all red-eyed and crying, sitting alone. So I go up to her and ask; 'That man with the rings ... does he really believe in satyrs?' and she looks at me, and says through many tears *'No; he's the real father.'"*

Everyone exploded with laughter, even Frej, Garad, and I. We'd been ordered to stay by the ship, but we weren't important enough to merit a seat near the fire; only Sammuel, Digr, Skalla, and a few select others were given that honor. Many were lying on cloaks outside the fire-ring, some already asleep. Branwulf, Father, and the others hadn't returned.

Kappi bowed to scattered applause and sat down next to Hjalti. Someone that I didn't know started talking next, telling a story about attacking a French merchant fleet in stormy seas.

Suddenly a hand fell on my shoulder.

"Have you cleaned your weapons today?" Smiðr asked.

"Yes," I replied.

"Since landing?" he asked. "Since you jumped into the water and got them all wet?"

"I held my sword ..."

"That doesn't matter," Smiðr said firmly, and he gave me a large oily rag. "Clean them good, all you boys, and then wipe down every bit of metal that you're wearing, swords, knives, even your belt buckles. You don't want them rusting, do you? Keep your blades naked tonight; your scabbards and sheaths need to dry out."

"Can we listen while we polish?" Garad asked.

"Sure," Smiðr smiled. "Just don't get in anybody's way."

"Make way for Captain Branwulf!" shouted a loud voice, and men cheered and moved aside; everyone around the fire stood up.

Branwulf approached, surrounded by Father, Rath, and the others, carrying torches to light their way. But Branwulf didn't come to the fire; he and Larg stalked across the dark sands to the ship.

"We're *rearguard!*" sneered the tall, gray-bearded man

beside Father: all smiles vanished, and a dead silence fell.

"Clean your weapons well," Smiðr said to us. "We'll need them doubly sharp now."

* * * * * * * * *

"Rearguard means that we're last in line," Father said to Garad and I after we walked away from the fire, "When we sail upriver, in single file, we'll be the last ship."

"To guard the exit," Rath sneered.

"Captain Flöskuskegg called it an honor, and said he needed his best rowers there," Father scowled, "but rearguard is the most dangerous position; if the Saxons ambush us, as they like to, they attack rearguard first. I've been there before: you're sailing upriver in silence, and suddenly a hundred Saxon arrows land in your ship."

"They hope that the rearguard will plug up the only escape route, and trap the rest of the fleet," Rath said.

"Stupid idea," Digr said. "Taking dragons upriver ..."

"Everything on the coast has been plundered to death ... or is so well defended that we'd need fifty ships to take it," Trandill said.

"Why waste your best rowers?" Brún argued. "Better rowers could get around a decimated ship. What about that new ship, the one that we saved?"

"They ...," Rath began, but Father shushed him.

We all looked; a strange man walked past us.

"He's okay," Garad said as he walked away. "He's from our ship."

"That makes him our shipmate," Father said to Garad. "That's important, because he sinks if we do, but we ten, and no one else, are from our village. Out here, that makes us kinsmen. We're loyal to our ship, but we rely on each other. Even friends like Sammuel and Branwulf aren't kinsmen."

"We only have three shields between us, and if arrows rain, then we may have to fight to keep them," Hal said.

"I'll row," Hjálmun said.

"Good," Father said. "Digr, Brún, and Trandill will also row. Rath, Smiðr, and I will hold the shields. Hal, keep your knives ready; if anyone tries to pull our shields from us, you take them out."

"And grab any shields that get dropped," Rath said.

"What do we...?" I began.

"You do nothing!" Father hissed furiously. "You and Garad get on the deck as low as you can ... and stay there!"

"Crawl under us, if you can," Brún said.

"But don't get in our way," Digr warned. "Fast oars are our best defense."

"Branwulf argued, but Captain Flöskuskegg said that he didn't trust the new ship's captain to be rearguard," Father said. "They'll be right in front of us, second to last; Branwulf has orders to attack them, if they flee without orders."

"That's another stupid order," Digr snarled. "They won't flee unless there's trouble: nothing would plug up the river worse than the last two ships fighting."

"Captain Flöskuskegg isn't the strategist that Branwulf hoped for," Father said. "Still, we swore oaths, and Flöskuskegg promised Branwulf first choice of all the plunder. That's the reason why Branwulf agreed; Flöskuskegg promised that our ship would be rewarded with gold, more than any other, if we took rearguard."

"Dead men can't spend gold," Digr grumbled.

"Our duty is set," Father said. "We sail in tomorrow night, at dusk, and wait offshore for the signal."

"What signal?" Garad asked.

"Fifty men, dressed as Saxons, will sail over in a fishing boat," Father explained. "They'll be let off at various places along the river. At midnight, their captain will sail back to the mouth of the river and wave a torch for us."

"What about the men dressed as Saxons?" I asked.

"Their job is to kill anybody who might raise the alarm. They're Captain Flöskuskegg's hand-picked guard; our mission depends on them."

"Only a fool would believe that they'll take out every guard," Rath said.

"We must begin the attack before the alarm's raised," Father said.

"It'll be a costly retreat," Brún said.

"But a rich reward, if we make it," Trandill said.

"So Captain Flöskuskegg says," Rath said.

"My confidence in Flöskuskegg's word is waning," Brún said.

* * * * * * * * *

Wrapped in cloaks, we slept not far from the fire, with guards walking by all night. Early the next day, Larg found Garad, Frej, and I, and we all spent another day aboard ship washing and oiling. I had to strip and swim out around the ship, making certain to polish the keel to the waterline, trying not to be slammed against the hard hull each time that a wave crashed into me. Garad scrubbed every inch of the side, leaning over the rail, which was unpleasant; sitting on the rail was the closest thing to a privy that we had. But Frej had the worst duty; Frej had to lift up the deck planks and crawl inside the hull with a handful of dry rags to clean out every drop of bilge water, and every time that he thought he'd gotten it all, Larg would crawl inside and discover some niche where a spoonful of bilge water still hid, and Larg would chew out Frej at the top of his lungs, then send him back down to soak up the water and oil the spot where it'd been.

The morning soup was much better; Captain Flöskuskegg's local friend, the man in the white and purple dress, which Sammuel called a 'toga', provided us with a hundred chickens. Each ship was given ten, but even that was too little, so they boiled them up into a rich, thick sauce. Larg put us to work until midday, when Father rescued us.

"It'll be a long night, and boys their age need rest," Father said to Larg.

Larg seemed ill-disposed, but he only snorted and walked away.

"Thron, Garad, wrap up in your cloaks and get some rest," Father said. "Frej, do the same. You won't get any sleep tonight."

* * * * * * * * *

I'd only dozed, fading back and forth from sleepy to wakeful all afternoon and evening; I raised my head under the starlit sky at the first sound of Father's voice.

"This is your first viking. Do you boys know what I want you to do?"

"Kill Saxons ...," I started.

"No," Father said. "You'll have your chance to fight when you know what you're facing, not when you're wide-eyed and confused. Keep low, as protected as you can without hiding in a sea-chest. Remember what happened to Halgrum on his first fight: your only job is to stay alive."

* * * * * * * * *

“Raise the sail,” Larg said quietly.

Silent as ghosts, men complied without a word or grunt, the only sound the sea slapping against our hull. We sailed out onto black waters, dim starlight peeking between dark clouds. No one spoke, but many furtive glances were exchanged. We sailed last in line as the fleet sailed slowly away, the Frisian Isles behind us.

Crossing the English Channel took long, dreary hours. Cold swept the night sea, penetrating our quilted coats. Digr used our piled cloaks as a shield for arrows, but they were poor protection for his large body, and none at all for his shoulders or head. Father had donned his mail shirt. We looked menacing, certainly, but no joy or excitement showed; these weren’t the brave, fearless adventurers of Father’s tales. *If I hadn’t known otherwise, then I’d have said that everyone was frightened.*

“Land ...!” whispered someone in the row behind us, leaning close, and Brún leaned forward and passed the message along.

“Not a word now,” Father whispered. “All of our lives depend on silence.”

Lights twinkled on the shore, but only a very few; the glows of shielded windows peeked from houses hidden by the night. Finally, Father put a hand on our heads and pushed us gently down.

“We’re being watched,” Hal hissed, pointing.

“No, they’re waving at us,” Brún whispered.

“It’s the signal-ship,” Rath said.

“Quiet!” Father whispered urgently. “One Saxon could

sound the alarm."

"Lower the sail!" Larg hissed.

Another hour passed. I could feel Garad shiver as he pressed against me, flat on the deck, amid the hard boots of the others.

"The signal!" We heard the message passed back, row to row.

"This is it," whispered Branwulf's voice.

"Oars!" Larg hissed. "Quietly!"

No oars were tossed; carefully they were dipped into the sea, then fitted smoothly through their ports. Larg hissed, not an order, but all oars dipped in unison.

"Oars up!" Larg whispered a few minutes later, and then he squeezed past several men and made his way toward the tail.

Branwulf himself walked to the edge of the lowered sail.

"Listen to me!" Branwulf hissed. "Our orders are to stay right behind the new ship, and we will, whenever we're in open water. But when the shores close in, especially at bends in the river, we fall back. Larg will be giving the orders from the rear, so watch the oar in front of you, and match their speed. Pass messages up the ranks as quickly as possible: whispers only! Our lives are in Odin's hands."

Hal reached down and patted my back. He had a satisfied grin on his face, and so did the others. Father leaned over and whispered:

"Stay low and silent!"

Larg hissed, and oars pushed us after the new ship. Branwulf's words echoed in my mind; I didn't understand it all, but I was glad that we were sailing with such a clever, crafty captain.

For over an hour, we rowed, then suddenly the pace of the

oars fell to almost nothing. We drifted a short while, and then the oars began paddling again. I looked up to see their faces, but Hjálmun ungently nudged my face with his knee, and I quickly lowered my head.

This wasn't how I'd hoped to spend my first viking raid, I thought angrily.

Then ... I heard the first scream.

* * * * * * * * *

"Back!" Larg shouted. "Back! Back!"

The rowers strained for all their worth; our ship lurched backwards; Garad and I toppled into legs. Several wooden thuds struck; *arrows had pelted our ship!* Someone's knees pressed me down, and suddenly the dim light vanished; Smiðr, Father, and Rath were holding shields over us.

"Row!" Branwulf cried. "Row for your lives!"

Knees pressed harder on us. Our dragon flew backwards, away from the narrow bend.

Suddenly Father said aloud:

"We're clear!"

"Keep all shields up," Branwulf shouted. "Any injuries?"

"Aye!" shouted several.

"Replace the wounded!" Branwulf shouted. "Keep an eye out, in case they come at us in ships."

"It's coming from those tall walls along the shore," Hjalti said.

"Fine," Branwulf said. "We're too far out for bows to reach, but let's see if any of the other ships make it. I don't want to backtrack downriver alone; the alarm's sure to have gone downstream."

"Thron, Garad, get up!" Father said. "This is what you

need to see!"

Hands pulled us up. We spied the source of the screams; the new ship was struggling, its tall, flaming sail eclipsing frantic men hiding behind shields. Arrows rained from the high stone walls along the shore, many flickered from flaming rags tied to their shafts; streaks lit the sky. Two other ships rapidly rowed around the new ship; one crashed into it, and pushed it aside. Death-cries filled the air.

Arrows suddenly streamed from the other side of the shore, illuminated by flaming rags, the dragons were ambushed between them. The closest two ships, one on each side, pushed past the new ship, and raced toward us, away from the chaos. The new ship came to life again, after being pushed parallel in the river by the other ships, and chased after them. Behind them, we saw distant ships burning and heard anguished cries.

"They're trapped!" Rath said. "Flöskuskegg led them straight into ambush!"

"We've not escaped yet," Trandill warned.

"Row!" Captain Branwulf shouted. "Stay ahead of those dragons, no matter what! Row until we're clear!"

"Row!" Larg shouted.

Our dragon lurched forward. Within minutes, we were racing, the men pulling like never before, but at one point, the shores closed around a narrow pass.

"Back on deck!" Father ordered, and Garad and I fell onto our bellies. Father, Rath, and Smiðr again raised their shields and plunged us into darkness.

* * * * * * * * *

Chapter 36

*   *   *   *   *   *   *   *   *

Men grunted and flexed sore muscles as they lifted their oars and placed them at rest; we were far out to sea.

"Where're they going?" Smiðr asked.

We looked up to see the new ship. Half of its oars were missing, and it still had fire burning inside it. Its few living oarsmen pumped furiously. They rowed away from us as fast as they could.

"They're leaving," Rath said.

"Deserters," Digr mumbled.

"Did you see them?" Hal asked. "A ship of corpses!"

"That could have been us ...!" Rath said.

"Look at this," Father said, displaying his shield; three Saxon arrows stuck out from it.

"I got more," Rath said; his shield bore five arrows.

"You missed one," Digr said, and he held out his arm. A long rip bled through his shoulder, soaking his tunic. "It's just a scratch. Here's the arrow that did it."

Digr reached down and picked up an arrow off the deck ... *by my feet.*

"Pull alongside!" Larg shouted at the other two boats. "Let us help you!"

The only other two boats to escape pulled alongside us, and ropes were tossed. Men from our ship jumped to theirs; Father held us back. Some men were crying on the other ships, and blood painted anguished faces.

"How many?" Branwulf asked.

"At least thirty dead!" a voice from the ship nearest us cried. "Twice that wounded."

"Is your captain still alive?"

"I am!" said another voice, but it was strained with pain. A tall man stood up. He was wearing chainmail, but had several arrows in his back. His men tried to hold him down, but he shrugged them off.

"The captain from this ship is dead," Larg shouted from the other ship. "Only one of their captain's kinsmen survived, and he's tending his men. More than half of their crew's wounded or dead; that new ship blocked their exit too long."

"We have to sail from here before dawn, and that's not far off," Branwulf said, and he turned to the surviving captain. "Is your sail intact?"

"Aye," the captain said.

"Part of this ship's sail got burned, but not too badly," Larg said.

"Bring the captain's kinsman aboard my ship, and you come, too," Branwulf said to the captain. "We need to discuss what to do now. Larg, send our men over to help both ships. Strip and dump the dead; all three ships must be under oar and sail within the hour."

"I'm the captain of this ship!" roared the wounded captain.

"If you wish, we can leave you here," Branwulf said. "The Saxons would be delighted to find you still limping off their shore in the morning light."

* * * * * * * * *

Sammuel whispered to Father as the strange captain was brought aboard, and then he went down the line, talking to others. Father leaned close and whispered something to Smiðr and Rath, who passed it on. No one even looked at Garad and I.

"Were you friends with Captain Flöskuskegg?" Branwulf asked.

"Known him for three years," their captain said.

"Ever been ambushed before?"

"Captain Flöskuskegg is a great man," sneered the captain. "I won't believe that he's dead until I've seen his severed head."

"Captain, this is Øgæfa," Larg said, pulling a young man with a dark curly beard onto the prow of our ship. "He's the kinsman of the dead captain."

"A pleasure," Captain Branwulf smiled. "Have you enough men to man your oars?"

The wounded captain never got to answer. Without warning, Captain Branwulf pulled out a long knife and stabbed him deep. Larg did the same with Øgæfa, knifing him from behind. Both cried out.

Suddenly weapons drew all around, even Father, Hal, and Trandill. Men leapt from our ship to the others, catching their sailors unawares, wounded or tending their wounded. The few small scuffles all ended the same: with the grunts of a dying man.

Captain Branwulf swept out his sword. The wounded captain was thrown against the rail and held by several men, so that everyone aboard his ship could see. Øgæfa was thrown against the other rail, pinned by many, although he looked already dead.

"Behold!" Branwulf cried, and he lifted his sword, put one foot on the rail, and decapitated the wounded captain. Then he went to the other side and severed Øgæfa's head, letting it fall into the night-black waters.

"I'm Captain Branwulf!" he shouted, standing on the rail, holding on to one of the dragon's wooden ears. "I command your ships now! Anyone loyal to these two, even friends and kinsmen, will be allowed to depart. We'll put you off back where we beached last night. Anyone willing to sail under my command, who'll swear an oath to me, an oath upon their very life, may stay aboard ... and enjoy a fair share. What say you? Choose now!"

No one spoke. Finally, one man raised his hand. Several men from our ship pointed their weapons at him.

"That was my brother, Captain Hítdælakappi, whose head you just sent to Njord," he said. "I'll curse you all of my life."

"You'll be set free," Branwulf said. "Any others?"

Thirty men accepted Branwulf's offer of freedom.

"The rest of you will swear to me?" Branwulf asked.

The remaining men, many of whom were wounded, said *'Aye'* or nodded.

"Fine," Branwulf said. "Men, set them free."

"No!" a man cried. "*You promised to set us ashore!"*

"Over the side ... or die!"

"No ...!" the man cried, but sword-points and spears suddenly surrounded him.

"Free him now," Branwulf ordered.

He screamed as sharp tips penetrated his flesh, and then he fell onto the deck.

"Anybody else?" Branwulf challenged.

"Please sir," came a weak voice. "I'm wounded! The salt water will poison me! I'll swear to you! Please!"

"You've already shown your loyalty," Branwulf said. "Now you show your lack of it. Larg, count to twenty, and then kill any of these men still aboard."

"Wait!" cried another. "At least let me get my armor off!"

Captain Branwulf ignored him and glanced at Larg.

"One," Larg began.

* * * * * * * * *

Men were allowed to strip off helmets and mail, but only because Branwulf wanted them. All of those men's possessions were piled in the fore on Branwulf's ship, and then those men were forced into the choppy black waters with only a thin sliver of land barely visible on the dark horizon. If they couldn't swim for miles, avoiding sharks and Saxon ships, then they'd drown. Most took their swords; if they survived the swim, then they'd arrive as hunted men in a hostile land.

The wounded, when their arrow-wounds hit salt water, screamed like dying pigs and thrashed in the sea like Urd throwing a tantrum. Some vanished underwater the instant that they splashed in ... and never came up again. Others swam off at once.

The remaining wounded were treated by their kinsmen, if they had any, and by no one, if they didn't. I watched one man pull an arrow out of his own neck, screaming as he did.

The seriously wounded were laid center, and the slightly wounded were stationed at an oar.

Sails were raised, and Garad and I were set to row. The new men were stripped of their weapons and put on oars near the rear of their dragonships with Branwulf's retainers standing guard over them. Larg was placed in charge of Captain Hítdælakappi's ship, and a young man named Bjarki was put in command of Øgæfa's ship.

The rising sun illuminated us: Branwulf and his retainers laughed grimly; this misadventure had proven more profitable than they'd dreamed. Branwulf now owned three dragonships, and he ordered one of his tallest men to scan the sea.

"Where are they?" Branwulf demanded. "They were badly damaged; they couldn't have gotten far!"

"It was dark," Kappi said. "Maybe they hugged the coastline."

"They were fools, if they did," Branwulf sneered.

"Maybe they sank," Hjalti suggested. "Maybe they were more damaged than we thought."

"Perhaps," Branwulf said. "A pity, if so. A damaged ship I could've repaired, if we'd gotten it home."

"Not enough treasure?" Kappi laughed. "Two dragonships, a hundred new men, and the weapons and armor of a hundred dead?"

"I need coins to pay the men so that they'll sail with me next year," Branwulf said. "No more dresses and candleholders!"

"With three ships, we'll need more men," Hjalti agreed. "But for gold, we'll need a better plan than Captain Flöskuskegg could execute."

"Damn these letters," Branwulf cursed. "I wish that I'd

learned to read! Next year, remind me to bring someone who can read aboard my ship."

"Excuse me, Captain!" Hal said. "We can read."

"What?"

"Yes, sir," Hal said. "Five of us were learning all winter: Brún, Trandill, Thron, Garad, and I."

"Raise your oars!" Branwulf said. "Kappi, replace them."

Other men took our oars, and Trandill pushed Garad and I up to the fore.

"All five of you can read?" Branwulf asked.

"Only a little," Hal said.

Branwulf handed Hal a sheaf of papers.

"This is an old date," Hal said. "August ... what number is that?"

"Twenty-four," I said as he held the papers out to us.

"Sorry," Hal smiled at Branwulf. "I'm not very good with Arabic numbers. Let's see: September twenty-fourth - made it to ... London. Guards everywhere. Town garri... garrison over three hundred in this quarter alone. Leaving tomorrow, heading back to the coast."

"Is it the journal of Flöskuskegg's spies?" Branwulf asked.

"Seems to be," Hal said. "September second – south of London less guarded. Lots of deep rivers, sandy beaches, good for dragons. Two key pass... passages controlled by chains across the river, but poorly manned. A few good men could take the guards out silently and disable the chains."

"Chains would've trapped us all," Hjalti said. "Captain Flöskuskegg's men must have disabled the chains, and then gotten caught."

"And alerted two whole garrisons that we were coming," Kappi growled. "No wonder we were ambushed!"

"Captain Flöskuskegg was ambushed, not us," Branwulf

said.

"Only because of you," Hal said.

"Never praise a captain until he's in sight of his homeland," Branwulf said.

* * * * * * * * *

Hal handed each of us a stack of papers; we had to hold them tightly to keep the wind from blowing them away. The papers were written by several different men, one whose runes were very crude and hard to decipher. We took turns reading aloud; slowly their record of observances led us to understand their purpose. Every waterside fortress in south-eastern England was documented, and one spy drew little sketches showing doors and towers of the fortresses that they'd observed; Branwulf studied them carefully.

"I like this church," Branwulf said. "Garad, read that description again."

"March twelfth – sat through Christian mass at St. Ursul's Cathedral; a palace if ever there was. Gold challises are displayed, and wealthy patrons donate silver as much as copper. Much riches lie about as if worthless, with none save for a few guards and priests to defend. But St. Ursul's isn't a possible target; just downstream of the cathedral lies a station of city guards two hundred strong, and Eorl Sir Dungrem lives with a dozen knights and nearly a hundred guards just upstream. His castle wields siege engines to thwart any assault upon his shore. St. Ursul's itself would be formidable, if well defended; mere rumor of a dragonship would seal doors as thick as tree-trunks."

Branwulf smiled wickedly, and those watching grew alarmed.

* * * * * * * * *

That night, we sailed close to a large, gleaming white mansion, lowered our sail, and rowed hard. We beached all three ships beside several fishing vessels tied to docks, and as one huge mass, we ran quietly at the mansion. Father kept us beside him, behind his shield, although no arrows flew, and we followed him and Rath toward the house. Frej ran close by, next to Skalla. I ran with barely concealed excitement; *finally I was standing on Saxon land, sword-bared, on a real viking raid!*

We charged from the ships three hundred strong with bows, axes, and swords. No neighbors ran to help, only pleas from behind thick, stoutly-braced doors to let them be. But Larg demanded entrance, and threatened to kill everyone in the house if not admitted.

Suddenly we were pushed aside. Men were leaned against the outer walls, and some men were lifted to stand up on their shoulders. Thick doors and barred windows defended the lower walls, but not far above hung balconies. Within moments, a dozen men topped the lowest balcony, followed by a smashing of glass and the chops of axes breaking wood. Women screamed and shipmates cheered, and more men climbed, vanishing the instant that they breached the rail.

The door in front of Larg cracked open suddenly; torches illuminated Sammuel's grinning face. The door flung wide, Larg entered, and Father and Rath followed, Garad and I pressed against their backs.

The residents were kneeling, even the men, and most were sobbing. Shipmates crowded the room with drawn blades.

"*You dare defy me?*" Larg shouted. *"Do you know the*

price ...?"

"Take all, but spare my family!" cried one old man.

"You dare speak ...?" Larg shouted. *"You dare beg ...?"*

"Please ...!" the man cried.

"I need your daughters," Larg smiled evilly.

"No ...!"

"Yes," Larg said. "Sammuel, do we have what we need?"

"Yes, Captain," Sammuel replied.

"Take these two," Larg said, indicating two young, horrified daughters. The old man tried to rise, but blades pressed into his throat. "And take that one, the little boy. Sir, you and the rest of your family we'll leave alive ... if you don't detain us."

"We won't, but ...!"

"Your children won't be violated," Larg said. "We require them for a task, and they'll be released afterwards, if we're successful."

"Then ... I dare pray you well," the old man said.

"But, for your defiance, you'll be punished," Larg said, and he turned to face all of us. "Men, we sail in five minutes! Those not aboard ship will be left behind! Take anything that you want, and kill any fool that raises a hand against you!"

A swelling cheer rose, and men started running through every door. Drawers were yanked out and curtains ripped down, but neither Father nor Rath moved. Garad started to run, but Rath stayed him with a firm hand.

"Be silent!" Larg shouted at the screaming daughters. "Silence ... or I'll kill your parents right now!"

Both girls stopped screaming, muted by fear more than any force of will. The whole crying family could barely be heard over the ransacking of their house. I glanced at Father questioningly; *I'd waited my whole life to raid and plunder a*

Saxon house, and to stand idle while others grabbed the riches ...

Beside me, I saw a tiny metal box inlaid with stones, sticking out of a box of yarn, beside knitting needles. Curious, I reached down, picked it up, and opened it. I'd hoped that it'd be full of gold coins, but it was only shirt buttons, some of antler, some tin, and some of tiny shells. I was about to put it back when Father grinned at me.

"Your mother will love it," Father said. "Garad, get the scissors; Vespa will want them, too."

Garad looked up at Father, hesitating.

"Look at them kneel," Father said. "Property belongs to the last man standing."

Men seized the two daughters and little boy. Sammuel took one of the daughters, who struggled so much that Rath had to help hold her, and together they carried her out of the door. Kappi took the other daughter, who wept pitifully but walked as directed. The tiny boy was no more than ten, and Skalla ordered Frej to take him. The youth struggled, but Frej picked him up and pinned him to his chest as we walked back to the ships.

* * * * * * * * *

No one seemed impressed with my little box of buttons or Garad's brass-crested scissors. Birtingr, a man in front of us, had scavanged a drawer full of silver forks, spoons, and knives; everyone complimented him on having the best haul of all. The man beside him argued with him, but I couldn't hear why.

Digr had suspected that some of Øgæfa's or Hítdælakappi's sailors would escape at the first opportunity, but all had returned to the ships. Branwulf ordered the girls to pick their best dresses out of the stolen clothes, and then called forth Father, Rath, and Skalla; each selected fine clothes to fit them. Garad, Frej, and I were called for last.

"Give us cloaks!" said the quieter sister when her sister refused to change clothes in front of three hundred vikings.

"Do as I say or I'll carve your brother to pieces before your eyes!" Branwulf shouted.

The noisy sister screamed in protest, and would've flung herself on Branwulf if Kappi hadn't seized her.

"Please!" cried the quiet sister, grabbing her sister's shoulders and dragging her back. "I'll do as you ask."

"Captain, this girl will suit our plans well, but this one," Hjalti indicated the combative one, "she's too defiant."

"We need two girls!" Branwulf shouted.

"With a whip and salt water, and a few days, we could break even the most defiant child, but we don't have days," Hjalti said. "You planned to use the boy as hostage for the behavior of the girls, but why not use the noisy girl as the hostage for her brother and sister?"

"My brother will do what I say," the quiet girl said to Branwulf, almost pleading. "We won't endanger our sister's life, I swear!"

"Do we have clothes for the boy?" Branwulf asked.

"I think so," Sammuel said. "We grabbed a little of everything."

"Very well," Branwulf said to the quiet girl. "Dress well; you're going to church."

* * * * * * * * *

After sailing south all day, two small Saxon fishing vessels sailed toward us; both had been docked outside of the big house that we'd raided.

"Ørðigskeggi!" Branwulf called to a tall, bristle-bearded man on one ship, "Is everything ready?"

"Awaiting passengers," Ørðigskeggi laughed.

"You know what I need," Branwulf said to us.

"We'll make it happen," Father promised.

"You'll both do as you're told?" Branwulf asked the quiet girl and her little brother.

"Yes, sir," she said.

"You know what I'll do to your sister ... if you disobey?"

"We won't be any trouble," the girl promised.

One at a time, we crossed to the other ship, hands from both ships holding us as we crossed. I was wearing brown trousers and a new, short white tunic with a fancy dark-blue vest. Garad looked comical, wearing a yellow tunic with green trousers and a matching coif, whose long tail hung all the way down his back. Father and Skalla both wore fancy green tunics, Father sporting a black cloak, Skalla a red cloak; both cloaks concealed their weapons.

"We'd best be acquainted," Father said to the girl, and he named each of us.

"I'm Fwen. My brother is Ginforn."

"You'll be my daughter," Father told her. "Ginforn will be Skalla's younger son. Neither of you are to speak. Do you understand?"

"We'll reverence you as if you were our fathers," Fwen said.

"If you make any attempt to reveal us, then I'll kill you both," Father said. "If you stay silent and draw no attention to yourselves, then we'll leave you in the church, and you can go home tomorrow."

"And our sister ... if we behave ...?"

"If you both behave yourselves, then we'll leave her on the dock, and soon you'll all be back with your family."

"We'll behave."

"This will be a deception worthy of Odin," Ørðigskeggi said, scratching his bristle-beard, "... if you can pull it off."

* * * * * * * * *

Chapter 37

* * * * * * * * *

The Saxon docks were full of fishermen, most tying up their boats, and merchants sounding like they were demanding lower prices for their day's catch, although I couldn't understand a word most of them said. A few spoke the common tongue, but we drifted by too quickly to catch more than a few shouted words. Some people seemed to have no business at all, but hurried along the shore as if wishing that it was dignified to run.

A shiver ran down my spine; *these Saxons would kill us if they knew who we were.* None seemed to notice us as Ørðigskeggi sailed alongside a docked ship to an empty berth, and Rath jumped out, holding our ship against the dock with a single rope. We disembarked in silence, and then Ørðigskeggi sailed away into the dusk.

Father and Skalla led the way. Frej looked excited; Skalla cuffed him curtly.

"Hold Ginford's hand," Skalla ordered Frej.

"Good idea," Father said, "Thron, Garad, each of you take one of Fwen's hands."

"I promised ...," Fwen began.

"Just a precaution," Father said.

We fell in line with a group walking across the wooden boards along the river, like a dock that paralleled the water's edge. Strange, curious buildings towered about us, but we kept our eyes down and walked in silence.

* * * * * * * * *

The cathedral of St. Ursul rose incredibly, gleaming white, with steep, sharp-pointed towers and blowing flags, covered with life-sized idols, beautiful women, with giant dove-wings, and horrible monsters so well-carved that I thought them alive ... until Rath's hand firmly tilted my head down. Father led the way with Skalla at his side, and all of us followed. Huge, massive doors, their brown wood polished and gleaming, hung on giant iron hinges with decorative curling bracings, freshly painted black. Guards stood on both sides of the door accompanied by an old man in a white robe. Father held out a silver coin to the old man, who accepted it with a gracious tilt of his head, and then we entered between the stout, ornate doors.

A magnificent palace lay inside. We passed through a large room, many times bigger than our house, and then entered the biggest room that I'd ever seen. A dozen Tavern Halls could've fit in it, and the ceiling reached so high that it was almost a sky, save that it was gloriously adorned with pictures of life-like people resting upon painted clouds.

"Eyes down!" Father hissed, and his hand jerked

threateningly at Garad and I.

Fwen drew out a cloth, which looked like a silk handkerchief, and covered her head with it. Then she pulled Garad's coif off his head. Father glared warningly at her, but she flared her eyes and gestured to the crowd; every woman had her head covered, but none of the men wore hats.

Skalla silently motioned to one of the many benches. Only Fwen and her brother didn't sit; they got down on their knees, pressed their hands palm-to-palm, and bowed their heads. Many others were doing the same, so Father knelt down and motioned for us all to do the same.

Rath was missing. Alarm rose in me, but then I recalled that he was never supposed to come inside; Rath was outside, waiting for night to fall.

Suddenly the silent hall erupted with voices. Garad visibly startled at the sound, but Fwen joined the throng, speaking in a language that I'd never heard. A single man's voice replied from the front, and Fwen and the entire congregation replied, as if conversing with him in some strange ritual.

I couldn't see the man in front; the one time that I rose off my knees Father pressed me back down. They rang what seemed like a chorus of tiny bells a few times, and many high, young children's voices sang a beautiful song, but the words were in the mysterious language that everyone here used.

Yet once, when Father wasn't watching me, I looked up: above the head of the talking man was a very life-like statue. This statue was incredibly painted, so well that at first I thought it was a real man. This man was hanging from crossed wooden beams with metal spikes nailed through his hands and feet. Blood was pouring down his mournful face, and his mouth was open in a silent cry of anguish. Thorns stabbed into his skull, curled around his head, and my memory of falling into the thorn-patch returned so vividly that I shuddered. Yet its wooden frame struck me the hardest; it was a cross, the same shape as the big one that Friar James had made, which he'd nailed above the door to Rath's old house. *This was the place that Friar James had come from! We were about to rob Friar James' family!*

* * * * * * * * *

Fwen and her brother finally rose off their knees and sat on the bench, and Skalla and Frej did likewise, so Father let us do the same. A long time passed; the sunlight streamed through colored windows and rose high on the walls: it was nearly sunset.

Eventually the crowd began to rise and silently depart, but Fwen returned to her knees and motioned for us to join her, so we did. Enough people left that I could see the raised floor behind the wooden fence near the front, and the big table behind it. One curiosity captured my attention; in a small alcove in the wall, under the cross with the statue of the tortured man, right out where everyone could see it, gleamed a treasure so bright that it made me blink: a tall chest of intricate design and craftsmanship, so detailed that I couldn't believe such treasures existed, fashioned of the same metal as the tiny rosary that Father had brought back from the viking last year: *this tall chest was built of solid gold!*

* * * * * * * * *

It was a treasure like in the old Norse tales, the bedtime stories that Father used to tell me. I'd begun to believe that those were only childish imaginings, that there wasn't that much gold in the entire world. But the world was much bigger than I'd truly understood; *this treasure was real.*

"Eyes down!" Father whispered angrily.

I was tingling with excitement. *Finally I was in a daring adventure!*

An hour passed, and the colored windows grew dark. The cathedral grew almost empty, but boys in dresses went around lighting candles, and then more people came in, and soon another crowd had gathered. Giant bells, so loud that I was deafened, rang from somewhere over our heads, and then a group of more boys in dresses paraded past us, before a group of older men in colorful robes, down the center aisle, ringing small bells, carrying candles, and swinging a smoking brass ampule from a long chain. We all stood up as they passed, and many made the sign of the cross that Friar James had shown me. One man carried a large book with a gold cross on it; *Friar James would like that book!*

A curious ritual began up front; it reminded me of weddings and funerals back home; very ceremonious, but I couldn't understand a word. They seemed to be repeating the same ritual that they'd performed only a few hours before. *Why were all of these people coming back to see the same show?*

Finally, people stood and filed toward the front, only to walk back to their seats minutes later; apparently they were handing out food and giving drinks from a strange golden cup. My stomach rumbled loudly; I wanted to go up there and get some, but Father glared at me, and I stared at my sore knees.

I could take no more sitting or kneeling when, suddenly, the parade passed by again, and it was over. People rose and slowly began to filter out the door. Father made us kneel and stare at the floor again while people left, and then he looked at me and winked.

* * * * * * * * *

A familiar horn blew outside, and Garad stood up expectantly; Father shoved him back down. Only a few dozen people were left sitting in the huge cathedral, and the one old man to whom Father had given a silver coin was walking around, talking to people in whispers. Most of the people crossed themselves and departed after he talked to them.

He softly said something to Father, and to my surprise, Father replied in their strange language, and the old man started to walk serenely away, when Branwulf's horn sounded again, this time much closer. The man looked puzzled and headed for the door. Shouts came from outside, and then a scream.

"Guards!" the old man cried, using the common tongue. "*Guards!*"

"Stay!" Father hissed to us.

Soldiers appeared in various doorways and alcoves, but all ran to the front door. I heard Rath's shout, and then came many yells and the sound of running feet. Most of the guards ran out of the church, but five, each wielding a long spear that had an axe near its head, stayed inside.

"Dragonship!" one said.

"Look at it go!"

"Pagan fools! They're rowing right into the sights of Eorl Sir Dungrem's ballistas!"

"Better than those heathens deserve!"

"They landed in the Master's District."

"Listen to those screams!"

"Mother of God!"

"They're tearing up the city!"

"Look! That building's on fire!"

Suddenly there was a loud crash of many boots, a jingle of mail, and the rattle of weapons.

"Come help!" shouted someone from outside.

"Can't leave our post!" one of the guards at the door shouted back. "Give them Hades ...!"

"Kill them!"

"Hurry!"

"Did you see fat old Waterbean run?" one guard smirked. "He'll collapse before he gets halfway there."

"Look, they've started another fire!"

"What are they trying to do?"

"Listen! Another horn!"

"Another dragonship?"

"Downstream! Pulling up at the dock!"

"Lord save us!"

"Right in front of the guardhouse? Are they mad?"

"Listen to them yell!"

"Maybe we should close these doors."

"Why?"

"Are you blind? Attacks just north and south of us ...? Simultaneously ...?"

"Another dragonship!"

"Hurry! Brace the doors!"

"Now," Father grinned.

He handed me my sword and gave Garad his axe. Skalla gave Frej an axe and a long knife, and then he and Father drew their swords. Fwen grabbed her brother and climbed under the pew.

Father and Skalla jumped up, and before I could even draw my sword, before any of the horrified congregation remaining could scream, Father and Skalla charged the guards, who were busy trying to lift the heavy brace into the thick iron brackets on the backs of the huge doors, their hands full, their backs to us. Skalla pushed aside the old man in the robes and stabbed a guard in the back of the neck. Father slashed at one of the other guards at the same instant; his head tumbled away in a bloody spray.

Skalla tried to attack another guard, but the old man jumped in his way, shouting something in his strange language, and Skalla cut him down instead. The guard that he'd been about to kill threw his spear at Skalla; he knocked the spear aside in midair, but the guard managed to draw his sword before Skalla was on him.

Father hacked at another guard, but that guard ducked, and the blow caught him across his mailed shoulder. The guard still fell, but he wasn't killed; the other guard pointed his spear straight at Father, and thrust hard. I gasped, but Father spun suddenly, knocked the spear point aside with his sword, and slashed hard at the spearman: *Father moved like a legendary warrior from the old tales!*

Frej ran toward them, Garad and I right behind. A moment later, Garad and I chased off the guard that Father had hit but hadn't killed; he screamed and vanished through an alcove just as Father body-slammed the remaining guard into the wall, then slashed deep through his face.

"Well done!" Skalla shouted, but he was talking to Frej. Blood dripped from Frej's long knife.

"Come on!" I shouted to Garad, turning to chase the guard who'd fled.

"Thron, no!" Father cried.

"Guard our backs!" Skalla ordered.

Skalla and Father seized the heavy brace and pushed it out

of its thick iron braces just as voices shouted and fists pounded from the outside. Father and Skalla pushed the doors open and a hundred shipmates poured into the cathedral.

"Hurry!" Branwulf cried. *"We sail in minutes!"*

Separated from Garad, I was swept along with our shipmates as we ran toward the front of the cathedral. I couldn't hear anything clearly: men shouted, Saxons screamed, and someone was ringing the giant bells above us as if to awaken up the whole city. Hjalti and Kappi went straight to the priceless gold box and took it. Sammuel grabbed my arm.

"Stay by me, Thron!" he shouted.

"Find the priest!" Branwulf cried.

I ran with Sammuel through several doors, two of which were locked, until a big Norseman in thickly-woven mail bodily crashed into them, and broke both doors into pieces.

"Here he is!" cried a voice.

"Search the room!" Branwulf ordered.

Branwulf ran into the room, and we followed. A very old robed man was there, looking terrified. Branwulf grabbed him.

"Where's the treasury?"

The man only whimpered. Branwulf shoved the priest onto a table and stretched out his thin arm. Sammuel held the priest down as Branwulf raised his sword threateningly over the priest's outstretched arm.

"I've no time to waste!" Branwulf shouted. "Where's the treasure?"

The old man didn't speak.

"Last chance, fool!" Branwulf hissed at the priest.

Branwulf's blade struck at the wrist. It smote into the

wood, severing the priest's whole hand off. Blood sprayed, and the priest screamed.

"Where's the treasure?!?"

Branwulf grabbed the priest's bloody forearm and raised his sword again. He chopped again, right below the elbow, and the old priest screamed incoherently.

"Where's the treasure?"

Branwulf grabbed the priest's shoulder and raised his sword again.

"I found it!" cried the big man in the heavy mail.

Branwulf hesitated. "Are you sure, þjófi?"

Þjófi held up two bags, shook them, and the jingle of coins filled the room.

"We're rich!" þjófi cried.

Branwulf ran to see. Sammuel and I crowded behind him; inside of a large chest lay a dozen of bags, all buldging with coins.

The writhing priest fell helpless onto the floor, his one hand clutching his bleeding stump. He looked like he was screaming, but his mouth emitted no sound.

"Back to the ship!" Branwulf cried.

Everyone ran. I started to follow, but I noticed something before I exited; on a small table by the door was the large book with the gold cross on it.

* * * * * * * * *

"Where were you?!?" Father angrily shouted.

"He was with me!" Sammuel shouted to be heard. *"Come!"*

"Back to the ship!" shouted the voices of many.

We dashed through the huge doors into the night;

Branwulf's dragon was docked right before the cathedral. The giant bell in the tower was still ringing. Screams echoed from all around; the whole city seemed to be burning, not half a mile in either direction.

Just as we pushed off, Captain Bjarki's ship came flying past us.

"Row!" Branwulf shouted as the last of the men jumped for the rail, and some were still clinging to the side, not fully onboard when we cast off, but they were quickly pulled in by others.

"Row your backs out!" Branwulf shouted.

Suddenly a huge thud sounded and a man cried out. A thick spear had plunked into our boat so hard that it shook us; it pierced clean through a man's upper chest, out his lower back, and nailed itself into our deck.

As we passed a long wooden dock, Rath's deep voice thundered, and there he was, fighting six men, his axe in one hand and a flaming torch in the other, beside another Norseman whose name I couldn't recall. Larg steered close to the dock, and suddenly Rath turned and fled. Just as our dragon passed, Rath dropped his torch and leaped off the dock, men jumping to get out of his way. He splashed into the water right behind us, but his axe hooked our rail, and men jumped to pull him aboard. The other Norseman arrived at the pier's edge a moment later, but we'd already sailed past. The flames of Rath's dropped torch beside his feet illuminated him as the Saxon guards stabbed him from behind.

"Row!" Branwulf shouted.

* * * * * * * * *

"I'm well pleased!" Branwulf said.

I joined the cheer as loudly as I could. We were floating in the center of the English Channel. Our three ships were again all tied together, our rowers in the rear keeping our carved, painted dragonheads from scraping against each other.

"Silver for every man!" Branwulf shouted, and the men cheered again. "Our losses were few and our rewards great. Captain Bjarki will report on our damage."

"Two ships are damaged," Captain Bjarki shouted. "Captain Branwulf's ship was hit by two javelins from the ballistas, one that killed Drumb and stuck through the deck, but it did no damage to the hull. The other pierced the hull near the prow, above the waterline, but fortunately it stuck itself in the keel. We've already pulled both out, plugged the holes with cork, and tarred them well.

"My ship ran the gauntlet at full speed," Bjarki said, casting a dark look at Branwulf. "Seven javelins struck us; two men are dead, and two badly injured. One of the dead was a lone mercenary; no one knew his name. The other was ... Torfi." A murmur of disbelief ran through the frowning crowd. "Both were rowing when struck, only minutes after fighting Saxons. Torfi honored himself as a great fighter: he smashed a shelf full of whiskey bottles and lit them, and those flames hampered our foes. We can all rejoice that Torfi earned Valhalla. Of the two wounded, one is Kráka, a sailor from Hítdælakappi's crew; he was pierced through the arm, but should heal. The other was old Tréfótr, who sailed with Branwulf's father; a javelin pierced right through his thigh-bone and pinned him to the deck. Tréfótr ... will probably die ... unless his leg is removed."

Many heads bowed. I didn't know Tréfótr; *certainly he hadn't come aboard intending to become like Clambsy.*

"All that can be done for Tréfótr will be done," Branwulf said. "We'll sacrifice a good horse to the gods for him. What damage did your ship suffer?"

"Well, Uncle ...," Bjarki began.

"Captain Branwulf!" Larg snapped as Branwulf's eyes rose.

"Sorry, Captain," Bjarki quickly apologized. "Still sea-worthy, but heavily-damaged; we've three open holes under the waterline. We plugged them with oiled rags; for the moment they're holding, but they'll leak soon. Two other holes exist, but those javelins are nailed in them tightly."

"We'll repair both ships as soon as possible," Captain Branwulf said. "If they don't slow us down, then we'll fix them in Norway. Captain Bjarki, your crew had the hardest, most-dangerous job; I'll remember that when our treasure's divided.

"Now we should recognize those whose deeds best merited praise. Captain Larg, will you begin?"

"All my men fought bravely," Larg said. "Our job was to distract the guards and start a fire, to draw attention away from the cathedral. We landed closer to the guardhouse than we'd intended and hardly made it off the dock. Little damage was inflicted; it was mostly a standoff, but Hlöðu and Øþveginn shot flaming arrows into the buildings; those fires diverted attention from us and the cathedral."

"Hlöðu and Øþveginn," Captain Branwulf grinned, raising a friendly hand to two men on Larg's ship, "well done. Good thinking is essential; you'll be ... richly rewarded."

Men on all three boats cheered, but the loudest came from Larg's dragon. I couldn't tell which man was Hlöðu and which was Øþveginn, but they couldn't look more different: one was huge, richly dressed in bright reds and yellows, and the other was small and greasy, wearing leathers and furs so badly matted and stained that their previous owners would have died of embarrassment, had they still been alive.

"Everyone on my ship fought hard," Captain Bjarki said. "We landed first, raided the shoreline, and stood off the city guards ... and Eorl Sir Dungrem's knights, when they finally arrived, and then we had to run the gauntlet through a barrage of three ballistas."

"I had to see if you had what it took to be captain; I owed that much to your father," Branwulf interrupted him, frowning. "You'll not suffer the most dangerous assignment next time."

Bjarki nodded and seemed contented.

"Above all others, I'd praise Bitra," Bjarki turned and looked back at his ship. "Bitra may be a sour old puss, but he felled the first two guards to threaten us. I'd also praise Hvamm; he organized the shieldwall when the knights arrived. Galti also deserves mention; he may not be young anymore, but he fights like a wounded boar."

Cheers rose for all of them, but the loudest came from Bjarki's ship.

"For myself," Branwulf said, "I'd most highly praise those who went ashore and kept the doors from being braced, although I must admit: I was a little worried when we docked and found the doors closed." A scattering of laughter arose at this. "But the doors opened just as we reached them. Thorir and Skalla, well done! And let's not forget Rath, who slew the guards outside and signaled when all was ready. All three will be richly rewarded!"

Many cheered at this, Garad and I the loudest.

"Captain Branwulf!" Skalla interrupted, "I have joyous news: we have a new man! My son, Frej, killed his first Saxon today, an armed guard!"

"Well done, Frej!" Captain Branwulf saluted him, crossing his swordarm across his chest.

Neither Garad nor I joined in the cheer.

"Now, to the rewards," Branwulf said. "Thanks to Þjófi, we found the cathedral's treasury: a whole chest of coins. We also got their tabernacle, which held three silver chalices. We could sail home today and count ourselves lucky; each man here could winter in þurs on their share. Yet, another successful raid like this one would double each man's rewards, and there are many here who haven't yet had the chance to be singled out for special merits. This viking season offers many chances to improve our profits: the greater our plunder, the greater your rewards!"

Bjarki signaled to his men, and three large bundles wrapped in cloaks were brought forth and handed from their ship to ours. Each was placed before Branwulf.

"Open that one first, Vápni," Bjarki said.

Vápni lifted up a long iron sword, undecorated but beautiful in its sleek, lethal design. Branwulf raised it up high. Next, Vápni lifted a shirt of mail.

"We stripped the weapons and armor of our foes, when we had the time," Bjarki said.

Vápni lifted up several more weapons, large daggers, and a pair of steel gauntlets. Then he opened the second cloak; it was filled with metal cups and plates, little boxes and flasks, but nothing of real value. The third cloak was filled with clothes; women's dresses. Branwulf scowled at them.

"I'll take the weapon-hoard," Branwulf said. "The rest you may divide amongst your men. You did well, considering that your job was to distract while we plundered. Still, all that we take is profit."

Vápni wrapped up the last two cloaks and passed them

back to Bjarki's ship.

"I have some tribute," Sammuel spoke up.

All eyes fell upon Sammuel's wide smile. Sammuel held out three hands, including one that didn't belong to him: golden rings with many stones sparkled in the sunlight.

"From the priest …?" Branwulf asked.

"Here're the rings from his other hand … and his necklaces," Sammuel smiled, displaying them. "I'm sure that priest would've given them freely, if asked."

Branwulf took the severed hand, pulled the rings from it, and tossed the bloody mess overboard. Then he took the remaining rings and necklaces.

"Your tributes have increased everyone's profits," Branwulf said. "You shall be richly rewarded!"

A few others came forward. One had taken many brass candleholders, another who'd taken the six copper crucifixes, and several who'd robbed those trapped in the cathedral when Branwulf attacked. One of them had a small coin bag, a large silver ring, and a pair of gold earrings.

"Captain …?" said a soft voice.

"Yes, Hafr?"

Hafr came forward. In his hands, Hafr held the bundle of silverware stolen from the manor.

"This belonged to Birtingr, my brother," Hafr said. "His death on the dock grieves me. I feel that it's wrong to keep his riches, certain that he'd want it shared by his shipmates."

Branwulf took the silver, then nodded to Hafr.

"Birtingr was a brave man, a credit to your family," Branwulf said slowly, with great emphasis. "I accept your gift; you'll be richly rewarded."

"Captain Branwulf, my son Thron stole something," Father said.

"Really?" Captain Branwulf grinned. "Bring it forward, boy."

I stepped up and handed him the book.

"It's a bible," Hjalti said as Branwulf flipped through its pages.

"Is it valuable?" Branwulf asked.

"Only to a Christian."

Captain Branwulf held the book as if it were accursed.

"What do you plan to do with this?" Branwulf asked me.

"We have a Christian in our village," I answered him. "He taught me how to read; I thought that I'd give it to him."

"Fine, you do that," Branwulf said, and he gave me back the book.

"Best let me store that in my chest so it doesn't get ruined," Digr said as I pushed back into the crowd, and he took the book from my hands.

Several others came forward with small trinkets, all of which Branwulf let them keep, except for one gold ring and a pair of silver cloak clasps.

"Sails!" someone shouted, pointing far behind us. *"Waving red flags!"*

"Release the lines!" Larg shouted. *"Row for your lives!"*

* * * * * * * * *

Chapter 38

*   *   *   *   *   *   *   *   *

We rowed all day under full sail, with Larg on our left and Bjarki on our right. Hjalti had taken Larg's place on our ship, but he had no drum; he clapped his hands to give us rhythm. Everyone manned an oar. Captain Branwulf stormed aft at least once every hour to look at the ships chasing us, and then he stomped back to the fore. The news flowed freely; nine sails now pursued us.

At Kappi's request, Branwulf grudgingly allowed the brazier to be lit and the giant stewpot to be placed upon it.

"They've obviously seen us," Kappi said. "We won't be able to escape until nightfall."

"By nightfall we'll be at the coast," Branwulf snarled. "We can't sail south and be trapped in the Straight of Dover, and they'll cut us off before we reach Den Helder. Our only hope is to get back to the Frisian Isles."

"In the dark, their red flags ...," Kappi offered.

"They signal with torches at night," Branwulf snapped. "If even one of their ships spies us, then they'll all give chase. And if they catch us ...!"

* * * * * * * * *

My hands were raw and swollen, legs cramped, back aching, butt sore ... and still I rowed. The evening was windy and chill; half of me was freezing, the other half overheated. Hour after hour, through dusk into twilight, under twinkling stars and a glowing crescent moon, we rowed. With seven flickering, threatening torches constantly behind us, we rowed.

Father was sweating beside me, Trandill on his other side, and Hal on center. In front of me was Garad by the rail, Brún beside him, then Hjálmun, and Smiðr on center. Digr and Rath were not far away, filling in where there had only been two at an oar. I wondered how we were doing, but kept silent, watching the dim, distant red flare of oiled torches not far behind us. I tried to ask questions, but Father dismissed me angrily.

"All of our lives depend on every man rowing his best," Father said sharply. "Captain Branwulf will decide where to go and why, and he doesn't need every man aboard ship telling him the obvious. Save your strength for rowing."

My mind reeled as the hours passed, sometimes numb with weariness into near-unconsciousness, yet the one time that I let my chin lean against my chest, Father elbowed me so hard that I cried out. We were in the English Channel sailing north up the coast of the Netherlands. Apparently, each ship that saw us lit a torch to tell the others where we were. I'd never before imagined wishing for a storm at sea, but I did now.

Rath's voice echoed inside me: *'Vikings are about more than profit. Vikings are our heritage, our faith, our culture. Vikings keep us strong, courageous, and feared by our enemies.'* But would we have enemies if not for the vikings?

'We are their curse!' Old man Ranglátr had said.

I recalled Branwulf hacking his way up the old priest's arm: the memory made me shudder. Father had told me tales of Branwulf all my life: had Branwulf always been so harsh?

'Vikings ruin good men,' Læknir had said. *'Off on their own, living like beasts ... it's amazing that they don't come back with horns and tails!'*

'Every year men throw their lives and families to the wind for a few trinkets and some hollow boasts.'

'One dead this year, six dead last year, and three the year before that. What'll happen to our village when there are no more of us left?'

'More widows than wives ...'

'The vikings sap off our best and strongest.'

'More men are lost and fewer treasures are gained each year.'

'Killing people is wrong! It's wrong to kill people!'

'See these corpses? Wealth belongs to the last man standing; sometimes we won, sometimes not. This is what happens when we lose. Remember these faces every time you draw a weapon. In all fights, death claims your enemy ... or you.'

Those dead faces haunted me still, lying on the tables in Tavern Hall; the memory of Holbarki was the most-vivid. *These thoughts were weak, unmanly;* I shouldn't be having them, but they weren't my words, not my voices, not my dead face. We all wanted to be rich, but would any of us ever truly gain vast wealth?

What I wouldn't give to be laying on a mattress at Þur's with Inn Danski! Or better yet: Ingrid. *Oh, the memory of Ingrid!* Watching her sway naked before me, feeling her soft breasts press upon my chest ...

Or should I be thinking of Helsa ...?

* * * * * * * * *

"Ready for walking!" Hjalti shouted, and two oars lifted and were held straight out, just above the water. A rope was cast from the other ship; a man on Larg's dragon tied it securely around his waist. Men from both ships pulled it taut.

I looked, amazed: a man walked across the extended oars from Larg's ship to ours. I stared, horrified, certain that he'd fall to his death, but quickly, as if running, his bare feet quick-stepped from oar to oar until he breathlessly jumped atop our rowers, who'd doubled-over, struggling to hold their oars motionless.

After regaining his feet, the man started to whisper, but Branwulf shook his head.

"Speak up, Gylðir. We're all facing the same doom."

Gylðir looked about nervously.

"My lord, Larg says that our men won't last until dawn."

"I know that," Branwulf replied.

"He's thought of several possibilities," Gylðir said. "He assumes that you've thought of them as well..."

"Speak."

"We could let half of the crew rest while the other half rows ..."

"Without all hands, they'll quickly overtake us."

"We could weave between the islands ...."

"We'd risk running aground on sandbars. They'll send some ships ocean-side; if any of their ships get ahead of us ..."

"We could double-back after their ships divide..."

"That would only even the odds," Branwulf said. "They don't even need to kill us, just to slow us down."

"We could burn one ship, abandon it, and use its rowers to relieve the others."

"Abandoning one ship will only help us stay as we are, no closer to escaping. If I'm to lose a ship, then I want to escape because of it."

Gylðir stood silent before him. Branwulf wiped the sweat from his brow with one hand.

"A small company could remain on one ship," Gylðir said softly. "We could promise to recompense ... their families ... for their sacrifice."

"Who would you suggest?" Branwulf asked defiantly, but Gylðir looked down and didn't answer. "We'd be better off sending one man off with Bjarki's ship, letting him sail his ship into a harbor. Our closest pursuers would surely follow him, but he could easily land, abandon his ship there, and escape across the countryside with enough gold to buy his passage back to Norway.

"But what of next year? Each of these ships is a treasure equal to what we got from St. Ursul's. We've a fleet now, not just one ship, and enough wealth to outfit next year's viking."

"You're our fleet commander," Gylðir said loudly. "We do as you say."

* * * * * * * * *

Vápni came aboard from Captain Bjarki's ship the same way that Gylðir had, running across extended oars with a rope tied around his waist, but he came across slowly, and three men had to pull on his rope to keep him from falling into the cold, dark water. Vápni was pale and sweating when they finally pulled him aboard. He spoke to Branwulf, but only repeated the ideas of Gylðir.

"I've made my decision," Branwulf said. "We won't abandon a ship; we'll slip behind the Frisian Islands, making them split their forces. They'll expect us to weave between the islands along the coast of Germany, but we won't; as soon as we can, we'll fight our way past the Saxons. If the majority follows us, then we'll round the first island and sail right into the teeth of those ocean-side. If not, then we'll turn our ships and fight our way back.

"We'll live or die rich men," Branwulf announced. "Every man who survives this viking will be rewarded with ... three silver coins!"

"Branwulf!" Hjalti's raised voice exploded as if he couldn't believe his ears. "Forgive me, Captain, but no mercenaries have ever been paid so much ..."

"I'm not paying for a single viking," Branwulf said, "I'm paying for all the years after this, when I'll need the best men. If these men can get us through that Saxon line, then they're the best. If we die in the attempt, then they're not worth keeping. If any man here's afraid, take one silver and jump ship; we'll do better to lighten our load. But for those who face this battle, they're worth three silver coins to me."

"Pay is worthless if we don't survive," Vápni said. "How do we break through?"

"Transfer all of our shields to one ship; that ship will take point, and the other two ships will follow it," Branwulf said. "All of our bows will be transferred to the other ships. Our lead ship sails toward them to draw their fire, then drops sail as they approach. Our other ships will sail around the lead ship, and loose every arrow that we have. We cut right across their path; if the lead ship doesn't row fast enough, then they'll be rammed."

"And whose ship shall take the lead?" Vápni asked gruffly.

"Who do you think?" Branwulf growled back.

"You said that Bjarki wouldn't get the most dangerous job!" Vápni complained.

"It'll take a great, experienced captain to steer the lead ship," Branwulf snarled. "Bjarki can't do it: *I will captain the lead ship."*

* * * * * * * * *

Vápni and Gylðir returned to their ships across the oars, but the ropes were kept strung from ship to ship. Onto the ropes they strung all of our bows and the belt-loops of quivers, each stuffed full of arrows, and by shifting the rope back and forth, all of our archery gear was passed to the other ships. They sent us their shields in the same manner, the ropes strung through the hand-grips, until forty new shields were transferred onto our ship.

"Do I get a shield?" I asked Father.

"Why would you get a shield?" Father asked.

"Branwulf said that the youngest would get ..."

"The youngest men," Father corrected me. "You haven't killed an enemy yet."

"Frej will also be on an oar," Skalla said. "He's never used a shield, and this is no time for learning."

"Hjálmun!" Branwulf shouted. "Take a shield."

"I'm better at rowing ...," Hjálmun complained.

"Take a shield!" Branwulf repeated, and then he chose most of Hjálmun's friends from other villages, the younger men. Sammuel, Hjalti, and Kappi were also given shields. Brún was the last to take a shield, and Þjófi replaced him at our oar.

"Ørðigskeggi, man the tiller," Branwulf said. "Listen for my orders; if you can't hear, do what you think best."

"I won't be able to see well from aft," Ørðigskeggi said, "not with all shields raised."

"Watch their sails and stay on the outside," Branwulf said.

"Land!" Hjalti shouted. "Dead ahead!"

"Head north!" Captain Branwulf shouted. "Turn the rigging! Stay with the wind!"

"I recognize this coast," Hjalti said. "The Frisian Isles are just north of us."

"Good," Branwulf said. "We'll sail outside the first and see if any of them try to cut us off by sailing inside."

"They're fools if they do," Hjalti said. "The first island's the big one; it'll take them forever to sail around it."

"Sailing west would lead us into the wind," Branwulf said. "Some of their ships could double-back."

"Let's pray that they're fools," Hjalti said.

"I sacrificed a bull to Odin last harvest; remind him of that," Branwulf said.

"Victory or Valhalla," Hjalti said to Branwulf.

"Victory or Valhalla," Branwulf said back to him.

* * * * * * * * *

Chapter 39

*   *   *   *   *   *   *   *   *

Where were the rivers of Saxon blood, the foemen fleeing from us?

I ached from toes to hair, and had to flex my arms around the cramps that knotted my muscles. Garad fared no better; several times I heard Rath shout at him to stay awake. I couldn't recall the last time I'd slept, but I'd have given anything just to fade into mindless slumber.

I liked sitting fore, where I could hear what was going on unless the wind whistled in my ears so loudly that it blocked out all else. Yet it was dangerous; when we sailed past the Saxon ships, those sitting closest to the dragon's head would be the Saxon's first targets.

We sailed ocean-side past the first of the Frisian Isles. One ship turned inland towards Den Helder, but no one cheered. Two more torches appeared on the horizon.

"Once we cross inside, we should have the advantage,"

Branwulf said.

"The western coast is straighter," Hjalti said. "We'll be hard-pressed to reach the next gap before they do."

"My map shows a tiny island just west of its northern tip," Branwulf said. "We'll have to sail between the islands."

"Risky under starlight," Hjalti said. "Besides sandbars, the Saxon's wind might not be blocked by the island. If they make it there ahead of us, then they'll hold that passage."

"Then they'll have to anchor there," Branwulf said. "We have to risk it: sail inside."

"I'll pray some more," Hjalti said.

* * * * * * * * *

"They're splitting up!" Hjalti cried. "Three ships turned east!"

I barely heard or understood; my hands burned, my ears deaf from the whistling wind. Every muscle cramped; I'd never imagined that a living body could endure such torment. Digr cursed with every breath, and Brún, rowing while leaning against his shield, looked mostly asleep. Even Father seemed weary; he constantly grunted, and occasionally jerked as if stabbed, as if every movement was a new pain. I carefully looked away, determined not to notice.

I was spared a few precious moments as a bowl with a very little soup was shoved into my hands. I had to eat quickly; Kappi was waiting for my bowl. When I gave it to him, he dipped it back into his larger bowl and handed it to Father.

"We could use some more water," Smiðr said to Kappi.

"We're low on water," Kappi said.

"How're we supposed to row without water?" Smiðr snapped.

"Shall I have Captain Branwulf explain it to you?" Kappi snapped back.

Smiðr snarled, but kept rowing. I turned back to my oar. Smiðr was our blacksmith, the strongest man that I knew. *If he was tiring ...*

"Can you see it?" Captain Branwulf shouted, awakening me from my half-slumber.

A younger man had climbed up onto the dragonhead and was staring across the night's sea.

"Yes!" he cried excitedly. "I see the island!"

"Is the straight held?" Branwulf asked.

"I can't see anything yet!" the youth shouted back.

"No torches is a good sign," Hjalti said.

"You don't use torches in an ambush," Branwulf snapped. "If they're there, then we won't see them until the last moment. Shout to Larg and Bjarki: tell them to close in."

"We could just sail around the little island," Sammuel said to Branwulf. "We can't risk the narrow straight."

"What would you do if you commanded their fleet?" Branwulf asked. "If they leave the straight unblocked, then we could slip out to sea."

"I'd divide up," Sammuel said. "A few flaming arrows into our sails would virtually stop us."

"That's what I'd do, too," Branwulf said.

"Only three ships sailed north," Sammuel said.

"Yes, but others have been joining them all night," Branwulf said. "We could be sailing into a trap."

"I see them!" the youth finally shouted. "They're there, in the middle of the straight!"

"How many?" Branwulf demanded.

"Two!"

"That leaves one on the eastern side," Hjalti said.

"Unless they got more ships," Sammuel said.

"Straight ahead!" Branwulf shouted across the length of the ship to Ørðigskeggi. "This is the moment! Row hard! Kappi, make ready to drop sail. Sammuel, Hjalti, help him!"

"They've seen us," Hjalti said. "If we go between them, they'll drive us onto shore."

"Straight ahead," Branwulf shouted back at Ørðigskeggi. "Prepare to turn starboard! We'll sweep past them around the little island. Don't turn until I say so!"

We rowed hard, and suddenly Branwulf shouted.

"Now! Hard starboard, now!"

As we turned, the Saxon ships loomed into view, floating in the starlight in the center between the islands. They were just out of arrow-shot, even for our best archers, and suddenly we swerved away. Distant, muffled curses came from their ships; their oars dipped and splashed, but from a full stop: we cheered as we rowed away.

* * * * * * * * *

"Saxon ships!" cried the youth on the dragon's head as we rounded the eastern side of the next island.

"What?!?" Captain Branwulf cried.

"Three ships, coming straight at us!" cried the youth.

"Full speed!" Branwulf shouted. "Shields up! Prepare to drop sail!"

"Damn!" Father cursed.

"We should've expected it," Rath said.

"Why?" Hjálmun asked.

"We robbed a church," Hal explained.

"A wealthy church ... and hacked up a priest," Digr said.

"Christians don't like that," Smiðr added.

"I've never seen them send this many ships," Brún said.

"They don't just want their gold back," Trandill explained. "They want to make an example of us."

"Shieldmen, fore!" Branwulf shouted.

Hjálmun and Brún grabbed their shields and pressed beside the rail, but stayed by us. Father pulled out his sword with one hand, still rowing with the other, and set it beside him.

"They may try to ram us," Father said. "If they do, we'll have to row and fight. Every battle's different, especially sea battles."

"Victory or Valhalla," I said to Father.

"Victory or Valhalla, my son."

* * * * * * * * *

I'd heard countless tales of battles. Ship to ship battles were especially exciting because there was always the chance that both ships would sink and everybody would die. I'd dreamed of being in my first sea battle.

Reality was a nightmare. I could see nothing, was so cramped that I wasn't certain if I could walk, and my hands so sore and swollen from rowing that I doubted if I could grip my sword if I had to block an enemy blade. *What would I do if we were boarded ... except die on a Saxon sword?*

"Drop sail!" Branwulf shouted. "Shields up! Row!"

Our speed relaxed as the sail fell, and many men, including Father, shouted to row harder. I pulled as hard as I could, certain that we were about to die.

"Arrows!" someone shouted, and thuds pattered into wood like hard, heavy raindrops on a thick lambskin window.

"Veer port!" Branwulf shouted. *"Ørðigskeggi, port!"*

We turned, but I was barely aware of it. I had no idea what was going on, where we were, how far away our enemy was, or how fast they were coming at us. My only weapon was my oar.

A strength that I hadn't known surfaced. I rowed harder, pushing and pulling with all of my might. It didn't matter that I didn't know what was going on; Branwulf knew, and why should he listen to me? My sword was useless unless we were boarded; I rowed like a madman.

Suddenly arrows, many trailing glittering sparks, flew over our ship. Larg's ship was on the other side of us, firing flaming arrows at our enemy. He had the greater range; we fired with the wind, so his arrows traveled farther and straighter. More arrows whizzed over us, and some shieldmen cheered.

"We got their sail!" Brún cried. *"They're burning!"*

"Only the lead ship," another shieldman said.

"Silence!" Branwulf shouted at them. *"Larg, again!"*

More arrows flew, many lit, many more not. I quit looking overhead, intent on my rowing.

"Hard port!" Branwulf shouted suddenly. *"Ørðigskeggi, hard port!"*

Port? I thought wildly. *Port would lead us toward them, not away!* We turned so hard that I was flung against Father, but I kept rowing.

"Shields steady!" Branwulf shouted.

Suddenly Trandill cried out. He fell back against our oar, clutching an arrow sticking out of his side.

"Trandill ...!" Rath cried.

"Keep rowing!" Digr shouted.

Several other men cried out from all over the ship. Arrows rained upon us. One man screamed and fell over, writhing so violently that he fouled the oar that he'd manned. Sammuel and Kappi pulled him center.

"Row!" Branwulf cried. "*For your lives, row!"*

Arrows flew in every direction. Two shieldmen fell. One got back up, ignoring the slender shaft sticking out of his arm, the other replaced by an oarsman who grabbed his shield and jumped to take his place. Larg's ship was ahead of us now, Bjarki beside us, and both were firing arrows as fast as they could.

"Starboard!" Branwulf shouted at last. "*Starboard! Starboard! Flee!"*

We turned hard and I heard the order repeated by Bjarki.

"Shields aft!" Branwulf shouted, and Hjálmun, Brún, and the other shieldmen began stepping quickly over the oarsmen, rushing to the rear. Branwulf grabbed some shieldmen and sent them running down the center of the ship toward the dragon's tail.

"Hoist sail!" Branwulf shouted, and he himself helped Sammuel and Kappi pull the rope. The strong wind filled our sail, puffed it out, and our speed increased.

"Row!" Branwulf cried. *"For victory, row!"*

* * * * * * * * *

"Oars up," Captain Branwulf said. "Oars rest."

We pushed our oars out of the ports and lifted them high, sliding them into their rests. They slid in with thuds as dreary as we felt.

"Three silver coins apiece," Branwulf said. "Well done. Rest now. Hjalti, take the rudder and keep us with the wind."

Father unsteadily stood and rubbed his legs.

"How's Trandill?" Father asked.

I'd forgotten; the wounded had been pulled off the oars and carried toward the tail.

"I'll check on him," Rath said. "Get some sleep."

"I won't sleep until I see him," Father replied. "Thron, Garad, get some rest."

Father and Rath went back to see Trandill. Garad turned to look at me, his mouth yawning, looking more haggard than I'd thought he could. Garad held up his cloak with sore hands, wrapped it around him, and then collasped onto the deck.

I tried to do the same, but my hands were so swollen that I couldn't grip the edges of my cloak. I tugged it snug around me as best I could and fell asleep almost at once.

* * * * * * * * *

"Dammit, it hurts!" Trandill cursed.

"It's no use; it's pointed right at his heart," Smiðr said. "If we push the arrow through, it'll kill him. If we pull it out, those barbs will tear his insides up."

"Just pull it out!" Trandill shouted angrily.

"There's no choice," Smiðr said. "Red-sword."

"No!" Trandill cried.

Everyone struggled to hold him still; Trandill's strength failed almost instantly.

"Sorry," Smiðr said. "It's your only hope."

"I'm sorry," Hjálmun said to Trandill, his voice cracking with regret as he pinned one arm.

"It could've been either of us ... or neither of us," Brún said. "I had more than thirty arrows in my shield."

"You shieldmen were incredible," Hal said. "Odin favored us: only four serious wounds and three dead. I can't believe that we got away so lightly."

"And two of the dead were shieldmen," Digr said. "You were taking as great a risk as us."

"I'll get the sword ready," Smiðr said, frowning.

"I'll help," Brún said grimly.

Trandill's face was ashen white. They'd torn his tunic away from the bleeding wound, which had a long, unadorned arrow with black crow fletchings sticking out of his ribs. Trandill looked like death, I thought, but I said nothing.

* * * * * * * * *

Garad woke up, but still looked sleepy. I yawned. Despite days of rowing, neither of us had slept long.

"What's going on?" Garad asked, but Father shushed him, then turned back to Trandill.

Trandill was trying not to drink from the mug that they were holding to his mouth, but he was exhausted, with five strong men forcing him to drink. Garad looked questioningly and I motioned him to the side, then stepped over the bench to lean against the rail.

"What's ...?" Garad started.

"Trandill's badly hurt," I whispered.

"How bad?"

"They can't get the arrow out."

"Can't they just leave it in?"

I shrugged. I'd never thought to ask, but then, I'd never seen anyone walking around with an arrow sticking out of them.

The moment felt odd; Garad and I hadn't talked, just talked, in forever. Once best friends, we'd barely spoken since Garad had found out about Father sporting with Grettir, and then her death, for which I still felt guilty. Garad looked at me, his expression sorrowful, but he quickly turned to face the sea. Neither of us knew what to say.

"No ...!" Trandill cried alarmedly, so loudly that both of us spun around.

"Hold still," Rath shouted. "Hey, help us!"

Trandill's drunken struggles, which Father, Hal, Digr, and Rath were fighting to restrain, became increasingly agitated, but hands reached from every angle, including Sammuel, Hjalti, and oarsmen from both before and behind. Soon more than two dozen grown men were holding Trandill still. Trandill's struggles became noticeable only by the terror in his eyes.

Smiðr and Brún walked carefully up. Men moved quickly to get out of their way; in Smiðr's hand was a short, narrow sword, glowing red from a fire and still smoking: *a red sword.*

Brún stepped right up to the crowd of men holding Trandill. He said nothing, but reached down with a wet cloth and wiped the blood from around the protruding arrow. Then he laid full down right on top of the frantic Trandill, pinning him with his full weight, his legs across the men holding Trandill, who seemed to have expected it.

Trandill screamed, futily struggling, and finally Smiðr stepped forward. He knelt down carefully, then took the arrow in one hand and lowered the glowing, smoking red sword toward the wound.

"Here we go," Smiðr warned.

Smiðr stabbed the red sword right underneath the protruding arrow, and then he pushed it in; Trandill's scream echoed across the ocean. The air filled with the stench of burning flesh. Everyone on all three ships turned to look.

Smiðr stabbed the red sword into Trandill's ribs hard, but

not too deep, and then pushed it farther. Finally, he slowly pulled the arrow out along the edge of the sword. The arrow had a wide head with two sharp barbs, and the instant that it was out, Smiðr withdrew the sword.

Smiðr rose and stepped next to me; he shoved the sword into the green water, making it hiss and sizzle.

"Take care of him," Smiðr said to me, motioning to my other side.

Garad was puking over the rail. Seeing him vomit made my own stomach roll. I didn't help Garad; I joined him, side-by-side puking into the sea.

* * * * * * * * *

"Disgraceful!" Father sneered at both of us.

"But ...," I started, but Father cut me off.

"I don't expect you to enjoy it, but someday you may have to red sword someone ... or watch them die," Father said angrily. "That could easily have been me, or Hal, and I'd expect either of you to red sword us, if needed."

"I'm sorry ...," Garad stammered.

"Don't be sorry," Father said. "Be brave. Be strong."

"I will," we said together.

Trandill lay unconscious, wrapped in three cloaks. Brún sat on one side of him, Hjálmun on the other. Trandill's face was chalk-white; he reminded me of that horrible day when Father and Sammuel had helped carry the dead villagers into Tavern Hall.

* * * * * * * * *

"We need water!" Vápni shouted from Bjarki's ship,

fighting to be heard over the wind. "We're almost out of food, too."

"Same here!" Branwulf shouted back. "We'll turn sail at dusk."

"To where?" Vápni shouted the question.

"We'll meet before dusk to discuss it," Branwulf shouted.

As the sun fell toward the horizon, we lowered sails, stuck out a few oars aft, and tossed ropes to each ship, pulling until the fierce painted dragonheads were almost touching. Larg was standing at the head of his ship with Gylðir at his side. Many others gathered around him, but Hlöðu and Øþveginn were the only two whose names I knew. Captain Bjarki stood foremost on his ship, with Vápni next to him, and behind them stood Bitra, Galti, Hvamm, and many others.

Captain Branwulf faced them with Hjalti beside him. Kappi, Sammuel, Father, and Rath stood right behind them, with many others crowded close by. Garad and I leaned over the rail, watching as best we could, with Frej right beside us.

"How are Kráka and Tréfótr?" Branwulf shouted.

"Kráka is healing," Bjarki said loudly. "His wound was bad; he won't be leaving the ship again, but he may be able to walk without a cane next year. Tréfótr's wound was much worse, and then got infected; we had to cut off his leg."

Many men grumbled and glanced around sternly.

"Will he live?" Branwulf asked.

"It's too early to tell."

"Did you have any losses escaping the fleet?"

"No losses," Bjarki reported. "Several wounds, but only one serious; one of the rowers from Øgæfa's ship, Skardal, lost an eye."

"All such wounds will receive extra reward," Branwulf promised, and then he turned to Larg's ship. "Captain Larg, did you have any losses?"

"None," said Captain Larg loud enough for everyone to hear. "About a dozen minor wounds, but nothing serious."

"Well done," Branwulf said.

"I didn't lead us safely past the Saxon fleet," Larg shouted back. "I didn't take the most dangerous position: that was Captain Branwulf!"

"Branwulf! Branwulf!" the men on Larg's ship began chanting, and soon everyone on all three ships shouted his name.

Branwulf let this continue for a minute, then waved for them all to be silent.

"We had losses," Branwulf said. "Two young shieldmen, Nafg and Falstag, died. Brave men they were; doubtless they're already feasting in Valhalla. No one knew the name of the rower who died. One more, a rower named Trandill, is seriously wounded, his future uncertain. We had to red sword him."

Another unhappy murmur ran through each ship.

"Still, we've done well, and still have half a viking to go," Branwulf said. "We need food and fresh water, so our first target shall be a large farm. We'll sail up a coast tomorrow and choose one carefully, then come back and attack it at night."

"Where?" Bjarki asked.

"Denmark's closest, but it's too well defended," Branwulf said. "Germany's too close to Denmark. I don't want to head for the Baltic Sea; too many other fleets were viking there. Nor do I want to return south; the Saxons would come after us again. That leaves Scotland."

"It'll take us two days to reach!" Bjarki argued.

"Ration what food and water you have," Branwulf said.

"Sails only; give our rowers a rest."

Another murmur, much happier, went through the crowd of rowers.

"Scots are tough fighters," Bjarki warned.

"True," Branwulf said, "but we're tougher!"

* * * * * * * * *

Trandill grew worse by the hour. He awoke later, but in a delirium, and Brún and Hjálmun struggled to hold him down. He puked all over his cloaks, but no one seemed surprised; the soiled cloaks were quickly washed in the sea and hung to dry. Father and Rath took their own cloaks and covered Trandill, Brún, and Hjálmun, but it didn't seem to help.

Later, Father made Garad and I lie on both sides of Trandill and share our cloaks as the night's chill fell. No one spoke the whole evening.

Smiðr examined Trandill's wound the next morning.

"Very good," Smiðr said excitedly to Trandill. "Looks clean, already healing. You'll be up and fighting again in no time!"

My heart leapt at the news, but Trandill didn't seem impressed.

"Liar ...," he called Smiðr.

"Go back to sleep," Smiðr said to him. "Rest is what you need now."

The realization struck me numb: *Trandill was dying.* I'd known Trandill all of my life, never well, but he'd always been there, at every village gathering, in Tavern Hall, laughing and gambling in the corner. He'd been friends with Father since they were kids, always welcomed into our house whenever he came to see Hal or Morgan.

I'd watched many men die since the viking began. All were strangers, men that I'd never known, and they'd died quickly, almost painlessly. Trandill was a friend, dying slowly, and there was nothing I could do about it.

Helsa, I thought darkly, wishing she were here with Læknir. The two of them, with all of their skills and herbs, could surely save Trandill, but they were back home, hundreds of miles away across open sea, and even with every man rowing under full sail the whole way, we'd never make it in time.

Smiðr looked at Father, Digr, and Sammuel ... and shook his head. Tears welled in my eyes. *Were three silver coins really worth dying? I'd gladly give up my share to make Trandill live!* I glanced up at the sky, at the clear blue dotted with huge, billowy clouds. *Where was Odin when we needed him? Why didn't the gods that we worshiped come down from the sky and save those loyal to them? Why did we worship gods that weren't there when we needed them?*

Trandill puked again ... and his bile was dark green.

* * * * * * * * *

That evening, we were each given a single spoonful of thin soup, and then sat silently around Trandill.

"I'll save benches ... for you all ... in Elvidner," Trandill said.

"We'll be there," Smiðr promised.

"Beside you until Ragnarrok," Brún agreed.

"You're ... good friends," Trandill said, and then he coughed.

"Brothers," Hal said.

"Family," Digr said.

Even Rath and Father had tears in their eyes, too many to be dried by the swift wind.

"Trandill ...?" Digr asked hesitantly. "What do you want us to do ... with your share?"

"Beigaldi," Trandill said, and all of the men nodded.

"She'll get it ... and more," Digr promised.

Trandill smiled and died.

* * * * * * * * *

Chapter 40

* * * * * * * * *

A wide hole hollowed my chest.

Brún and Hjálmun cleaned Trandill up, then polished his sword and belted it upon him, overtop his cloak, to send his sword with him to Valhalla. At sunset, they lifted him over the rail and laid him to rest on the waters, as if the sea were a great mattress that he was going to sleep upon. The waters didn't support him; Trandill slipped under the waves and slowly sank out of view.

"A great man," Captain Branwulf announced. "He took the same risk as we all do, danger for riches ... or Valhalla. His sacrifice rewarded us with life. His reward will be the beautiful Valkyrie each night and a place among our honored ancestors in fabled Valhalla."

* * * * * * * * *

Father, Brún, and especially Hal spent the evening telling Garad and I about Trandill, every story that they knew, every memory that they had. Sammuel and Kappi also sat with us, and everyone nearby sat respectfully silent. Captain Branwulf and Hjalti came by for a while, and both spoke of Trandill, of the many years that he'd sailed with them, and how honored they felt to have known him.

Trandill had been a wild youth, a practical joker, and very generous, especially with Beigaldi, from whom he'd purchased evenings since her husband died. He was born free in a nearby village, but his father had lost everything to one poor harvest; to save his family from ruin, Trandill had allowed himself to be sold into service, and he'd gone through several owners before Digr bought him.

Digr had liked Trandill from the very start, and always treated him well. Trandill loved Digr's steam room, and always chopped extra firewood so that he could relax in the hot, foggy shack. He also liked to fish with Gandr, and would play with Beigaldi's children whenever he could, believing that several were his, although he was never sure which; sometimes he just claimed them all.

On vikings, Trandill was a great spear-thrower. He'd steal anything; he'd once stripped a pair of nuns down to their skins, believing that they were hiding jewelry under their habits, and left them that way: Beigaldi had loved the habits and worn them for months, until one of her kids got sick; afterwards, she feared that Freyja might be punishing her for wearing the garb of Christians.

Trandill had always asked Digr for permission to go help whenever someone was building a barn or clearing a new field. Sitting next to Garad, I began to regret all of the animosity between us; I wanted to be the kind of true friend that Trandill had been.

* * * * * * * * *

There was no food or water.

The coast of Scotland looked rich and plentiful. Branwulf and Hjalti examined each farm on the coast; some were too small, too close to villages, or too far away, which meant they were heavily-defended. I just tried to rest and recover: my hands were still swollen, but I could almost make a tight fist.

With not much else to do, I pulled out the little box of polished-shell, antler, and tin sewing buttons that I'd stolen so long ago. The polished shells sparkled in the light; Mother and Ingrid would love to sew these onto their dresses; I couldn't wait to see them again, especially Ingrid. The cold nights aboard ship were a torment compared to lying in Ingrid's warmth. Yet buttons and a few coins seemed a pitiful compensation for the loss of Trandill.

* * * * * * * * *

"Hold your weapons until you're on shore," Father said to Garad and I, handing us each covered lanterns. "Keep these lanterns covered until we're inside."

We rowed toward the shore under a cloudy night sky. Rowing was no fun anymore, just a chore, like killing a pig, but it wasn't the torment that it'd been when the Saxons chased us.

"Oars up!" Branwulf hissed. "Oars rest! Prepare to viking!"

We posted our oars and stood, letting our momentum and

the waves carry us the rest of the way. Sitting in the fore, we were among the first who'd disembark.

We sailed right up to a tiny dock with two small fishing boats tied to it. Kappi and Sammuel jumped onto the end of the dock and quickly tied us up. Larg sailed up next to us, tying up right against one of the fishing boats; his men crawled across its deck onto the dock, but we were first, running toward the large farm house before Bjarki even docked.

Branwulf motioned for silence, and waved for us to follow him. Hjalti ran the other way, motioning for others to follow him. Larg's and Bjarki's men filled in behind.

"Watch this!" Father whispered.

Kappi reached the window first, but he didn't try to force its shutters; he knelt down on the grass under it. Þjófi came charging up next, and he jumped, placed one large foot upon Kappi's back, and used him as a springboard. Þjófi hit the shutters with his full weight and crashed through with a boom like a thunderclap.

Loud crashes resounded as we followed him through the window, jumping from Kappi's back; other shutters had been broken. Several women screamed and shouts rose:

'Invaders!' 'Norsemen!' 'Raid!'

As we'd been told, Garad and I pulled the covers off our lanterns. We were in a large bedroom with four beds, but these people were older than I'd ever seen; Old man Ranglátr and Widow Væna looked young beside them.

Sammuel pointed a sword at them as they cowered behind their blankets.

"Get up and we'll kill you!" he shouted.

Without another word, he grabbed Garad and ran through the door into the hallway beyond.

"Hold that light up!" Sammuel shouted at Garad.

Þjófi and Father pulled me and followed Sammuel, but in the hallway, they knocked open every door, then ran inside, swords drawn; Sammuel and Garad continued running down the length of the hall.

Not wanting to be outdone, I ran to a closed door and slammed my shoulder into it. Sword-first, I ran inside.

A dozen girls screamed, some jumping up and down on their beds, while others tried to hide beneath their blankets: pretty servant girls from ten to twenty-five. They had nothing to steal, but I stood mesmerized as they frantically screamed and cried, wild with terror, looking at me.

Rath stepped into the doorway behind me, glanced around, and pulled me out.

"No time for rapes!" Rath shouted, but he took one last look at the girls before following me down the hallway.

Someone cried out directly ahead of us; a death scream.

"Thron, wait!" Rath shouted, but I ran ahead, too fast to stop.

I charged in; Sammuel stood there, leaning against the wall, a horrified look in his eyes. A dead Saxon was crumpled against him, fallen onto Sammuel's feet with an axe splitting open the back of his head. *It was Garad's axe;* Garad was still holding its handle.

"Well done!" Sammuel breathlessly gasped. "You saved my life!"

Sammuel kicked the Saxon body off his legs, and then pulled a silver ring off one of his own fingers, pressed it into Garad's palm, patted Garad's shoulder, and then he dashed out of the room.

I'd forgotten that Rath was behind me until he patted Garad's head.

"Take his sword," Rath said as he hurried on. "Check him

for jewelry, pockets, and pouches."

A lot of yelling and screaming was coming from all over, but Garad just stood there, Sammuel's ring in one hand, his father's axe in the other. The dead Saxon was very big and covered in blood. Still in his hand was a long steel sword; I pulled it free and lifted it to Garad. It was a brightly polished sword, bigger and longer than mine, with a brass pommel crusted with garnets.

"This ... is ... yours," I said.

I pushed it into Garad's grip, and suddenly he was holding it. I glanced down at the dead man, then suddenly knelt and pushed my hand into his pockets, which held only a length of string. His pouch jingled of coins; I cut its cords and opened it: a dozen coppers lay inside.

Garad had killed an enemy; *I was the only boy left in our fleet.*

I ransacked the room, tearing open every chest and pulling open each drawer. Large, water-filled tubs lay against the wall, towels and tunics hanging on ropes strung across the ceiling. There were many types of clothing, lots of thick wool stockings, and cloaks decorated with embroidery that only Helsa's skill could equal.

I found a large sack and stuffed into it the best that I could find, including all of the stockings and one very impressive cloak. I took several large tunics that only Father and Rath could wear, and even some baby clothes for Urd. Garad still stood frozen, looking at his new sword.

"See if you can find its scabbard," I shouted at him, but he only looked about blankly, as if he didn't hear, when suddenly Father pushed into the room.

"Garad, well done!" Father shouted. "Holbarki would be proud of you!"

* * * * * * * * *

Garad and I headed back to the ship laden with our lanterns, a huge bag of clothes, baskets of onions and barley, a heavy sack of ground wheat, three knives, and the dead man's coins, pouch, and knife. Garad also carried his new sword, but we hadn't found its scabbard. We led a crowd carrying kegs of ale and fresh water, butchered slabs of ribs and calves' legs, and large baskets of vegetables, along with plunder of all kinds, anything not nailed down. Father and Rath walked behind us.

"Some son you got there!" Rath laughed, telling Father. "Found him in the servant's bedroom: two dozen young girls; he would've raped all of them!"

"The girls at þur's were right!" Father laughed. "Like father, like son!"

I cringed; I'd not thought of raping anyone until Rath suggested it.

Hal and Digr laughed with Rath and Father, but Smiðr and Brún were arguing over whether we should stay and raze the place fully or escape before the alarm spread.

Garad clutched his new sword as if it were the greatest trophy in the world.

I squeezed my bags through the press of men toward my place near the fore. I looked askance at my plunder as I stashed it with my box of sewing buttons. *What was I doing? Risking my life for things no one would ever miss?*

As we rowed away, Garad was taken to Branwulf by Sammuel and Father. Branwulf shook Garad's hand, praised his manliness, and then carefully examined the prized sword. He seemed to want it for himself, but Sammuel reminded him of Holbarki's many years of service, and Branwulf reluctantly returned the garnet-crusted sword to Garad.

By the time that we were far out to sea, our sails raised, many bottles of wines were shared by all, and the smell of cooked meat filled the air. For the first time, they filled all of our bowls as close to the rim as they could in a rocking boat.

"He came at me from the shadows," Sammuel said, gesturing wildly. "I blocked his sword, but he had a knife in the other hand, which I wouldn't have seen if Garad hadn't run in with a lantern. I caught the man's arm, but he sliced my wrist pretty bad. Suddenly: *wham!* It was just like having Holbarki guard my back."

"Holbarki saved us all, at some point," Digr said.

Garad's new sword was being passed around, examined by everyone. I felt ashamed. I tried to stand up and turn away, but Father's hand grabbed me and pulled me back down.

* * * * * * * * *

Branwulf repeated his presenting Garad with the garnet-encrusted sword in front of everyone. Garad also had the silver ring that Sammuel had given him, although he had to wear it on a thong, as it was too big for his fingers. All three ships cheered as Garad blushed.

I went forward when it was my turn and showed Branwulf the pouch of coppers and the bag of clothes. Branwulf patted my head, took the coins, and let me keep the rest.

Father took hold of my arm as I tossed my prizes onto the deck; he pulled me down the center past the rows of men as Branwulf claimed a pair of gold earrings, but let the sailor keep several armbands made of carved horn. Father pulled me all the way aft to the tiller, which I'd seldom seen because

I sat fore. Ørðigskeggi leaned against it as he carved slices from a thick sausage.

"Wish that it were you ...?" Father asked me.

"Huh?"

"You wish that you'd saved Sammuel?"

Ørðigskeggi cleared his throat loudly, having obviously heard, then he rose and wandered fore. Several of the nearby rowers looked away.

"What if you'd killed that Saxon?" Father asked. "Garad's your best friend. Wouldn't you want him to be happy for you?"

* * * * * * * * *

Soon it began pouring rain so heavily that we couldn't see the tail of our dragonship. Even in our cloaks, we all got soaked, and I was freezing, especially my feet. Yet, with a moment of inspiration, I opened the bag of clothes that I'd stolen.

"G-G-Got e-extras?" Garad asked as I pulled on a pair of thick, dry stockings.

I took a deep breath.

"For you, anything!" I said.

Soon I was handing out dry clothes to everyone from our village. Smiðr seemed especially delighted with his forest green stockings, and I showed them all of the rest of the clothes that I'd gotten.

"Uh, oh ...!" Hal gasped.

"What?" I asked.

I was holding up a fancy cloak, thinking that I should wear it.

"Is it ... *gold?*" Brún asked.

"Looks like it," Digr said.

Father rubbed the cloak-clasp hard with his thumb, then examined it closely.

"Gold," Father said. "I can't tell if it is solid or plated."

"Better tell Branwulf," Smiðr said.

"Good thing that we found it now," Brún said. "Don't want Branwulf thinking that we're holding out."

Branwulf, Hjalti, Kappi, and Sammuel came up immediately, rain dripping off their hoods. Father showed them the cloak.

"Thron stole it," Father explained, holding out the cloak. "We didn't notice the clasps until now."

Branwulf took the cloak and examined it.

"You understand that I have to take this ...?" Branwulf asked me.

"O-Of course."

"Don't worry," Branwulf smiled. "If it's solid, then you'll be ... richly rewarded."

This pronouncement seemed to impress everyone.

"Captain, this rain doesn't look like it's going to let up," Rath said.

Captain Branwulf sighed heavily.

"No, I suspect not," he said. "Alright, let's put up the awning. Garad, climb up onto the dragonhead and keep watch."

"Yes, sir," Garad said.

* * * * * * * * *

"*'Richly rewarded'* means that you get two shares," Father explained. "If there are ten people, and five of them get richly rewarded, then, at the end of the viking, all of the plunder is divided into fifteen shares, and those who are richly rewarded get two."

"You never got six silver coins!"

"Branwulf never got so much treasure," Father said. "My great-grandfather told stories of plunder like this, but only when he was young. We've been attacking too long, and our enemies defend themselves too much. This raid will be the pride of Sweden, once it becomes known, a story every Norseman will tell."

"But you told us ...!"

"I told Vespa," Father said. "Do you think that she'd have let me come if I'd told her that we spent the first week whoring and drinking, then almost got killed by Normans, and then gotten chased all the way around Ireland?"

"Why ...?"

"Do you want to be poor forever?" Father asked. "Our chance of getting wealthy is small, but it's better than no chance at all. Besides, how else would you earn your manhood? How can you look other men in the face until you've proven your worth? How else would you impress the Valkyrie?"

"Is there really a Valhalla?" I asked hesitantly. "Are they ... are Valkyries real ...?"

"I don't know," Father said. "I hope so."

"But .... *Trandill's dead!* Is Valhalla worth three silver coins when we don't even know if it's real?"

"Do you honor me?" Father asked.

"What ...?"

"Do you honor me?"

"Of course!"

"Our beliefs are who we are, all that can never be taken

from us," Father smiled. "I don't know if my father really believed in the Valkyrie, but he always said that he did, so I honor him every time that I repeat his words. But duty to our descendants trumps duty to our ancestors; that's why you're here, Thron: for our family yet to come.

"Besides," Father grinned, "the girls at Pur's let me do things that your mother never would. You'll find that it's the same with Helsa ... or is it still Ingrid?"

I shrugged.

"We'll be sailing back soon; if you don't choose, then those girls will eat you alive."

"Who would you marry?" I asked.

"Me?" Father grinned. "I'd marry Tungu!"

* * * * * * * * *

Chapter 41

* * * * * * * * *

"Helsa ... and Ingrid ...?" Garad asked. "*You lucky bastard!"*

I smiled; Garad and I hadn't talked like this in a long time. Garad had spent four uneventful hours watching for other ships, clinging to the wet top of the rocking dragonhead. Frej stood there now, hanging onto the bobbing dragonhead.

"Who would you choose?" I asked. "Helsa or Ingrid?"

"Why marry either?" Garad laughed. "Enjoy them both!"

"Until one of them gets pregnant? Or, until one of them leaves, and then I'm stuck with the other being mad at me? Or ... until Widow Væna decides for me?"

"Rath seems happy," Garad said.

"In a land full of widows, Rath couldn't find a wife," I reminded him. "Everybody says it."

"How about if I marry one?" Garad offered.

"Which one?" I asked.

Garad furrowed his brows.

"Hard to say," Garad murmured.

"See ...?" I retorted. "This is driving me mad: get married, or go on the vikings ..."

"What?!?" Garad shouted in surprise. "Why would you ever not want to go viking?"

"I didn't say I didn't want to," I said.

"But you're considering it?" Garad asked incredulously.

"Maybe ... after a few years."

"But why ...?"

"Remember what Kampi said? *'There're other ways to make a living; less dangerous and more profitable.'*"

"Vikings are about more than profit," Garad said. "*Our gods, our faith, our culture...*"

"The Scots, Danes, English, and Irish are growing stronger every year."

"Viking warriors are never afraid."

"Warriors fight smart ... or die."

"Do you want to be left behind with the women?"

"Women have their uses."

"That's what Þur's is for," Garad argued. "I watched you and Inn Danski ..."

"Inn Danski said I should marry Ingrid."

"Who cares what she said? Women aren't for talking ..."

"They do a lot of it!"

"All the more reason to not listen."

"What good have our gods ever done us?"

"Careful! You'll curse yourself!"

"Did Trandill curse himself? Did Halgrum? Or your father?" Garad blanched; *I'd gone too far.* "Inn Danski is there anytime you have money. Wealth is why we come viking, but look around: do you see anyone with wealth?"

"Branwulf ..."

"Branwulf, but no one else."

"What about Larg and Bjarki?" Garad asked. "Larg was just a retainer, Bjarki a nephew, and now both are captains of their own ships!"

"They're captains of Branwulf's other ships," I corrected him. "What does that have to do with you or me? We'll never be captains."

"I'd make a good captain!" Garad said.

"Where will you viking? Every treasure's been raided. There's no place left!"

"If we turn against the vikings, then we turn against Odin! Who'll protect us from the Christians?"

"Protect us from men like Friar James ...?" I demanded. "We're the ones threatening them."

"You sound like a Christian," Garad said.

"Your faith or your life," I said. "If you could only have one, which would you keep?"

"We have to viking," Garad said. "Boys must prove that their men."

"Tell that to Halgrum," I said.

* * * * * * * * *

"A sail!" cried several of the rowers.

"Is it alone?" Branwulf rose up high so he could catch a glimpse of it.

"It looks like it," Kappi said. "Maybe it got lost in the storm."

"Let's check it out," Branwulf said. "Maybe they have something worth stealing."

We splashed our oars into the water and readied to row. Kappi started clapping his hands, setting a rhythm.

"Pull ... pull ... pull ...!"

Their ship wasn't a fast ship. Branwulf had us slow our rowing so that Larg and Bjarki could encircle it. Finally they lowered their sail and waved to us.

"Shields up and spears ready," Branwulf ordered, and he slipped on his polished helmet and raised his shield.

"Drop sail!" Hjalti ordered.

"Ho!" Branwulf cried to the ship.

"Peace!" cried a man on the ship. "We surrender!"

"Who's your captain?"

"I am," the man shouted. "Captain Richards, at your service. You're welcome to all the fish in our hold!"

Branwulf and Hjalti exchanged frowns.

"You're a fisher?" Hjalti shouted.

"All that we have are nets and fish!"

"Well ...?" Hjalti asked Branwulf. "Do we want fish ...?"

Branwulf sighed and turned away. "Take what you want."

* * * * * * * * *

"What do you think we should do?" Brún asked with a mouthful of hot tuna.

"Whatever Branwulf wants," Rath and Father chorused together.

"You know what I mean!"

"I'd play it safe," Hal said. "We've already made a profit."

"Branwulf can't let success make us lazy," Digr said. "When good times finally come, you take advantage of them. Once word spreads of him paying three silvers per survivor, men will flock to his banner."

"If Branwulf fills his ships with good men, then where will we sit?" Hal grinned.

Everyone laughed, but Father broke in unexpectedly.

"Thron, what do you think we should do?"

"Huh ...?"

"Come, son," Father said. "You're growing up, becoming a man. What do you think that we should do?"

"Tell us!" Brún smiled.

Father was giving me a chance, since I hadn't yet killed a Saxon, to prove what kind of man I was. I looked past him, across the ocean, at all of the distant fishing boats that had finally come out, the boat we'd robbed already lost amid their numbers.

"I'd take all these fishing boats," I said.

Smiling, Brún and Hal shook their heads.

"What good are fishing boats?" Rath laughed. "There's nothing on them but men and nets."

"Kill the men," I said. "Keep the ships and nets, sail them home ... and own the largest fishing fleet in Norway."

Rath, Brún, and Hal fell silent, jaws falling open, and Digr laughed so loudly that half of our rowers turned to glance at him. Father smiled proudly, and Garad looked astounded.

"Branwulf ...!" Rath shouted. "Get over here!"

Branwulf hesitated, then stormed across the deck.

"Did you just order me?" Branwulf demanded.

"No, sir!" Rath grinned. "But you'll wish that I had once you hear what this boy just said!"

* * * * * * * * *

Branwulf patted my back and declared me one of his chief advisors. My plan was quickly repeated down the rows; Hjalti presented me with a bottle of mead that he'd brought from Norway.

"We could put three men on each fisher and sail with the dragons as escort," Hal suggested.

"The fishers would never expect it," Brún said. "We could take twenty a day ... with no losses!"

"Branwulf will be rich," Digr said. "He'll be able to feed his family year-round, sell the remainder, and he'll have Thron to thank for it."

"My son!" Father reminded him, beaming.

Smiðr alone scowled, frowning.

"Fishermen ...!" he spat the word as if it were a curse. "You won't catch me stinking of seaweed!"

"No, you stink like a forge," Hal chuckled.

"Better me than Gandr," Smiðr argued. "We already have Friar James. Now we're talking about fishing fleets ..."

"Norway can't fight alone against England, France, Germany, ..." Hal said.

"We aren't alone!" Smiðr said. "There's Sweden, Lapland, Denmark, ...! If we all banded together ...!"

"Denmark's king is a Christian now, and the Swedish royal court includes two bishops," Digr interrupted.

"That's blasphemy!" Smiðr scowled.

"All of Europe has converted," Rath said. "We and Iceland are the last holdouts."

"What about Greenland?" Brún asked.

"I don't think there's anybody left there," Rath said. "The last settlements that I heard of fled ... or died."

"That was a nasty trick," Brún said. "Naming the farmable island Iceland, and the frozen tundra Greenland."

"The clans that settled Iceland didn't want others knowing how great it was, and the first settlers in Greenland wanted more people to join them in their icy wasteland," Digr said.

"It doesn't matter," Hal said. "Iceland and Greenland are peaceful settlements."

"Peace!" Smiðr spat the word. "Our fathers didn't want peace! They took what they wanted, and they killed anyone that stood in their way!"

"Like when they took Northern France?" Father asked.

"Yes!"

"Those vikings betrayed us," Father reminded him. "A thousand Norsemen conquered the richest, most fertile lands in Europe, and then what did they do? Married local women, called themselves Normans, and turned their backs on the rest of us. They'd attack us if they saw us; you need a fleet of thirty dragons just to land on their shores."

"They should've taken Norse women and colonized, like they did on Iceland," Smiðr said.

"I though that the whole point of the vikings was to get away from Norse women!" Hal exclaimed, and everyone laughed.

"It's a war of gods," Rath said, "the Asier against the Christian God. What can we do? How long can we cling to the old ways before they get us killed?"

"As long as I'm alive!" Smiðr growled.

* * * * * * * * *

Sitting on top of the dragonhead wasn't easy. It wasn't carved to be a seat, was too small to hold on to, and it rocked back and forth with each wave. Many fishing boats were about; most sailed away as we approached, a few just ignored us and tended to their nets. In the southern distance, I saw mountains: Scotland, according to Rath, but it was too far off to see anything but trees and tall, rugged peaks. Yet one ship didn't look like a fisher.

"Hjalti!" I cried, and I pointed at the ship.

"Good work, Thron," Hjalti said. "Branwulf! What do you make of that?"

Branwulf came up and leaned across the rail. Behind him, several men stood up and followed his gaze.

"A merchant, I'd wager," Branwulf smiled. "Let's see what they're carrying."

"Oars!" Hjalti shouted to the men.

Soon we were rowing again, all except me. Hjalti had me stay where I was, clinging to the dragonhead, which became even more difficult the instant that our oars splashed. Oared, the ship rocked violently, sped faster, and bobbed more, the fore lifting up and crashing harder; my fingers locked into the intricate crevices of the dragon's open mouth.

"Don't fall in," Branwulf grinned at me. "We won't have time to fish you out."

Bjarki and Larg sailed off our starboard bow; Branwulf gestured for them to spread out. Hjalti shouted back to Ørðigskeggi, who was again manning the tiller, and we turned slightly south, cutting off their last hope of escape. The merchant ship turned and fled, but it was too slow; soon they lowered their sails, and a man waved a white cloth.

"Prepare to board and fight!" Branwulf shouted. "Slowly! Take us in slow!"

"Lower the sail!" Hjalti shouted.

Bjarki was already talking to their captain as we sailed up. It was a large ship, but with only nine men on it, all weathered sailors with long beards and clothes tattered by the wind. In the hold of their ship, easily visible, were stacks of great earthenware jars, all painted with fantastic designs.

"What have we here?" Branwulf asked.

"Wine and olive oil casks," Bjarki answered.

"Yours, if you wish, my lord," a short but very powerfully built man interjected. "How many would you like?"

"You're the captain?"

"Yes, my lord."

"Where are you from, and where are you headed?"

"From Melvich, headed to Boddam."

"Who are these casks intended for?"

"Baron McMardin of Boddam," the captain answered.

"Must have a deep purse," Branwulf said. "He's a powerful lord?"

"Very," their captain said. "A great man."

"How do you deliver the casks to him?" Branwulf asked.

"Beg pardon ...?"

"The casks!" Branwulf said. "Do you drop them off on the docks, or transport them inside his castle?"

"The docks," their captain replied.

"Too bad," Branwulf sighed. "Too bad for you, of course. Men! Weapons out!"

Their captain paled white as foam as every oarsman on our ship jumped to his feet and raised spears and axes, and a singing chorus of swords sliding from their scabbards filled the air. A confused moment later, Bjarki's men did the same; nine frightened men were trapped between hundreds of heavily-armed fighters.

"Mercy!" their captain cried. *"Take everything! Please! Just ...!"*

"We want your ship," Branwulf growled.

The pale captain glared, confused, but then he stepped back. He looked at the distant shore, at his men, and then back to Branwulf.

"Take it!" he cried. *"Sailors, follow ...!"*

Their captain ran to their bow, jumped up onto his rail, and then leaped overboard. He splashed loudly into the sea and vanished. His men hesitated only a moment, then followed. They jumped overboard without a moment's hesitation, splashed into the sea, and swam away, following their captain. Many of us began laughing, and Branwulf joined in.

"Let them go ...?" Hjalti asked.

"Let them go," Branwulf confirmed. "If they actually got into McMardin's castle, then we could've impersonated them and gone after another hoard. But we must take what we can. Ørðigskeggi! Take a few men! You're captain of this ship now! Follow us, and stay as close as you can."

"Aye, Captain," Ørðigskeggi said.

"Begging your pardon, Captain," Hjalti said. "What do we want this vessel for?"

"Cargo," Branwulf grinned, and he glanced across at me, "and wine for the men all the way home!"

* * * * * * * * *

We sailed at ease for two more days, sometimes leaving Captain Ørðigskeggi far behind, before we spied another merchant. This one wasn't alone or unguarded; there were five ships, four low, slow, deep-drafted cargo boats, each with heavily-rigged white sails, and one slim, fast-looking vessel with a green and red striped sail that looked as if it could outrace us even at oars and sails.

"Let's take them," Branwulf said.

"Oars out!" Hjalti shouted.

I'd been sitting with Garad and Frej, again talking about

what we'd do with our three silvers, but Skalla shouted for Frej to join him at his oar. Garad got shifted up to sit beside Smiðr and Brún, and I was left squeezed between Digr and Hal. Hjálmun was rowing several rows away, and Rath and Father were standing beside Branwulf, not rowing at all. We tossed out the paddles to splash into the sparkling water, slipped the handles through the oar-ports, and braced, ready to row.

"Weapons ready!" Hjalti shouted. "Shields ready!"

Digr reached past me and grabbed one of the two shields leaning next to us against the hull. He set it to lean against his knees, then drew his heavy sword and set it next to him.

"Grab that other shield," he instructed me. "Hold it ready. You'll have to shield us and Hal."

"Especially Hal," Hal grinned.

"Row!" Hjalti shouted, and he began clapping his hands loudly, setting a fast beat.

I fumbled the shield against my knees with one hand, rowing with the other, and then I struggled to draw and lay my sword beside me, but soon I had both hands on the oar.

"They've seen us," Father said. "They're turning."

"Svartiþurs, stay on the lead ship!" Branwulf shouted to the huge, burly man wielding the rudder.

"What's he doing?" Rath asked. "He's circling their ships. Why not try to lead us away?"

"Get one of those kids up here!" Branwulf shouted.

"Thron!" Father shouted. *"Now!"*

I slid between the oars right into Father's hands; he pulled me to the fore.

"Up on the dragonhead!" Father shouted, and Rath helped lift me as I climbed. "Stand as high as you can! We'll hold you!"

Father and Rath clung to my legs, half-standing on the rail. Nervously I placed my boots on the narrow wooden head and stood up, balancing with my arms.

"Look carefully!" Father shouted. "Look at the merchants first! Can you see what they're carrying, how many men are on their decks?"

I scanned the boats, fighting to see through the bright glare off the water.

"Four men on that one," I called down, pointing. "Five on that one."

"What's on their decks?" Branwulf demanded.

I scanned as best I could, shielding my eyes with my hands. The surface of their deck was still distant, indistinct, and something on it was glinting, reflecting the bright sun into my eyes.

"I can't tell," I said.

"Do you see bare deck?" Father asked.

"No," I said. "It's a loaded ship."

"What does it look like?"

"Colors, different colors," I said. "It could be large bags."

"Could it be men?" Branwulf asked. "Men bent low, hiding, trying not to be seen?"

I stared as hard as I could. Their closest ship was bobbing in the waves, making it difficult to see, yet as I looked, thinking about men hiding, suddenly I saw them, their backs and hooded heads. Glinting light reflected off brightly polished metal ...

"I see them!" I shouted as loudly as I could. "Swords and spears ...!"

"Hard about!" Branwulf shouted.

"Trap!" Hjalti shouted, running to the rail and leaning over, waving at Bjarki and Larg, both of whom were on our

port side. "*Trap! Trap!*"

Svartiþurs turned us so fast that I toppled off the narrow head. I splashed into the water, but Rath and Father had tight grips on my legs, and ungently pulled until I could grab the rail. With their help, I slid onto deck soaking wet and trembling; if they hadn't caught me, then the ship would've pushed me under.

All the heads on the Scottish ships raised up; fifty men on each ship, many with bows. Some fired arrows at us, but we were upwind, and their arrows fell short. Only one of their ships was built for speed, and it had circled around, apparently hoping to meet us just as we reached the decoys.

"It's a sign," Rath muttered so that only we could hear.

Branwulf shot him an evil glare, but then subsided.

"We can't go home yet," Branwulf said. "The men have no booty, and men with empty arms will always want more."

* * * * * * * * *

"*Branwulf! Branwulf! Branwulf!*"

Branwulf raised a hand and waved, accepting their praise.

"We're not home yet," Branwulf shouted, turning around so that all the men on each dragon and the small ship with olive oil casks could see him. "We're going on one more raid, a small village, hopefully tonight. Tomorrow, we'll take as many fishing boats as we can; I want at least twenty. Once we have enough, we'll turn north and sail home."

A mild cheer followed these words.

"Our voyage back home should be easy," Branwulf continued. "We'll look like a huge fleet, surrounded by three dragons, and no one will sail close enough to perceive what we really are. No oars, or we'll leave my fishing boats behind.

The voyage home will take longer, but we'll have plenty of fish, and I expect all of the wine on Ørðigskeggi's ship to be drunk before we reach Norway!"

All of the men cheered.

"And ...," Branwulf continued, "as reward for all that you've done for me this year, I'm promising this: *no limits on this last raid!"* The men fell utterly silent at this. "I give you my word: this last raid, whatever village we choose, I won't even ask what you've stolen. I'll give you as much time as I can, up to three hours, before I wind my horns. Whatever you find, whatever you can carry back and load on this ship, will be yours! *No tributes! No limits!"*

A moment of disbelief swept four decks, and then men began cheering.

"Branwulf! Branwulf! Branwulf! Branwulf! Branwulf!"

* * * * * * * * *

All afternoon we sailed up the coast, Branwulf, Hjalti, Father, and Rath carefully eyeing each village, judging its potential. I stood against the rail, half-naked, shaking my slowly drying tunic; I'd been dunked head-first to my waist.

"I don't care what bed sheets they steal," Branwulf said in a whisper. "We need a place big enough to provide an armful of junk for each man, but not big enough to put up much of a defense."

"Not even the biggest farm has that much," Father said.

"Maybe we should sail to the Orkneys," Rath suggested. "Attack one of the smaller islands?"

"Those places expect attacks," Hjalti reminded him.

"We need a small coastal village," Branwulf said. "I don't want to sail up another river."

They settled on a small town built in between the sea and a steep, forested hillside beside a small river. No one could easily come to their aid from across the river without crossing on boats, and on the other side was a single large farm with a small dock just big enough for three fishing boats. The town had a small church with a steeple, several large barns, and dozens of houses.

"It's perfect," Branwulf said. "We'll come back tonight."

Father and Rath grinned approvingly, but I said nothing. *I was the only boy in this fleet.* Tonight would be my last chance. *Before I stole anything, I'd have to kill someone.*

* * * * * * * * *

Chapter 42

* * * * * * * * *

We rowed under bright stars toward the south-west Scottish coast. The sleeping village showed few lights. Whatever they had, anything that we wanted, would soon be ours. Branwulf had given permission for some ambitious men to steal the docked, unguarded fishing boats before the sleeping houses; he'd keep the ships for his fishing fleet, but they could crew those vessels for him. Branwulf also allowed the capture of Scottish women to become imprisoned wives or servants, or worse, slaves to be sold at auction. Most would probably end up like Inn Danski; stolen women trapped far from home, doomed to whoredom or starvation.

Inn Danski: she'd been so soft, so beautiful, that it hurt to remember her. She'd been such a sweet girl, a wealthy daughter with a promising future ... a future stolen by men like me. A pang of regret struck my heart: *could I doom an innocent young girl to Inn Danski's fate?* No, I wasn't an evil man. Yet ... was I not a viking warrior, a Norseman? *Hadn't I raided, stolen, and watched men hacked apart ... for my own profit? Wasn't I rowing hard toward men who'd never harmed me, hoping to kill one of them for my own glory?*

"Remember, follow me!" Father whispered.

The twilight shore came closer. I gritted my teeth and rowed; *this wasn't the time for a conscience.* Either I'd earn everyone's respect tonight ... or I'd suffer their taunts all winter ... and have to go viking next year.

"Oars up!" Hjalti whispered hoarsely. "Quietly! Oars rest!"

We pushed out our oars and hauled them onto the ship. Father helped me find our oar's rest-hole in the dark, and we slid it into place silently. Then Father grabbed my arm and pulled me forward with him. Men pressed close behind us, eagerly awaiting.

"Draw your blades and hold them high!" Father whispered to Garad and I. "Be careful; don't hit anyone except Scotsmen!"

Sammuel climbed up onto the rail with a rope, and a moment before we felt our mighty dragonship slide against pylons, Sammuel leaped onto the dock and wrapped a rope around a weathered post.

"Hard and fast!" Branwulf hissed as we stormed past, jumping onto the shore. "When you hear my horn, come running! We won't wait for stragglers!"

Garad and I followed Father; we ran ahead of the pack up a dark, grassy hill. Behind us came Rath, Hal, and the others, even Digr running with a speed and strength that I didn't think he had. Father veered left and we ran past the first house.

Behind us came a loud crash, a tinkle of glass, and a

terrified scream. The sleepy house had been broken into; our shipmates were swarming inside, recklessly killing and stealing. For a second, I wondered what they'd found, what treasures were hiding in that house that we'd reached first but passed by.

Our destination suddenly loomed large and imposing: a church with a large stained glass window over its tall twin doors. Father reached it first and pushed on its closed door.

"Braced!" Rath cursed.

"That way!" Father whispered to Rath. "Thron, Digr, Smiðr; come this way!"

Divided, we ran around the church; we spied a narrow back door. Father pressed hard against the door, but it was also braced. More screams and crashes pierced the night.

"The whole village will be awake soon," Brún snarled.

"How can we get in?" Hal asked.

"Maybe we should just pick a house," Hjálmun suggested.

"I can get us in!" Garad said suddenly.

"How?" Rath demanded.

"That big window in the front, over the doors," Garad explained. "You could throw me through it, and ..."

"No, wait!" Hjálmun said. "Here, help me!"

Hjálmun ran back to the side of the church that they'd run past. An old, crude fence stood there, a pig-pen, just like the ones that we had back home.

"Cut the supports!" Hjálmun cried, and he hacked at the thin beam stuck into the ground. "No, not there: on the end!"

"I get it!" Hal cried, and he ran to the other end.

Moments later, both ends of the fence were cut free, and Hal and Hjálmun lifted a long section high, making several pigs grunt and flee in terror, but as I looked at it, I didn't see a length of fence: I saw a ladder.

Lights flared in windows all around. Suddenly a loud bell rang out, startling us all.

"Hurry!" Father cried. "It's the priest!"

Carrying the fence, we ran to the front and propped it up against the church just over the doors. Hjálmun jumped onto it, climbed the fence-braces like rungs, and slashed his sword at the window.

"Cover your eyes!" Hal shouted.

Colored glass rained all over us as the bell rang again. Hjálmun jumped through the window, and a moment later we heard a heavy scraping of wood.

"Now!" Hjálmun's muffled voice shouted, and we pushed the door open and dashed inside.

"Where's the stairs?" Rath roared looking about.

"Spread out!" Father ordered as the bell rang again. *"Hurry! Keep your weapons ready!"*

Hal led the way to the altar, jumped the tiny fence protecting it, and rushed to the small door beside it. Hjálmun ran through the door on the other side of the altar, followed by Rath, but our door was braced.

"Stand aside!" Smiðr cried, and he ran at the door and threw himself against it; it burst open with a loud crash, and Smiðr fell inside.

We ran in as Smiðr climbed shakily to his feet. The small room had a tiny flame in its fireplace, a bed covered in thrown-back blankets, and a little table taking up most of the space; if any wealth was there, it was well-hidden.

"Damn!" Smiðr cursed. "Bruised my shoulder for nothing ...!"

"No!" Digr cried, and he pointed up to the high ceiling. A large square was cut in it, barely visible in the light of the fire.

"A trapdoor!" Hal cried.

"Let's get the ladder!" Smiðr said.

"No!" I shouted. "Lift me!"

Hal and Smiðr hesitated, glanced from me to each other.

"Thorir'll kill us if he gets hurt," Smiðr warned.

"Is Thron not a warrior?" Hal challenged.

Smiðr's grip was like the iron that he forged; he lifted me with no more effort than if I'd been an infant. Sword-first, I pushed open the trapdoor and climbed into a tiny storage room filled with piles of stuff; dusty wooden chests, old bolts of cloth, a real ladder, and a strange rope hanging from the ceiling.

"There's a ladder up here!" I shouted, and I slid it through the trapdoor until I felt its weight supported. Then I pulled hard on the rope: a section of the wall swung toward me like a door, which opened upon the main hall overlooking the altar; I shouted down to Father and Rath, who'd broken open a locked cabinet behind the altar. The doorway led to the rafters, high above the heads of the others. Its wide beams looked like a crisscrossing spider's web holding up the ceiling.

"That's it!" Rath cried. "Those beams lead to the steeple!"

"Go!" Father shouted to me. "We're right behind you!"

Hal climbed up into the storage room as I stepped out onto the nearest beam. The church bell rang ceaselessly; everyone in the village must be awake. Occasionally, between deafening rings, I heard shouts, screams, and clashes of weapons from outside; I carefully made my way across the wooden beams out to the center, right above the altar, then turned and began pacing off the distance toward the front of the hall. Dead-center over the front door, above the broken window, hung a large banner bearing a golden cross, and upon its cloth I made out the imprint of a ladder built onto the wall behind it.

Father dashed into the bedroom as Hal followed me across the wide beam, but slower; to me, this was as easy as climbing a tree. Smiðr stood in the doorway, one foot on the beam, safely holding onto the edge of the wall. Right below me, Rath matched my steps, prepared to catch me if I fell.

"Go on, Thron!" Hal whispered. "You can do it!"

I crossed as quickly as I could, pushed aside the banner and climbed the ladder, which was solidly affixed to the wall. At its top was another trapdoor; I took a deep breath, steadied myself, and with a roaring cry, I slammed against it, knocked it open, and jumped up into the bell tower.

The bell was so loud that I could hear nothing else, but as the trapdoor crashed against the wall, a horrified priest looked at me as if I were death itself. I jumped at him, sword pointed at his face, but he threw himself back, away from the vibrating bell, slammed into the wall, and crumpled to its floor.

"Take it!" he cried, holding out a small box to me. *"Please! Take everything, just don't kill me!"*

I snatched the box from his hands and raised my sword. It rattled of coins, but my need wasn't wealth. This was my chance; *kill him ... and I was a man!*

I didn't swing. Sobs filled his voice, and his glistening tears reflected the starlight. Yes, I could kill him, *but why?* He'd never done anything to me ... except given me whatever he had. He was certainly no threat; *why should I kill him?*

Hal stuck his head through the trapdoor, then climbed up.

"Good work, Thron!" Hal said, and I heard his smile in his voice.

I kept my sword raised at the cowardly priest, but handed Hal the box.

"Silver!" Hal cried as he opened the box. "A chalice, coins, and a cross! This is what we came for!"

In the silence of the bell not ringing, Hal's voice echoed in my ears, but as Father came up behind me, pointing his own sword at the crumpled priest, I glanced aside, then froze: *fear widened my eyes.*

This church was built on the very top of the hill. Behind it were tall trees, but from the bell tower, I could see beyond the treetops: torches flamed high in the hands of guards surrounded by stone parapets and tall towers.

Behind this village, a huge, mighty castle loomed.

"Father ...!" I shouted.

"Raven's blood!" Father cursed. *"Look to the trees!"*

With difficulty, I pulled my eyes away from the gigantic, stone castle; I'd never imagined a building so large, so big that only my giant-born ancestors could've built it, but flickering red lights and movement drew my eyes. Hundreds of men swarmed through the trees, Scottish warriors with huge swords, long spears, and many torches. Some were riding horses and wielding long lances. They flooded up the hill to our right, pouring towards town.

Suddenly a clear note, very familiar, sounded out high and distant.

"Branwulf's horn!" Hal exclaimed.

"Go!" Father roared. "*Hurry! Or we're dead!"*

Hal paled as he spied the parapets, and then he pressed behind me as Father climbed through the trapdoor down the ladder.

"What is it?" Rath cried from below.

"An army!" Father shouted. "There's a castle just beyond this hill, on the other side of the trees! Knights are coming! Brace the door!"

Rath ran to the front door, pushed it shut, and Hjálmun threw aside an armload of plunder to help Rath slide the stout brace into place.

"Out the back!" Father cried, and he stopped in the middle of the beam, sheathed his sword, and jumped backward. I gasped, but Father caught the beam with his hands at the last possible moment, then hung a second before dropping safely to the floor.

"Thron, jump!" Father ordered. "Do what I did!"

I sheathed my sword, but I didn't jump; quickly I grabbed the beam, lowered myself down, and then I felt Father and Rath's hands catch my feet; I fell into their arms.

"Digr, catch!" Hal shouted, and he dropped the box of silver, then descended as I had.

Smiðr was signaling to us just before the door beside the altar, to the other room. Hjálmun, Brún, and Garad were there, peeking outside of the narrow backdoor.

"See anything?" Brún asked.

"No," Hjálmun said.

"Go!" Digr hissed. *"Before we're surrounded!"*

Cries and sword-clashes echoed. We dashed left, past the house nearest to us, and stayed behind it, out of sight of the road. Branwulf's ship, our only escape, was in the opposite direction, but so was the fighting.

Following Father and Rath, we ran. Digr alone carried any plunder, Brún and Hjálmun had dropped their armloads to leave their hands free. All of our weapons were gripped, Garad bearing his fancy new sword in one hand and the dagger that Father had given him in the other. Behind us, a war raged: shouts and screams and metal hammered metal.

We ran from house to house, behind bushes and sheds, jumping fences. Twice I spied kilted Scotsmen on the road, once seeing several men in full armor on horseback, but they didn't see us, and as soon as the way was clear, we ran even farther.

"We have to cross the street!" Hal hissed quietly.

"We'll be seen!" Digr whispered.

"We can't stay here!" Hal retorted. "Come sunup, Branwulf will be gone!"

"Quiet!" Smiðr hissed at them. "Branwulf's already gone! We need another ship!"

"Now!" Father whispered, and he ran out into the open and quickly closed to the next house, all of us on his heels.

"We've got to get to the ocean!" Father whispered.

"How far can we run?" Rath asked.

"As far as we must!" Father answered.

We made it past several more houses before someone nearby screamed; an old woman had leaned out a high window and spotted us in her garden.

"Vikings ...!" she screamed. "*Vikings ...!"*

"This way!" Father shouted.

Father dashed toward the road. We raced after him. Many Scots stood there with lanterns, but only a few were soldiers, most were old men and young boys still in their nightshirts. Many screamed as we ran past, but only the soldiers chased us.

Heedless of their shouts, we ran through a gap between two houses, past several hen-houses, and straight down a hill. We were farther away from the ocean here, and had to pass another peasant-filled street before we spied the starlit sea. Then we ran down a hill even farther from the bulk of the fighting, but some Scottish guards chased close behind us. Three houses away, we saw a long, narrow dock, and tethered to it was a small, grimy fishing boat.

Three dragonships were rowing away. Two were distant, one very close; Hal shouted and waved, not slowing as he ran.

Shouts behind us made me look back: six Scottish guardsmen were close behind, several with spears, and dozens of angry villagers followed in their wake, many with large, bared daggers. We had no shields. We ran toward the dock, almost stumbling and falling down the hill.

"We need time to cast off!" Rath shouted.

"Go!" Father shouted. *"I'll be right behind!"*

Suddenly Father stopped, so fast that we flew past him. Hjálmun ran down and out onto the dock first, Rath and Brún right behind him. They severed the rope and piled into the tiny boat. Garad, Hal, and Digr jumped in behind them, seizing the oars and fighting to get them set.

Father shouted at his attackers, standing between them and us, blocking their path. Dimly I heard Rath and the others calling to me, but I couldn't move: Father faced six soldiers, three with long spears, running straight at him.

Father swept aside the first speartip as it stabbed at him. He slapped its point to the side in the exact angle so that it fouled the other two spears. Then Father spun and ducked low, even as he swung at his right-most attacker. His sword swept through the man's knee, cleanly cleaving off his leg. The man screamed and fell, and two of his companions toppled over him as he bounced upon the grass. Father jumped right into the middle of the others and hewed down one swordsman as if felling a weak sapling. The three spearmen fought to get out of Father's reach, enough to bring their long weapons into range, but Father pressed them, raining blows. One raised his spear-half to block, but Father pulled his sword in tight, sliced straight at the haft, and the man screamed as all four fingers of his right hand fell away.

The villagers running down the hill all stopped, taken aback by the savage carnage. I couldn't look away, despite

Hal, Rath, and all the others shouting at me from the boat; all of my life I'd heard stories of Father's fighting prowess, how Saxons and Frenchmen fell like wheat before his blade, and how no enemy lived once Father had decided to kill them, but after watching the care and caution that he'd shown since the viking began, and learning that so many of the old stories were untrue, I'd begun to doubt. Now I saw, with shocking clarity, the ferocity that Father held inside him, the untamed beast that he could unleash at will. Six against one had charged downhill at him; Father hadn't even flinched, and now he threatened to kill them all.

Father jumped high and crashed down on the back of one fallen Scot with both boots, stomping with all of his armored weight. Father stumbled slightly, but then he leaped at the two remaining spearmen, swinging his sword. But the spearmen twisted their bodies to block Father's blade with their hafts, then pushed back against him, trying to knock him down. Yet Father sent them both sprawling, and then he jumped at them, stabbing down.

From their backs, the spearmen kicked and blocked. Father stabbed both several times, but only weakly, inflicting little real damage, until one tried to scramble to his feet too soon, and Father buried his mighty sword-point through his back. The other spearman managed to roll to his feet and leveled his spear at Father; Father hesitated, wary of the deadly point, focused entirely upon it.

Suddenly the man that Father had stomped crawled forward and seized Father's leg. Father raised his sword, but just then, the spearman attacked. I ran to help, back up the wide hill, but I was too far away. Weaponless, the spearman whose fingers had been severed rose with a cry and jumped Father from behind, smashing into him with all of his weight.

Father fell. The lone, last spearman raised his weapon high, and thrust down hard: the Scottish spear drove right through Father's mail so hard that it pierced Father deep into his chest.

"NOOOOoooooooooo!!!"

I charged uphill furious, swinging my sword. The wounded, maimed spearman who'd struck Father from behind lay sprawled on the ground, still clutching his bleeding stubs, but he kicked at me as I came on. Nimbly I dodged his feet and, single-handed, swung at his face: the force of my sharp blade struck right across his nose, slicing deep with the *'squish'* of an axe chopping mud. The foundering swordsman that Father had stomped pushed to his feet just as I reached him, and I swung hard right at his sword, then half-spun, and stabbed backwards with all my might. He gasped as my sword-point disappeared into his mouth as if he were swallowing it, only to burst out of the back of his skull.

Father! Alive or dead, I wasn't sure, but I couldn't check on him without getting both of us killed. The spearman's deadly point aimed straight at me, but I couldn't wait: *a drum pounded in my head and red colored my sight.*

I charged. He stabbed forward, but I swung my sword at just the same instant. Our points met, but mine was heavier and shorter; his speartip battered aside. He pulled his spear back as I charged inside his defense, ready to block any blow that I could throw at him, but I suddenly dropped low. He pushed out his haft horizontally to knock me over, but I slid to my knees upon the blood-slick grass right between his feet, under his plaid skirt, and with all the strength that I could muster, I swung overhead, my sword clenched in both hands: I cut upwards into his exposed groin, through his vitals, and deep into his stomach.

His leather belt fell, severed both in front and behind, with his sporan. I pulled my blow through, slicing even deeper, then rolled heels over head, and somehow I landed on my feet. He half-turned to look at me, awash in his blood, an expression of purest horror on his face. Then his guts fell out, sploshing to the ground between his feet, entrails hanging between his bare knees like limp strings of soggy sausage. He dropped his spear and fell forward onto his knees, clutching at his exposed vitals: the back of his white neck gleamed like a prized treasure; I slashed down as hard as I could.

Father!!!

Father's eyes were open, his face smiling. *He was alive!* A feeling of glee and relief washed over me so totally that I felt both dizzy and giddy. But, as I knelt over him, the blood coloring his teeth and gums leaked from the corner of his mouth.

"My ... boy!" Father gasped. "*My ... son!"*

I froze, uncertain, for the briefest moment and longest eternity, and then Father's eyes rolled upwards until I could no longer see his pupils. The grin on his face became a grimace, and Father's head fell back.

"NOOOoooooo!!!" I screamed, and all the world seemed to vanish except for he and I, together, frozen forever ... and then an angry cry rose in a great chorus. I turned my head and, as if viewing another world, saw the throng of armed villagers.

I squeezed my fists; the comfortable familiarity of my sword was encased in my grip. Slowly I rose, purposefully, and turned to face the villagers. More than forty were gathered, yet looking at me, the expression on my blood-drenched face, hearing the guttural snarl escape from my lips, they all stepped back. I glared at them mercilessly, as

I'd stare at pigs in a pen waiting to be slaughtered. I raised my sword, ready to rend them all, to fight until Ragnarrok or every Scotsman was dead.

I stepped uphill, toward them, determined to kill them all.

"Thron!" screamed an oddly familiar voice, and an arm wrapped around my chest, and a strong hand gripped my sword-wrist. I rose into the air; Hal lifted and pulled me back.

I struggled to get away, to pull free, to hack and slash until all the world fell dead at my feet, until the oceans flowed red, but my limbs hung frozen, my joints locked. Hal paused only to bend low enough to snatch up Father's sword, and then he dragged me back down the hill. Unable to move a single joint, like a statue I was carried down the hill and dropped into the arms of the others, into the fishing boat. Brún and Hjálmun kicked off together, and we rowed away.

Father ...!!!

Dimly I was aware of arrows flying from the sea toward the land, of villagers fleeing back up the hill, as Bjarki's ship sailed near. I was lifted aboard the dragon, and somehow, for reasons that I couldn't guess, Bjarki himself embraced me. Men seemed to be cheering, but it sounded distant and bittersweet.

* * * * * * * * *

Hours crept by; stars ... moon ... and slowly a bright light filled the sky. A golden dawn rose, but none that I'd ever wished to see. I sat numb, empty ... despite the small bits of food that had been forced into my mouth, or the great amount of beer that they'd made me drink. I was on Branwulf's dragon, surrounded by my closest friends, with the sun breaking the horizon in all its glory, brightening the new day with the promise of a future yet to be revealed. Yet all that I saw was Father's bloody smile, witnessed the pride in his eyes, and heard the joy in his voice as he'd called me his son for the last time.

My dream was dead, my whole life passing like a horrid nightmare into the irretrievable past. *Father and I wouldn't conquer the world together.* That dream was over, and it wasn't the ending that I'd hoped for; *it was the worst ending.* A new day had come, but I cared only for the old.

Hjalti's voice pestered like some annoying insect buzzing around my ears, but I paid it scant attention. Branwulf had assigned men to command the distant fishing vessels that we could just see sailing out into the dim ocean's morning mists, still readying their nets to be cast, the vast fishing fleet that Branwulf hadn't yet taken, but surely would. Life went on, as always ... for everyone ... except me. I'd live no more; *I would stay with Father.*

Father was hailed as a hero; Bjarki described our whole fight to Branwulf, witnessed by his entire crew, once we were far out to sea: how Father had held off six Scottish guards so that we could escape, but I heard only pieces of it. I was proclaimed a great hero; Branwulf hailed me before everyone as The Avenger, The Champion of the North, and no mirth tinted his voice; the praise that I'd sought all of my life; *how gladly I'd give it back!*

"Boys must prove that their men."

Was that worth losing Father?

"Your faith or your life; if you could only have one, which would you keep?"

A hand squeezed reassuringly on my shoulder; Garad sat beside me, his still-youthful face grim, his eyes full of sympathy. At first, I didn't recognize him, but then I remembered Holbarki, Garad's father, who'd died years before. Then I remembered Halgrum, my other best friend, who'd died the year after that. I saw all of us spread out on the tables in Tavern Hall. *We were all dead.*

This had to end: we couldn't go on this way, slowly watching our friends and family die, one by one, or by the hundreds. Times must change, or we'll all go down in the flames of Muspell, consumed and forgotten, a story of a legendary people who once conquered ... but existed no more.

It had to be done ... and now that I was a man; it was my duty!

Tense, knotted fingers rose slowly. As Friar James had so often done, I touched my forehead, then my chest, my left shoulder, and then my right: *the sign of the cross.* Garad's eyes flaired, his expression paled. I had no choice; *I could follow this path no longer.* The age of our people was over; I would have to end it, for my family, my village, and for all of Norway. I'd have to be a supporter of Friar James, a tool of Mother and Læknir, a Christian, the bringer of the new age.

Slowly I looked up into the bright sun rising above the horizon, wondering what the faces of my future sons would be, if they would look like Father, trying to picture them in the brilliance of the great golden light as it rose to fill the sky. *They wouldn't need to kill others to become men!* My eyes stared, red, but dry. I hadn't cried all night; Father wouldn't have wanted me to cry.

Father had said that it would be us or our enemies, the Norsemen or all of Europe, who'd win in the end. He'd been right, and I saw that clearly. Our kind was failing, our beloved customs killing us. I couldn't let that happen.

Duty to our descendants trumps duty to our ancestors.

We could no longer continue fighting, generation after generation, losing valuable Norsemen, or our whole race would soon perish. *Either we'll conquer Europe or Europe will conquer us,* but we'll never conquer Europe; the time for the end of our traditions had come. I must end them ... my duty was to end them ... at any cost. The raids must end. The days of the vikings were over.

THE END

ABOUT THE AUTHOR

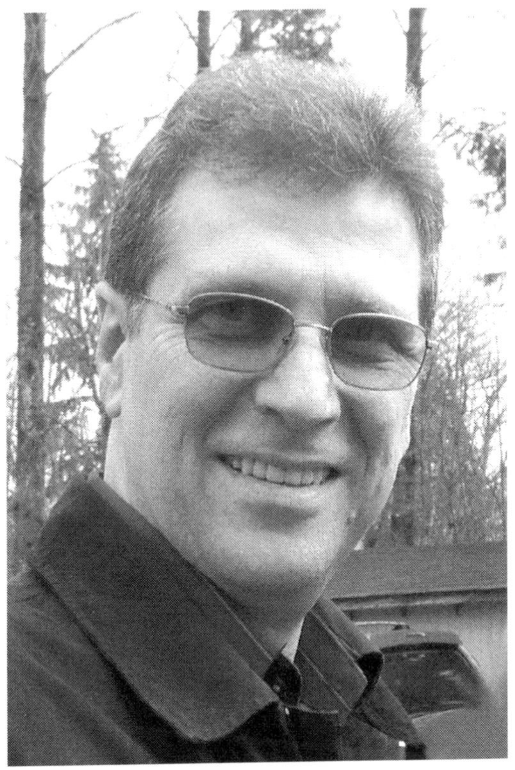

Born in Tripler Army Medical Center, Honolulu, Hawaii, Jay Palmer works as a technical writer in the software industry in Seattle, Washington. Jay enjoys parties, reading everything in sight, woodworking, obscure board games, and riding his Kawasaki Vulcan. Jay is a knight in the SCA, frequently attends writer conferences, SciFi Conventions, and he and Karen are both avid ballroom dancers. But most of all, Jay enjoys writing.

JayPalmerBooks.com

Made in the USA
Middletown, DE
25 April 2017